THE ALCHEMIST

THE ALCHEMIST

MARK ILLIS

BLOOMSBURY

First published in Great Britain 1990
This paperback edition published 1991

Copyright © 1990 by Mark Illis

Bloomsbury Publishing Ltd, 2 Soho Square, London W1V 5DE

British Library Cataloguing in Publication Data
A CIP catalogue record for this book is available from the British Library

ISBN 0-7475-0805-4

10 9 8 7 6 5 4 3 2 1

Typeset by Hewer Text Composition Services, Edinburgh
Printed in England by Clays Ltd, St Ives plc

'Are you paying attention? Do you understand me? Whatever you wish, whatever you have not yet even dreamt of, can be yours.'

Gold, the Great Pretender adds, is a key to many doors; even at seven Billy Gunn understands that gold is a key to power. Moving between Mr Melody's infinitely tempting shops, Sweet Surrender and The Circus of Delights, the shock awaiting him and his father at Jerome the Evangelist's stagy tent-show, the sinister discovery in Archer's luxurious house and the aborted confession in the dentist's chair, Billy becomes increasingly disorientated and increasingly sure that mysterious forces are working against him. His family, he finds, is no protection. Alone and with his worst fears realized, Billy is left to ponder Archer's genial statement: 'I love people, love them to death.'

'Don't look for motive,' Billy is told, 'don't look for motives and alibis and methods. It isn't like that.' Surrounded by a cast of colourful characters – the avuncular Mr Melody, the sleazy crook Jay and his cronies, and of course, the all-knowing Archer – Billy struggles to create a new, safe world out of the frightening ingredients of the old.

The Alchemist is a subtle and richly-layered tale of a child's nightmarish quest for truth; the wit and originality of Mark Illis's second book consolidates the promise demonstrated by his outstanding debut novel *A Chinese Summer*.

FOR MY PARENTS

A cheat, a thief, a swearer and
blasphemer, who smelt of the rope from
a hundred yards away, but for the rest
the best lad in the world.

Clément Marot, *Epitres XXIX*

ELABORATIONS

One

Unchronologically, I'd like to begin about halfway through. A normal enough day, although hotter than average for April, encouraging me to walk home from school. I was passing an excavated and overgrown pit, one of two on the heath, great shallow-sided holes used for bike rides in summer and sledging in winter. It used to be a gravel pit, I think, although even now I am not sure. Certainly then, aged twelve, I had no very clear idea of the true nature of my surroundings. It was said that plague victims were buried beneath the heath, in which case digging pits into it did not necessarily seem a good plan. I was walking, in any case, alongside the gentle slope on a hotter than average day when there suddenly appeared, like a witch out of a fairy-tale, a short-haired, large-faced, denimed woman with a strange look in her eyes. Flared nostrils and hard set mouth like someone on the point of erupting. It was as if, behind some bush, she had just been in the middle of a heated argument. It was as if, through some sequence of events that I couldn't understand, I was the subject of the argument. She stood her ground as I approached. Her brown shirt collar was awry, and there was sweat on her upper lip. I moved outwards as I came nearer, circling well out of reach. She watched, her debate apparently continuing internally, and approaching some sort of climax, as her eyes widened and her paunchy face tightened. When I was almost parallel her arm shot out towards me, fist clenched, finger pointing. 'Billy Spoon!' she roared, 'Billy Spoon, stop following me!' I kept walking. She kept shouting. I walked faster. She shouted louder. Then, hawking up phlegm, she spat at me.

When I thought it was safe to look back I found that she had gone, a frightening assistant removed by a clever magician. Back behind her bush I suppose, back to her furious debate. I never saw her again. When I got home I found a large dribbling gob of her saliva on the back of my jacket, right between the shoulder-blades. I've no idea what her name was. My name is not Billy Spoon.

Unchronologically, I open with this episode because it gets me started on the right foot. The sense of being surrounded by mysterious, probably ill-wishing people was one which filled my childhood, and not only because of a vivid imagination. I walked in fear of persecution. While I'm on fears, I also walked in fear of being presented suddenly with crucial, life-changing choices and, most of all, of being abandoned by my parents. Ironic then to look back, older and safer, and see that this illustrative episode came only two weeks before all three of these fears were fulfilled.

Chronologically, I ought to begin with my parents, Eldon and Lucy Gunn. I always knew that my father was a shrewd man. He made his money with a string of, of all things, bookshops. He used to boast, even when I was quite little, about how he had invested his profits heavily in the bubble market of the late seventies and the eighties, and then withdrawn before the stockmarket crash. He used those profits to move into property, and to keep new shops springing up. Clever capitalist. But money wasn't his first love, he was a man deeply involved in hobbies. Computers, cinema, acting, cars, tennis and, for a while, an evangelical religion which operated out of a tent. What else can I say? He loved to wear slick suits and, at home, Crocodile casuals, that made him look like a tycoon out of an American soap. He hated to lose. He had, probably, an obsessive personality. He would smoke a lot and drink a lot, and then give both up totally, for a long period of time. And then one day, inevitably, he would return to tobacco and alcohol as if some other person had been depriving him of them against his will.

My mother was a different type. She had been the manager of one of his bigger shops which, at twenty-five, three years out of university, was pretty good going. As with my father, money was not her interest. Her degree and her skill in the book trade had not changed the fact that she wanted her abilities to be immersed in a family. She was fairly sure of how things would turn out. She saw herself in twenty years time as the mother of three children, with a bread-winning husband, a large house in the commuter belt and a discerning antiquarian and secondhand bookshop.

Eldon was thirty-five, had had no education to speak of (proud of it), and was ready to find a wife and a home to house his hobbies. He had a handsome, longish face with a nose that suggested Jewish antecedents. Hair greying at the sides and thinning on top. He had a boyish, unfettered enthusiasm when talking about his favourite topics; it was only when he sensed competition that those slick clothes seemed to fit him. Then he would become ruthless, and probably take up smoking and drinking again. Lucy Gentleman had a short, business-woman's haircut that revealed all of her face. Wide lips that were usually bright red. Lively eyes that were often serious when the rest of her face was not, sometimes only tolerant when the rest of her face was amused. She was a good listener. She and Eldon could not have been better matched if they had advertised for each other.

In his flat after the meal and after the play, he joked about her name and she teased him about his anonymous taste in furnishings. They had known each other within a business relationship for some time, and were having trouble breaking out of those confines. He was regretting not having had anything to drink with dinner, and was considering lighting up. I can almost see it, I've heard the story so often. She is wearing a short black dress with a flounced skirt, and feeling like an over-dressed undergraduate. He is wearing a moderately shiny grey suit and a red paisley tie which he thinks she doesn't like. This is because he has misinterpreted the appraising quality in her eyes. Now his arm moves along the top of the sofa towards her short brown hair. Things happen quite quickly as if, because it is such a well-worn sequence of events, there need be no hesitations. Starting as he touches her, she spills her coffee. He apologizes, moves closer, wipes her dress with his hand. First she laughs and then he does, and then, finally, they are kissing.

'Look,' he said, 'I haven't got anything. I wasn't expecting, I mean this is fantastic, couldn't be better, but I wasn't ex-pecting . . .'

Looking up into his face, she weighed him once more with her serious eyes. Then she smiled fully. 'Equal responsibility,' she said. Her hands on his buttocks pushed him smoothly into her.

'Yes.' The word was drawn into three syllables. Then he struggled to return her composure. 'Will you marry me?'

'Yes. Yes. Yes.'
So I was conceived.

I should probably begin with J. T. Archer. He has played a big
enough part in my life. Or perhaps I should say that he has played
enough parts in my life. But anyway, he'll turn up very soon.

Two

We lived a couple of side-streets away from my father's first shop.
He called it, and all of the shops that followed it, Gunn's World
of Books. He had big ideas, my father, and his businesses had
to expand fast to keep pace with them. But through all of his
successful property speculation, and by the time I was born he
was heavily involved in this, we never moved. The house was the
still centre of the world he was developing.

It wasn't quite in the commuter belt, but it was as large as my
mother could have wished. My room was a big one at the top,
with a partly sloping ceiling and a window on to the long, narrow
garden. There were superfluous rooms, furnished with style but
rarely entered. I used to feel a continuous sense of discovery as
I toddled around. There was plenty of space to become lost in.
Once, aged about four, I entered a room unaccompanied to find
it being decorated. Dust sheets, paint-streaked overalls, a man up
a ladder, another crouching by the skirting. I sat in the middle of
the room, open-mouthed, listening to their talk, which carried on
as if I wasn't there, and watched the transformation with a feeling
of wonder. What was happening? Were these men here every night,
climbing ladders and changing the walls while I slept?

I am probably remembering thoughts which are too sophisticated
for the mind of a four year old. Our neighbour, at first sight at least,
is a more verifiable subject. Mr Melody lived close to us and his

shop, the flamboyantly named Sweet Surrender, was next to my father's. They were old friends, although exactly how far back they went I don't know.

The first time I went into the shop my father was with me. We were hand in hand, as we always were then, in spite of the awkwardness this entailed. My hand enclosed in his palm, his fingers around my wrist.

Just that fragment of memory threatens to bring back an unhelpful wave of nostalgia, but Mr Melody's shop is equal to the challenge. It was a treasure house of trays and jars and shelves and glass-fronted cupboards crammed with multi-coloured, brightly wrapped, familiar and mysterious confectioneries. A jangle of bells as we entered. I smile and almost lick my lips at the remembered sound. Dumbly I pulled my hand from my father's and wandered round in a mist of glorious smells and eye-popping sights, nose pressed to glass to look at rich swirls of chocolate, fingers stretching to lift me up to the level of glistening, ingenious confections in pastel pinks and shining primary colours. My tongue was hanging out, greed all over my face like spilt sugar.

'Billy. Come and meet Mr Melody.'

(Did I mention that the woman by the pit on the heath was half right? Billy Gunn, not Billy Spoon. Much too close for comfort.)

I turned, dazed, saw two dark-trousered pairs of legs, and moved towards the nearest and clung.

Laughter. 'Hello Billy.'

I looked up into a doughy moon of a face topped by wavy red hair and split by a grin. 'This is gratifying,' it said, 'whatever becomes of this exuberance? Eh, Eldon? Where does it go?' That was how I met Mr Melody, who was to become a rock of reliability in an uncertain world. His moustache was fascinating. It was short and thick, like the bristles of two shaving brushes pointing in different directions, and it never seemed to grow or change; always that minor red explosion beneath his nose.

An example of his reliability: I was walking home from school with Kim, talking about the latest game we had invented, which involved pretending that there was a labyrinth at the bottom of the garden. The way home from primary school was along quiet, tree-lined roads, and across one major street, on which stood my father's and Mr Melody's shops. We always crossed this street at the lights. On the day I am thinking of, we saw one of our friends

7

knocked over. Physically he was barely hurt, barely even touched, but it was quite spectacular to watch. He was stepping out on to the road, shouting some insult at us because we had made the detour to the lights, and we looked up just as the car grazed him, catching his arm and spinning him like a top so that for a moment we thought he was still joking as he spun crazily, still on his feet, into the path of the next car, dancing in the traffic like a drunk playing at being a matador, until he collapsed with an unresisting loose-limbed finality.

There was a lot of screeching, swerving and shouting as we ran up the hill towards him, but the first person on the scene and taking charge was Mr Melody. Perhaps he had learnt first aid, because he saw soon enough that there was no damage and he carried the boy into his shop. Kim and I followed. In the back room he laid our friend on a sofa, wrapped him in a blanket, put on the kettle, called an ambulance and, not having the parents' phone number, phoned the school with the relevant information. Somewhere in the course of this we received sherbet fountains and reassurance.

As the boy began to come round, Mr Melody talked him back to consciousness. 'Quite a performance,' he said, 'where did you have your dancing lessons? Look, here's Billy and Kim, they saw it too, wasn't it a performance? Here's tea, drink, drink, drink, it's good for you. Your mother's on her way, and so's the doctor. More tea, and chocolate. Tea and chocolate, universal panacea. These two are wishing they had been knocked over. Aren't you?' His arm round the boy, his hand tousling his hair. Kim and I nodded.

Where did Kim come from? She walked into the story earlier than I expected. Her mother, Melinda, was a great friend of my mother's. Kim was at school with me, we used to walk home together, I spent a lot of time in her flat, she spent a lot of time at my house. We played in the garden, had massive, final arguments and regular reconciliations. Every now and then we would remind each other that we were in love, and were going to be married. This was OK, not too soppy because, basically, Kim was a boy. I mean we had actually checked each other out, and I knew that she *wasn't* a boy, but to all intents and purposes her plump little fold of skin where there should have been a willy made absolutely no difference. Her hair was a little bit shorter than mine, she wore trousers, she played football. I had even been read a book in which Kim was a daring young male hero. If I was going to have to marry, and my mother was out of bounds, then Kim looked like a good bet.

If this sounds like the musings of a very young homosexual, then perhaps I've misread my memories. I'm trying to recall the rules that applied to life in childhood, and reapply them. I'll sort it out eventually, because I am good at puzzles. I like to think that I have an affinity with labyrinths. At the bottom of the garden the bushes grew thickly around an old hut and a tall, climbable tree. More bushes against the back wall, and low fences on either side. Tunnels underground, dark passages where I, or sometimes Kim and I, would explore. A cave, the knotty face of a cliff, fingers tugging at us as we passed. The idea was always that we were in total darkness, and utterly lost; intrepid archaeologists evading enemies, and searching for an elusive, probably cursed, treasure.

We did discover the odd thing. It was there one dusk, trousers and underpants around our knees, that, in the dim light, we inspected each other, touching each other curiously. I tried to explain how, unaccountably, my thing would sometimes become stiff, like a finger without knuckles, and I peed into a bush in my eagerness to demonstrate its workings. Kim, to my disappointment, would not reciprocate. It was there, on a later occasion (you can't rush into these things), that we had our first kiss. There that, after impulsively pushing Kim over a root, I realized I was stronger than her, and there was some pleasure to be found in demonstrating it. No treasure though, no jewels or gold coins, although we stayed out long after we had been called in and dug and searched tirelessly.

Three

I've never had more friends than I had on my seventh birthday. The extravagant house seemed a sensible size for once, filled as it was with more or less my whole class from school and a sprinkling of children of my parents' friends. Melinda was there, helping out,

9

and Louise, Kim's fourteen-year-old sister, was assisting. There were to be games, a meal, a magician, and a disco.

At two o'clock, before anyone arrived, Kim and I were sitting in the kitchen talking to Melinda, who was taking biscuits she had made out of four large plastic boxes.

'I hope everyone comes,' she said, 'or there's going to be a biscuit diet in this house for a fortnight.'

'Everyone is coming,' I said. 'They are coming, aren't they?'

'They are coming,' said my mother, coming in. 'In their droves. Mel, what is this?' She picked up a biscuit and tasted it. 'Mmm, you're a dream, I think I'm dreaming and I'm about to wake up. How you can spare the time I don't know.'

'Because Harold is being nice to me,' she said, 'since I agreed,' a glance at Kim and I, 'to take over the other office.'

'Harold is it? I thought it was Mr Grey.'

Melinda shook her head. 'Harold is Senior Partner,' she said, 'and retirement age. So save your prurience. It's been cosy first name terms ever since he imposed this decision on me.'

'*What* did he do?' asked Kim. 'What did he do to you?'

'Nothing,' said Melinda, 'I'll tell you about it later.'

'We'll tell both of you later,' my mother added.

After this nothing more could be got out of them, and the talk turned to the magician, the Great Pretender, and what he might do in his act.

These are the best memories, these intervals in which nothing at all is happening, and there are familiar people around me, and I am cherishing something that has not yet happened. This foursome, of myself and Kim and our mothers, was a familiar one. Melinda and my mother had been friends since university, where she read Law and my mother English, and there was an established closeness between them. But even in this memory, the four of us in the kitchen together, there is an unresolved sense of doubt in the air. *Later*. Things were always going to happen later, so that time advanced and receded perplexingly, like a freakish tide.

At the back of the wardrobe among the coats, it smelt of my parents and, somehow, of the past. Rubbing up against wool, tweed and cotton in a half comfortable, half stifling closeness. *The Lion, the Witch and the Wardrobe* had been read to me, and so I had explored in here before without success: no magic, no escape hatch into a more exciting, more black and white world. There was something else though, something that I was always after at one period in my life: security. The back seats of cars have no resonances of teenage groping for me, instead they recall my parents driving and myself dozing, the reassuring buzz of their voices. I was not cosseted, and not unhappy at school, but I was always hungry for security. Perhaps our household was a little too rationalist. Too many books, not enough hugging, no teddy bear. In retrospect it is easy to believe that I had an instinctive, childish awareness of tension in the air, of changes waiting to happen.

The door of the wardrobe swung open abruptly, and I stood up and pushed the coats aside, relieved to have been found at last. The face in the doorway was no one I recognized, unless you count its similarity with the villain of ancient silent films I had seen on television. This man had the appropriate drooping black moustache, the prominent made-up eyes, the thin, white smiling face, and the compulsory cape and top hat.

'Billy,' he said, 'Birthday Boy. Enchanted. Come away from your womb now, it's time for your adventures to begin.'

First the meal. My parents, Melinda and Louise had all been busy while the game of hide-and-seek went on, and when we entered the room, about thirty of us squeezing through the bottleneck of the door, everything was laid out ready for us. Three long tables loaded with hamburgers, crisps and relishes, formed three sides of a square which contained a fourth table loaded with desserts. Jellies on beds of meringue alongside piles of Melinda's biscuits surrounded two huge cakes. BILLY written on one, GUNN on the other. Mr Melody, apologizing for being unable to attend, had donated an enticing, tooth-rotting collection of his stock. The room was decorated with streamers and balloons.

My father was patrolling amiably, dressed for the occasion in a blue suit with a thin red stripe and a bright blue and red striped tie. Louise, who was being paid an undisclosed sum, was ferrying things from the kitchen. She wore a suitably lively white dress with red polka-dots. Kim told me her mother had said it was too short, and Louise had answered that she didn't think she had to worry about advances from six-year-old boys. I glanced now and then at her calves, and the lower part of her thighs, and wondered why Melinda thought they should be hidden. Kim was in a yellow dress, a thing with lace at the collar and a pleated skirt which subtly

11

changed my attitude towards her. I felt this was a different girl from the Kim in jeans who played football, explored labyrinths and could be pushed over roots. I solved the problem by largely ignoring her.

'Pass the crisps!' Charlie Larbey was on my left. He was a friend my parents didn't particularly approve of. He took the crisps I passed, poured them on to his plate and put a fistful into his mouth without pausing in eating his hamburger. This was a serious, two-handed job.

'Charlie,' I said, in the tone of a choosy host, 'you're like a big hoover. You're like a great big hoover bag.'

A noise emerged from the crammed mouth which might have been, 'Fuck off toe-rag.' Charlie's older brother allowed him and his friends to watch his videos, and our vocabularies had expanded accordingly.

Dishes of dessert had now arrived on the table, and I picked up Charlie's jelly and dropped it on to the remains of his hamburger.

'Scumbag,' I said. He answered with a bloody dollop of tomato sauce in my face, then he ate some hamburger and jelly. Dripping sauce like, I thought, an injured gangster, I pushed a creamy piece of birthday cake into his face. A friend of his a few places away came to his aid by throwing some meringue at me, 'You're gonna die!', and then Kim, possibly anxious to show that her pretty dress didn't exclude her from such games, stood up and threw her paper cup full of coke at him. 'Motherfucker!' Jelly, hamburger and bits of biscuit began to fly around the tables. The food fight had begun, to the accompaniment of every word of abuse we had heard and didn't understand, and my father's bellowing had no effect on thirty screaming kids.

It began to look ugly. The room was possessed by a growing hysteria, kids were waving plastic cutlery in each other's faces as well as food, and there was a snarling, sincere quality to some of the insults being thrown. My father was trying to protect one unpopular boy from attack by three others and a girl. Choking him with food seemed to be what they had in mind. The gunshot pops of balloons punctuated the cacophony. Charlie's friend was weaving his knife around in front of me in imitation, I recognized, of a drunken lout in a film we had seen; Louise, her dress drenched, had backed up against a wall and was watching us; Kim was ready to throw a punch as two six-year-old boys approached her with evil grins. My father, no longer shouting, was looking bewildered. Something crazy was happening to all of us in the room. Then there was an explosion.

Everybody looked at the door. Out of a purple plume of smoke stepped the Great Pretender, the silent movie villain who had found me earlier.

'You children will stop your games now,' he said. 'I have arrived.'

Charlie's friend dropped his knife, Louise peeled herself off the wall, and the two boys approaching Kim froze, their evil grins melting into puzzlement.

'I will be needing you, Louise,' he said. 'We're going to find you a costume.' He looked at my father. 'If you would lead them to the sitting room, Mr Gunn, and have them sit there, quietly?' He asked this as if he was not sure that my father could manage it. My father nodded, and only now began to appear authoritative. Perhaps he sensed competition.

We sat on cushions in front of a makeshift stage. There were a few props: a box in garish wrapping paper with a big bow, a coffin on a couple of trestles. There were no curtains, but there was a door behind the stage, and steps up on to it. A chastened air about us. Melinda and my parents sat on chairs behind us, occasionally exchanging a quiet remark, and I could feel their eyes on us. My father had taken off his stained jacket and tie, and was in his shirt-sleeves. We all waited patiently.

The Great Pretender walked on to the stage and stood and looked at us. A disarming silence. He was like a feared teacher in front of an unruly class. 'I can't possibly begin without applause,' he said, eventually. Obediently, we applauded. He opened his arms in a gesture of gratitude, and then opened his hands in abrupt movements which revealed, first a bunch of flowers and then a gold chain.

'For my beautiful assistant,' he said. 'First lesson: gold is a key to many doors.'

Purple smoke again, at the back of the stage, and then Louise emerged, stepping out with a daring, exhibitionist smile. But could this be Louise? This girl had straight blonde hair instead of Louise's brunette curls, she was expertly over-madeup, and she looked about twenty. Scarlet lips, her plump cheeks rouged in an otherwise pale face, eyeliner and false eyelashes. She wore a black miniskirt, fishnet stockings and a spangled scarlet bodice which revealed a cleavage between small breasts.

I heard an intake of breath, and then Melinda's voice from the back of the room. 'I don't approve of this,' she said. 'I think you'll have to do without an assistant. Louise, you can come off the stage now.'

'Oh Mu-um,' said the vision in spangles. 'It's only for a game.'

The Pretender looked over our heads at Melinda. 'Only a game Ms Sexton,' he said. 'There is no harm intended I assure you. I do not allow stereotyping in my act, as you shall see.'

All of us were looking back at Melinda now. She was staring at the magician, unmollified. 'What do you call that costume, if not stereotyping?'

'I call it a costume. Nothing more. Your daughter is playing a part.'

Melinda looked at my mother, whose shoulders moved slightly. 'Very well,' she said finally, 'we'll see.'

The magician looked at us again. 'My name is the Great Pretender,' he said. 'Also the Alchemist, the Necromancer and the Keeper of Souls.' He lifted his cape, disappeared behind it as it grew, and then suddenly it was standing unsupported on the stage and he was in front of it, dressed in the same clothes, but entirely in white. 'Second lesson: we have more skins than a shop full of onions.'

I'm not going to describe his whole act. It lasted about half an hour and much of it was conventional business involving rabbits and playing cards, sleight of hand and more rapid costume changes. In spite of his promise, Louise's function was mostly decorative. Lessons were drawn. 'Beware of strangers.' 'Wisdom overcomes strength.' 'Knowledge is power.' And even, as he gave Louise what seemed to be a thick metal bar and she bent it with ease, 'Sex is power too.'

Two things stand out. The first is the act which was supposed to prove that he didn't believe in stereotyping.

The Great Pretender lay in his coffin, head and feet protruding at either end. He looked at his audience and flashed his yellow teeth at them. 'Now my gorgeous assistant will proceed to saw me in half, thus striking a blow for feminists everywhere. I insist on complete silence, and on no account must anyone interfere with this girl during the procedure.' A huge lewd wink, from his mascara lined eye, directed at the back of the room. Then, 'If you please,' he said.

The blonde, leggy, and in retrospect overwhelmingly nubile Louise, who could only have had five minutes' rehearsal for the entire act, picked up a saw from behind the cape-screen and advanced on the coffin. We could see clearly that it was a short-bladed saw with long and vicious teeth, scarred with signs of rust. Was this new Louise, revealed beneath the skin of the old Louise, to be trusted with this weapon? The audience was collectively holding its breath.

She inserted the saw into a crack we had not noticed before, and then she lowered it until it seemed to reach some sort of obstruction.

'Now,' said the Pretender, 'my stunning sidekick will saw through my body, and separate my two halves. Continue please.'

Louise, using a little effort, began to saw. Immediately, there was a spurt of blood from the side of the coffin, and a hissing shudder from the Pretender. Louise stopped, her face white, and the adults at the back of the room stood up. We, the audience, shuffled forward, wide-eyed.

'Silence!' shouted the man in the coffin. 'Silence is imperative if this performance is to be completed safely.' His breath was audible. He looked up into Louise's eyes and seemed to brace himself. 'Continue.'

Staring back into his eyes, she did as she was told, moving the saw back and forth, wincing as it met resistance. The trick continued smoothly, in an atmosphere of viscous tension, and of course, when the Great Pretender finally climbed out of his coffin, we saw that his injury had been another pretence, because the grey body-suit which he had somehow changed into was unmarked, except for a red rose motif on his chest.

'Seventh lesson: always give the punters some blood. They may not think they like it, but they do.'

The finale is the second thing which stands out. I was personally involved, because the big gift-wrapped box on stage was apparently a birthday present for me.

'Unwrap it Billy.' The Pretender stared down at me. He was dressed in gold tails now, setting off his black, shoulder-length, greased-back hair. His yellow teeth grinned at me, and his black circled eyes stared. Louise looked at me resentfully, I thought, because I was sharing the spotlight.

I unwrapped the parcel warily, worried about explosions or

spring-loaded surprises. Nothing. In the parcel, in layers of tissue paper, was a lump of lead.

He took it from me. 'Now I am the Alchemist,' he said, and his voice resonated with a deep, tantalizing desire. 'Who craves gold? Who longs for servants and mistresses and gigolos and mirrors of subtle angles to multiply your possessions? I am offering you perfumed mists to lose yourselves in and baths like pits to fall into, gossamer and roses to dry yourselves. The lowest of your servants will eat salmon served living, so that it leaps, wriggling exquisitely, down his throat. And you shall dine on the swelling unctuous paps of a pregnant sow, newly cut off, dressed with a piquant and poignant sauce. Are you paying attention? Do you understand me? Whatever you wish, whatever you have not yet even dreamt of, can be yours.' As he spoke he took from his pocket a paste, and smeared it on the lead. 'All from this unpromising material.' He looked at my blank face, and those of the audience. 'Trust me, these are things you want very badly.' His hands moved over the lead more and more quickly, his forehead lined with concentration, his lips gradually moving back from his teeth in a self-satisfied smile.

'There,' he said with an exhausted finality and a sudden relaxation of his body. And now his hands were full of gold. Grinning in avaricious delight, he poured the coins from one hand to another in a chinking, glittering golden waterfall. 'My final surprise,' he said, holding his handfuls of coins out towards his audience, 'is my parting present. Coins for every boy and girl in the room. *Gold*. Who wants it?' There was an excited clamour from the audience, and I felt a sick sensation in my stomach, thinking I would be forgotten, sitting behind him. But he took a few steps back, clapped his hands together dramatically, and gave me some coins before throwing the rest out to the audience. 'Final lesson,' he announced, 'same as the first: Gold is the key to many doors.'

Another purple plume of smoke, and he was gone, leaving the smell of gunpowder in my nostrils and foil-wrapped chocolates in my hands. Louise had taken off her wig, revealing her brown curls plastered to her skull; she was fingering her gold chain and looking embarrassed in her absurd get-up, but she was laughing at my expression of crushed disappointment.

The disco was an energetic, welcome return to reality. Some lights had been hired, and Louise, back in her stained but dry party dress, played the records. There was soon a crowd of dancing six- and seven-year-olds clustered in the middle of the room. No wallflowers. No one wanted to be conspicuous on the fringes of the crowd.

I danced with Kim of course, and, in my black jeans and shirt, I found that I was glad that she was wearing a dress. We danced a slow one cheek to cheek, ungracefully going through the motions. My hands on her back, hers around my neck. There was a confusion between us that was something quite new. I looked over her shoulder and exchanged facial sign language with Charlie, who was moving his hands up and down his girl's back. When his hand moved too low, on to her skirt, the girl moved it up again. Everyone preferred fast records, because they involved a kind of running on the spot that was similar to what we sometimes did in gym at school.

After about half an hour of this, Melinda came and took Kim away, and for a while I danced aimlessly in the crowd while watching them talking. The noise and the flashing lights and the darkness made it difficult to see what was going on, but something was being said that Kim didn't like.

Eventually she came back. She had been crying. She had to put her hands on my shoulders and shout into my ear to make herself heard. 'We're *going*,' she shouted. 'I have to change schools and houses and friends, and go and live somewhere else. It's not fair, she never asked me and Louise knew and never told me, we're just going.'

She was leaning on my shoulders and shouting the news directly into my ear, so that it physically hurt. It was only North London, across the river, but it was the end of my first romance with her.

Four

My father, who used to quote Polonius as part of his business creed: 'Neither a borrower nor a lender be', my father borrowed money from his old friend J. T. Archer. This is because my father was one of those men who it is invariably better to avoid: a man with a dream. Eldon Gunn, the man who made Britain literate. He saw Gunn's World of Books extending in franchises across the country and across society, absorbing hearts and minds, refashioning prejudices and, in short, absorbing the real world and transforming it. For himself, he predicted an eventual move into publishing. Top rung of course. I still like to think that it could all conceivably have happened – he was a man of ingenious ideas and inexhaustible energy – if not for that early mistake, when he broke the rules of his own creed. I don't like to accept that he wasn't shrewd, that he wasn't quite the businessman he thought he was. It was just that his dream had unlucky foundations.

I'm jumping ahead again. I have to try to keep things in order, hug the facts. The effect of my father's dream on me, as a child, was that I didn't seem to see much of him. At weekends he would usually arrive late on Saturday evening to go out with my mother, and then he would have more business to attend to, or would become engrossed in one of his enthusiasms, shortly after lunch on Sunday. He was like an apprentice god, omnipotent, but not omnipresent. Which is why most of my memories of childhood involve my mother. In my mind's eye she is always about thirty. Brunette hair in a simple style, brushed straight back, covering her neck. Small and rather thin, with a slim and mobile face, her bright red lips and lively eyes vying for attention with their conflicting signals.

We would go for walks, across the heath and into the park. I am remembering the winter that Kim moved, my mother in a chunky sweater and myself wrapped like a Michelin man in gloves, scarf, woolly hat and a padded coat. This can be placed in time. It was two months after my birthday, about a month after the massive gales in the South East. Four hundred trees down in the park, and their stumps and trunks still littered the grass. Our breath steamed, so that my mother's sighs were visible, wreathing her face. She must have been thirty-three. She bit her chapped lips as she walked, and gazed at the fallen trees as if she bore a grudge against them. Her eyes swallowed them bitterly, her lips lay in an impassive straight line.

Naturally, I was oblivious to all this at the time. Maybe she had quite a different expression. I don't rate this as hypothesis though.

The expression I describe is the right one, even if she never wore it. I was jumping on tree-trunks, demanding attention as I danced on wide, severed stumps, trying to get a reaction out of my mother like a comic with a morose straight man. She kept walking, straight up towards the statue of General Whale, which commands a panorama of London as if he is for ever considering his best plan of attack on the city below him.

She stood and looked over this view while I, as usual, examined the statue. Four stone steps led to the bulk of the pedestal, which was pock-marked and scarred and drilled all the way through by one narrow hole. This was as mysterious to me as the origin of the pits on the heath. On the whole I blamed low-flying German planes from the last war, strafing the area on their way to bomb the city. But I did not dismiss some connection with General Whale himself. I did not understand the inscription engraved on the statue, so nothing contradicted my hunch that a battle had once raged on the spot on which I stood. One bullet or shell of tremendous power had pierced right through the stone, no doubt killing a soldier who had thought himself adequately protected.

I looked through the tunnel the bullet had created, and remembered the magician's lessons. 'Knowledge is power.' What nonsense. He was just encouraging us to go to school. A gun with bullets that could smash rock and hit someone who thought they were in safety – *that* was power. Through the tunnel I saw my mother, and I moved around the pedestal. Why stand there so still? She had seen the view many times before. And why stand there if you are not even going to look, if you are going to stare resolutely at your feet? A thought occurred to me, as I considered the city, and I ran down the steps to my mother.

'Can we see Kim's house from here? Where is it? Do you think we can see it from here?'

I would have thought I was a bit old to be lifted up by her, but that is what I remember. Her lifting me up, her warm breath on my cheek, her pointing with one hand while I clung to her. In my catalogue of self-obsessed memories, it is a moment which stands apart, because as she pointed out vaguely towards the north, I was looking at her face, and I touched some wetness beneath her eye. This is what I have trouble describing, because I am two people, the seven year old and the older man, each experiencing the taste on my fingertip and the guilt it evokes.

'Why are you crying?'

She shook her head, and smiled.

'The wind, Billy. Look out over that way, follow my finger, that's where Kim lives now. Don't you feel the wind in your eyes?'

Of course, I was more than ready to be deceived by her.

So my concern for her evaporated as I followed her finger northwards, and realized that I was looking at a labyrinth more elaborate than any I might invent. An indistinct grey jumble, dotted by cranes and tall buildings, starting at the river and spreading outwards, spilling outwards much further than my eye could see in the dull, hazy light.

There was no wind. My concern evaporated, but some stubborn residue of doubt remained. I don't think I am taking liberties with the truth, if I say that some residue of doubt always remained, from that day on.

My mother put me down and we walked on, my hand in hers now.

'You see,' she said, 'what a distance it is. I'm afraid you'll be seeing Kim less often, and I'll be seeing Melinda less often. That's what happens when distances get involved.' She wasn't looking at me, I wasn't understanding what she was saying. 'I'm worried about my eyesight Billy, I'm losing sight of things that used to be clear to me. That's what happens as you get older, your eyesight goes.'

'*I'm* not losing my eyesight. You ask me, you ask me to see something for you and I'll see it. I'm not losing my eyesight, am I?'

'Not till you're older Billy. Don't you worry about a thing I say my love. Not till you're much older. Your mother's babbling, like a babbling brook.' She made a nonsensical sound, to illustrate. 'And my sight must be better than yours because I've seen Mr Melody before you.' Another change of tone. A dryness. 'That's life you see, lose a friend, gain a Mr Melody.'

'Delightful,' he said, as he approached, 'how delightful to meet friends in the park. Billy!' From his pocket he produced some peanut brittle. 'That is, if your mother has no objection?'

My mother had none, and I accepted his gift.

I have mentioned some dark trousers of Mr Melody's, but these may have given the wrong impression. His clothes were not so much loud, as chatty. Companionable colours. You looked twice and, rather than raise your eyebrows or wrinkle your nose, you probably smiled. Flowery waistcoats. Two-colour frames on his bifocals. A check on his jacket that brought to mind interference on a TV screen. Sweaters in Afghan stripes. Woolly red hats from which strands of his red hair poked out. A deep-pocketed overcoat covered in geometry.

'Say thank you.'

I said thank you for the peanut brittle.

'Not at all. Not at all, not at all. My pleasure. What's the use of business if it isn't pleasure? And my apologies Billy for missing your party. I hear there were excitements?'

This was an opportunity to be relished. I had thought I had run out of people to tell about the day. Mr Melody walked between us as I told him about the food fight while he tut tutted, and then expanded on the wonders of the Great Pretender's act while he listened in respectful silence. On the subject of alchemy I was particularly enthusiastic, my imagination caught by the promise of unlimited powers in return for a trick with a piece of lead.

'And Lucy, were you entranced?'

'Not exactly,' said my mother, 'more disturbed. I was wondering who this was that I'd let into my house. He was rather creepy. There's no doubt that he was talented, but I don't think his act was quite tailored for seven year olds. He was trying to play to two audiences at once.'

Mr Melody smiled like one who knows. 'A dangerous game,' he said. He turned back to me. 'I expect you didn't know Billy, that confectioners dabble in alchemy?'

I didn't know.

'It wouldn't be too much to say that the confectioner's art is founded on the search for the Perfect Sweet. You must not get bogged down in too straitened a definition of the word "Alchemy", Billy. It is a wonderfully broad and encompassing, in fact an *engulfing* word. We shall call it the making of something golden from mundane or unpromising materials. Does that suit you?'

It suited me.

'Good.' Then he told me about the Perfect Sweet, how it was the sweet with the perfect taste, consistency and appearance, how it had been scientifically proven by study of taste buds and surveys of eating habits and examination of historical records that such a thing existed, how it involved a particular blend of certain simple but unknown ingredients, and how, cheap to produce and universally enjoyed, it would inevitably make the name and fortune of its inventor. 'Imagine,' said Mr Melody, 'eating the Perfect Sweet,

21

and being the one to give it to everybody else in the world. Imagine their gratitude, and the warm sense of achievement you would take to your grave.'

By now we were almost out of the park and my mother, slightly impatient, interrupted Mr Melody's fantasy.

'I meant to ask you,' she said, 'before we parted, whether you were free on Friday night for some babysitting. I don't like to ask, but it's rare for Eldon to agree to go out on a Friday and as you know, my friend Melinda isn't really available any more.'

'Ouph.' Mr Melody made a sound as if someone had punched him gently in the stomach. 'You put me in a difficult position Lucy. Prior engagement. Infuriating.' He appeared to consider, staring at the sky with his arms folded and his fingers drumming on his biceps. 'I wonder if things could be altered.' His eyes returned to earth. 'No, I'm so sorry Lucy, I don't think it can be arranged, it doesn't seem to be on the cards. What a shame.'

'Never mind,' said my mother, again with that slight tone of impatience. She and Mr Melody were never the greatest of friends, though not for want of trying on his part. 'It's nothing personal,' she would tell my father, 'I just don't like his manner. Don't you find it ingratiating? I just don't like the way he makes a meal of things. I get the impression he'd like to organize our life for us. And what is this silly affectation of not telling us his first name? "Call me Melody," he says. He just gets on my nerves I'm afraid. Those impossible clothes. I'm never going to like *all* your friends. I don't notice you getting on like a house on fire with Melinda.' So forth.

'Never mind,' said my mother, 'Eldon said he'd talk to J.T.'

Mr Melody raised his eyebrows and passed a finger across his moustache. 'Do you think he's quite . . . quite suitable?' This was as close as he ever allowed himself to get to expressing dislike for J. T. Archer.

My mother's smile was at its brightest. 'I don't know the man as well as you and Eldon do, but I'm sure my husband knows what he's doing. I think we're going different ways here, aren't we? Say goodbye, Billy.'

I said goodbye in a preoccupied way. I was a neurotic child, always apprehensive when my parents were out, fearful for their safety or worried that circumstances beyond my understanding might keep them away; but staying with Kim at Melinda's usually made me forget my anxiety. J. T. Archer was a man I had heard of but could not remember meeting, and Mr Melody's doubts did not reassure me.

Five

After school on Wednesday afternoon, I was at Charlie's house. I had told him about my conversation with Mr Melody, and we had decided to discover the Perfect Sweet. It wasn't really gratitude and a sense of achievement we were after. The Great Pretender's visions of wealth and power had infiltrated Mr Melody's whimsy, his mystifying spell of words still worked on us: it was gold we wanted. There was also, of course, the prospect of finishing up with something we could eat.

On Sunday evening, my father had taken me into his study and shown me how to draw shapes with computer graphics. From experience, I understood the etiquette of these exchanges. With a flourish, he pressed a button and shapes appeared on the black screen. 'Magic,' he said. I sat on his knee and pointed at the screen pretending interest, looking at the revolving squares as if I didn't think they were absurd compared to the pictures I saw every day on TV, and I asked my questions at what seemed to be the most propitious times.

'Daddy, what is alchemy?'

'Turning things to gold. Now look, if we press these buttons here, we get a circle inside the square! It's like magic isn't it?'

'Yes,' I humoured him, 'it's just like magic. Did the magician turn things to gold then? Did he really do those things?'

'Tricks, cheap tricks. Just concentrate, this is science, you can do terrible and wonderful things with science. Scientific alchemy.'

'What can you do? What things?' My curiosity was roused in spite of myself.

'Watch. Here's one I made earlier.' His fingers moved over the keyboard and the circle and the square disappeared, to be replaced by a red stick man waving a wand up and down over a triangle. As the wand waved the triangle changed colour, from white to gold. I was pleased to see that my father's imagination had been touched by the Great Pretender's illusion too. The triangle continued to change, white to gold, gold to white, as we talked.

'What about that?' said my father. 'Not bad after an afternoon's practise, eh?'

'Terrible and wonderful,' I said dutifully.

He turned me round on his lap so that I was facing him. He was grinning, so I reached up and patted his balding head. 'Billy my boy, I sense a certain lack of sincerity in your attitude. One day you may make an excellent MP, but in the meantime, I'd like you to be truthful with your father. No pretending, all right?'

Astonished that he'd seen through my deception, I nodded solemnly.

'Now what is it that you're after?' He frowned as he played back our conversation. 'Alchemy? You want to try your hand at that?'

I told him what Mr Melody had said. 'I want to make golden sweets,' I finished.

'Make them then,' he said. 'You can find ingredients in the cupboard, or buy some things with pocket money. I warn you though Billy, it's just a game. Only children and fools try to make something out of nothing. Alchemy only works if you have the right ingredients.' He tapped his head. 'Business sense, that's what you want, a little depth to your thinking. All in good time though. Come on, let's find your mother, tell me what she's been so glum about recently. Is she worrying about Christmas presents?'

We were sitting on the floor in Charlie's kitchen, surrounded by the uniform colours and shapes of its units. Beige formica and imitation wood, rounded edges and smooth, wipeable surfaces. I had bought a Mars bar, and he had bought a Milky Way. We had some white chocolate and some sherbet. From the cupboards we had also taken cereal, marmalade, cocoa powder and, because we were great believers in secret ingredients, baked beans. We had a large bowl and a wooden spoon, and we were very excited: we were going to make our fortunes, so that whatever we wished for could be ours. I didn't tell Charlie, because Charlie was my new best friend, but I was wishing that Kim might come back to stay.

'Break it into small pieces,' said Charlie, '*small* pieces! The smaller the better because then we can mash it.'

'And put it in the fridge in shapes, and take it out later and it'll be ready.'

'More cocoa powder.'

'It's too solid already, stupid.'

'*I'm* not stupid, you put it in first. I'm putting milk in.'

'That's right milk, chocolate has milk in it.'

Charlie splashed in half a carton, and the mixture in the bowl became a dirty brown liquid with blobs and fragments of solid material floating in it. We sat on either side of it, looking in, like a couple of apprentice witches.

'Doesn't look too good,' said Charlie.

'It's not *supposed* to. Unpromising, Mr Melody said, and something else: mundane.'

'What's that?'

'I'm not sure.'

'Well you should have found out, shouldn't you? How do we make it if we don't even know what it's supposed to look like? That's just stupid. You could have *asked* him. That's really stupid, Billy.'

'Shut up, I'm not stupid, you don't know anything, you don't know what you're talking about. I'm putting the baked beans in, that'll make it thicker.'

The beans slid below the surface, leaving an orange oil slick floating above them. We stirred it, and the oil slick swirled into spirals.

'That's good,' I said, 'I bet that's how it's supposed to look. If we can make it small with spirals like that then it will look good. *I'd* buy it. You see I know how it should look.'

'It's too milky. It's just a milkshake, let's pour some of it out.'

We slopped most of the liquid away into the sink, where it clogged the plug, and we were left with a gooey, lumpy substance the colour of burnt baked beans.

'Well,' said Charlie, 'here goes.'

He put in a finger, scooped up a dripping brown lump, and

dropped it into his mouth. I watched his face as he chewed. It was thoughtful.

'Sugar,' he said. 'And you know what we forgot? Soy sauce. I have soy sauce with everything.'

I looked at him admiringly. I had expected him to spit it on to the floor in theatrical disgust. This was surely a scientific approach. There was depth to our thinking. His A Team T-shirt, his Henry V haircut and his podgy cheeks did not inspire much confidence, but his whole-hearted approach to the problem did. We shared a sense of partnership in endeavour. It wasn't the rapport I had had with Kim, but it had its own advantages. I saw in him a recklessness that I might learn to imitate.

When we had added the new ingredients, I followed his example and tasted the mixture. 'Eugh!' Something hadn't blended properly. I tasted sickly sweetness and a strange, bland, faintly sour flavour at the same time. 'What did you put that sauce in for? It's horrible now, I bet it was all right before you put the sauce in.' I had trouble talking. A sticky lump of something lay on my tongue. Liquid trickled down into my throat, but I didn't want to either chew or swallow the solid matter. I opened my mouth and let it fall into my hand, where it rested, soft and squashy, leaking juice, like a just-removed organ.

'It's horrible now.'

'Well what did we do wrong? The sauce was right, I have it with everything. All the things we put in were all right.'

'I don't know,' I said. 'Mr Melody said people had been trying for years to do it right.'

'Well, Mr Melody's full of shit then.'

I thought about my mother's coldness to him, and felt able to nod.

'He dresses like a clown.'

Another nod.

'I stole the Milky Way from him. Let's steal some more stuff. Do you want to steal some stuff?'

'Sure,' I said. I didn't hesitate, but even at the age of seven, anxious not to look like a coward in front of my friend, I was aware of what I was doing: this was something new, something more realistic than I was used to. The sick, what-am-I-letting-myself-in-for fear that accompanied this knowledge, was just part of its novelty.

'Good,' said Charlie. 'We'll do it on Saturday. Do you want to see a video?' He said this without much enthusiasm. At school he was always bragging about the films he had seen with his older brother, so he knew what was expected of him. He described it for me. 'There's lots of blood, and a girl with the biggest tits you've ever seen. There's too many scenes with her,' he added, 'but it's mostly this guy with a shotgun. Pow! And there's someone who he's after, but there's some other people after him, so there's a chase. It gets a bit complicated really. We could watch a bit anyway, if you like?'

He didn't want me to go, so he didn't want me to realize that the video had bored him. We ended up enacting our own version of the film in his room, having purged it of sex and the complications of plot. He crouched behind his bed firing a tommy-gun, I attacked his position wielding a Luger, and in the end we had a fight which he won by sitting on my chest.

'Listen,' he said, pinning my arms, 'do you want to see a secret?'

'Yes.'

'Do you surrender?'

'Yes.'

He got off my chest. 'Come on then.'

We went into his brother's room. 'It's all right,' said Charlie, 'he plays football on Wednesdays. Usually comes home drunk.' A smell of staleness in the air. Two posters of Madonna on the wall over the unmade bed watched us. In one she wore leather and leered at us, in the other she wore a modest white towel and looked coy. Charlie took a key from underneath a dirty ashtray on the table by his brother's bed. He unlocked the wardrobe and pulled out a cardboard box from the back, where it lay behind coats and under some football shirts. I watched, frightened to be trespassing in his brother's room, fascinated to see what had been hidden so carefully. Charlie pulled off the shirts, and some comics carefully laid over the top.

I was disappointed: a video, naked women in peculiar positions on the covers of magazines, a pair of knickers and a toilet roll. Not exactly a treasure trove.

Charlie explained things to me in the manner of a guide. 'There's some really funny things in here,' he said, picking up a magazine. 'Girls being smacked and things. They're special ones, he sends off for them.' He pointed at the knickers. 'I bet those are his girlfriend's. And *this*,' gingerly picking up the toilet roll with the air of someone coming to the prize exhibit, 'you won't guess what he does with this. He puts it on his *thing*, and pulls it up and *down*!'

I thought of the tough looking boy I had seen around school. 'No he doesn't.'

'He does.'

'He doesn't.'

'I've *seen* him, I've looked through the crack in the door and once I came in on purpose, to see him better, and he hit me.' Charlie proudly showed me a bruise behind his ear, which I couldn't see.

'Well, let's go now,' I said, 'he might come back.'

Charlie put everything back. 'Told you,' he said, 'told you I had a secret. Now you have to show me one.'

'I haven't got any secrets.' All I could think of were the labyrinths, and they didn't seem appropriate after Charlie's revelation of his brother's hidden habits.

Charlie could afford to be magnanimous. 'You come stealing with me,' he said, 'and then we'll both have secrets.'

Once, with Kim, I watched workmen digging in the road, exposing pipes running beneath the surface. We stood by the little red wooden fence they had put up, and stared at the fat pipes criss-crossing below us. We had an argument, because Kim was convinced that the pipes must run everywhere beneath the ground, under our feet, under cities and roads and countryside. I won the argument, because my scorn at the idea made her feel foolish. As I walked home now, fretting about unguessable things happening behind the doors I was passing, I decided to ask my parents for their judgement on the pipes under the ground. My father would apply depth of thinking, he would be able to explain.

Six

I elaborate memories, starting from vivid moments and allowing them to grow along an increasingly tenuous chain of association.

As a result, I sometimes remember things that never happened. I also presume on privacy like an enthusiastic gate-crasher, trusting to presentation and bluff to see me through. This is by way of explanation for eavesdropping on my parents. I feel justified. They fractured my childhood, I am trying to recreate something coherent, and whole.

One large bedroom, flanked on each side by 'studies'. The setting for a farce. A double bed dominates the room, a bedside table on each side, three or four books on each. My father is rereading *Great Expectations*, is dipping into Larkin, and is meaning to start a number of other things, fat new works by contemporary novelists. On my mother's table, a well thumbed copy of Lowell's *Life Studies* lies beside a favourite biography. My parents' literary tastes were not negotiable, and their banter on the subject turned early on in their marriage to irritable sniping. The kingsize duvet is white, the carpet grey, the curtains mildly floral, touched by pink. It is Friday evening, my mother sits in her underwear on the bed, her dress hangs from the back of the chair by the dressing table, its sleeves seeming to search for something on the floor.

'It appears,' she says, 'that Mr Melody doesn't like J.T.'

'Is that how it appears?' My father enters from his study, buttoning his shirt. He is not wearing trousers, but it is still a dignified entrance. His prominent nose scents an argument, but he doesn't have the patience to be reasonable. His long face is mournful. 'What's your objection to that? You don't like Melody, do you? So his opinions shouldn't bother you.'

'He said J.T. wasn't suitable. As a babysitter.'

'Mm-hm?'

'Why would he say that?'

'You've caught me out there, I'm afraid. I don't read minds.'

'They're both old cronies of yours; how far do they go back?' She stands up, and looks at herself in the mirror over the dressing table. Fingers her eye. It appears a contact lens is misbehaving. My father looks away, always made uneasy by the red interior of the eyelid and the encroaching veins on the lower part of the eyeball. 'Why would Melody call J.T. unsuitable? That's all I'm wondering. It's not his style to criticize.'

Eldon is sitting where my mother sat, as he pulls on his trousers. 'How far back? Since before your time, Lucy my love.

We all started our balls rolling together, as it were. Melody and I our shops, J.T. his dentistry. Don't ask me why, but there's never been any love lost between them. I don't think I've ever even seen them together, certainly never heard them speak well of each other. I have a feeling there's a history involved. One of these days we'll get one of them drunk and he'll tell all. You don't mind J.T., do you?'

' "Don't mind him" is about right. He thinks the world of himself, doesn't he? Still, my estimation of him rises if he doesn't like Melody.' Lucy has finished adjusting her eye, and now she is dropping her dress over her head. Onion skin. My father has stood up to tie his tie, it is my mother's turn to sit on the bed again, as she pulls on stockings. Like a stately dance.

'What do you have against my friends? These are my oldest friends you're talking about.'

'Past the sell-by date. Should be remaindered.'

Eldon is watching the unrolling of her stocking over her thigh. 'Why put on the dress before the stocking? You're creasing the skirt.' No answer. Perhaps it was an oversight. He tries a rather random stab. 'Are you taking out Melinda's move on me? Because her boss is a man too?'

Dissatisfied with the first knot, he begins on his tie again, watching Lucy in the mirror. She meets his reflected eye. 'Do I need ulterior motives to dislike your friends?' But, abruptly, she is tired of this exchange, and does not want to hear his answer. 'Let's not argue,' she says, 'not when there may be cause to celebrate.' She is still looking into the mirror, and she appears to adjust the smile of her lipsticked lips as she watches herself.

On Eldon's lips there is a witty response unconsummated, and he is forced to divert his energy into another remark.

'What kind of friends is Billy getting involved with? He's been asking me some crazy questions about pipes underground, and funny magazines, and alchemy and God knows what. I thought we agreed that Charlie was a bad influence?'

Lucy has decided not to be provoked. 'It's just his games, nothing to be concerned about. And Charlie's all right really, he's ever so polite. Yes, well apart from the birthday party, but it's unfair to judge anyone by that. Anyway, I've always said, all Billy needs is a little brother or sister.'

The door bell rang and they emerged from their room, fully dressed. In my room, immersed in a town built from Lego, I had ignored their raised voices. Now they took me downstairs, explaining that J.T. was late so they were in a hurry, and would see me in the morning, I was to be good and to sleep well. They opened the door and the man who came in kissed my mother, shook hands with my father and hoisted me into the air as he said goodbye to them and told them to have a wonderful evening. He stood in the doorway holding me until we'd watched them drive away.

I had met him before, but this was the first time I was old enough for J. T. Archer to make an impression on me. A worn black leather jacket, jeans and an open-necked shirt. A tall slim man, with a self-conscious, actorish suavity about him, so that he seemed to be always skirting the edge of self-parody. It was easy to imagine medallions, and a couple more shirt buttons undone, revealing a dark, clustering, curling mat of hair.

'Bill,' he said, 'do you know when we last met? You don't, do you? Well I'll tell you, we last met four years ago when you were about this big,' his hands six inches apart, 'and you cried all the time. I had the same jacket. Do you know, you're younger than my jacket? Don't ask me to choose between you now, that could be fatal.' All this delivered too fast for me to make much sense of it. 'Right, I'm going to make myself a drink, do you want something? Do you drink? Do you talk? Well run along and watch TV, and then we'll have a chat.' He winked. 'I have ways of making you talk.'

There was a cop show on television, so I curled into an armchair and settled down to watch it. I was holding my timidity at bay successfully. It was too soon to worry about my parents, and it seemed that J.T. was not a man to be afraid of: the hearty type, best humoured and largely ignored. He came in swirling my father's whisky in his glass, chinking ice cubes, and he sat down with the bottle beside him, and sneered at the TV.

'This must be pretty tame for you after Charlie's videos,' he said. 'Do you want me to run down to the shop and get something more interesting? As it happens I have some good contacts in that area. Just ask Charlie's brother Gary.'

'I'm watching this. How do you know Charlie?'

'I can see that Bill, I can see you're watching it, I'm just wondering if you wouldn't prefer something a bit more exciting. But I'm forgetting your age, aren't I? Silly me.'

'I don't like videos, I like this. Have you met Charlie?'

'Charlie and me? We go way back, same as Gary and me. Charlie tells me everything. I've got lots of friends. I like to build up relationships. Take my word for it Bill, you'll get nowhere by being quiet and mousy, you've got to build up relationships, meet people, make networks. This is good advice Bill, you should keep this in mind.'

'Do you do their teeth? You don't do my teeth.'

'Now you take your parents. Funny couple your parents. Wouldn't you say? Funny couple. I mean you wouldn't have said they were all that suited really, would you? Not at first sight I mean. There's your dad, dear old Eldon, with his shops and his hobbies, and there's your mummy, with her old-fashioned ideas of domestic bliss. But you know what they've got in common, when you look a bit closer? Neither of them build up networks. Oh, daddy's got his shops all over the place – nice little business that – and he's got his property here and there, but no personal networks. By which I mean *people*, he doesn't know people, so it's a very surface thing. That's what I'm saying to you, Bill,' he refilled his glass, 'that's what I mean, you see. Without networks you're vulnerable. Your daddy, he may not realize it, but he's vulnerable. As for your mummy, she certainly knows she's vulnerable. Off goes Melly and your girlfriend and lovely Louise, and all of a sudden she's alone. No networks. Relied too much on the future, you see. Mind you, she'll be all right, I have a lot of faith in Lucy. But you ask yourself, what are three of you doing in a house built for five?' He took another swig of whisky, and looked at me as if he expected an answer.

'It's a nice house.'

He shook his head. 'That's my problem, I'm always surrounded by kids. I'm a martyr to my networks. Yes Bill, it's a nice house, but it's an empty house. You're rattling around in here, because you've got no brothers and sisters have you? Don't tell me you've never noticed that? But,' gesturing with his glass, pointing at me, 'I can tell you, in the confidential spirit of the dentist's chair, all that may be changing. No one else knows yet, because it's a bit early in the day to be sure, but I think you should be informed that the bun might just finally be in the oven. Probably six buns, the way these things work.' He looked at me. 'There's going to be another *baby*.'

'How do you know?'

He grinned smugly. 'Precious few secrets between your daddy and me.' The grin grew broader. 'Precious few on his side that is. Well, are you pleased? It means the limelight will be off you. It means not being mummy's darling boy any longer. You might even end up feeling like your mum, all lonely, what with Kimmy gone and a brother or sister ruling the roost. That's where my advice comes in you see, it all fits together like a jigsaw. Networks. You may find you need me, and if you do, I promise you I'll be there for you. You ask Charlie, see if I'm not a good friend. And never forget, friendship is a two-way thing – a friend does something for you, you do something for him. Now is that good Christian advice or what?'

I nodded, not understanding.

'Of course it is.' That grin again, wider than ever, as if he was repressing laughter. 'Any son of dear old Eldon is a friend of mine. You want anything, come to me. We're not just talking about advice here. Pirate videos of the latest films? Come to me. Something a bit risqué? I'm your man. Want an acting opportunity? I always find room for talent. You're looking puzzled Bill, and I'm not surprised. You'll understand everything in the fullness of time. But just try to remember, eh? I can open doors, I can make things change.'

With that he lapsed into silence, apart from the regular plash of whisky into his glass, and occasional comments on the teeth of the characters in the cop show. The villain received a right to the jaw: 'He'll be wanting some reconstruction.' The hero smiled: 'Look at that – more caps than Bryan Robson.'

I watched the programme without seeing it, and tried to think about what he had said. There were too many questions. I didn't know whether to think about the baby, about whether Charlie had told Archer about stealing from Mr Melody, or about the more confusing things that he had said and implied. Secrets from my father. Vulnerability. I wasn't even clear whether this man was my father's friend or his enemy. It wasn't something I felt I could ask him to clarify. He knew about Kim and her family, my parents, Mr Melody, Charlie and Gary . . . the image in my mind was of a network of underground pipes, stretching indefinitely beneath the labyrinth I had seen from the hill in the park.

When the programme ended, Archer took from his pocket a camera, a slim black compact model. 'I like to have records of things,' he said, 'my life is a scrapbook of pictures, like a film star's. Do you mind?' Before I could answer, he had taken a picture of me. To my embarrassment he stood up and took a couple more, from different angles. I recognize his style now, from the world I move in: 'Smile at me Bill, look happy, look like you're enjoying yourself.'

I told him I was going to bed.

'Fine,' he said, sitting down. He raised his glass to me. 'Remember what I said.' A wink. 'Everything becomes clear in the fullness of time.'

I sat down beside the town built of Lego which sprawled over my floor. Six houses and three shops of box-like design. An out of proportion railway ran through the street, and a train stopped at a Lego station where people waited on the platform. There were cars on the street as well, and a bus waiting at a bus stop. Just outside town, plastic characters from a cartoon series were disembarking from their spaceship, and were considering either an invasion or a friendly visit. I had big plans for an M25 ring-road constructed from Scalextric. After that I would be ready to introduce Charlie and other friends to the world I had created. It was a question, as my father reminded me, of funding and resources.

I sat beside my town, and then lay beside it, trying to see through the windows of the houses, hoping for some insight on what was hidden behind suburban walls. Delicately, as if handling a bird's nest, I lifted one of the houses, and examined the carpet beneath it. Of course there was nothing to find, and of course I expected nothing. But I was disappointed. Without the pipes, without the locked cupboards and hidden secrets, my town looked like a childish, superficial enterprise. With less delicacy, I removed a ceiling and looked at the hollow shell I had revealed. I had heard about a man who walked down his village high street killing people indiscriminately. There was no clue to that mystery in my toy town. There was no clue to any mystery. I was on the verge of demolishing the entire town, having the spaceship drop a few well-placed atom bombs on it, but I restrained myself. Coupled with my disappointment, there was relief because I knew of an area that was immune to real life. Nothing sinister in this town, nothing to hide behind its closed doors. No uncertainty, no tunnels beneath it. I replaced the ceiling. Perhaps the spaceship was generating a protective force-field around the town's borders barring any contamination. If I was going to dream tonight, I decided, my dreams would inhabit these safe streets.

So finally I went to bed, and admitted delayed but inevitable fears. What time was it? I had managed to stay awake until ten-thirty. No prospect of my parents returning for some hours. My mind began to move in familiar channels, nudging me towards familiar rituals. If I said the Lord's Prayer to myself, slowly, without mistakes, then my parents would return home safely. No mugger would attack them, no driver would crash into them and no stranger would persuade them not to come home. I said the prayer, but my mind was not on the words, so I said it again, thinking about it and thus causing myself to hesitate and stumble on one of the lines. A third time, and I was satisfied.

One ritual led me to another. I counted, slowly, up to 109. I stopped there, paused, and then started again from one. Up to 109 again. And then I began again from one. These numbers were my friends, a family which accepted me as an honorary member when my parents were away. I was well acquainted with them, and with their relationships with each other. Here was a network I understood; an intricate pattern whereby each knew each, and none were ever far apart. There were always new ways of joining them, and I enjoyed exploring the ways, but most of all I enjoyed the fundamental, unchanging pattern which they followed as I counted them, slowly, from one to 109.

By this pacifying, almost hypnotizing process, I gradually moved towards, and imperceptibly entered, sleep. I was disturbed twice. Once the door of my bedroom creaked and, lying on my side, I half opened my eyes and half thought that my parents had come home, and were looking in at me. Was it my father's shape in the doorway? I grunted something, and slid back into sleep. The second time I was disturbed I heard voices coming up the stairs. Unmistakably my parents. They were laughing while trying to keep their voices low; they had obviously had a good evening. But, instead of making me happy, this just brought to my mind, unbidden, a new fear: the thought that tomorrow I was supposed to steal from Mr Melody. I slept uneasily after that, even though my parents were home now and J. T. Archer had left.

Seven

In the morning, I found that the force-field around my town had been silently breached. In the middle of the main street, surrounded by a crowd of staring figures, stood a cardboard box the size of a house. Although he had not had it with him when he arrived, I had no doubt that this was a gift from Archer, rather than from my parents. Already I perceived that surprise and bribery were part of his style. I opened the box.

Nothing earth-shaking inside. It was a model, an expensive accessory sold with the plastic science-fiction characters who were still frozen on the edge of town. It was a model of The Skull Beneath the Skin, the pub which was the headquarters of their arch-enemy, The Gargoyle. It was an elaborate Gothic construction with arched windows revealing glimpses of unnatural practices, and a swinging sign outside, emblazoned with a skull. It was something I had seen advertised and had coveted, but not especially for the centre of my town. It changed the nature of things. Still, there were possibilities. Street battles might be staged, involving house-to-house fighting. It might be time to involve Charlie, even before the ring-road was built. I postponed any decision about it, as I got dressed and remembered the news about the baby.

'He had no right to tell you,' said my mother. 'That's something *I* wanted to tell you. Anyway we don't know yet, I mean we aren't even sure yet. What do you think, Billy? Won't it be wonderful?'

I agreed that it was wonderful.

'You aren't going to be jealous now are you?'

'Why should I be jealous?'

'Yes, why should he be jealous? You see what you're doing, don't you Lucy? You're putting ideas into his head. You're right Billy, no reason at all. Sensible lad.' My father looked at his watch. 'If we're going to play, we're going to have to move. I've got a meeting at one o'clock.'

My parents were playing tennis. It was one of the few of my father's hobbies they could both enjoy. I was to be dropped off at Charlie's for the morning.

I made a last effort to postpone this. 'Can't I play tennis too? You wanted to teach me.'

'You didn't want to be taught,' said my father.

'I *do* want to be taught, I've changed my mind.'

'Excellent. Tomorrow. Or next week at the latest. Now tell me,' he said as he finished his toast, 'how did that alchemy go with Charlie? I've been meaning to ask.'

I told him about the failure of our experiment.

'I warned you,' he said. 'Business sense is what you need, good business sense produces results. Like stocks and shares Billy, or a bestseller.' He nodded complacently. Behind his back, my mother caught my eye and looked sceptical. 'Alchemy in a way *is* my business, making gold out of some pretty unlikely things. You come to me next time, not Melody, I'll explain it for you. In the meantime,' swallowing the last of his coffee, 'let's all get going.'

Charlie and Gary were both in front of the television when I arrived, and I was happy to join them. Perhaps Charlie had forgotten his plan. No one said much. There were cartoons on, each introduced by a young blonde woman who, Charlie told me, Gary fancied. Her hair was held up in a snaky pile on her head and she wore a furry blue jumpsuit. Her face was certainly glorious, the smoothest and pinkest thing imaginable, with a big jumpy red smile and a winning eyelash flutter. Gary fidgeted as he watched her. When I said to Charlie that she reminded me of Louise in her magician's assistant costume, Gary interrupted without looking round, 'Shut up, I'm listening.' Charlie shrugged an apology to me. I sneaked a look at his brother. I couldn't tell if he was listening, but he was watching the presenter intently.

When the cartoons were over, and a band had come on with their new single, Gary left the room.

'Are you ready to go?' said Charlie.

'Where shall we go?'

'You know where we're going. Mr Melody's. You know what we're doing.'

'Let's watch a bit of this. I like this.'

Before the song was over, Gary was back. A different presenter began an interview with the lead singer.

'Who's this wanker?' said Gary. 'Where's Debbie?'

'Shall we go now?' said Charlie.

'Where you going?'

'Out.'

'Where you going?'

'Sweet Surrender. We want to buy some things.'

He sneered. 'Bye-bye kids. Don't spend all your pocket money at once.'

I suddenly knew what Charlie was going to say. 'We're not spending. Who needs money? Mr Melody's a wanker.'

With that he ran out and I followed. He shouted to his mother that we were leaving, picked up his coat, and we were gone.

'I'm not doing it,' I said, 'I'm not doing it now that he knows. He'll tell, won't he? We can't do it now.'

I expected Charlie to agree. 'What are you scared of, he's only my brother, who cares if he tells? We'll say it's not true, or we'll tell on him, we'll tell about his secrets. We *have* to do it now.' Almost a note of pleading in his voice. 'We've *told* him.' As if this was an unanswerable argument in his favour.

Trays and jars and shelves and glass-fronted cupboards. Mr Melody knew how to lay a place out. He knew how to display things to the best effect, how to marshal his goods so that shapes and colours and quantities enticed and intrigued the eye. I'm talking about a confectioner's equivalent of an art gallery, about the particular placing of the ordinary and the unusual, of vibrant colours and warm ones, soft textures and hard ones, rich odours and sweet perfumes. These may sound like large claims for a sweet shop, but here I am at an advantage in relying on memory, because the fact that my image of the place remains so vivid is a testament to Melody's skill.

My first hope was that, by some miracle, the shop would be

closed. Seeing the door wide open and customers inside, my second hope was that Mr Melody would not be there. More often than not he had other business to attend to, and left his shop in the hands of his staff. But there he was, finding time while serving someone to give us a cheerful wave.

We browsed. I don't think we could have acted more suspiciously if we had tried. I was being casual, which involved putting my hands in my pockets and looking around a lot. Charlie nudged me and whispered.

'This is the best place,' he said.

I looked more casual than ever.

It was an alcove where the best-selling sweets were displayed on a wide counter; the Mars bars and Milky Ways and Marathons, the Smarties, the various chews and gums and mints. We looked round. Mr Melody and his assistant were busy and, with Charlie standing behind me, they couldn't see us. Since we hadn't noticed the mirror up in the corner by the door, we thought they couldn't see us. Faced by the choice in front of me, some of my apprehension disappeared. I took my hand from my pocket, it hovered a moment, lingering, one last pause, and then I picked up a Crunchie and put my hand back in my pocket. Then, my face like a beacon advertising my guilt, I had to stand in front of Charlie while he did the same.

That was my introduction to crime.

After we had sidled out, Charlie was exultant.

'What a blind old bat. Did you see him? Did you see him standing there smiling at that woman? Old bat. Just as well he didn't catch us. Borstal if he had, big trouble. And my dad would have gone mad.'

I interrupted him. 'It was easy though, wasn't it? We should have taken more, we could have taken anything, he couldn't see us. I was worried you know really, I didn't know it was going to be so easy.'

In this jubilant mood we returned to Charlie's clutching our stolen chocolate bars like trophies, not even considering eating them until we were safely in the security of his bedroom. It was a small room, and the bed and the clutter of clothes took up most of the space. We were watched by a poster of a Master of the Universe. I took a bite of Crunchie, fingered the golden honeycomb in the middle. Gary came in while I still had a mouthful.

'Successful trip then, boys?'

We looked at him.

'I don't need to ask really do I? Guzzle guzzle. Don't you know you'll ruin your appetites?'

In his dress, Gary was almost a younger version of Archer. He had the jeans and the leather, a T-shirt instead of a shirt, and a thin gold chain. Physically however, there was no similarity. Where Archer had a thin face, well-defined bones, smiling thin lips and short dark hair, Gary was a chubby-faced sixteen year old, cherubic you might have said, and he was heavily built. At school they told him to cut his hair.

'Cat got your tongues?' Gary leaned on the wall by the door. 'What are you frowning about, Billy? Worrying about what Mr Melody might think of you? I bet he'll be disillusioned, won't he? You're pretty close, the two of you, aren't you? And as for you Charles, can you imagine dad's reaction? I can. We're talking about a week off school to recover, Charlie, that's what we're talking about here.'

'You've stolen things. You've told me so.'

'Me? You're kidding, aren't you? What an idea, what a hopeless attempt to defend yourself. Lying about me.'

'What do you want?' Charlie held out his half-eaten chocolate. 'Do you want this?'

He laughed. 'You are so pathetic Charlie, it hurts. When are you going to grow up?' He looked at us. 'Get up off that bed. What are you, bum chums? Back to back. Well come *on*, stand back to back. Do as I say, you maggots.' We stood back to back. 'You're a short-arse, aren't you Billy? You'll do.'

'What for? What do you mean?'

'Don't act so bloody scared. What's the matter with you? It's just a little job you can help me and my mates with, that's all. Nothing to wet your pants about. You might even come out of it quite well, if you're a good boy.'

'What job?' said Charlie.

'Shut up and I'll tell you.' Gary smiled at me. He had a piggy face. It was going to get piggier and piggier as he got older. His smile broadened his nostrils. 'There's this house right, which belongs to friends of one of my mates. Well, they've gone away for the weekend haven't they, and he needs something they've got. He's got keys of course, but they've gone and bolted the front door. Very careless. So it's lucky for him they've left a window open, isn't it?'

'You can wait till Monday, when they get back.'

He shook his head, as if disappointed in me. His mannerisms, his tone of voice and his words all seemed to belong to someone else, as if he was borrowing them, and they didn't quite fit. It was something he would grow into. 'Now Billy, don't argue with me. I'm asking for a little favour, in return for not grassing on you – and you want me to wait till Monday? Is that friendly? I'm offering you an opportunity here. I'm waiting till tomorrow evening, that's what I'm doing, and then you're going to climb through the window and let me and my friends in.'

'It's stealing.'

'You're not as stupid as you look. Of course it's stealing, have you got something against that? Are you turning over a new leaf suddenly? In the window, pull back the bolt on the front door, and you can go home. Piece of piss. Don't argue with me son – ' he was eight years older than me, and I could see in his face the pleasure he got from calling me 'son' ' – don't argue with me or you'll get a smack, you understand? You'll get something out of it, don't worry. Something for nothing. It's as easy as falling off your BMX.'

Eight

My solution to my problem was to run away from it. What I wanted was a fresh start. It was very simple, like learning to write: if a page became too messy, too covered in scribbles and crossings out, then I screwed it up and started again with a clean piece of paper.

Gary was only part of it. When the time came to explain, I sprayed explanations about without much concern for the truth, and so my memory is clouded by inventions, but I know there was a mood of restlessness at home. My father was hardly ever there, and my mother was nagged by discontent. She talked about a job, talked about the baby, talked, unjustly, about what a seedy neighbourhood we lived in. One afternoon she tried a tea party for other wives and mothers and one house husband in the area. I witnessed the result when I came home at four o'clock. A china teapot and cups lay neatly on the coffee table. On the floor around it there were about five empty wine bottles, a bottle of gin and some whisky. The house husband was holding forth in plangent tones to my mother about his lack of self-respect, while she avoided his pawing hands; two women on a sofa were hugging each other; another was sobbing to a sympathetic friend. One was sitting in a corner practising yoga with a disgusted expression.

It was like my birthday party, a fragile order easily disrupted, replaced by anarchy.

Now, inescapably, my father and a pack of his business cronies barge into my memory as they barged into the house late one night, invading its peace. Disturbed by their crashing entry, I left my room and went to the top of the stairs, to see that I had been preceded by my mother. My father's arms were around her, he was almost hanging from her neck while his friends cheered him on. 'Come on Luce,' he said. 'Loosen up Luce, let's have a party. Ring your girlfriends, ring 'em up and get 'em over. Party time!' Raucous agreement from his friends, including one who was holding his stomach and looking ill. My mother murmured something. 'What! Whassat? Whatsamatter, not good enough for you? Not good enough for college girls?' My mother disentangled herself and left him there, wordlessly ushering me back into my room. In the morning there was a smell of vomit downstairs. The bodies of most of my father's friends lay in the living room. One of them, dishevelled but well turned out, greeted me courteously in the kitchen and told me we were short of milk.

Another reason for running away was the love that Kim and I were supposed to share. In the month since she had moved I had only seen her once, briefly, when Melinda had asked us all round for dinner among the packing cases. My mother had not taken me back since then. 'It's too soon,' she said, 'give them a chance to settle in, they've only just arrived.' I felt it was time for me to demonstrate my loyalty.

Fear, restlessness, love; I was a runaway with fine qualifications.

The door to my parents' room was closed as I tip-toed past it. I knew I would have a fair start, because it tended to remain closed for a good portion of Sunday mornings. Eldon and Lucy were not devotees of Sunday newspapers, and they had a tea-maker by their bed. I liked the mystery of the closed door, and had no inclination to solve it by looking through the keyhole or entering unannounced. Far from it: I was glad that they had a secret to share.

It is early on Sunday morning in the middle of November, and it seems to me that it is promising weather for escape. I am waiting for my train, moving from foot to foot, tilting my face into the sun and wondering why it has no warmth. Promising weather: bright, light and airy, but not warm. I look at the track, heading off towards London in parallel, glittering lines, and I feel a strong sense that I am in the right place, doing the right thing.

I admit that this behaviour was out of character, given my love of security, my concern for my mother's happiness and my natural timidity. I can only say that I wasn't myself. I can only say that I either wasn't myself then, or I wasn't myself previously. I have to add, though it undermines my status, that I am not that seven and a bit year old any more, and I cannot explain or answer for his behaviour.

There he was, there I was, on the train, moving forward, suppressing my fears, somehow working on them in order to produce excitement, and what might pass for bravery.

In the huge deserted cavern of Charing Cross, my mood changed. Wide, empty floor space, shops shut, a flickering notice board addressing no one. What was I to do next? While I was thinking about it, my few fellow passengers disappeared, leaving me alone except for a cleaner pushing a mop in a corner. Was this his job? To clean the floor at Charing Cross every Sunday? Tentatively, I approached him.

'Excuse me. Excuse me?'

'What do you want?'

'How do I get to Elliot Road?'

'Where?'

'It's in Kentish Town.' From the tube I intended to ask my way to Melinda's house. I felt sure that Kim and I between us could persuade her to let me live with them.

'You on your own?'

I did my best to mimic his face. I had heard the expression 'poker face'. This, I thought, must be it: a long face, down turned lips, heavy eyes. 'Yup.'

'Something wrong with you, boy?'

I altered my face a little, felt that I was frowning now, and decided that that would do. 'Nothing wrong. I mean nothing's wrong. I'm visiting my aunt. My parents sent me.' Then, in a moment of inspiration, 'She was supposed to meet me, I'm going to her house.'

'Tube,' he said, pointing. 'Kentish Town, Camden Town, Chalk Farm.'

'Sorry?'

'One of them is the tube you want, boy.'

'All right.'

I found myself now in a true labyrinth. I wandered through passages and down escalators, ogling posters for films and bras, guided by signs and symbols, turning corners to be greeted by long, empty stretches of brightly lit tunnel. I walked halfway down one and then doubled back on myself, sure that it couldn't be right, it was going too far, leading me somewhere I didn't want to be. I took a turning and discovered a staircase that wasn't there before, and realized with horror that I didn't know the way back to where I had started. I tried running, and was frightened by the echoing of my own steps. I walked, slow and deliberate, tearful, considering sitting down and waiting until someone might pass, speculating that the passages might continue all over London, like the pipes, thinking that even jail for burglary was better than starving to death alone underground. I turned another corner and almost bumped into a tourist, back-packing, who noticed my tear-streaked face and stopped.

I promptly frowned, but I was not sufficiently off-putting to stop the man from taking me to the right platform.

'Thank you,' I said ungraciously, when he was out of earshot.

Noisy and jolting in its enthusiasm, the train rushed me to my station without incident, and the doors opened obediently. Encouraged by this, and finding 'Exit' signs easier to follow than colour coded information about lines, I returned to the surface.

I don't know what I expected from Chalk Farm. Blackboards I think, and cows and sheep grazing. I might have been less surprised to find this than to find just another street, so very like home. Having travelled so far, I was surprised to find the same shops and houses, and the same roads. I was surprised by the lack of imagination this implied. After my journey above and below ground, such a large step for me, I expected a correspondingly large change in the environment.

The first person I met thought she had heard of Elliot Road. I received some complicated directions, attempted to follow them, and found myself on the edge of a fenced off, hilly looking field. I found hope in this huge expanse of green: here perhaps was the farm. It was still quite early, and the grass and stark trees were attractive in the fresh-faced morning light, so I shouldered my duffel bag and went looking for the animals.

Dogs. Labradors and alsatians, poodles and pugs. I concluded that I was in a dog farm and, not sure if I might be trespassing, I frowned all the more as I encountered the various varieties of owner. Green wellies, overcoats, anoraks and bomber jackets. I saw a man in leather trousers leading a daschund and a woman in tweed from head to foot with a doberman that seemed taller than me. I saw two collies but no sheep. It occurred to me that if I lived with Melinda I might get a job on the farm. Groom to some of the larger dogs. What would I say though, if someone braved my frown and challenged me, asked me what I was doing on private property? Farmers carry shotguns. I was only reassured when I saw a man playing golf. Clearly the rules in the farm were not strict, even to the extent of allowing potentially hazardous golf balls to be flying around the dogs' ears. Or around mine. I ducked as the ball sliced towards me, and turned to see that it had landed in some bushes.

'Don't move! Don't take a step, or I'll never find the little bleeder.'

The golfer was approaching, waving his club authoritatively. I waited.

'Good man, good man. Where is the little bleeder?'

I pointed out his ball, nestled among roots and fallen leaves.

'Plum in the rough eh? My luck.' He reached in with his club and dragged the ball out. 'What are you doing out here on your own, young man? With that bag? Tell me off if I'm being inquisitive if you like, bad habit I'm afraid.'

He had a scary face. A bulging, inflated nose, a protruding chin, prominent, oddly triangular cheeks and pouches under his eyes. At the temples and forehead his skin flattened out, as if the face itself was a mask, a thick layer of plastic or clay over the flesh.

He spoke again before I had time to think of an answer.

'What's that expression for? What's that scowl doing on your face? Eh? I'm prepared to believe that it's a defensive scowl, but nevertheless, it's not something to be encouraged. It's something your mother or your father should have winkled out of you, or winkled you out of. You can't go through life like that, it's just not on. You can't go through life scowling like that, think of the effect you'll have on everyone you meet. Where *are* your mother and your father?'

'I'm going to see my aunt,' I said. 'But I came in to see the animals first, but there's only dogs and I'm looking for Elliot Road but I don't know where I am now.'

'Animals? The zoo? Fine idea, educational, but your aunt will have to accompany you, because it's too expensive for small boys. And you'll only get lost again. Do you mean to tell me that your parents sent you off alone to look for your aunt? Careful what you say, young man, think before you answer.'

I looked up into the mask-like face, unable to read the expression. I thought I should approach the truth a little more closely. 'Not exactly,' I said. 'I decided to visit her, to surprise her.'

'And them no doubt. Does it occur to you that they may worry?'

'I was going to ring them when I arrived.'

'Then perhaps I had better see you on your way, although it means aborting a highly successful round.'

We were, he assured me, nearly there, when Mr Melody came rushing out of a shop to greet me.

'Can it be Billy? It can! Well this is most peculiar. Pleasant to be sure, but peculiar without a doubt. In North London, miles from home. Wait, don't tell me, no, no, don't say a word . . . I have it! You are visiting Melinda and the delightful Kim. Am I right?'

My golfing friend answered. 'I was showing Billy, whose name I neglected to discover, the way to his aunt's house.'

'Aunt's? Billy I didn't know you had an aunt here? Are your parents with you? Are they already there?'

'I think at this point I shall leave. If you would be good enough to take Billy to his aunt or, failing that, to the delightful Kim?' The mask creased into a dry smile. 'Goodbye Billy, perhaps we'll meet again if you are visiting any of your . . . connections here.'

'Goodbye,' I said, 'thank you very much.' We shook hands, my hand lost in his big palm, and then Mr Melody and I watched him leave. His socks, I noticed, were rolled over his trouser legs, and his putter swung in a business-like way as he headed back to the park.

Mr Melody's North London shop was a gift emporium selling gadgets and novelty items, tableware and games. Its scope was wide. Attached to it there was a photography section, in which jazzy designer 35 mm cameras and video cameras were sold, and speedy development of snaps was promised. The shop was called The Circus of Delights. 'Open all hours and every day,' Mr Melody said. 'Christmas is approaching you know.'

We were sitting in a small room behind the shop, neither a stock room nor a living room. 'My studio,' he had said, proudly. A light on a stalk gazed down at us as we sat on two canvas chairs in front of a white background. He chattered about the shop as if his mind was elsewhere. For my part I was feeling pangs of guilt, wondering whether I should risk jail or borstal by confessing. The room was uncomfortably bare, like an interrogation cell in a police station. Finally, Mr Melody noticed my preoccupation. 'You can tell me all your troubles later,' he said. 'I'm certainly intrigued to hear why you're here on your own and why you're looking so glum. You've always been intriguing Billy. First let me show off a little. Look at my newest pride and joy.'

From beneath his seat he brought out a small black box, inside which there was a video camera, a compact, handheld thing which whirred and flashed and then played back a film in the viewfinder. Mr Melody was like a child with a new toy, and his enthusiasm kindled mine. He recited something from a play while I filmed him, and then he filmed me, tongue-tied, until he prompted me to tell him a joke.

'Knock knock.'

'Who's there?'

'Boo.'

'Boo who?'

'There's no need to cry about it.'

Mr Melody laughed delightedly. 'You'll be a fine comedian Billy, you're photogenic. Do you know what that means? It means the camera loves you.' Finally though, he looked at his watch. 'I have appointments Billy, I have friends coming soon. Unless you want to meet them?' I didn't. 'Now, tell me the truth. Have you run away?'

The abrupt question caught me off guard, as he had intended. Tearful again, I confessed to the theft of the Crunchie. I didn't mention Charlie or Gary, but I burbled a little about my mother's irritability. I even said something that I hadn't realized before: I was worried that *I* was irritating her, and that she would be glad I had gone. Mr Melody listened, saying nothing, just looking at his watch occasionally.

'As to the matter of the Crunchie,' he said, adjusting his thick glasses, 'it is loyal of you to try to protect Charlie, laudable in you, but I saw you both. I've been hoping for a chance to talk privately with you. I know it was not like you, Billy, but I must say, I was very disappointed. It's a selfish act, Billy, not just a criminal one. What would happen to me if everyone stole from me? I'd go out of business, Billy, I'd starve. Is that what you want? Do you want me to starve, Billy?'

I shook my head.

He smiled. 'I should think not. I hope you're very sorry, Billy.'

I told him that I was very sorry, and repeated that I certainly didn't want him to starve.

'Then we'll say no more about it.' He looked at his watch. 'We'll say no more about the matter, not even to your parents.' He stood up, brisk now. 'You really shouldn't be here. Shall we get you to Melinda's? Contrary to what you may think, your poor mother will be frantic. You must try to remember how lucky you are with your parents, Billy. Some children don't have parents like yours, they go into care. Are you familiar with that phrase? No, of course not. Well it is one of those phrases that means the opposite of what it says. A scandalous state of affairs. Not a fate I would wish on any child. Now, we must go.'

Melinda, Louise and Kim were all bemused to see me. They were sitting down to lunch, so Melinda first phoned my parents, and then set me a place. I had to explain to all three at once.

'I came to see you,' I said.

'Came to see Kim, you mean,' said Louise.

'Why?' said Kim.

'No, not just to see you.' I couldn't tell them about the stealing, or about Gary, or about love, so I found myself talking about my mother again. 'She's having a baby,' I said, 'but she's unhappy. I think she's lonely because daddy's never there and now you're not there.' As I enlarged on this theme I remembered Archer's words, 'You might end up feeling like your mum, all lonely.' I found it worryingly plausible. 'She doesn't like the people who live near us, or daddy's friends, and she gets bored, so she's unhappy.'

Melinda talked at length about how daddy was my mother's friend, and how I should be too, and running away wouldn't help and she, Melinda, wasn't very far away at all and anyway, I was probably exaggerating things. I nodded agreement but it was no good. Doubt was there. Melinda and Mr Melody might disagree with Archer but it made no difference: doubt was there. I had persuaded myself. I felt I had stumbled on a truth.

My mother arrived alone, and Melinda talked to her before I saw her. I was with Kim.

'Is all that true,' she said, 'about your mother?'

'I don't know,' I said, 'I think it might be. You haven't forgotten that we love each other have you?'

Kim shook her head, an impatient movement which seemed to deny the whole idea rather than the suggestion that she had forgotten.

'Because I haven't. Even if we never see each other.'

'I don't know what you mean,' she said.

'You don't know?'

'It's not the point. It's not the point is it?'

To begin at the beginning is difficult, as I found as soon as I started to write this memoir. Where is the beginning of my relationship with Kim? My first sight of her? I don't think so. There is no significance to be gleaned from two very young children peering at each other from behind their mothers' legs. The first time we played together? Perhaps. It was some board game, something like Snakes and Ladders, and we were interrupted by a bee. A fat furry bumble bee, buzzing around our heads. It left us to charge against the window, the ping of its head on the glass clearly audible. This phenomenon was new to us, and we watched it with interest. It got lost behind the curtain and, to Kim's admiration, I found it again by jostling the folds of material. I don't know. The faltering tentative occasion I am describing now is also a beginning of a kind. The beginning of a new stage in our relationship.

Distance had stretched our friendship thinly. I thought I had a lot to tell her – about my journey, about the Perfect Sweet and about Gary Larbey's secrets. I planned to confide in her about the stealing of the Crunchie and my putative role in the burglary. That wasn't how it was. After that first exchange, our conversation was stilted, overshadowed by her disarming surprise at my presence. I felt irrelevant. She talked about new friends and her new school, I talked about Charlie. We used conversation to avoid saying anything. Almost a sense of rivalry in our tones, almost a sense of relief when it was time to go.

It wasn't until we were halfway home that my mother questioned me about the story I had told Melinda. By this time my lies and intuitions and avoidance of the truth had confused me utterly.

'What's all this?' she said. 'Are you laying the blame on me? Tell me, sweetheart, have I been all that miserable?'

'No.'

'No, of course I haven't. So what the hell are you up to?'

This sudden sharpness surprised me. 'I don't know.'

She sighed, not looking at me, watching the road. 'Why did you run away, and why did you decide to tell stories about me? I want to know, Billy.'

'I ran away to see Kim,' I said, choosing the lesser of various evils. 'You kept saying they were too busy, they had to settle in, and I wanted to see her. That's all.'

'I doubt that that's all. And your tall stories? What about them? Do you understand how you've embarrassed me, and hurt my feelings?' She still looked straight ahead, out of the window. I looked straight ahead too. There was hardly any traffic. The Sunday afternoon streets were empty.

'I'm sorry. I didn't want to say the truth.'

We drove home in silence after that, my last words remaining with us in the close atmosphere of the car, reproaching both of us. Words, I felt, were failing me with those I loved. They were all right for Mr Melody, and for the golfer, but with Kim and with my mother, they seemed to be sadly inadequate. My excursion into burglary, I realized, had only been postponed, but I took consolation in a certain pride in my adventure. I still feel it: I did all right for a seven year old, and if I ended up immersed in guilt, that was partly because of my mother's dishonesty. I am less inclined to feel sympathy for her now than I used to be.

Nine

This was a busy time in my life, a crowded time. My troubles came in a pack, one after another, one leading to another like dominoes toppling in sequence. I think that in these months leading up to the first tragedy for the Gunn family there was something malign in the air. In retrospect, I can recognize it at certain moments. It possessed me for an instant when I felt exhilaration and triumph after my petty theft from Mr Melody. It had a hand in the conductivity between myself and my mother, which made me sense the unhappiness she was trying to hide. Certainly, it was leading me by the nose as I wandered illicitly, almost in a trance, around the strange house during the rescheduled burglary. There was even a malign element, as in a mischievous practical joke, in the way in which I landed up the following morning in J. T. Archer's dentist's chair. Stealing, blackmail, running away, burglary. I felt myself, not at the centre of my own network, but on the periphery of someone else's. I was being pointed in different directions, and made to move. The burglary and its sequel were not a culmination; from my present vantage point they look more like a beginning.

I am slipping out of time again, when what I want is to recreate my partial view. Still, it is not cheating to say that, during the burglary, I felt I had come upon the centre of the malignancy.

Outside, Charlie, his brother, and three of his brother's friends, are waiting for me to unbolt the front door. It is dark and silent. I am at the back of the house, in the kitchen. It is a gourmet's kitchen, well appointed and well stocked. A pleasant, spicy smell which makes me think the owner has been cooking curry. A pang of guilt at this domestic nuance, as if I am afraid of being accused of racism, to compound my other crimes. No more than a passing pang however – my feelings in fact are quite numb. I feel nothing. I am waiting to feel something.

I leave the kitchen slowly, wide-eyed, as if hoping to discover

51

feelings outside it. I am in a large hall. Ahead of me the front door, rooms on either side of me, the stairs behind.

'Ssst! Shift yourself you dozy bastard.'

Here then is a feeling. Anger at these crass words loudly whispered through the letterbox. I ignore them and turn into one of the rooms at my left, pushing open the door. It is a swing door which swings to and fro behind me. I watch it soundlessly moving in and out. It reminds me how easy this is turning out to be. Finding myself in a study, and seeing its heavy brown curtains, I recklessly turn on a light. Now I smile, and, in all honesty, I have to admit that I am enjoying myself. This is luxury. I sit in the brass-studded brown leather chair, sink in it, my legs not touching the floor, and I inhale its smell, and examine my surroundings. A sturdy wooden writing desk stands in front of me, varnished so that its natural colour, almost black, shines in the light. Behind me, an array of hi-tech hardware: a computer, a compact disc player, a stereo television and video recorder, and a stack of videos. Above them, two prints. In one a thin-faced bearded man, melancholy in his incongruously colourful coat, stares solemnly at the painter. In the other a man is seated in a room painted in such infernal red that it seems to be on fire. His face is daubed and blurred, its features indistinguishable. I swing the chair. On the desk in front of me stands a marionette which slightly unnerves me. It wears a flowing blue cape over pink jerkin and stockings. Beneath its swash-buckling hat is an ugly *commedia dell'arte* mask. It stares at me and, with an unabashed gesture, invites me to inspect the room at my leisure.

I do so. On my right, shelves lined with books. I take one down at random, open it, and find a diagram explaining how to separate three metal rings, apparently joined. Another book is more disturbing – it features pictures of facial tumours, post-operative photographs and pictures of prostheses. Another book, in an unglamorous hardback cover, contains pictures of children, boys and girls, indulging in strange games with adults. That is the mental label I fix on what seems to be happening: strange games. Fear finally makes its entrance. I have replaced the other two books, but I just drop this one at my feet, push open the swinging door, and leave the luxurious room. The marionette continues to smile.

'What the fuck have you been up to?' This is Gary, loudly whispering again, coming in with his friends. I see Charlie, looking anxious, standing by the gate. 'Go on, get lost.' I am shorter than he is, and slimmer, when we fight I always have to submit, but as I walk down the path towards him, I feel taller and braver. This is a kind of alchemy, this conversion of trepidation into bravery, fear into high stepping pride.

J. T. Archer has no ancient copies of *Reader's Digest*, *What Car?* and *Woman's Own* in his waiting room. He has the latest issues of *Playboy* and *Playgirl*, along with a few copies of *Forum*. 'Gains me more custom than it loses,' he says. 'Who wants to look at feminist teeth anyway? It would be like supplying guns to the enemy.'

Tipped over on to my back the next morning, staring up into his high cheek-boned, intense face, all my thoughts of pride had evaporated. His fingers on my face, and in my mouth. He was monologuing, as was his custom.

'I hope you know you're honoured, Bill. I'm making a special dispensation, because we're friends, you and I, we have an understanding. I'm not usually an NHS man. There's no excuse for not making money, that's my philosophy. You'd do well to remember it. Have you got any playground scams? You ought to have, that's all I'd say, you ought to have. It's never too early to start. Sell conkers, re-sell sweets, hire videos, find someone who does homework and be his agent. Your father and I, we started young. Take away the benefits and the dolies would soon find work. Just look at the semantics of the thing: *benefits*! What is the idea of giving someone a benefit for not getting a job? A pat on the back for being a layabout. You see what I mean? As soon as you think about it you realize it's an insane system. No one thinks about it. My house was turned over by dolies last night, Bill. Do you know what? I haven't even told the filth. This is the kind of thing I handle for myself. That's another advantage of networks I forgot to mention last time we spoke, Bill: I'll get to the bottom of this in no time, handle the retribution and everything. There's an unpleasant side to it though, Bill, I may as well tell you. It looks like someone I know was probably involved. No breaking in, just opening the front door, easy as you please, bolt and all. It's a tangled web, Bill, oh yes, it's a tangled web, but I'll unravel it. That's the beauty of networks, Bill – the intersections, the cross references, the bridges and links and corridors. I'll get to the bottom of it, or the centre of it if you like, in no time. I'll tell you what, I save my special punishments for friends who cross me. Any friend who crossed me would be better off owning up.'

'Ag whar mu.'

It was me. Instant confession brought on by fear of this tall man with his secrets, more sinister than Gary's, and his unruffled manner, more threatening somehow than Gary's bullying. My whole body was tense, petrified by its utter vulnerability.

He took his hand, and his sharp metal probe, out of my mouth. Broad, closed mouth smile, curling upwards slowly, as if he was unable to restrain his amusement. 'Don't be dense Bill, I know it wasn't you, there's no need to tell me. No son of Eldon would behave in that despicable way.' He gave me a cup of purple mouthwash. 'Clean bill of health for you.' He winked, and showed his yellow teeth. 'You little devil.'

Ten

I may be giving the impression that I endured an incident-filled childhood, or an extremely eventful year, or even just an action packed autumn. None of that is really true. For long periods, nothing much happened. I feel like a guide in an art gallery, hurrying past unremarkable landscapes in my eagerness to reach more eye-catching, if less representative, canvases.

Here is an unremarkable fact: my father had an enthusiasm for baths. Sunday, in his ordered world, was the day of the Perfect Bath. Heat just barely tolerable, chin-deep. As the water cooled the plug was removed; shoulders, thigh and stomach were slowly revealed, and then the plug was replaced and the hot water gushed back in, all managed with nimble, prehensile toes. A gulp of whisky, ice melting fast in the steam-warmed glass. When I came in he would put down his damp paperback and welcome me, as if into a more formal presence. 'Delighted you could join me, sit down, take a seat, feast your ears.' I would watch him, hairy, soapy bear, splashing and clowning. He didn't sing in the bath, he recited, he loved to show off with reams of *Under Milk Wood*, or sonnets, a fistful of them, Shakespeare and Donne. Once he threw me the book he was reading, *Romeo and Juliet*, and we did the balcony scene, I was his Juliet, before he skidded off into Mercutio's Queen Mab speech, no longer seeing me while he spoke of dreamers and dreams. These are my best memories of him, his big body unselfconsciously on show, so competent, so uninhibited. He might have stayed there for ever, might never have left his bath, if my mother hadn't come along. Every time, eventually, she would come along and shoo me away and close the door of the damp and steaming room, 'No more larking,' and, eventually, emerge with my father, towel wrapped and tamed. Chastened sheik. I would resent her for working this transformation.

Another picture: Lego lies in a chaotic mess on the floor, like a smashed mosaic; two model trains face each other on a railway track, one has derailed; plastic figures are scattered at random, as if thrown from a height; a plastic spaceship lies on its side, beached; in the middle of all the destruction squats The Skull Beneath the Skin, like a tumour at the centre of a disease.

One Saturday morning at my house, I showed Charlie the town I had created with my father's help. By lunchtime it was destroyed, ravaged by bombs, invasion and fighting in the streets. I didn't think I cared. We had lunch and Charlie left, and in the afternoon my father began to teach me to play tennis. It was his habit to draw morals from things, and the fact that I wasn't successful at tennis became more evidence that I must not expect results without effort. 'At the risk of harping on a theme,' he said, as we walked home, 'look at me: self-made man made good, success dug out of a poor background, like ore out of dirt.' Having not even worked up a sweat in our game, he was striding home briskly. I was almost running to keep up, all attention, hoping to discover how to win his approval. For a short period after I ran away he was more attentive than he had been, and I was anxious to prolong this effect.

When I saw the wrecked town on the floor of my bedroom

that evening, it looked different. I entered the room and saw it as if for the first time, and immediately felt a weight of guilt descend on me. I went to bed but couldn't sleep. Perhaps my father would be hurt, because he had shared the job of building. Now there would be no ring-road, no Scalextric cars racing around the town. I turned on the light and got out of bed and, sitting on the floor, began to rebuild one of the houses. The wall was only half broken, it was a question, as usual, of getting the corners right. My fingers were moving quickly, and I began to see myself recreating everything perfectly, I could see everything exactly as it had been, if I could just fix this stubborn brick, if the light wasn't so bright. It seemed to be brighter than usual, hurting my eyes. Things ceased to fit together, my fingers became clumsy. It was as if a vital piece had been lost. I dropped the wall I was trying to repair and it broke into pieces. Perhaps in the morning. There was too much to do now. Perhaps in the morning I would start rebuilding, because there was too much to do now.

I made this decision firmly and got back into bed. I felt obscurely that I had let my father down. I fell asleep finally, imagining morals he might draw from my carelessness.

A third picture: at the bottom of the garden the bushes grew thickly around an old hut and a tall, climbable tree.

The New Year began mild and windy. The weather changed with surprising speed from refreshingly cool sun pouring out of a clear sky, to violent and thundery showers pulsing from dramatic cloud cover. From sun to rain to sun again. It was lively weather, and when we weren't in school Charlie and I were always outdoors. We were having bike rides, raincoats tied around our waists flapping in the wind behind us as we flew down the sloping sides of the gravel pits; we were playing football on the heath, watching the ball, caught by the wind, arc away from us, towards the road or the pond; we were grabbing newly fallen branches in the park and holding them up like sails in the hope of being blown away, blown far away, past the statue of General Whale and over the city and up and up above the clouds and into orbit, where we'd meet a Russian spaceman who had been there for 300 days and would be surprised to find us knocking at his capsule door.

On the bushes, droplets of water hung glistening in the recently returned sun. Every leaf held two or three droplets, and there were far too many leaves to count. The white trunk rose out of the bushes, forked, and developed into black branches which tapered and leaned, twiggily, back down towards the earth. Odd that, when the branches were weighed down by leaves, they seemed to rise upwards like strong arms, and when they were bare, they drooped.

'Are you coming up or are you just going to stand there, you big bog-roll?'

This was our latest insult, and it had gained some currency at school, but only Charlie and I understood the secret of its derivation.

'Bog-roll, bog-roll.'

It usually had one or other of us in stitches, and now Charlie was in danger of falling out of the tree, he was making such a meal of being amused. I threw the tennis ball at him and it bounced off the trunk and on to the back of his head before it rolled down his spine and dropped into a cleft in a branch where, crazily, it stuck.

I waded through the bushes, shaking beads of water off leaves, feeling their dampness penetrate my jeans. A couple of gnarled footholds helped me reach the first branch. Easy, I said to myself, no problem. I sat on this branch, pausing to gather my nerve a little, before standing unsteadily, hugging the trunk, and reaching up towards the next.

'Come on!'

Charlie shouted just as I gripped the wet bark, and I jumped a little. It was harder when he was watching. With Kim I used to pretend that I wasn't scared and, as a result, I would climb quickly up to the fork in the trunk without any trouble. She would follow slowly, with deliberation. Charlie's presence changed things, making me self-conscious. His audacity intimidated me. Now he stood in the fork and made room for my arrival by shinning a little higher.

'*Finally*,' he said. 'Slow-coach.'

The view was not spectacular. The back of my house behind us, gardens all around, more houses in front. The view was not spectacular, but it was large. The houses stretched away on either side, two long, bulky spans fractured by apertures. The gardens sprawled over fences towards roads, spilling on one side down a hill. I had a sense of being in a channel, grass bounded by bricks, shutting out the wider world. Above us the round sky, seen through crowded branches and twigs. On the tree, in the fork in the trunk, I felt myself dwindle, felt an impatience with my precarious position, and with the limits which seemed to be defined within this large view.

'So how are we going to get that ball?'

A return of focus. Clinging to the trunk again, I looked down. A flimsy branch, no more than a flexible stick suitable for a tentative foothold, extended outwards below me. The tennis ball nestled in a cleft of this branch, partly supported by some twigs.

'We'll throw something at it.'

'Throw what at it?' said Charlie scornfully. 'There isn't anything.'

'We'll climb down and get something.'

'You climb down if you like. I'm going to shake the branch.'

Charlie slid down the left hand trunk, so that I had to move over. He made his way to the branch above the one that held the ball, and then lowered himself.

'Coward,' he said, without looking up. In keeping with the care he was taking over his movements, his voice had become uncharacteristically earnest. 'You never want to do things, you just watch. You don't do *any*thing.'

Hanging fully extended, he kicked and stamped so that the branch below him wavered, but the ball was firmly wedged. I began to climb down towards him.

'It's stuck,' he said. 'I'm going to get on the branch.'

'It won't hold you.'

'Course it will.'

'Won't.'

'Coward.'

As I reached the branch from which he was hanging, he swung down, using an outcropping as a handhold, on to the one which had caught the ball.

'Wish me luck.'

He was enjoying himself, getting a thrill from his audacity. I was suddenly angry with his certainty, the way he said something and then simply made it happen. I watched him standing on a foothold beneath the branch, moving his hands along, putting more and more weight on it until he was at an acute angle to the ground below him. This was my tree in my garden, and he had somehow appropriated it. He thought he was proving something. I lowered myself as he had, and then stamped on the branch he was holding, not on his fingers, but enough to set the branch shaking. Appalled, I watched him fall out of the tree into the bushes, where he rolled over, and lay still.

I hung a moment in stillness, looking at what I could see of his body. 'But . . .' I didn't know what to say, I wanted to protest that something so serious could happen so quickly. It didn't seem fair. I scrambled down the tree, almost slid down it as if it were a pole until, six feet from the ground, I dropped, jarring my knees and rolling on to my back.

'Charlie? Charlie, are you all right? I didn't mean it.'

He lay on his face in the middle of the wet bushes. I crouched next to him, shaking his shoulder. After a moment he began to rock to and fro, his mouth moved, and then suddenly he sat up with a jerk, roaring, 'Bastaaard!'

He was laughing as he leapt on me and we fought, rolling over and punching and kicking. Where I had been angry at his competence, I was now angry at the way he had tricked me, and for once his weight and height were not sufficient advantage for him. I got in a couple of punches to his face and I finished up on his chest, pinning his arms with my knees and hands so that he couldn't move. I was pleased with myself, and pleased with his look of surprise, but I was also slightly shocked. Was this me, kicking him out of a tree and then beating him up? I must have lessened the pressure on Charlie's arms because he rose up off the ground and overturned me, and then tried to force grass into my mouth while he held me down.

We called a truce, based on the fact that we had hurt each other approximately equally. When we finally went inside we were wet and bruised and covered in grass, and exhausted. We didn't have the energy for animosity, we were hungry. I was glad to see my mother. There was a cake baking, and she was writing something in a student's pad of A4 paper while she waited for it. Her stomach was in her way, bulging outwards like a small ball beneath her dress. She scolded us, and told us to clean up. Charlie was saying something but I wasn't listening. I had just realized, with the slow but sudden perception of a comic character with a light bulb over his head, that my brother or sister was inside my mother's stomach.

Eleven

Time to jump forward a few months, while my mother's belly swells and her hopes for change become invested in her baby, while my father's business interests expand prodigiously, running away with themselves, and while I grow and unimportant events continue to happen to me. Time to jump forward to the first tragedy for the Gunn family.

First I must introduce my grandparents. My father's father, Joseph, lived in the Sun Hill Rest Home. He used to complain that it sounded like a Chinese restaurant. It was a well lit place of pleasant pink and grey surfaces but, in common with luxurious hospitals, it couldn't escape the smell of established decay. Sun Hill was a hospice for people with incurable, terminal diseases.

It is a Sunday afternoon, so he is sitting in his favourite chair in the common room. There are four other residents there, and two attendants. Joseph is wearing a check shirt and a tie. He is my father. He is thinner, more angular and very nearly bald, his head pecks forwards continually, but he is my father. I think Eldon perceives this too. Joseph is talking to Mrs Warburton, and when we come in he includes us in the conversation. He is courteous, he would not dream of excluding either Mrs Warburton or his son and grandson.

'Terrible lunch as usual, wasn't it terrible, Mrs Warburton? Hello Eldon, Willy, terrible lunch today. It didn't stop Mr Wallace from gobbling it up of course, you'd think he'd know by now, you'd think he'd know better, but no, he gobbles it up and then sicks it all up again later. The slow race to the lavatory. Does anyone try to stop him eating so quickly? Does anyone think of that? No. I don't know what's worse, Eldon, the smell of the food or the smell that lives here, in the building, between meals. Funny thing. One smell reminds us of another. That's so isn't it, Mrs Warburton? The boredom you see, unrelieved by the dreadfulness of the television, the boredom leaves me nothing to do but analyse smells. Missed my profession, Mrs Warburton, I should have been a chemist like your good husband. The boredom was not relieved Eldon, by the books you brought me. I do not wish to reread *Great Expectations*. What are my expectations? And I am not intrigued by a modern man described as Dickensian. Haven't you got Bellow's latest effort? You know I have a weakness for Mailer. Where is Lucy? She has some interest in the Americans. Busy. Lucy is my daughter-in-law, Mrs Warburton. Of course she is busy, she has a life to lead. Best to lead it, best to lead her life before she is handicapped by the twin terrors of bones and bowels.'

And so on. This, I now understand, is not simply a list of complaints, this speech is a display, a marshalling by my grandfather of the contents of his life. He professed no interest in how I was getting on at school, or in my father's business, and he even refused, at least in our presence, to dwell on the past. Occasionally he visited us, and we took him to parks and sometimes, if he was up to it, to the theatre, but these excursions he considered to be outside reality, separate from the daily events of the real world. 'Not part of the business of dying.' This was the phrase he loved to use. He loved to disarm my father with these words. 'Not part of the business of dying.'

My father's response combined curiosity and confrontation, but his attitude remains a mystery to me. This sentence makes me pause. Much about my father remains a mystery to me. He avoided exposing his feelings or revealing his secrets as assiduously as his father avoided anything he thought unconnected to 'the business of dying'. They each drew their limits around themselves, chalk circles defining their behaviour and their disclosure, beyond which they would not step. Hence I suppose my father's tactics: he was trying to find out what lay within Joseph's casual, contained approach to death.

I am thinking of a visit in early spring. As we drove to the hospice my father handed me a slim paperback. 'Find "The Old Fools",' he said. Obediently, I leafed through. 'Where all the alchemists wind up,' he said, 'whatever becomes of their experiments. Read it aloud.'

I began to read it, slowly, emphasis in all the wrong places, stumbling over the long words. He took the book from me, 'What do they teach you at that school?', and read the poem to me, a stanza at the traffic lights, the second in a slow moving traffic jam, and so on. Then he explained to me some of the meaning of it, prune-faced geriatrics trying to dwell in the past.

'But why?' I said. 'Joseph's not like that.'

He shook his head. 'Did I say he was? It's just a way of looking. I'm trying to tell you that time is passing, Billy. Joseph's dying, as we've told you, and soon you'll have a brother or a sister. Put it another way, my father is dying, and I'm going to have a child.'

This meant nothing to me, beyond the fact that he was getting impatient about something that I was slow to understand. Eldon had a passion for education. He read me all his favourite writers long before I could understand what I heard. Not just while he was in the bath, but before I went to sleep, and even, apparently, in my cot. Passing the book to me, he stalled as he was about to leave the lights, and swore.

We sat and listened to Joseph and, big eyed, I looked around, taking things in as I had been taught. Mr Wallace sitting in his corner opposite us, open mouthed and drooling, dabbed by a watchful nurse. Mrs Warburton who listened with us placidly, glad of company. After ten minutes my father gave up the effort of conversation with Joseph and instead fed him cues, allowing him to regale us as usual with the details of his daily life. Only towards the end of our visit did he manage to swerve the talk on to literary territory, where a full-blooded argument could take place, maintaining a decent distance from the business of dying.

My mother's father, Roly, had once been, she insisted, a handsome blue-eyed sandy-haired lout. A loblolly, my grandmother agreed, a layabout. A yob, added my mother. My grandfather, a spindly, puppet-like man with straggly white hair, blushed like a girl at these remarks.

'Don't listen Will, don't pay any heed. They're filling your head with stories. I was a choirboy, a paragon.'

'Oliver Gentleman, you are a liar. Your grandfather was a disgrace, William, was and is. "Gentleman!" Have you ever heard such a name for such a man?'

My grandmother, in her late sixties, was short and overweight. I had a fascination with her legs, great pink stout things encased in tights which did not hide their pinkness, or the thick blue veins which mottled them. She used a stick, drove an automatic car, and got around more quickly than I did.

The visits of Ethel and Roly, and our visits to them, were regular occurrences. Sometimes we would go to the coast, to Southend, but I was content simply to be in their house. It was the house Lucy had grown up in, a small semi-detached just outside Romford. Archer might have approved of my grandparents, because they were firmly embedded in the community, surrounded by a network of friends and children of friends. There was often someone there when we visited. 'Meet William,' Roly would say, proffering me to some stranger. 'Our grandson,' Ethel would explain, perhaps ruffling my hair.

I never resolved the question of Roly's past, whether the story of his misdeeds was a private joke, pure invention of my mother and grandmother, or whether his emphatic denials were indeed lies. It was hard to imagine a wild man buried beneath my grandfather's frail and gentle exterior. Hard – but not impossible.

'Oh please,' says Ethel, in my memory, as her husband pours tea from his saucer into his cup, 'these are not your loutish salad days. These are your silver years. Think of William. *Please!*'

I think I am avoiding the issue. It is May. The earth is blooming and the sky is a faultless blue, hiding nothing. It is Charlie's eighth birthday party.

My father, preoccupied and smoking, drove me round at midday.

'Welcome, welcome, welcome,' said Charlie's mother, as I came in. 'Last to arrive, but never mind. Father not stopping?' He was already driving away. 'Never mind. You know everyone I'm sure.'

Gary, I was pleased to find, was absent, so it was just the nine of us, two girls and seven boys, with Charlie's parents. Our first game involved searching a room for hidden coins. Five, ten, twenty and fifty pence pieces, and two pound coins, were sellotaped to the bottoms of chairs, concealed inside books and cups, and tucked beneath a rug. Mrs Larbey supervised us as we delicately ransacked her living room. I grovelled under a desk to find five pence taped underneath it, scrabbled at the back of a drawer to find twenty and, jackpot, discovered a pound coin under the cushion of a chair.

'Well, well, well,' said Mrs Larbey, 'I didn't know that was there.'

Mrs Larbey wore a floral dress that didn't suit her. It fitted her well enough and, objectively, looked well enough with her dark hair and plump figure, but we knew Mrs Larbey wasn't flowery. She was thorny. Charlie had told a previous best friend that she kicked him when she was angry. The story got around. Part of its fascination concerned Charlie's father, because no one liked to think what Mr Larbey might do to his son. He was something in insurance, and he worked out. He pumped iron. Every day he went to work sober-suited, but at home, where I had often seen him at weekends, he wore short-sleeved shirts and tracksuits which revealed his impressively swollen arms and shoulders. He had big hands, with long fingers. Once he had hit his wife in an argument, Charlie told me, about a lover. I wasn't sure whether to believe Charlie, he seemed to treat the story as something to boast about, but I was wary with both of his parents, wondering whether they were concealing violent and lustful tendencies.

On Charlie's birthday, I must be fair, his father was genial.

'Well, Billy,' he said at one point, 'it's not on the scale of your party, by all accounts. Are you enjoying yourself?'

'Yes thank you,' I said, 'very much.' I dug the three coins out of my pocket to prove it.

'Well done, well done indeed.' He laughed. 'Yes, we know how to keep children entertained. Simple really: imagine they're adults.'

We ate lasagne with chips, Charlie's favourite dish. His father drank beer with the food that his mother served up. There was no food fight.

After the meal there were more games involving prizes, and there was an attempt to organize a Whodunnit, a murder mystery complete with detective, suspects and victim. I was chosen, in a lottery, to be the detective, and so stood in the hall while my friends had a conference with Mr Larbey in the sitting room. After a while the light was turned off and I heard them circling in the darkened room. I looked at the closed door, and waited. There was a sudden, high-pitched scream and then Mr Larbey, playing a policeman, showed me into the room.

'Young lady seems to have been murdered, sir,' he said, Plod-like.

It was Jane who was dead, sprawled theatrically on the floor, her arm outstretched as if reaching something, and her blonde hair covering her face. The other seven stood around her, suppressing smiles.

'Hello, hello,' I said, taking my tone from Charlie's father, 'what's all this then?'

Titters from the suspects.

I started with Charlie. 'Name?'

'Mr Hillen. Mr V. Hillen.'

'Any relation to the victim?'

'I'm her husband.' More giggling.

'And where were you, Mr Hillen, when your wife was murdered?'

'I was in the pub having a drink. Sitting alone. I don't know if anyone saw me.'

'Hmmm,' I said, 'very suspicious.' I moved on to Louise Thompson. 'Name?'

'Fatal,' she said. 'Miss Cruella Fatal.' She was failing to keep her face straight.

'And where were you . . .'

'In bed with Mr Villain!' And she collapsed into giggles, starting everyone else off, including the corpse.

The game was over, because Louise had more or less given away the solution. Miss Fatal was having an affair with Mr Hillen, and they had conspired to kill his wife. I never got as far as the red herrings. Case closed. Being a detective, I decided, was pretty straightforward.

'Children,' said Mr Larbey, shaking his head. 'There's just no point in making the effort.'

There was one more effort made though, a novel idea of Mrs Larbey's. From the kitchen she brought out a bowl of what looked like dough. On some newspaper on the table, there were some paints in little glass pots and five brushes. The paints were white and brown and red.

'We're going to show you how to do make-up,' she said.

There were groans.

'It's not what you think,' she said. 'Who's going to volunteer?'

Jane was coming forward, but Mr Larbey interrupted. 'Show them on me first,' he said. He put out his arm, as if for us to admire. His wife took some of the white paste from the bowl and spread it in a thin layer in a small circle on an almost hairless part of his arm. She smoothed it on to his skin. While she made the scar, his hand was on the small of her back. He watched her, smiling. With her little finger she made a trench through the middle of the paste, keeping the sides even, and not penetrating through to his skin. Then she began to mix the red and white paint.

'Anyone who spills paint on the carpet,' said Mr Larbey, 'gets a smack.'

When she had arrived at the right mixture, she began to paint the paste on his arm.

'Shame about your tan,' she said, 'it's not really a match.'

When she had finished with the pink, she painted the interior of the trench a bright red. A few speckles of brown, like crusted old blood, and she had finished.

'There,' she said, 'now who would call that girlie?'

Mr Larbey appeared to have a vicious open cut on his arm, something he might have sustained in a knife fight, or a car crash.

'A flying splinter of glass,' he said, 'embedded itself in my bicep. It was a terrorist bomb.' He staggered around a bit, clutching his wound. He had suddenly decided to become the life and soul of the party. 'But I ripped it out again with my teeth,' he mimed the action, 'and refused all medical assistance.' He grinned at us, lips curled back. 'When I get those terrorists I'll teach them to throw bombs at me.'

'Right,' said Mrs Larbey, 'now you try.'

So far, give or take some narrow squeaks, everything has been rosy. Which means, probably, that most of it has been well wrapped up in fiction. In terms of documents my childhood is a series of Januaries. From the age of five, under duress, I began a diary every year. Year after year I became lazy, lost interest, and gave it up. I can tell you when I saw *E.T.* for the first time, and loved it. Ask me what I did a month later, and I would have to invent something. I would have to remember something that never happened. But memories are perverse, and other things, which I would not choose to remember, remain vivid. The unkindest memories are the easiest to recall.

I came home, with my scar proudly displayed, and my grandfather, my mother's father, let me in.

'What have you got there, Will?'

'It's a scar,' I said, showing it to him and grimacing. 'There was a fight and I hurt my arm.'

He stuck his finger into the dough. 'I have to tell you something.'

'Look at my scar.'

'Listen a minute.'

'Why are you here? Aren't we coming to see you at the weekend? Look, I won some money too, I found it, and Charlie's mum said she didn't even mean to leave it there!'

He looked at the paste on his finger. I continued.

'I'm going to spend it on sweets. I'm going to show mummy my scar. Is she still in bed?' She had been feeling ill all morning, and had not got out of bed when I left at lunchtime. My father, who had been in one of his smoking and drinking phases for a couple of days, had not been communicative.

'She's not here, Will, that's why we came. Daddy called us this morning, before you left. She's in hospital, and I'm going to take you along to see her.'

My first experience of a hospital. A huge, uncrowded foyer. A smell I recognized from Joseph's rest home. Big signs bearing lists with unpronounceable names, and arrows. More corridors even than I discovered in the tube. I was continually surprised at the gaps in my experience. Roly and I got lost, and he had to ask a nurse the way. I wasn't impressed by her uniform. Her apron made me think she had something to do with catering. She smiled at me and I frowned.

My mother was crying quietly and continuously. Her shoulders and head were involved, in shuddery movements. Hands over her face. Small, throaty sounds. The whole thing was restrained, but the restraint was frightening, as if a word put wrong might result in an explosion. I stood at the end of the bed and watched her, my flour and water red paint scar still conspicuous on my forearm. My mouth was open, I was breathing through my mouth, standing in an attitude of waiting. I was waiting for this moment to pass, so that my mother might become my mother again. The moment didn't pass. It stretched. I didn't know then that she was mourning both my brother and the vision of her life that went with him.

At night, at home, I missed my Lego toytown again, for the first time for months. Nothing like this could have happened there. There were no surprises there. Not until Archer's intrusion anyway, breaching the force-field. Him with his pictures, his strange games. My father was staying at the hospital with my mother, where it smelt like Joseph's rest home, smelt of death. My grandparents were sleeping in my parents' room. I was dozing, moving towards dreams. 'My father is dying and I'm going to have a child.' But the child died instead, a reversal of the natural order of things. What can you do when you can't predict something as fundamental as that? 'I'm trying to tell you that time is passing.' Perhaps, and here I found my first touch of consolation, perhaps my father is wrong about that too. Time might stop passing, my mother might come home and then things might freeze. This was a good conclusion to reach. I began to count up to 109. Before I had finished I was asleep, dreaming of a party game in which we all wore bright red scars, and fathers were children and children fathers, and mothers were nowhere to be seen.

DIFFERENT WORLDS

Twelve

Eight, nine, ten. Time, discreetly, continued to pass.

When I was ten I began to write. At school a teacher was away and a replacement came in and gave us a story title to be getting on with. 'The Journey to the Wreck'. He wanted a piece of descriptive writing, something demonstrating ability to create a setting around a narrative thread. From the start however, I've been more interested in plot than description. Narrative is the bone, events are the meat, and description is the fat. I'm tempted to give an example of my writing from my present trade, but I don't want to injure my credibility any more than I already have, not just yet.

My journey to the wreck developed into an underwater battle with a race of sea-monsters who had kidnapped my family. I had only just begun it at the end of the class for which the teacher was absent, so I continued it at home that evening. We hired the boat, we reached the wreck, green webbed and scaled hands rose out of the water all around us, like strange seaweed, and snatched my mother and father away. Alone, I didn't hesitate, I dived in after them and followed, and found to my amazement that I could breathe underwater. I freed them from their prison cell, but we were recaptured so I offered to fight their leader, King Tharn, a creature of unravelling green fronds, in hand to hand combat. I won in spite of dirty tactics by the King, so my parents and I returned to the surface and, with brash equanimity, finished our trip around the wreck. Virtue triumphant, normality restored. I delighted at the craftsmanship which enabled me to dip into an alien world, beneath the surface of our own, and then to return to reality unscathed, in a neat circular movement.

For some reason, I felt that at home my writing should be a secret. I was toying with the idea of surprising my parents one day with the final, published version of 'The Journey to the Wreck'. So I wrote in bed, under the blankets. I lay propped on an elbow, using the light of a torch laid on the pillow. Every now and then I would push back the covers for a breath of fresh air. The undertaking became more serious because of the discomfort involved. As I watched the words appearing on the page I felt my breath on my hand. My eyes, elbow and wrist ached. I was pleased: if I had writer's cramp, I must be a writer. At the end of a week, it was done, and it had reached an imposing total of eleven pages.

I read the story out to the class on the last week of term, just before Christmas. We had just had gym, in which we played a game called 'Pirates' which involved people chasing each other across wall bars, up and down ropes and along benches, without ever touching the floor.

Charlie was lounging as usual. I was 'it' and I knew that he was my best chance of catching someone quickly. Strong he might be, and daring, but not fast. I ran along the bench, ignoring Frank Spark hanging off the wall bar above me jeering, and I jumped on to the horse. Charlie saw me coming and began to move from his corner but too slow, much too slow for me, and I lunged, swinging on a dangling rope, Tarzan, and touched his ankle as he tried to climb above me. He glared at me, because I had broken an unspoken agreement, that we wouldn't bother each other on these occasions. I pretended not to notice. Now I could relax, he wasn't allowed to catch me back, so I could lurk as he had, in the corner, out of the action. Better not get breathless, I was thinking, not if Bradley's going to make me read it out, read it out to the whole class.

What are you going to be? people asked. For a while I said I was going to be a computer, because I found that it made people laugh. Then I said I was going to drive the Space Shuttle. Bravado this, because like everyone else, I'd seen the teacher blown up in mid air. NASA: Needed, Another Seven Astronauts. I didn't fancy that, I didn't fancy people telling sick jokes about me in the playground, but again it seemed to be the right thing to say. People would smile and nod and say, I always wanted to be a train driver when *I* was young, as if there was some lesson to be learnt in the progress from a train to the Space Shuttle. But now, now I knew what I wanted, and it had nothing to do with making people laugh, or making them nod approvingly. What do you want to be when you grow up? A writer. I'm going to be a writer. I wrote a story that was eleven pages long and I read it out at school.

'All right!' Mr Hamill shouting: 'All right that's it. Five minutes to get changed. Go!' As always the last word, the command, was a single syllable delivered in a kind of screech. We went.

The changing rooms were bare concrete with wooden slatted benches and even twenty of us, talking, jostling and running in and out of the steaming showers, didn't warm the place up.

'Tell us a story, Billy.' This was Charlie, still resentful that I had picked on him in the game.

'Haven't you got better things to do than write?' Frank Spark, always keen to join in baiting someone.

'No, because he's boring.'

'Boring Bill.'

'Bog-roll Bill.'

Mr Hamill came out of his cubicle. 'Are you kids still here? I said five minutes, not days. If you're not out of here in five seconds I'll roast you all over a fire. Move!'

Out of the door, across the playground, up to our classroom block. We were the last three, and Mr Bradley watched us enter in silence.

'Sorry I'm late sir,' we chorused.

'No you're not,' he said. 'Bunch of hypocrites. What's a hypocrite Frank?'

'Someone who's late, sir?'

'William?'

'Someone who says something and doesn't mean it?'

'Right. You must be an expert in hypocrisy. Sit down then, sit down, don't stand there like the three little maids from school.'

Laughter from the class. We sat down. There were twenty-two of us, two to a desk. Normally I sat with Charlie, but he was sitting down with Frank, so I found myself next to Jane, the corpse at Charlie's party.

'Are you reading out your story?' she whispered loudly.

I nodded. I was becoming nervous. Four twenty-twos are eighty-eight, five twenty-twos are . . . 1010. Can't be right, 110. That's too much. Five twenty-ones . . . Jane was nudging me. I looked at her. She was looking at Mr Bradley.

'Are you with us Billy? Are we keeping you awake?' Laughter again.

'Yes, I mean no. Sorry sir.'

'What did I say?'

'I don't know.'

'Oh?'

'I wasn't listening.'

'Oh. And yet you expect us to listen when you read us your story?'

'But I didn't mean it. I was *thinking* about my story.'

'The genius at work. "A poem is never finished, it is only abandoned." That was a French poet, Valéry. Val-air-ree, not Valerie. He meant that there was always something that could be made better, always room for improvement . . .'

Bradley was off on one of his famous digressions. I strained to appear attentive. Looking around, I thought I was the only one doing so. Didn't seem fair. Charlie and Frank were whispering. What about? It's not fair, just because I guessed what hypocritical meant, just because I caught Charlie in the gym. They're jealous. My eyes met Charlie's. He smiled maliciously. Bradley, looking at his watch, wound up what he was saying.

'You'd better come to the front Billy.' As I approached his desk he said, 'Just read it slowly, and loudly enough for us all to hear.' He gave me a smile of encouragement. I decided I liked him after all.

I stood in front of his desk and looked at the class. Twenty-one faces looking at me. No one absent. I looked at my exercise book. 'The Journey to the Wreck,' I said. I was hoarse before I had even started. The first paragraph seemed to go very quickly, so I slowed down and spoke a little louder. Began to get a rhythm. I looked up as I turned the first page and saw Frank making a face, trying to make me laugh. I paused in mid sentence, and then continued. I glanced up each time I turned a page after that, resolutely avoiding the eyes of either Frank or Charlie, and each time I saw two or three people who were clearly bored, staring at the ceiling or their hands. At about the middle, when I was freeing my parents from their underwater cell, there was some chatter and Mr Bradley had to stop me while he told someone off. When I defeated King Tharn, Charlie and Frank both laughed, and others joined them. Even I felt a desire to giggle. In the last pages my voice descended to a low monotone, and I knew that I had lost their attention. The neat ending engineered by the circular plot movement sounded lame, and no one was sure I had finished until I looked up and, with a small gesture like a wave, said, 'That's it.'

'Thank you, Billy,' said Mr Bradley, 'thank you for reading that out to us. Comments from the class? Yes Charlie?'

'It was silly. It didn't make sense. How come he could breathe while he was underwater? Where did these monsters come from? It was just stupid.'

'You weren't supposed to believe it. It was just a story.'

'Too long,' someone said. Others agreed.

'Why do you think they laughed at the fight with the King?' said Mr Bradley. 'What was it about that episode, do you think?'

'I don't know. Was it because I beat him? I don't know why they did.'

Mr Bradley found some good things to say about the story. He liked the way I had given the monsters a language and a currency, giving the impression of a complete society existing under the water. He said I had clearly put a lot of work into it. He would have liked more description, less action. 'It was a good effort,' he said. 'You can make something of it.'

'Money?'

'No. Revise it, if you still like it. That means work on it, improve it. Sit down again Billy. As I was saying, you should always look for ways to revise something . . .'

He was off again, and now he would not stop until the end of the class. 'Well done,' whispered Jane, as I sat down. 'I couldn't have done that, I could never have stood up in front of everyone like that.' I didn't hear her or Mr Bradley. *If you still like it.* He didn't understand, he clearly didn't understand. It's because I didn't read it well, and they laughed, that's all. That's all it is.

My mother wasn't aware that there was a ritual going on at supper that night. My father was late so we ate alone. She had her spaghetti bolognese with shredded cheese, I had mine with shredded newspaper. I had a few small pieces in my hand and, when her back was turned, I sprinkled them on my plate and mixed them in. We watched Terry Wogan interviewing an actress about her new play.

'How was your day, Billy? What did you do?'

'I had to read out a story in class, and they didn't like it.'

'That's a pity. What story?'

I had something thin and tasteless in my mouth. I rolled it into a ball with my tongue, and swallowed, felt it moving down my throat. 'There was this story that we wrote in class. I finished mine at home, and it was quite long. So Bradley told me to read it out.'

'Did he say why he didn't like it?'

'No. He didn't say. He didn't even understand it.'

'Poor Billy. Don't be discouraged.'

I nodded. I swallowed some more newspaper. The idea was that I was taking the art of writing into myself, making it a part of me, digesting it. With each swallow I was thinking, I am a writer, I am a writer. Creating my identity, something new from something familiar. My father wouldn't have approved, of course, hardly a scientific approach. I still think the idea was all right, it was just the execution that was at fault. My big mistake was to use newspaper, rather than the pages of a book. The gods of these rituals are notoriously pedantic.

Thirteen

My mother was in the kitchen and my father was getting changed when the first guests arrived, so I answered the door.

'Hello Billy. Billy, this is Benedict Floyd. We're horribly early, aren't we, but I thought Lucy might want a hand.'

'Hello Billy.'

'Hello Billy.'

Floyd and Kim spoke together. I smiled at Floyd and said, 'Hello, hello, come in, mum's in the kitchen,' and I trailed after them as Melinda led the way. Melinda wore a green silk shirt-dress. Have I described her yet? Taller than my mother, with the same brunette hair but worn longer, in a braid tonight that lay between her shoulder blades. Her face was longer too, elegant rather than attractive, with almost concave cheeks. My eyes had rested on Floyd for a moment, but I hadn't noticed him. Kim wore jeans and a red sweater with a zip-up collar. She'd had a drastic haircut since I had last seen her. I made a face as we went in to the kitchen, and she wrinkled her nose at me.

'You can't come in here,' said my mother, 'everything's poised, everything's at a vital stage.' She kissed Melinda, holding her mayonnaise-spotted hands out of the way. 'So *good* to see you,' she said.

They hugged for a few seconds, and then Melinda disengaged herself. 'Benedict Floyd,' she said, 'Lucy Gunn.'

'Call me Floyd,' he said, 'try to forget my first name. It's very kind of you to invite me.'

My mother smiled and ran her hands under the tap. 'I've been wanting to meet you. You're a reporter?'

He nodded. 'A versatile one. Investigative stories when I can get them, and royal babies when I can't. And sometimes I freelance. Mel has used me in the past.'

'Last of the renaissance men,' said Melinda.

'Let's have a drink,' said my mother. 'Eldon will be right down. Hello Kim, how are you, did you have a good Christmas? Billy, why don't you show Kim your Christmas presents? And hurry up your father?'

Kim stopped me on the stairs. A low whisper. 'I want to listen.'

'Why?'

'Floyd.'

She tip-toed back down the stairs with comical caution. Her mother's guardian. Kim had only ever met her father twice but she had compiled a firm view of him through guesswork and talking to her sister. She was protective, and unwilling to trust Melinda's friends. I glimpsed her face as she went into the now vacated kitchen. It was intent and serious. Floyd clearly hadn't won her over yet. He had made no impression at all on me; I realized that I still hadn't taken in what he looked like, although I had watched him talking to my mother.

I shouted through the bedroom door, 'Dad! Mum says hurry up. Melinda's here, she's got a man with her.'

My father came out of his room, pulling on a ribbed grey sweater over his shirt and tie. He put his hands under my armpits and picked me up.

'Don't dad, you'll strain yourself.'

'Happy New Year,' he said, and kissed me.

'It's too early for that.'

He put me down, sighing slightly with the effort. 'You'll be asleep later. What do you mean "she's got a man with her"? Eh? Do you mean "brought a guest"? Who dragged you up?'

'You did.'

'Aren't you going to change out of those jeans?'

'Kim's wearing jeans.' I was going down the stairs behind him. 'Dad?'

'Hm?'

'Happy New Year.' He turned round. I was two steps above him, holding out my hand. He shook it.

Kim was in the kitchen, sitting on the counter beside the serving hatch. Red and blue, with her legs dangling, all she needed was a fishing rod. I noticed that her jeans were better quality than mine. She put a finger to her lips as I came in.

Floyd had just been introduced to my father. 'No,' he was saying, 'the truth is it's neither sordid nor exciting. Imagine being cornered at a party by someone telling you all about themselves. That's what it's usually like, only self-imposed. Researching and following and meeting some not particularly interesting person. Anyway it's only a sideline, the journalism is more important to me.' My father asked a question, and Floyd began to talk about a drug company. I peered through the crack between the doors of the hatch. Floyd was a brown haired man of medium height. A small mouth, though not too small for the rest of his features. A smooth oval face. Not a face to look twice at, unless because it was so quintessentially not a face to look twice at.

I nudged Kim's leg and motioned with my head. She shrugged and nodded.

In my room she said, 'He's a private eye, but he never tells anyone.'

'How do you know then?'

'I heard him tell mum.' She shook her head dismissively. 'But it's only boring things he does. I could be at a party,' she said abruptly, 'mum's letting Louise go to a party and stay with a friend. She wouldn't let me do that.'

'With your friends in Kentish Town?'

She nodded. She was sitting on the floor leaning against my bed. In between us was a game I had been given for Christmas which involved accumulating money on the stock exchange. Restless, she stood up, and walked to the window.

She said, 'Do you remember treasure-hunting? Do you remember looking in the bushes and in that hut?'

'I remember. And sometimes we dug, because maybe a burglar might have buried things.'

She turned round. 'I want to go out into the garden again, in the dark, we could have candles or a torch, it would be spooky.'

'We're eating soon.'

'We won't be long, come on, I haven't been in your garden for years.'

'It's cold. There's nothing there any more. I mean there was never anything there.'

'Come o-on.'

'I'll find a torch.'

The last weather of the year was clear, and so cold that it was almost painful to breathe in. Winter so far had been snowless, but an afternoon shower of sleet had left the grass and bushes damp. The torchlight picked out cameos of glistening leaf clusters.

'Point it at the sky!'

I did as Kim asked, and we looked up to find that the beam had disappeared, but that there were more stars than there had ever been before. I switched off the torch, and we stood in the dark halfway down the garden with our heads craned back and our mouths open, as if we were waiting to catch raindrops. Staring up so high, I thought I could feel the earth spinning beneath me. After a moment I took a step back, stumbling, and, sure enough, I was off balance. As I looked down I half expected to find stars beneath me as well as above. Space swarmed in on us where we stood, at the centre of a giant world. Dwindling and growing at once. My hand brushed Kim's, skin on skin, and the cold contact made us look at each other. We laughed, as if we had done something much more intimate than brushing hands, and we moonwalked down to the bottom of the garden.

Kim made a click with her tongue, and shook her head slightly. She held the torch at her side, switched on again but pointing straight downwards, so that it spotlit the grass.

'What?'

She didn't look at me, she lifted the torch and played its beam on to the bushes. 'I don't know,' she said. 'I'd like a space-ship to come down and land and take us both away. Wouldn't you?'

I didn't answer. It was the last thing I wanted, to leave my comfortable, increasingly predictable life.

We were looking in the shed when Archer surprised us. We weren't looking for anything, we were just looking at what was there. Kim shone the torch into the darkest corners, at ghostly spider-webs and shelves loaded with small fat sacks of fertilizer and mouldy plant pots. There was a pungent smell of decay. In one corner a selection of garden tools leant like old bones. Standing still, we remembered the cold. Darkness encroached.

'How cosy,' he said, and we both jumped. His voice as ever was filled with ironic harmonies. He stood in the doorway, tall and black in his dinner jacket. Dracula. 'I hope I'm not interrupting you two young people?'

The table was laid with silver cutlery, linen napkins and red candles. There were crackers beside the eight places. My mother, Melinda and Floyd were sitting with a lady I didn't know. She wore a black evening dress, and a prow of sculpted black hair jutted from her scalp. She said, 'Well, he told me it was formal. I do apologize, it's just like J.T., he has to be different. Any excuse to dress up.'

I looked at her with interest, seeing her immediately as a part of Archer's network. Although I had not seen much of him, I had not forgotten what he had told me three years earlier; it was hard to forget something said with such authority. He handed me secrets like tempting morsels of food, and revealed areas of his knowledge like someone revealing titillating areas of flesh. I know Charlie . . . I know Gary . . . I have divined your fears . . . I know more about your parents than you have dreamed of . . . He was hard to ignore. He made me wonder how much was unrevealed, modestly concealed like his album of child pornography. I was still unsure whether he knew that I had let thieves into his home. In the few times I had seen him since we had barely spoken but, literally with nods and winks, he had managed to imply that he continued to know more about me than I could hope to guess. My father liked to speculate about him.

'Hello,' she said, 'you'll be Bill. Kim and Bill. I've heard about you.'

'Anita Bell,' said my mother.

'Nita,' she said with a big grin between lips even redder than my mother's, and she nodded her astounding hair at us. Surely only much younger people had hairstyles like that? I looked at Kim. Kim, reading my mind, shrugged.

Crackers were pulled, jokes read out, and paper hats put on. Nita's hat perched unsteadily on her haircut.

My father came in with a big platter. Chicken livers in a sweet vinegar on frilly lettuce. Archer followed carrying plates.

'J.T.,' said my mother, 'I wish you'd let me.'

'Nonsense,' he said, 'why should I?'

'I thought Mr Melody was coming as well?' I said.

I got a withering glare from my mother. 'No,' said my father, 'he couldn't make it unfortunately.'

'Ah,' said Archer, 'wisdom from children. What a shame he wouldn't come. What an apt time to heal old feuds.'

'I feel I'm missing something,' said Floyd, 'but if it's personal of course . . .'

'If it's personal of course, you'll want to know all about it.' Archer's smile was light-hearted.

'Dig, dig, dig,' said Floyd. 'I never sleep.'

'We're all missing something,' said my father. 'I've known both Melody and J.T. for many years, and I've never even seen them meet. It's a hole in my life, in the tapestry, not knowing what happened between them to keep them apart.'

Archer began to eat. He continued talking as he ate, and he gesticulated and jabbed with his fork. He had an imperious way with a conversation. His red paper hat looked almost sinister over the slim lines of his face and his immaculate dinner jacket. 'But why should we meet?' He said, waving the upright fork in a circle in the air. 'You've got the wrong end of the stick my old mate, you're seeing things in extremes. We are neither friends nor enemies.' Jab. 'Neither friends nor enemies, I think that sums it up, sums up most relationships in fact, wouldn't you say? We have nothing in common besides our friendship with you, and your fascinating family.' He smiled at my mother and me, thin face beaming with the pleasure of being right, a shred of lettuce hanging from his mouth. 'Do you see what I mean? If I did see the man, you'd perhaps accuse me of hypocrisy, or of using him. Hm? It's not my practise to cultivate people I don't particularly like.'

I looked at him, about to contradict him, and he looked right back at me, raising his eyebrows, smacking his lips in appreciation of the food. Now the pale green shred of lettuce had descended on to his jacket, looking uncomfortably like snot. He picked it off and dangled it into his mouth, contriving still to watch me as he did so. I looked away.

'This, incidentally, is delicious, Eldon,' he said. 'You'll make someone a wonderful wife. Are you going back to your Jewish roots?'

My father laughed. 'Not quite, not quite that. I think I may be turning kosher as I get older.'

'Did you know, Lucy,' said Archer, 'did you know that your husband used to be ashamed of his antecedents?'

'I was never ashamed of them.'

'No, of course not, I'm sorry, wrong word.' He looked quite pained at his mistake. 'I meant to say, um, well . . . what word would you use?'

My father was unruffled. 'I used not to mention it. You mean what I said about school? It's just the pressure not to be different.' I was listening alertly, surprised that my father had talked about such things with Archer. He moved into the safety of a generalization. 'Children are merciless to anyone who doesn't conform.'

'My first name always seemed to be a talking point,' said Floyd. 'I've never liked it since.'

'It was in the showers of course that one noticed,' said Archer, ignoring Floyd. He looked across at me. 'Bill, you mustn't just sit there silently watching and voraciously listening. Join in. Kim, you too. Are you merciless to anyone who doesn't conform?'

We both looked blank.

'Well Bill, are you circumsized?'

It was not a word I was familiar with. I looked at my mother whose nostrils, interestingly, were flaring, but it was Nita who spoke.

'I apologize for J.T.,' she said, 'although of course you know him. His exuberance.' She took on a professional tone. 'He has this urge to be the centre of attention, and a concomitant desire to shock. Rather infantile of course. With a year of psychology behind me, I have no hesitation in diagnosing too long at the breast as a child.'

'Darling,' said Archer, smiling as if with amusement, 'sweetheart.' He was sitting in the middle of the table, and she was sitting opposite him; he half stood up and reached over and cupped her cheek in his hand, then he turned her face from side to side, like an exhibit, as if showing off the hat and the haircut, first to Eldon on her immediate right, and then to Lucy at the other end of the table. 'The loyal little woman,' he said. 'Misdiagnosing I'm afraid.' He released her, leaving the white imprint of his fingers on her cheeks. 'No, the truth is I'm an actor. Simple. I act. So are all of you, of course. We all act, with varying degrees of talent in varying numbers of parts, it's just that we don't all admit it. I admit it. I don't have a problem with it. Do you know how I see myself? I see myself alone on a stage, a black stage, in a brilliant, tight yellow spotlight, holding an invisible audience in the palm of my hand. Palm of my hand. Do you understand what I'm talking about? Like being on top of a geyser, spurting up on the crest of other people's emotions. Other people, I love them, love them to death. I need them you see. Where's an actor without his audience? Lost.'

In almost all my memories of him he is holding forth. Hogging the stage.

He was extending his long-fingered hand, the same hand that had held Nita's face, for us to see. Pink, hairless skin; clean, manicured nails. The black cuff of his dinner jacket retreated to reveal gold cufflinks on his shirt. His tone is hard to characterize. Jaunty solemnity. His thin face and aquiline features commanding his audience exactly as he might have wished. His assumption that he was so worthy of our attention was oddly beguiling. The only thing that undermined him for me could not have been predicted: I was irresistibly reminded by his words of the tiny spotlight of the torch, itself invisible in the round vastness of the velvet sky.

As I watched him I saw the smile return to his thin lips. A discreet upturning of the ends of his mouth, one slightly more than the other. A corresponding crinkling of the skin. Motion returned to his eyes.

Abruptly, and for the first time, I was reminded of my mother, her mobile eyes, seemingly independent of her mouth. I am ten now, and so more observant than I was. I shall say it then: my mother had a glorious mouth. Wide lips, I said earlier; I meant bee-stung, what I would like to unselfconsciously call luscious. I used to want to kiss them, when I was little, but she would not let me. I would ask her why not. 'Because it's special,' she said, 'only daddy can.' Swollen, kissable and unkissable bee-stung lips, the prominent feature of her always thirtyish face. And brown eyes that reserved judgement, were dilatory in response, shyly sliding, never darting, out of range. Something of Archer in her eyes then, and in her lips.

As my mother brought in the second course, which was salmon, the conversation split into two. She began to talk to Floyd, who was on her left, while Archer and Melinda, with contributions from Nita and my father, began to argue. For our different reasons, Kim and I were silent, listening.

Archer said, 'Oh you're not going to bore me with a diatribe are you? I mean that in the nicest of ways, no offence meant, but I can't stomach a diatribe. Doctor's orders, eh Nita?'

'He says it's bad for his digestion.'

'No, no, no diatribes,' said Melinda. 'I just wondered about your attitude. Do you see the magazines as attracting more people to your waiting room? Or do you relish the idea of causing offence? There's something, if you don't mind my saying so, there's something mischievous about you J.T. Something hidden.'

Archer twinkled. 'Hidden? Even from you, dear Mel?'

'Even from me.'

'Perhaps your new boyfriend should – how would he put it? – investigate me.'

This was intriguing, in the light of a conversation overheard between my parents, concerning who they should invite. Eldon: 'Is it over, between J.T. and Mel?' Lucy: 'Over? It barely began. I don't know what she was thinking of. The man has a positive network of women.'

Now my father, as host, steered the conversation into a safer controversy.

'That's something I've always wondered about, J.T. These girlie magazines of yours. What is your attitude?'

'Harmless titillation Eldon. Tit-i-llation. That's my attitude. Fun. That's it.'

Melinda: 'So not a more or less ritual humiliation of women?'

'No.'

Nita, with something personal in her tone: 'Not a way of eroding a man's view of a woman until he sees her as an object?'

Archer remained genial. 'Good Lord no.'

Melinda again, cordially: 'Not something that perpetuates myths, such as that women enjoy violence? Not hypocrisy on a grand scale? Or "acting", as you might prefer to call it?'

'No, no, no, no, no. No to all of the above. Dear ladies,' he grinned, clearly enjoying himself, 'dear ladies, I do believe this may be a diatribe after all.'

'Dear J.T.,' said Melinda, 'we're just trying to be clear about your attitude.'

'Is it clear?'

'Quite clear. A small child could understand it.'

My mother was talking to Floyd. 'I do a little writing,' she was saying, 'that's the most satisfying thing, but it's not something I can concentrate on for very long. Time is sometimes a little, you know, a little glutinous.'

'I know about glutinous time. What do you write?'

'Just something I'm working on. You and I should team up. I'm sure you have some material? We could write a thriller.'

'They'd have to coin a new term if it was based on my experience. A borer. I'm afraid you're a victim of the media's distortion of the facts.'

'Can I sue?'

'Yes. Gunn and Floyd versus Hammett, Chandler and Bogart. It has all the makings of a classic. Incidentally this salmon is terrific. Was it you or Eldon?'

'The salmon's mine. Cooking is another creative outlet you see. I have only one child after all,' she saw me looking, and smiled to soften that 'only'. 'Don't I, Billy? Only one child, and he's at school, so I find other activities. Because things haven't turned out precisely as planned.'

'Is the food always this standard, Billy?' Floyd deflected the conversation as my father had at the other end of the table, avoiding awkwardness, perhaps for my sake.

'Yes,' I said. 'And she's going to teach me to cook.'

I turned away. It was not my intention to become involved in a conversation. Kim was saying something to Floyd, but I was listening to Nita who, face flushed, was expounding enthusiastically.

'My opinion,' she said, 'my opinion is this. We take all the high rise blocks, all the high rise blocks which we have no idea what to do with, so it is said, we take them and we re-equip them with good lighting and reliable lifts, and we sink them in pits in the ground. Simple.' She slurred slightly and tried again. 'Simple. It's simply the lower floors of buildings not yet built. That's how we market it. Isn't it simple?'

'Remarkably,' said my father, straight-faced, and Archer laughed.

'Oh Eldon, I do like you,' he said. 'The archetypal uncommitted man. That's what you are. Never firm, always eliding issues to avoid arguments.'

'Not true, not true at all.' He was good-humoured but serious, his patrician's forehead and assertive nose were not suited to accepting jokes at his own expense. 'I am committed, if you want to know, to my work and my family.' Out of the corner of my eye, I saw my mother shoot him a glance. He didn't notice. 'And by my work I mean both literature and business, and it's not many who reconcile those two.'

'Exactly,' said Archer delightedly, 'that's my point exactly. The great reconciler, the great tier-up of different strands. Seldom a foot wrong, eh Eldon? Seldom.'

'And tell us what you're committed to, J.T. This I would like to know.'

Archer put down his fork with the remains of his salmon, the better to deliver his next speech. 'I'm very clear,' he said. 'I believe in being very clear about that subject. In fact I'm surprised you have to ask. My sights are set on money, Eldon, and power. My view is unclouded by spurious altruism, which I am not accusing you of, of course, and it is equally unclouded by, I know Nita will forgive me, love. With those twin aims, money and power, with no diversions, with just a few rules, but almost no boundaries, it is not too much to say that anything is possible. Imagine that, an untrammelled world. I can see right to the horizon, on every side. I am aware of all the possibilities, all the options, and I don't dismiss anything without a good reason of my own. Other people's reasons aren't good enough. I love other people, but I wouldn't dream of letting them forget their place. The only rules worth following are your own rules. I'm sure Lucy, as a writer, would go along with that.' Lucy wasn't listening, so he turned and met my eyes. 'Imagine that, Bill, *anything* is possible.' His smile bared yellow teeth.

'So what's on the agenda?' asked my father.

'Ah well,' he said, 'things are developing. Bill will tell you, I'm a believer in contacts and connections, diversification, fingers in pies. The gospel I have often preached to you, Eldon. I've been a bit quiet the last few years, but things are almost ready to start happening.'

'Are you talking about your practice?'

Moving his wine glass in a small circle, he smiled. 'Up to a point, up to a point. The nice thing, is to move in different worlds. But yes, Nita and I are considering dental and facial surgery. It seems to be lucrative. Nita and I will be a team. She has some dental training in her background, and I have some surgery in mine, and we'll learn from each other's skills. Do you know, some dentists retire or move into different specializations, many actually commit suicide, because they can't stand inspiring fear and inflicting pain? Hard to credit, but it's statistically proven. Quite a few also flinch from dental surgery, and there's not many qualified in any case. Gap in the market you see, I'm always more interested in gaps in markets than gaps in teeth. There's a mint to be made from filling those kinds of gaps.' He took off his jacket, and favoured me with another smile. He was aware of my observation, and unconcerned by my sceptical look.

'I take it you're not talking about the NHS?' said my father.

Archer spluttered, then spat out half of his final mouthful of salmon as he went into a fit of coughing. Melinda, concerned, broke off her conversation with Lucy to thump him on the back and raise her glass of water to his lips. He drank gratefully. 'Eldon,' he said weakly, 'you're a riot. I mean it, you are. You're a riot.'

'Are you all right?' said Melinda. 'I thought for a minute it was a bone, I thought you were choking.'

'Ah Mel, you have no feeling for an ending. Do you think I could allow myself to bow out in such a banal and undramatic manner, simply spoiling dinner for you? Such an anonymous way to go.' He began to laugh, a hoarse, unhealthy sound, as if now he truly was choking. 'I'm sure when I bow out,' he said, 'it will be in a suitably dramatic manner.'

In the last hour of the year, over coffee and chocolate mousse with cream, the attention turned to Kim and me. Aware that our presence had been almost forgotten by our parents, we had tried to efface ourselves, neither dozing nor making our presence felt by undue liveliness. Kim was flagging however, finally losing interest in the exchanges between Melinda, Floyd and my mother, she was beginning to nod.

'Time you were in bed sweetheart,' said Melinda abruptly.

'No!' said Kim, waking up with a start. 'It's nearly New Year.'

'Time you were both in bed,' said my father.

'Oh dad. We've stayed up this long, and we haven't disturbed anyone. Can't we stay up till midnight?' A wheedling tone. 'Just till midnight?'

'Yes let them,' said Nita, an unexpected ally, 'it's a special occasion.'

'They deserve to stay up,' said Archer, 'for the way they've been hanging on our words. I get the feeling this one,' a nod at me, 'is storing up knowledge for some dark design.'

Flattered, I made no comment.

'We'll go into the sitting room,' said my mother, 'and you two can curl up in an armchair. It's just a night like any other really.'

My father had just completed a meandering story about me, about my interest in alchemy, and how he had used it to teach me that there was no substitute for hard work. Convinced of his astuteness, he would never have guessed what job I would finish up with. He smiled apologetically. 'I'm sorry J.T., Nita, parents can be terribly boring.'

'Not at all,' said Archer, not looking at me. 'Your boy fascinates me. Children in general, and their growing up, fascinate me. The most interesting aspect, I think, comes before the adolescent fretting about bombs and starving peasants and such distractions. The most interesting part is while the more intimate perspective is changing. Wouldn't you say? That period of reassessment in which Bill realizes the fallibility of, I'm afraid, you and Lucy. That's what interests me. He realizes that he is not, after all, surrounded by that tedious phenomenon: sensible people. That's when childhood begins to give way to a more adult world.'

There was a short silence, only Archer seemed to have the energy left for argument, and then, 'I don't know if anyone's interested,' said Floyd, 'but it's five past midnight.'

There was a flurry of movement, as champagne and glasses were found. Archer remained seated, watching me with a small, sardonic curl of the lip.

Everyone kissed almost everyone else. I kissed sleepy Kim, and was kissed by Nita, Melinda, my mother and my father, who tried and failed to pick me up again. Floyd said, 'Happy New Year Billy,' and chinked his glass against mine, which held an inch of champagne. Things were blurry by now, I was tired, and weary of words. Even so, I retained a certain wariness in shaking hands with the still sardonic Archer. He seemed to be suppressing something, some sense of amusement. There was always this air about him, but more than ever now; a childish, irrepressible smirk on his face as he looked down at me. Then he did a strange thing. He puffed out his cheeks and widened his eyes, he let the smirk subside and changed the shape of his face with a fat smile.

'What an enchanting surprise, Billy,' he said. 'Fancy meeting me here.'

It was an extraordinary impression, achieved in spite of differences in height and build, hair and clothes. Dazed by sleep, for a moment I thought that there was a new guest at the party. Only for a moment: he passed a hand over his face, and he was Archer again, smirking, like a child who has performed a clever trick.

'Night night Bill,' he said. 'Do try to stay on top of things, won't you? Don't let events run away from you.' A wink and a final, trademark smirk. 'Stay in the driving seat.'

Fourteen

There is a postscript. I was in bed, sleeping through the first hours of the year, and dreaming of Archer surprising Kim and me in the shed, somehow making us feel guilty as he did so. I was asleep, but I know what was said in my absence, at the tail end of the party at the beginning of the year. It has been reconstructed for me.

There was a 'slightly premature' toast to the end of the Second Millenium, proposed by Archer, and then it was Floyd, stifling a yawn, who brought up the new subject.

' "The Second Millenium". It sounds like an aftershave doesn't it? You sound like that man Jerome. Are you a disciple?'

Archer said, 'Is he being investigated by you?'

'No, not at all. The subject is a hobby of mine, that's all. Not just Jerome. Evangelists, tent religion, TV shows; all those things, all those networks.'

'I'm sorry,' said Melinda, half lying in her chair, fingering her braid, 'I'm sorry if I'm being ignorant, but who's Jerome? Should I know?'

'Nobody,' said Floyd. 'He's trying to build up a following with a sort of religion.' He was drinking brandy. 'Incidentally,' he said, 'I'm assuming you're driving.'

'I've heard of him,' said Eldon, 'there was an article in the evening paper. He had a meeting on Hampstead Heath?'

'In a big top,' said Floyd, 'like a circus. Someone called him a ringmaster.'

'Actually,' said Nita, who up to now had appeared to be going to sleep with her head on Archer's shoulder, 'I think he's quite interesting. He has some quite interesting things to say.' She lifted her head. 'I read something of his, some pamphlet, and it seemed to make sense.' She raised an admonitory finger. 'What I can't stand about Christianity,' she said, slurring slightly, 'is all this business about meekness, and how it's wrong to make a living and all that. I mean you have to be *poor*. That's a bit outdated, surely? All this emphasis on guilt, and so on.'

'Let's all give up guilt for this year,' said Melinda.

'Good idea,' said Lucy.

'I don't think we should just mock,' said Eldon. Only he seemed to take the subject seriously. 'This type of thing has taken off in a very big way in America, maybe there's something in it. Because it makes money doesn't make it wrong.'

'Makes it right,' said Archer, matching his tone. 'He's making people happy and he's making money. Doesn't matter if he's sincere or not, it's a business. Look behind any large-scale operation like that and what do you find? Every time: someone making money, raking it in, piling it up. Cash, cash, cash. Secret of the world Eldon, isn't it? You know about that, after your own business adventures. You and I, Eldon, are the perfect people to judge a big operation like Jerome's. Anyone who carps about this man is probably just jealous. He's found a market, and he's exploiting it.'

Floyd made an expansive gesture with his glass, and burped. Nita giggled. 'I love these people,' he said, 'either they're masterful hypocrites or they're holy fools, but either way they fascinate me. You're right, they find a market, they find a *need*. When they get it right they can be quite frightening, their power.'

'But isn't that all beside the point?' Eldon was trying to sound speculative, like Floyd, but he was slipping in spite of himself towards assertion. 'What I'm saying is, what if it's all true? What if he's neither hypocrite nor fool? I'm saying there could be more to it. I'd say the man deserves a look before we judge him.' Eldon paused, and looked around the room in search of support. Nita gave him a small affirmative nod. 'I'm intrigued,' he continued, 'I tell you straight I'm very intrigued by anything that looks a little deeper than we're used to looking. Do you know what I mean? I'm interested in looking below the surface, I really am. That's why I'm not interested in the money, and the performance he puts on.' He paused again, clearly not quite sure, in the absence of any response, whether he was making a fool of himself. He looked at Archer, and an edge of belligerence entered his tone. 'Fools and knaves, is that your world picture? Is that all there is? I mean in general, in life in general, I want some idea of what's beneath the surface, because I think there are layers of life, like layers in a novel. I'm sure it's not just some big insect at the bottom of it all, some spider, gathering money into its web. I'm sure it's more than that.'

No one has reconstructed this next scene for me. It is partly a stab in the dark, and partly a conflation of other moments. A bedroom scene again, only this time it is at the end of the evening, not the beginning, and Eldon and Lucy are undressing, not dressing.

There is a slightly short-changed feeling in the air: the dinner party has been a success, but it is over; the two couples have withdrawn and, what's more, a New Year has begun, and all there is to show for it is weariness. They would both like to go to sleep now, but there are still words in them, a few more things that have to be said. So, unenthusiastically, they will have a stab at a conversation. Most of it has been said before. What is left out, is any mention of the miscarriage and its aftermath, the new vision of the future that it entailed. The subject is like a weapon too powerful to be used. Both secretly feel that they would like to take some blame on their shoulders, in order to contain it, and so begin to deal with it. Again this involuntary feeling, almost a sense of guilt: it is the New Year, surely there is something new to say?

Eldon has his sweater and tie off and his shirt is unbuttoned, revealing a mat of short grey hairs, curling in towards his flesh. Lucy is sitting in front of the mirror over her dressing table. She is wearing a white bra and knickers, and she is removing make-up with pale cream on cotton wool. She is still wearing one gold ear-ring, which swings as she moves her head.

'Lovely meal,' says Eldon. Lucy doesn't answer, so he answers himself. 'Lovely. What did you think of Floyd?'

'I've had a good evening,' says Lucy, 'I've really enjoyed our evening.' She puts down her cream-soaked piece of cotton wool and looks at him.

'I know,' he says.

'What?'

'I know what you're thinking: why is it so rare for us to have an evening like this?'

She laughs. 'I wasn't thinking that. I was thinking, why are we going to have an argument now? I don't want one, I don't suppose you do, but it's as if the evening isn't quite complete yet. It needs that finishing touch.'

He comes towards her, and sits beside her on the stool. There isn't much room, he puts an arm around her waist for balance. Then kisses her breasts. 'Well let's not argue love, let's leave it for another time.'

She is not looking at him, she is arching her neck and breathing in, a deep breath, but she is looking at their reflection. Her tone is persuasive. 'You see, you're always a step away, there's always this distance between us. There's Billy and I, and then there's you. There's your work, as you said, and then, secondly, there's your family.'

'No distance. There's no distance.' And indeed, the image she is seeing in the mirror seems to deny her words.

But now she lifts his head, holds his face a few inches away from hers. 'Usually you're operating somewhere else, on one of these other layers of yours. This one isn't good enough for you, this one where you live in this house with me.' She feels his body become tense. 'It's not an accusation, I'm trying to get things clear.'

He sighs, and puts an elbow on the dressing table, leaning away from her. 'You have your other layers. You have friends, you have your writing and Billy and your meetings. You know you could have your own business, just say the word . . .'

She is shaking her head almost as soon as he begins. 'Listen to yourself, laying out the cards, sharing things out like a divorce settlement. That's what I mean, you have this planned, objective approach, so the whole thing, this marriage, is like a convenient arrangement. You *know* what happens to plans, what happened to our plans.' And finally, and still in a level tone, she finds the centre of her argument. 'Why are you always God knows where, in your different worlds, fulfilling your private fucking dreams and diving into your latest enthusiasms? I've tried to fulfil myself *here*, in this big house. Is it not big enough for you too?'

She begins to cry, which is disconcerting because it's a departure from habit, from the usual boundaries. 'It's a big house, I thought it was going to be big enough. I made compromises and sacrifices to accommodate myself. I really made an effort. I thought you would too.'

He makes a negative sound and, taking his weight off the dressing table, puts his arms around her again.

'Maybe you're right,' she says, wiping her cheeks with her fingers. She looks him in the eyes as he lowers his face towards hers, her beautiful lips. 'Maybe you're right and it isn't big enough. You're beginning to persuade me you see, that's the danger. That's always been the danger.'

Fifteen

Joseph surprised us all with his longevity, there was even towards the end some talk of remission, some whispering in the common room at Sun Hill of miracles. 'Stubbornness,' was my father's diagnosis. 'He just wants to keep us on our toes until the end.' His death, when it came, was undramatic. His doctors had been predicting a decline for some time, and warning my father to expect the worst, hinting at increased pain and various indignities, but Joseph managed to circumvent these stages of his illness. He died abruptly, and unexpectedly, in his sleep. It was discovered by the nurse in the morning, when she came to give him his medication. 'He was smiling,' she reported, unprofessionally, 'he looked quite peaceful.'

'How do you think he did it?' I overheard my father talking
to my mother the evening we heard the news. 'Do you think he
squirrelled away some pills? They'd never tell us, would they, if
he had. Clever bastard, slipping off like that. Smiling. I bet he
knew there were things I wanted to say, I bet he was avoiding
seeing any more of me. He always hated to make a concession,
he never could stand not having things his own way. Made my
mother's life a misery. Smiling. He knew I hadn't finished with
him. Sick of the sight of me, I shouldn't wonder.'

He died on 2 January, and was buried a week later. A Christian
affair rather than a Jewish one, because one thing Joseph and Eldon
were agreed on, was their lack of respect for religious ceremony.
'If only he was alive,' my father apparently said at the funeral, 'he
would have a whole set of new smells to analyse.' Still stoic, Eldon
made all the arrangements, part of which involved the decision that
I should not be present. 'Nothing to learn from the dead, Billy,'
he said. Melinda was not available, so I was sent to my mother's
parents and Kim, who had met them many times, came too. This
was intended as a consolation, because I had protested at not being
allowed to be at the funeral. I was fascinated, and a little frightened,
by the idea of a body being laid underground, and left there, among
the pipes and tunnels.

Whenever I went to my grandmother's house, I would ask after
her tapestry. Ethel spent much of her time sitting in her favourite
chair, an old high-backed wooden one with a brocaded green velvet
cushion, working on 'The Romford Tapestry'. 'Second cousin,' she
used to say, 'to the Bayeux.' She sat at the kitchen table with a mug
of tea beside her and an anglepoise lamp peering over her shoulder.
Every visit I made to the house began with a cup of tea at the
kitchen table and, after discussion of light news, a progress report
on the tapestry. Roly would usually make his appearance about ten
minutes after a visitor had arrived, in order not to impinge on this
ritual.

'Now don't be disappointed with me William, but I'm still stuck
on World War Two,' she said on this day, as I brought a teapot out
of the kitchen. 'Those lovely searchlights against the night sky, and
the aeroplanes and the fires, I can't resist them. Because the thirties
were so dull mostly, and these are such bright colours. Of course
Romford wasn't terribly affected by the Blitz, relatively speaking,

but you can't be *limited* by the facts can you? No. No, it's poetic licence. Thank you dear,' as I passed her her tea, 'you must keep that in mind when you write the words to go with the pictures. You will, won't you? Don't follow the history books too closely. You don't want to trust history books. Mostly written by men for a start. And precious little about Romford in them. That's the trouble with history,' this was another favourite refrain, 'nothing to say about Romford.'

'What did you do in the war, granny?'

'What did I do? I was a land girl. Twenty at the start of it, just twice your age, working on a farm, mucking out pigs, and not a man to be seen. Big loose trousers and shirts, itchy things that were never clean. And no men, none of the right age anyway.'

'What about grandad?'

'Roly? Roly was busy up in the skies shooting down Germans.'

'I want to learn to fly.' This was Kim.

'So do I.'

'No you don't, you want to be a writer.'

'I'm going to be a writer *and* fly in the airforce. Girls can't fly.'

'Oh yes they can,' said Ethel, re-entering the conversation. 'You look at the Duchess of York for starters, flapping around in her helicopter. She's not one to be left on the ground waving her tear-stained hankie, is she? I think it's a very good idea Kim. And when you've learnt we'll fly away, the three of us, to a beach somewhere, where no one else ever comes.'

'Yes!' said Kim and I simultaneously.

This problem resolved, Ethel returned to the war. 'So there's the Blitz after the Battle of Britain, and then there's the dear pigs and the farmyard scenes, which will be fun, and then there's my fateful meeting with Roly at the dance. I thought the whole war section might be nicely rounded off with Churchill doing his "V" sign.' We giggled. ' "V" for Victory, children. Have you no respect?'

'Did Churchill ever visit Romford?'

Ethel paused. 'Probably,' she said, after some speculation. 'He was a great man after all.'

Just in time to save us from a digression about Churchill, Roly turned up, looking faintly surprised to find us in his kitchen. 'Hello,' he said, 'hello Will, hello Kim, how nice to see you. What are we going to do with you today? What are we going to do with them Ethel?'

For once, she paused. Outside, appropriately enough, it was stereotypical funeral weather. A low grey sky, drizzling. From the drainpipe above the garage water was splashing down into a drain in irritating, irregular bursts.

'I was going to say they could run wild outside,' she said, with a vague wave of her hand, 'but the gods don't seem to be with us.'

'I wonder,' said Roly, 'if Joseph ordered this weather up specially. I shouldn't think he would have had it any other way.' He sat down with us, with a cup of tea that he had just poured, stretching out his long legs.

'Don't you get comfortable,' said his wife, 'this is no time for getting comfortable. We need ideas.'

'Yes,' said Roly complacently, 'as it happens I have an idea already.'

'This was your mother's old room,' said Ethel, 'this is where we keep games and things. That was Lucy's favourite doll Kim, do you like it?' It was a rag doll in a patchwork smock. 'No, of course not,' said Ethel hastily, seeing Kim's expression, 'you're a bit old for that sort of thing, aren't you? What about these?' On a shelf some soldiers stood in various war-like attitudes. 'They're lead,' said Ethel. 'It was one of her phases, she painted them and everything, and had battles, wars really. She liked to be Napoleon I remember. She got quite keen on him. She's left it all here, dolls, games, books, old records, photographs.' Kim picked up a photograph. 'Oh, I shouldn't look at that one,' said Ethel, 'that's ancient history. Ancient. Look at this picture.'

It was a framed print, an abstract composition involving confused swirls of colour merging in places to suggest shapes. Parts of the body possibly.

'She bought it with her own money that she'd earned in some temporary job, £25 or something, a lot at the time. I wish she hadn't left it though, we don't like it. She wouldn't take it and she wouldn't let us give it away. The same goes for all the other bits and pieces. Left them all behind her, but wouldn't let us get rid of them. Bossy, your mother, William. I expect you've noticed. Always gets her own way in the end.'

My mother's old room had no effect on me. Lucy as a girl or a young woman did not exist, she was my mother and that was all, that word defined her quite sufficiently. Her old room, with its drab striped wallpaper, the lamp with the bulky shade and the cupboards which smelt of the past, her old room was irrelevant. It wouldn't fit into my inflexible world. The girl captured in the photograph that Kim had picked up, and evoked in my grandmother's words, this girl was a stranger, and it was still my habit to frown discouragingly at strangers.

'Here it is.' Roly was dragging a box from beneath the bed.

The chemistry set had been intended as a present for the grandson of a friend of Ethel's, but the boy's father had objected to the idea of him playing with a Bunsen burner and potentially dangerous chemicals. 'Potentially dangerous,' Ethel snorted, as Roly revealed the contents of the box, 'the man's an ignoramus.' They were going to give the thing to Oxfam, thinking I might be a year or two too young for it, but here was my chance to prove them wrong.

In the box were twenty-four test-tubes containing different coloured powders and, in one case, crystals. There were two empty test-tubes and a large beaker. There was a tripod that Roly fitted together for us and there was a small, bulbous jar which had a wick emerging from its screw top. Pink liquid sloshed inside when I picked it up. There were some safety guidelines and some suggested experiments. I knew immediately that we wouldn't be needing any suggestions.

Roly had some ideas of his own for what we should do, but Ethel wouldn't let him stay and get in our way. 'This is madness,' she said gleefully, 'I know they're going to blow up the house. We'll all be blown sky-high, to kingdom come.' We were left to ourselves at last in the kitchen, with the box laid on a thick layer of newspaper on the floor.

I took the lead soldier I had smuggled from my mother's room out of my pocket. 'Right,' I said, putting it in the beaker, 'we're going to turn this soldier into gold.'

This time I was going to do it right. With lead and chemicals, heated in a scientific experiment. With an exotic secret ingredient which had just occurred to me. And without Charlie's help.

'Don't be silly,' said Kim, 'let's make a stink bomb. Alchemy isn't really possible.'

'The magician did it.'

'It was a trick.'

'Maybe it was a trick, but it doesn't mean it's not possible. It's historical, people wouldn't have been trying to do it for so long if it wasn't possible.' I gained confidence from my words. 'Would they? Do you think you're right and all of them are wrong? It's centuries, they've been trying to do it for centuries. Philosophers. Who's being silly? I'm not.' She said nothing. I shrugged, generous in victory. 'Let's try at least.'

I sometimes had an ability, with a bullying weight of words, to persuade people of things I was not at all sure of myself. It was not just what was said, it was a withering tone of certainty which seemed to resonate in my voice almost without any effort on my own part.

'What shall we use then?' said Kim.

We looked over our chemicals, like a couple of fastidious cooks choosing ingredients.

After a while we had a solution of four of the different powders and some of the crystals boiling gently in the beaker. The soldier, a credit to his Emperor we thought, stiffly retained his position, his rifle brandished in front of him like a staff, as the pale green liquid bubbled around him. The long, yellow-blue flame of the spirit burner touched the bottom of the beaker and crept a little way up its sides. Kim had forgotten her reluctance and we watched intently the growth and bursting of the bubbles and the subtly altering colours of the liquid. There must have been sincere alchemists among the conmen of previous centuries, but none were more sincere than I was then, and none more absolute in their belief that success was possible.

'When we've done it, we'll be able to fly away on holiday with my grandma.'

'And my mum.'

'And mine. We'll have separate holidays, with everybody.'

We began to discuss the intricacies of the travel arrangements this would involve. Our mixture continued to bubble.

'What about the secret ingredient?' said Kim.

'I've been waiting for it,' I said, 'and here it comes.'

There was a back door in the kitchen, leading to the garden, and in the back door was a cat flap, and through the cat flap, as I spoke, came Ronnie. Ronnie had white whiskers and foolish, rheumy eyes. He was the same tortoiseshell orange and black as the frames of Roly's glasses. He had a craggy face, wrinkles around his nose, and a scar on his mouth which left him for ever grinning. He was an old cat, seventy something according to Roly, and he was cunning in his way but definitely slightly senile. 'Owrrh,' he said, as he saw us, and he came and scratched his claws on the newspaper and nuzzled his face into Kim's side. 'Soppy,' she said, scratching him behind the ears and holding him away from the flame, 'soppy cat.' She looked at me. 'Ronnie is the secret ingredient?'

I smiled, mysteriously I thought, and fetched Ronnie's dish from the corner of the room. He lapped the water and milk greedily.

'Ronnie's pee,' I said. 'It's the only thing no one else will ever have tried. And it's acid, pee is, so maybe it will burn the lead, it will burn it and then the chemicals will do the rest. It's my plan, I've worked it out.'

Kim screwed up her face. 'Eugh,' she said. But she was smiling back at me, as interested as I was, and enjoying herself. A sense of complicity between us, of joint effort. We were no longer strenuously trying to fill the new gaps in our knowledge of each other, no longer trying to recreate something indefinable we had shared before she had moved, we were just, without volition, finding ourselves in partnership. 'Eugh,' she said, smiling her disgust, 'as long as you collect it. How are you going to?'

'I don't know,' I said. 'Let him go and see if he wants to go out again. We'll follow him with the beaker.'

Ronnie did want to go out again, but unfortunately he didn't want to remain in the garden. Kim opened the door and I followed, carrying the beaker in my gloved hand, just in time to see the aged but sprightly Ronnie leap on to the garden wall. Here he stopped and turned, fat cat fixing us with a baleful glare over his disarming grin.

'Ronnie! Come on Ronnie, come back.' I called and Kim made squeaky cat noises with her lips, but Ronnie remained unimpressed. He sat on the wall and watched us, his smile slipping from paternal to supercilious.

So I began to walk towards him, stalking him, I thought, with the utmost discretion. He turned to face me a little more squarely, and watched my approach, grinning in anticipation now. I held out the beaker as if it contained something tempting. 'Come on Ronnie, I bet you need a pee, don't you? Come on now.' Ignoring Kim's giggles behind me, I sidled right up to him, raised a cautious hand to stroke him, and then grabbed him around the middle and squeezed. Outraged at being treated like a bottle of washing-up liquid, Ronnie leapt with septuagenarian agility over my shoulder, back into the garden. Pirouetting swiftly, so swiftly that I almost got a claw in the face, I slipped in the muddy flowerbed and fell, somehow saving most of the precious liquid but covering myself in damp black earth. I raised my eyes from the mud to see Ronnie, with an infuriating suave insouciance, in the act of squatting against the wall of the garage. 'Quick!' Kim's voice turned into a squeak in her eagerness. I raised myself, slipped like Bambi on ice, raised myself again and whispering words of hate, half ran, half crept towards the urinating cat. As it hobbled desperately away from me, dragging its leaking hindquarters, hissing its anger or shame, I managed to get the beaker, along with my hand and wrist beneath the strong flow of the warm, steaming urine.

The experiment was ready to continue. I had wiped myself down as well as I could and was now kneeling my muddy knees on some more newspaper. I had forgiven Kim for her hysterics at the sight of my efforts to collect the pee, and we were now both engrossed in watching the new solution bubbling over the flame. It was a pale greenish shade of yellow, and it stank. Napoleon's foot soldier continued to brandish his weapon dutifully, but it was impossible to discern quite what colour he was. It was on the new yellow pigment of the liquid that we were pinning our hopes.

'Are you two mad scientists ready for a cup of tea?' Ethel's face crumpled in revulsion. 'That is a hideous smell, have you been making stink bombs?'

'No grandma, it's alchemy.'

'What? Nonsense, it's a stink bomb, take it outside at once.'

'It's raining.'

'I don't care if there's a monsoon out there, I want you to take it outside right now, William.'

It was greyer and wetter than ever in the garden. The rain splashed into the beaker, diluting our magic solution. Only the soldier, perhaps used to adverse weather conditions in Napoleon's army, seemed unaffected.

'She doesn't understand,' I said.

Ethel opened the back door. 'Leave that out there and come in out of the rain. Or pour it down the drain, better still. Come and have a cup of tea.'

'It's not going to work,' said Kim. 'Look, he's still grey. We'd probably have to melt him first.'

'I thought it would work this time.'

'Let's go in, I'm cold.'

We left the beaker, undrained, by the garage, so that we would have the option of returning to it. In the kitchen Ethel was sitting in her favourite chair. I shut the back door to keep the warmth in. She was in a forgiving mood now, and she had a variety of teas to offer us: Chinese, Indian, English. 'Smelly or ordinary?' she said. 'Posh or common?' I gave up my intention of explaining alchemy to her. It didn't seem to fit. It seemed to belong to another layer of life, one that my grandmother evaded, I thought, with the help of cups of smelly tea.

Sixteen

My parents were talking about Jerome when I came down to breakfast. Mum was dipping a finger of toast into a soft boiled egg, and dad was doing the talking. With the instincts of a born eavesdropper, I paused at the door, unnoticed.

'Doesn't it make you want a second look?' he was saying, holding a piece of paper, flapping it at my mother. 'Doesn't it even intrigue you?'

'I'd be embarrassed,' she said, 'to use such an obvious crutch.'

'No, that's not it at all, that's not what this is about. I mean this leaflet is a joke I admit, but the idea behind it is interesting. The idea of taking a closer look at things. I mean, if only because we might be missing out on something. You know what I mean? I'm sure there's something I'm missing out on.' A judicious pause. 'I don't like having taboo areas between us.'

'I didn't think that was what we were discussing. Taboo areas?' She took the leaflet and paused in her demolition of her egg. 'No, I don't know what you mean, I don't know what you're getting at at all, but this, this is just cheapening.' Her tone became derisive. '"An exploration of life . . . An expansion of the self . . . The only truly encompassing philosophy, ancient in its roots and modern in its principles." You really find that intriguing?'

'Yes, because maybe it's a joke, maybe there's something behind it. If there's something behind it, I don't want to miss out on it. I don't know, it's a nice day, it'll do no harm.' My father moved in his chair, as if uncomfortable in the position in which he found himself. His defensive tone changed into something more assertive. 'I don't pretend to know without seeing the man. I think I might just go and find out.'

He became aware of me, on the periphery of his vision.

'Look,' he said, 'Billy takes an interest. Are you coming, Billy?'

'He just wants his breakfast,' said my mother, 'don't you, my love?' She got up, carrying her last yolky piece of toast with her. 'Boiled egg?'

I looked at the two of them, aware abruptly of a division of loyalties, a discreet pull in different directions.

'Yes please,' I said to my mother, but I sat down beside my father and picked up the discarded piece of paper. Was I going with him? I thought I had heard a note of appeal in his invitation to me, whereas there was a subtle directive in my mother's words. So I sat down next to him, and obediently took an interest in his latest enthusiasm. My mother put another egg on to boil, and he watched me read. This inconsequential scene is one of the clearer ones in my memory; my parents make their moves and speak their lines without hesitation. The scene is like one of the crystals I added to the alchemic concoction: a discrete ingredient, mixed into a solution. As the crystal is absorbed into the mixture a chemical reaction takes place, and it slowly releases awareness of my parents' fallibility, as predicted only a couple of weeks earlier by Archer. The mixture begins to solidify, the process is irreversible.

The leaflet was a cheap thing, black lettering, fuzzy at the edges, on pale green paper. Below the name 'JEROME' in fat capitals, some text included my mother's quotations and a few other bland generalizations. It finished in bold black type: '**Delve beneath the surface of your experience.**' That was what settled it for me, those words with their consistently confusing connotations of hidden pipes and forbidden photographs, labyrinths and sea monsters. 'What's that mean?' I said, reading it out as if deeply puzzled. 'What *is* below the surface?'

'Yolk,' said my mother.

'Gold,' said my father, and winked.

The tent on Clapham Common was striped in a faded pink. It was a square which developed into a sagging cone. Once the rumpled sides of the cone might have been impressively swollen, like protuberant lips, but now they hung inwards limply. The whole thing looked slightly lopsided, and the taut guy-ropes around it seemed only to emphasize its instability. The banners on the four sides of the tent however, were new. In white on gold each simply said: 'JEROME'.

'Hold my hand,' said my father, 'and if you lose me we'll meet back at the car.'

'I'm not going to lose you.'

'Not if you stay close.'

South London had been blanketed with the leaflets in the past fortnight, and the articles in the evening paper and the local press had been well timed, but even so, my father was surprised at the numbers who had come to see Jerome. He was muttering to himself as we shouldered through the crowds, 'Jesus, look at all these people. Who says there's nothing in it? Look at it Lucy, just look at this, and tell me there's nothing in it.'

I clutched my father's hand and moved among people's backs, their coats brushing my face. Anoraks and overcoats, Barbours and khaki combat jackets. Looking upwards, I found a preponderance of long hair, a lot of it dyed black. I knew enough to spot a hippy, but these were slightly different – pasty faces and over-madeup eyes, leather and black denim, punky hippies with fragments of crystals on chains round their necks. And yet alongside these people there was a sprinkling, quite a healthy sprinkling, of middle-aged couples. Earnest expressions; these people were here on serious business. With these two extremes there was a third faction, including my father and myself: the spectators, those with nothing better to do on a Saturday afternoon, those whose genuine involvement, if it existed at all, was submerged under layers of curiosity and scepticism. Jerome, somehow, had discovered an almost limitless constituency, crossing barriers of age and class as if they didn't exist.

At ten I was still waiting for the spurt of growth my mother assured me was on the way, and crowds like this one intimidated me. I was being jostled and kicked, and was dancing from side to side to avoid being stepped on, and I was still hanging on to my father's hand, feeling like a small boat being towed in choppy waters. Scraps of people's conversations floated above my head.

'She's boring, she's a white witch, and all she wanted to do was sit around and talk about paganism. I just left.'

'Billy,' my ears pricked up as I heard my name, 'Billy will always be irreplaceable for me. I think of him as my father, because it was through him . . .'

'What an industry,' this was my father, 'regardless of what else is said, what an industry.'

The tent was crammed, and the fragile looking edifice of wooden seating was groaning. We decided to stand in the aisle, towards the back. 'Out of harm's way,' my father said.

The warm-up man was at work when we arrived. He was not quite the smooth frontman we might have expected. He was small and fat, with slicked-back hair and a probably permanent shadow around his chin. His striped shirt bulged over his stomach and was framed by his grey jacket hanging on either side. The slick Italian styling seemed to have rebounded against him, because when he held out his hands to emphasize a point, fingers grasping something unseen, he looked like a member of the Mafia making a threat or demanding money. That said, there was a certain show-biz fluency to his delivery which caught the attention.

'Ladies and gentlemen, this man you are going to see this afternoon, and I know you're getting impatient to see him, but I promise I won't keep you much longer, this man has something special. I'm not talking about charisma and sincerity, you and I know that those are sadly devalued words in this world we live in, I'm not talking about image and personality, you don't care, and you're right not to care, about those things, because anyone can look right and sound right, except me maybe,' a self-deprecating smile, and a few titters in the audience, 'I may not have the build or the face you expected, but Jerome, this man you're about to meet, certainly he looks the part, and he surely sounds the part, but that's not what's special about him, my friends, that's not what's unique, it's his message ladies and gentlemen, it's his *words*. They can't be dressed up, like some advertiser's product, they *need* no dressing up, because that would just conceal the truth.' And here he held out those ambiguously grasping fingers. 'His words are pure, pure as daylight.' His arms fell back to his sides, as if he had exhausted himself. 'There's so much more I could say, there's so much more

I'd *like* to say; I was going to tell you about the effect this man has had on audiences up and down the country, I was going to tell you a little about the struggles he has overcome in his startling career, I would so like to tell you about the life-changing influence he has had on me, my friends, personally, in my life. I could talk about this man all day, but it's not me you're here to see, is it? It's not me you're here to listen to, so let's waste no more time, this man needs no introduction, without any more delay, here he is, the media sensation, the most talked about phenomenon of the decade, your man, the premier prophet of the New Age, Jerome!'

The welcome was meagre. Whoever he was, Jerome would have to be good. He was playing in a draughty tent to a wide variety of people, some of whom were actively hostile members of more established churches, or even followers of rival prophets. He was not preaching to the converted. Some of this my father whispered to me, as Jerome arrived on to the makeshift stage. 'Rather him than me,' he was finishing, but his sentence ended in an abrupt gulp of surprise. 'Fuck me,' he said, the first time I ever heard him use the word, 'it's Archer.'

Walking on to the stage, some twenty metres away from us and partly obscured by the crowd, was a tall thin man in a white suit with a blue tie. He had short but thick blond hair, golden hair you could have called it, and a rather bland round face.

'It's the wrong colour hair,' I said.

'Ssssh!'

Jerome had begun talking, so we missed his opening gambit. His voice wasn't Archer's. It was deep and well modulated, almost musical, just the right side of ostentation. Archer spoke quickly and cajolingly, persuading almost by the quantity of words, rather than the meaning; this was not Jerome's style. Jerome eschewed any of the more obvious rhetorical flourishes, he managed to sound almost conversational, while using the microphone and the sonorous depths he could call upon, to reach every part of the tent. We struggled closer up the aisle towards the stage, eager to get a better look. This is what he said:

'Let us think of ourselves as different people. Sometimes you may toy with the idea of being someone else: a member of the Royal Family, a prostitute, a criminal, a pop star or politician. You may imagine being black if you are white, white if you are black. Look at your hand now, and imagine it a different colour.' A few people in the audience obeyed. 'How would this alter your identity? What would it do to who you are? A man may finger the flesh between his anus and his testicles, and wonder what it is to be a woman. A woman may wonder how it feels to have a weighty cock and balls hanging between her legs. Perhaps you have wondered how it is to have a disability, to have one leg or no legs, to be unsighted or deaf, to be within an unresponsive body. What must it be, to be mentally ill, so that your view of yourself and of the world is unbearably fragile, tilting unpredictably this way and that? You probably have wondered what it is like to be old and frail. That at least you can expect to find out.' He paused for the first time, and looked over his audience. He continued, in an explanatory tone. 'Each of us lives in a narrow world, within self-imposed confines, and these speculations widen our horizons.' Another pause, another assessing survey of the upturned faces. They were reasonably attentive, waiting for the punchline. A slight increase in volume. 'But I am not asking you to speculate. I ask you again: let us think of ourselves as different people. Not as speculation, but as potential *fact*. I am asking you now to have faith, not in God, nor in yourselves as you exist now, but in the possibility of *change*.'

That was the essence of his sermon. The rest was an eclectic mixture of conventional Christianity, evangelistic jargon, and self-help philosophy, with a courteous mention of Jerome's 'American colleagues', the Channels who speak in the voices of their ancestors. The phrase 'to be born again' was used, but only to be rejected, because Jerome was talking, he said, about something less radical, although more demanding. He was talking about the gathering together of the disparate parts of ourselves, our different images of ourselves, our deepest wishes, into one coherent whole. Every adult is a different person from the child he or she was, but they are also the same person. This proves that change is possible, Jerome said, we can transform ourselves into something *whole*. These were the words that he kept returning to: 'Division is human, unity divine.'

He asked the audience to repeat them, and he got a reasonable response. 'Division is human, unity divine.' The tone of this response was timorous, and I found it more affecting than anything Jerome said. It was the wistful nuance of people who wanted to believe. Eavesdropper I might be, and thief, but I could never be a conman, because that tone would always tug at my sympathy.

It would be inaccurate to say that he had the audience in the palm of his hand. He did however, capture a few imaginations. His was a gospel of self-centredness, diluted with just enough Christianity to make it seem unselfish, to make fulfilled selfhood seem an altruistic goal. 'Gilt without guilt,' he pronounced at one stage, arms raised above his head in a rare moment of fervour, revealing glittering gold cufflinks. 'Profit is a Christian principle. Whether you are a teacher or a businessman, a nurse or an accountant, realization of the self is the aim. Only then, when *you* are fulfilled, when you have made something of yourself, can you begin to fulfil your Christian duty of helping your neighbour.'

At the end he was clearly aiming at a transcendent moment, his voice modulating into a lulling, almost sing-song, penetrating softness. 'We are at the centre,' he said. 'Around us is this frail tent, a fragile membrane holding off the outside world, the force of experience which tries to shape us in its image. The membrane can remain intact even when you leave this tent, spiritually we are all virgins as of this moment, we are whole. Around the tent is the Common, the Common is surrounded by houses, the houses are part of London, London a great city part of Great Britain, part of Europe, the circles continue, concentric circles emanating from this spot, wider and wider, girdling the Earth like the rings of Saturn, and continuing to grow and to grow,' his voice rising in volume again, 'and we are at the centre, my friends, my voice is at the centre, this contact between us, my body on this stage surrounded by you people, we are at the centre of something vast. Each of us is the centre, able to create the world he moves in.' His voice returning now to its gentle mode, like a wave drawing back into the sea. 'A great poet called Yeats once wrote that the centre cannot hold. He was wrong, the centre *will* hold. Please repeat with me: division is human, unity divine.'

'Division is human, unity divine.'

A good number of voices joined him this time. My father's was not among them. I think Jerome probably had my father well on the way to conversion until that final moment, 'A great poet called Yeats . . .' There was a challenge there, a division in fact, between my father's most enduring enthusiasm, literature, and this brash pretender calling on him to alter himself. My father was turning to me as the applause began, undoubtedly with some critical comment concerning the cynical distortion of literature, when the disturbance happened.

It was an excellent piece of timing, coming so neatly at the end of the oration. Behind us, where we had been standing until we had pushed forward to get a closer look at Jerome, a body of banner waving people was trying to push its way in to the tent. There were shouts of 'Hypocrite' and 'Sinner' and, more prosaically, 'Bullshit' and 'Bastard'. There was a voice I recognized, louder than the rest.

'Dad, is that Charlie's father?'

'No, it can't be. Yes, I think it is.'

The tent was still crammed, no early leavers, and Mr Larbey's interlopers were having trouble getting in. In a tidal quirk of the turmoil of bodies between us, I was abruptly granted a narrow view of him, T-shirted and snarling, exercising his meaty arms in sweeping people out of his way. There were shouts of anger, and then a woman's scream and, where we had been standing, a fight was suddenly erupting. All that I really remember of it is my occasional glimpses of Larbey, grinning, and the sight of people collapsing, like a colourful wave raggedly breaking, against the supporting struts of the temporary seating. There were more screams, and beneath them there was the ominous groan of warping, cracking wood.

I didn't see much more than that because I was being yanked in the opposite direction by my father, not the most physical of men, who was forcing a path away from the trouble, towards the stage. Most people were moving the same way, and we became part of a concerted surge. So, as I told the people at school who asked me in the days that followed, I had no chance of seeing the section of seating fall. I was distracted. I just heard the screams, first of fright and then of horror, two-tone yells, as if Jerome had after all whipped his audience into hysteria, redoubled on a higher note just at the moment when you thought they were finished. I was distracted by the breath-squeezing crush that my father could not entirely shield me from, and by the sight of Jerome's Italian thug warm-up man up on the stage appealing for calm. It was only when we clambered on to the stage that I could briefly glimpse back and see the pile of bodies, like some many-limbed monster, sprawled among the splintered wreck of the tiered seating.

We burst out of an exit behind the stage like a cork out of a bottle. A single cork, because my father was more or less carrying me in his eagerness not to lose me in the panicky crowd.

'Are you all right Billy?' he said finally, when we were well away from the tent. 'Nothing broken? Is everything all right?'

It was nice to feel this wave of overt affection directed at me. I almost wanted to be injured, to enable him to project more emotion my way. 'My leg,' I wanted to say, 'dad, I can't move my leg!' 'Don't worry,' he'd answer, all calm competence, 'lie still, don't try to move. I'm here. We'll get some help in no time. Don't worry about a thing, because I'm here.'

'I'm fine, dad,' I said.

He was already looking back at the candy-striped tent. 'Should I try to help? It's too crowded as it is. It's all right Billy,' he said, although I had said nothing, 'there were police outside, they will have called ambulances. Do you want to rest here for a while, before we move on? We'll have to call your mother soon, tell her we're all right.'

'I'd like to stay and rest for a bit.'

'Sure.' That was it, that was the end of the concern. We sat on the grass beneath a tree and watched for a while as ambulances and police cars drew up, and as the chaos was very slowly resolved into order. By the time he spoke again, I was fidgeting with an abandoned crisp packet, and I already felt embarrassed about my wish for his sympathy.

'I'm wrong, of course,' he said, 'Jerome's just the dead spit of him, that's all. Or not even that, not even that really, what with the hair and the build of him. It was the way he walked on to the stage, you know, his walk and something about his look. That poise of his, the assurance. They're the same type, that's the very least you could say. But it's not really his face, is it? Is it, Billy?'

'I don't know,' I said, and my father laughed.

'Come on,' he said, 'we'd better go.'

I don't know why he laughed, since he obviously shared my doubt. I think it was a possibility that, for his peace of mind, he couldn't afford to admit. Anyway, he didn't persuade me one way or the other. I'd grown beyond the stage of absolute trust in him. Hadn't he claimed we'd be out of harm's way at the back of the tent? Hadn't he failed to rush back inside and save some lives? And hadn't I had to stand up for him against my mother, earlier that same day? My perception of the world then was not conducive to absolutes. Things shifted and altered, independent of

109

wishes and preconceptions. Perhaps after all Jerome was preaching to the converted in one sense. There was no need to convince me of the possibility of change, it was the possibility of stability that I doubted.

Seventeen

When I was six, a boy in my class left a present for the teacher on her desk. Miss Martin was young and pretty and most of the boys had a crush on her. She always had praise for a piece of work, and her criticism was such that it seemed like special advice, given to someone showing particular promise. I remember her leaning over my shoulder, her face next to mine, pointing out that I had misspelt the word 'you'. 'Try to get it right,' she said, 'because it's such a *common* word, you'll use it so often.' For weeks afterwards, every time I used it, I marvelled at her perception.

It was not unusual for Miss Martin to receive small gifts, and she had developed a particular grace in accepting them, even though apples and comics and flowers yanked off bushes may not have been quite what she would have preferred. Kevin had thought of something special, to demonstrate his feelings. Miss Martin unwrapped the swathes of toilet paper with a puzzled smile. I remember the shifting series of expressions which followed: gratification and puzzlement were followed by shock, and finally anger, but more vividly than that I remember the boy's reaction. His tearful bewilderment as he stood in front of her, his back to the class, as she questioned him. His white legs shaking. The shrinking inwards of his shoulders as the giggles began behind him. On the desk in front of Miss Martin, who was sitting as far away from it as she could get, was a long thin turd, chocolate brown and glistening. The surrounding paper was covered in ugly smears, like a painting abandoned in anger.

When I was six, laughing with everyone else at the boy's agony, I felt simultaneously a twinge of empathy, a fear that some other set of circumstances might land me in such a position. Twenty-five years later the memory is the same, still clear, but my perception of it has altered. For one thing, I feel sorry for the child, and wonder what effect such an event might have had as he grew up; and for another, I layer on to the memory my knowledge of the bewildering nature of the adult world, its illogical habits and inflexible rules. I am also wondering *why* this picture sticks to me as it does. This memory is not a fragile crystal, both altered and altering while it dissolves within a mixture; it is a lead soldier, stubbornly holding its pose while I change around it.

When I remembered the scene only four years later, its main consequence was guilt. Why had I laughed at the boy's humiliation? My behaviour made me feel uncomfortable, as if I had let myself in for a delayed punishment. The memory was brought to my mind by the embarrassment I felt for my father, triggering a mysterious series of associations. As we walked into the kitchen after the violent finale to Jerome's appearance, what we saw was my mother sitting beside Floyd, and leaning across him. There was an intimacy about their position that made it ambiguous. A slight adjustment and they might have been teacher and pupil, or lovers.

'What,' said my father, 'if you'll excuse the cliché, is going on here?'

I don't know what made him so quickly jump to the conclusion that there was something going on. It doesn't say much for my parents' relationship at the time. I do know that he very quickly realized his mistake, and that it did not reflect well on him.

My mother straightened up slowly, not at all like someone caught in an indecent act. Her reaction was beautiful, something of grace about its spontaneity. She stood up, laughed, and hugged my father, still held him as she looked up at him with amused affection. 'Eldon, sweetheart, have you been reading romantic novels again? Jealous husband, erring wife?' She kissed him. 'I'm flattered, but I was showing Floyd my writing, not my etchings.'

Floyd put the wad of A4 paper on the table. 'I just dropped in,' he said, 'I've been to see Jerome. Lucy tells me you're fellow converts.'

While there was some discussion about this, and my father recovered his composure, I was walking around the table, my

111

suffering on his behalf quickly replaced by curiosity as to what my mother was writing. She intercepted me, and picked up the typed sheets. 'Uh uh,' she said, 'off limits.' Her hand ruffled my hair to soften the words. I moved away from the gesture.

'Why?' I said. 'What's it about? I want to know.'

'I know,' she said, 'you're a writer too after all.'

'Are you?' said Floyd. 'What do you write?' This invitation to talk about myself did the trick. While I was telling Floyd about 'The Journey to the Wreck', and about some things written in class since then, my mother was disappearing with her manuscript. And my father was disappearing with my mother.

I am tempted to follow them out of the door, up to the bedroom or wherever they went, listening in on their conversation. He apologizes. He questions her about her writing, and she tells him about it. They discuss it, and for once something of hers becomes an enthusiasm of his, for once he is looking towards his marriage instead of away from it. It is a seductive thought, but unrealistic. I don't even know what she was working on. My mother never told me, and I don't know if my father winkled it out of her at that or any other time. My own guess is that it was fiction, her first attempt, and it was rejected by agent or publisher, but I am biased by my own preferences. Perhaps, like me, she strayed into some form of writing basically foreign to her. I sat and talked to Floyd, and my interest in my mother's writing waned as our conversation continued.

Floyd had the knack, which I have never learnt, of only smiling when he meant it. His face was so unremarkable partly because it was so impassive, no clear expression there to snag the eyes. Judgements and emotions held in reserve. The effect of this, I found, was to make me want to win approval, to earn one of those rare smiles. Something similar in fact, to my relationship with my father.

'What did you think of Jerome?' he asked.

'Dad thought he was Archer,' I said, inviting Floyd to laugh with me.

'Yes,' he said however, 'he has that swagger, doesn't he?' He shook his head. 'I have a problem with these evangelists, I forever picture them selling something. I mean as a journalist I should be unbiased you see, but I can't manage it, I can never get past their mannerisms. Do you know what I mean, Billy? I mean like actors. Underneath the make-up and the suit and the tone of voice, underneath all that is probably something quite different from what you might expect. Layers.'

'Like onion skins,' I said.

He looked at me, and I was pleased to see a touch of surprise in his eyes. 'Yes,' he said, 'like onion skins. A bad guy underneath a good guy, a handsome one underneath an ugly one. And then something else underneath that, and then something else, and something else. Which is what he was talking about of course: being different people.'

'Do you think the people who came in thought he was a bad guy?'

Floyd raised his eyebrows. 'No, not really.'

'Why not?'

'Because I'm a suspicious type,' he said. 'You're talking to the wrong man Billy, you're too young to be talking to such a cynic. Your father's more sensible, because he has an open mind. I could be doing permanent damage to your faith in human nature.'

I was finding it a struggle to keep up with Floyd, but I latched on to this last comment. 'Oh don't worry,' I said, 'I haven't got any of that.'

That was when he laughed. 'You'd make a fine journalist,' he said. 'Well, as one cynic to another, I think that crowd were rent-a-mob. People that Jerome had hired to turn his little show into a newsworthy event. Mentioned on TV, a couple of paragraphs in the papers. Create a little controversy, have the Born Agains condemning him for practising magic.'

'Do you know Mr Larbey?'

'Who?'

So I told him about Mr Larbey, and gave him his address, and was gratified to see his interest grow. It seemed a fair exchange – he had piqued my interest in journalism. His job was clearly eventful, driving around London watching things happen, finding out things, then writing about them. I was pleased at the sense of distance implied by this: watching events, investigating, writing, but never actually taking that risky closer step that involved participation. My years spent cultivating a cautious and careful front to present to the world had apparently paid off, if Floyd saw immediately that I showed promise. I would marry Kim, and I would slip without difficulty into a journalist's job, while continuing, of course, to write stories. Naturally, I hadn't yet told Kim about my plans.

And naturally, I didn't quite realize then that writing invented stories and writing journalism could be more or less the same thing. Complications like those had no part to play in the future I was devising. My future, I had firmly decided, was to be uncomplicated, and unequivocally successful. I saw my life as an adult as something like the Lego town before Charlie and I destroyed it: an autonomous world untouched by outside influences, containing myself and Kim, family, and friends yet to be nominated. Beyond the limits of this small circle the other world could play whatever tricks it liked, I would observe them, perhaps write about them, but remain entirely unaffected by them.

'I'm going to be a journalist,' I announced to my parents.

'Good,' said my father, 'then you can keep us in our old age.'

Floyd had just left and the three of us were sitting together in the kitchen. Quite a rare event, to find ourselves together in this way.

We are surrounded by cooker and cupboards and a sink with some plates in it. We are sitting by the window looking out on to the garden. There are no unsettling connotations. The weather is mentioned, so is what I have been doing at school, and a dress my mother has bought. I want to know what is for dinner tomorrow, and my mother says she hasn't got anything. My father is surprised, tomorrow being Sunday. My mother didn't have time, she says she will go out in the morning to the new shop that is open on Sundays. My father suggests we go out for a meal, if it is fine we will have a pub lunch and sit by the river. My father starts to tell my mother about the use of Yeats in the sermon, says he may write a letter to a newspaper, and this is where I stop listening. Outside is the tall, climbable tree, the white trunk stretching towards the grey sky, stretching higher than I could hope to climb in my most audacious moods.

It is a timely moment as things quietly approach crisis to correct any wrong impressions. I would not want to suggest that my parents had an unusually unhappy marriage. It is easy for me to remember positive things. They take me to a concert, trying to create a taste in me for classical music, but I fall asleep and wake in the interval to find them kissing like a couple of teenagers. On a rare holiday abroad, my mother almost chokes with laughter as my father tries out his Spanish, product of a transient enthusiasm, on a waiter. They browse in a favourite secondhand bookshop, murmuring criticism of each other's choices. The three of us are in the kitchen, my attention is wandering, I am impressed by the height of the tree. My attention is caught when my parents begin to laugh simultaneously at something I haven't heard.

It is a short list, but I hope a convincing one. It is much easier – this should be taken into account – it is much easier to evoke sadness or despair than it is to evoke happiness, or mere contentment.

As well as memories I have photographs, containing unfeigned smiles and natural poses. When I picture myself at this age, I see myself standing between my parents, a small boy on the brink of a growing spurt, with those extra inches tight-packed inside him. He is full to bursting with the future, but he has little confidence. Tomorrow at school he might break some rule he is ignorant of, and become an object of ridicule to the entire class. At home he might offend someone whose love he covets. Error and humiliation are not hard to imagine. They look like a piece of shit lying on a school desk.

Eighteen

We go to dentists in the knowledge that we must relinquish control. Our destiny is temporarily in someone else's hands. We give the dentist the right to inflict pain, and to scrape, drill and dispose of teeth as if they were shoes in need of repair. The same is true of doctors, but hospitals tend to prepare the patient for his ordeal in a ritualized way, whereas we step off the High Street into a dental surgery in the middle of a shopping trip, and find our habitual view of life turned abruptly upsidedown. Lying semi-prone like an animal signalling its submission, we are at our most powerless. Where a few moments before we could believe ourselves to be autonomous, choosing a way forward from day to day and hour to hour, suddenly that power of choice is removed, and we are reminded of the fragility both of our bodies and of our view of ourselves. In the dentist's chair everything, even our identity, is under scrutiny.

I don't know exactly what happened on my father's last visit to Archer, but I do know that he spent the next day in bed, and my mother suggested that he cancel his evening meeting with Melody. This he was not prepared to do. White-faced, in grey polo neck and jeans, he was sitting in the kitchen, trying to eat a bowl of chicken soup, when the doorbell rang. I had been sitting with him, munching toast and trying to persuade him in a hearty sort of way that he needed a holiday. At the sound of the bell he poured the soup into the sink with a look of relief and asked me to open the door.

Whenever Mr Melody showed up, bewhiskered and jolly as ever, like an unseasonal Father Christmas, it was as if time had shrunk. In the midst of change, he managed to look and sound and act the same way as he always had. The same whiskers, the same build – always a little overweight, but not too much – the same rosy complexion. The same mode of speech: monologuing cheerfully like most of the adults I knew, unaffected by my lack of response, spraying exclamation marks everywhere.

'Hello Billy! My you've grown! I don't see you in the sweet shop so much any more do I? No, no, don't apologize, children grow up, it's sad, it's an unfortunate state of affairs, but there's nothing to be done about it. Of course I try to cater for all ages, remember that. Next time you are visiting the delightful Kim don't forget to drop in to The Circus of Delights again. I'm sure I have something to interest you there, my stock is expanding like crazy. Remember what fun we had in the studio last time?' He made a camera shape with his hands, framing me in an imaginary viewfinder, and he made a sound with his tongue, 'Click!', as he pressed an imaginary button.

I closed the door and led him in.

He showed up often, because my father and he had regular talks about business, in the study where I had once seen a magician drawn on the computer screen. My father's time in the two years since our visit to Jerome had been increasingly submerged by his business activities. It was unlikely he would find time for such a visit now. The walls between the different compartments in his life were breaking down. Over breakfast, or when I was trying to watch TV, or when I was alone in my room, he would appear, make smalltalk clumsily, and then begin to talk about marketing strategies and loss leaders, percentages and royalties and minimum terms agreements.

Melody is still waiting in the hall patiently, but I have just remembered one of these occasions. My father was sitting on the edge of my bed, not even looking at me, and I was watching him, half afraid of his tone. 'Business was just the enabler,' he said, 'that's all it was, it was just the motor for my plans and ideals, driving them forward. They were what mattered.' A humourless laugh. 'There must have been a smash up somewhere, a car crash Billy, because somewhere things got shifted, ideals took a back seat.' He made himself more comfortable on my bed, moving further back to lean against the wall. I was sitting at my desk, where I did homework, with a book on my lap. He had interrupted my reading. 'Property isn't everything it seemed to be,' he continued. 'I should have known. Beware of easy money. How am I supposed to concentrate?' His hands were out, palms upward, and he was looking at me suddenly, as if he expected an answer. 'Things get diffused, Billy, things go into channels you might never have predicted. That man had it right, Jerome. Unity is divine. I've always told you Billy, it's no good expecting things to come right by magic. I said once you should model yourself on me. Arrogance, Billy, that was arrogance. Concentration of effort, purity of effort, that's what's needed. Focusing.'

But his own words were unfocused, jumping from specific difficulties with a shop or an individual to larger problems, and to vague references concerning sour deals and rash decisions. He was too preoccupied with his problems to keep them to himself. At first I genuinely tried to listen to him – 'Knowledge is power,' I was thinking – but soon, each time he began to talk at me, I simply adjusted my expression and tried to appear interested, tried, at decent intervals, to ask intelligent questions. I didn't want him to guess that I hadn't understood a word he had said in the last six months.

Superfluously, I showed Melody into the study. Upstairs, my mother was running a bath. In the kitchen my toast was cold and inedible. There was nothing on TV and it was a bit late to call Charlie or anyone else. Gently, cautiously, I laid my ear against the door that had just closed. Here perhaps would be a clue to my father's moods. Liberated from their legitimate context, his words might become at once more interesting and more lucid. I strained to listen. The investigative journalist at work.

The more I strained, it seemed, the less I heard. Muffled exchanges. The door was thick and their voices were quiet. It was hard enough just to distinguish them. My father's voice, a monotone, drained of energy, Melody's . . . Melody's voice changing in register and pitch, changing and changing again . . . 'Knowledge is power', could that be what he said? Not that old chestnut? I gained nothing comprehensible from my eavesdropping, just confused impressions which merged in my mind but would not resolve themselves into sense. Was that Melody's voice? Or was there a third person present? Was Archer in there? Every now and then a few words became clear, almost as if they were addressed to me: 'wisdom and strength' . . . 'other people'. If I was hoping for an easy solution, the equivalent of turning to the back of the book to find the answers, then I was disappointed. Nothing so straightforward. I retreated from the door when I heard my mother coming down the stairs and, because I was in the kitchen, I did not even see Melody leave.

My father came in, whisky glass in hand, as I was spreading peanut butter on toast.

'Did you once steal from Melody?'

I stared at him, unable to come up with a quick answer.

He nodded. 'Yes,' he said. 'And Archer?' Again no answer was needed. He waved his hand in a gesture of dismissal. 'It means nothing. Who am I to judge? Only don't make an enemy of that man,' it wasn't clear who he was referring to, but he carried straight on, 'keep an eye on him, keep both eyes on him in fact, because one won't do. I'm no fool, I like Archer but I don't really trust him, I wouldn't confide my secrets to him, I know how single-minded that man is. Melody now,' he laughed, 'Melody is a man I thought I could trust.' He nodded again. 'Mistakes catch up with you, they have a tendency to do that. Keep it in mind, Billy, whatever else you do. I have to leave you now, I have a lot to think about.'

He left, and I sat in the empty kitchen and ate my toast. Almost immediately I heard my parents' raised voices in the sitting room.

I ate quietly, listening to the argument. I was happy this time to hear no words, only sounds. I was halfway through my coffee when I heard my mother in the hall. She was at the foot of the stairs. Perhaps they hadn't been arguing, because she sounded amused rather than angry.

'You're crazy,' she said, 'and you're drunk. I've never heard anything so ridiculous. It's all right, it'll be all right. Perhaps it's an opportunity, in a way. Sober up before you come upstairs, I'm sick of your drunken snoring.'

Before I could slip out, my father came into the kitchen, holding the whisky bottle by the neck. 'Still here?'

'Still here,' I agreed.

He switched on the kettle and sat down at the table with me. 'Past your bedtime,' he said. He was leaning back with his eyes closed, and for a long time he said nothing else, as if he was deep in thought. The kettle began to boil, and for a few seconds I thought it wasn't going to switch itself off. Steam poured out of the spout.

'Do you know,' he said, and he sat up straight and looked at me seriously, 'I don't want to bore you but I'd like to tell you about this; do you know, I had a strategy all worked out for when I made my move in publishing? A foolish one, not a realistic one, but even so it gave me a purpose, even if I knew it was patronizing and it couldn't ever happen.'

The kettle had turned itself off. He was leaning forward now, and his long, pale face looked lean and dynamic. He was possessed by his idea.

'A commando raid on people's sensibilities,' he said. 'I would have moved in on Mills and Boon, and all the others who sell people that muck. A corporate raid, but a stealthy one if such a thing is possible, so that no one knew about it. Then, the long-term plan. Little by little, year by year, decade by decade, I would upgrade their product, infiltrating literature into their output. You see? I mean a paragraph at a time, a phrase here, a nuance there. A surprising plot twist, something disarming where the reader expects a platitude. I would recruit a team, only the best, people who would share my vision. I'd call them The Mechanics.' He took a swig from his bottle, and continued without pausing. 'Eventually I'd be publishing *Emma* and *Middlemarch* and *Wuthering Heights*, under different titles

119

perhaps, but in the Mills and Boon imprint. Modern classics would come next, including a list of Mills and Boon poets to rival Faber, until one day, maybe not in my lifetime, there would be a whole generation of girls and women converted to the cause.'

He sat back again suddenly and let out a breath, like a small laugh. 'What do you say? What do you think?'

To me it seemed feasible and, in a neat and fully rounded way, logical. 'Could it work?' I said. I was imagining the process beginning in a couple of months. Roly had a taste for Westerns, and it was him I was imagining being gradually introduced to the classics. Matt Stone, the legendary Cavalry scout, smuggling to the Indians not rifles or alcohol, but Charlotte and Emily Brontë.

My father seemed not to have heard my question, he was staring at the bottle, rocking it so that the remaining whisky sloshed against the sides. 'I taught myself,' he said, 'autodidact, that's me, well known for it. Why shouldn't I teach everyone else? I've never had that modern problem of not knowing what to do, that wishy-washy thing where you wonder what's going to happen in the future. I've always known, that's been my strength, I've known what I've wanted. I want to teach the world. That's all I want. That would be something, it would really *be* something.'

He stood up, leaving the bottle on the table. 'Your bedtime, young man,' he said, and then he left the kitchen.

When I followed my father to bed I heard talking inside my parents' bedroom. I stopped on the landing and, although I did not press my ear to the door, I listened. It was the third time that evening that I had been aware of someone else's conversation, and I felt a pang of guilt. I just want to hear the tones, I told myself, to be sure that there is no argument going on. Eldon's voice was a drone interrupted by exclamations. Lucy's was almost too quiet to hear at all, but it may have been reassuring, there may have been a hopeful, or perhaps a badgering quality to it. There was a lot of silence. I would like to think that Eldon revealed everything that troubled him, and Lucy suggested a fresh start, out of London, a fresh start for their marriage and for her personally: new roles to play in a new place. My mother had faith in the possibility of change. But I am biased, and those are the things that I would naturally hope for. They might have been arguing or making love, they might have been exchanging revelations or deceptions: I don't know. I was outside the door, where I thought I wanted to be, a step away from the action. I stood on the landing until I was shivering, and then I tip-toed to my room, trying not to let the floorboards creak.

Nineteen

Each large step I take in this story, and one of the largest has finally arrived, is a step closer to where I am now, where I am paying for, or more properly *being* paid for my gross error in the ceremony of the eating of the writing. The error being the choice of newsprint, rather than a piece of a page of a novel.

At twelve she was embarrassed by her figure, now at sixteen busty beauty Beatrice finds her breasts have changed her life! Beatrice hopes to be a singer. We say: you're a sweetie Beatie!

This is the confession I've been avoiding. As I write, this latest example of my work is on the floor beside my desk. The model simpers at me, apparently unaware of our mutual exposure. I try not to think what my father would say.

I am feeling guilty, and I am using the guilt as an excuse for a digression. The last time I digressed at any length it was on the subject of my grandparents, to postpone writing about my mother's miscarriage. This time it is because I have arrived at the next tragedy for the Gunn family, the one which precipitates me, after choices have been made, into a whole different story. Digressions are comforting. It is good to be able to allude to

121

adulthood, and to evoke the vast area of normality which lies behind and between the events of this story. In April of the year I am talking about Oscars were awarded, the talk in the newspapers (the real newspapers) was of Presidential nominations, and the Russian manned flight to Mars was looking increasingly likely. In Edinburgh some people were killed when a man started shooting indiscriminately in a shopping centre. ('Rambo monster slaughters six.') My grandmother was having fun with psychedelic colours in 1969 in the Romford tapestry. Digression is a form of dilution, and as such I welcome it. I am not seeking intensity. I am trying not to let my present preoccupation with sensationalism influence this writing. I do not want this to become a story about varieties of pain.

It was towards the end of the Easter holidays and, since my relationship with Charlie was fairly good at this time, I had spent the afternoon bike-riding with him in the gravel pit. I pointed out where the mad woman had appeared a couple of weeks earlier, and I told him how she had accused me and spat at me. Emboldened by his company, I looked round the area with him but, to my secret relief, there was no sign of her.

When I got home it was about six and my father, who had been too ill to go to work, was slumped asleep in front of the TV news. His hand rested on another bottle of whisky on the floor. My mother was not home. I sat in my room for a while, and read a little, before deciding I wasn't in the mood. I didn't know what I was in the mood for. Bored with reading, I went downstairs to see if my father had woken up. He hadn't, and in front of him a sitcom was beginning, its credits unwinding to the sound of canned laughter.

I sat on the sofa. My father's presence made it hard to enjoy the TV. Just how unwell was he? At least he wasn't snoring. His chin rested on his chest, his hand hung inches from the bottle's neck, the fingers frozen. He was pale. The skin of his scalp was smooth, and shone a little beneath the electric light. Not long ago I had been bending over a teacher who was marking my work, and I had felt a sudden compulsion to kiss the great, pink bald spot that was presented to me. The strength of this urge frightened me at the time – what on earth, I wondered, did it reveal about me? Here was something to rival the piece of shit on the school desk. Now I looked at my father and, in an exceptional rush of affection, following the previous evening's intimacy, I considered waking him with such a kiss. The front door opened, and then closed with a bang. He didn't stir.

I went into the hall. 'Mum, dad's fast asleep and I don't think he's well.' I met both my mother and Mr Melody, taking off their coats. Melody's, I remember, looked like a patchwork quilt, in multi-coloured diamonds. 'It's all right, Billy,' said my mother, 'he's probably just drunk.' We entered the room to a burst of laughter from the TV. 'See what I mean?' She nodded at the bottle. 'Dead drunk. Eldon? Eldon wake up, I've brought Mr Melody back to talk things over.' She put her hand on his shoulder, and then took a step back as he slumped towards her. 'Eldon?'

Melody leant over on the other side of my father and felt his throat. I was reminded of Joseph in the Old People's home, with the nurses attending to him, chivvying him into taking some pills. 'Lucy,' he said, and as he spoke he was raising my father's arms above his head, 'why don't you take Billy into the kitchen and call an ambulance?' My mother didn't even speak, instead she began to pound on my father's chest while Melody, as if intending to surpass any show of affection I had in mind, appeared to kiss him full on the mouth. I stood in the doorway, frozen. I knew what was going on, I knew I should be running to the phone for an ambulance, but I couldn't move, I could only stand and watch. Melody's moustache was squashed between his cheek and my father's. My mother was surely bruising the back of her hand as she hit it. Her back swing made it look each time as if she was going to hit Eldon in the face. In my stillness amid their frantic activity, I felt like my father. I half expected to see him wink at me from beneath Melody's nuzzling lips. When he moved away for a moment I saw Eldon's mouth agape in his grey face, grey as his sweater. With his arms over his head he seemed to be weakly fending Lucy and Melody off in his efforts to watch television unhindered.

He used to tell me that there was a camera behind the screen and, if I misbehaved, it would see me and transmit pictures of me to millions of homes around the country. I imagined this scene being replayed in sitting rooms everywhere. My father reviving to the applause of millions. Lucy and Melody collided as they tried to return to their ministrations. Melody apologized. Bursts of uncontrolled hilarity accompanied his words as the comedy reached its climax.

Suddenly, unbidden, I turned and ran out of the room and into the kitchen. I looked at the phone, my mind a blank, and then I picked it up and dialled Ethel's number. She answered on the second ring.

'Hello granny.'

'Billy, is that you? How lovely to hear from you, this is unexpected, how are you?'

'Fine thank you . . .'

'Good, I'm fine too, but Roly's had the most awful cough, it's his misspent youth catching up with him I tell him, although he denies it up and down. I expect you'll be wanting to hear about the tapestry?'

Next door I heard my mother shouting. My grandmother had paused at last, waiting for my response.

'Billy?'

I found I had no wish at all to interrupt her flow of words with my graceless and unlooked for news. It was silent next door now. Unlikely things might happen, if they were only given the chance.

'Yes please, tell me about the tapestry.'

I don't know how long our conversation took. Perhaps after five minutes I made some abrupt excuse, 'I have to go now,' and put the phone down. I went next door. Sometime during the period that I had been talking, my mother had accepted that she was manhandling a corpse. She was on her knees next to Eldon's chair, her face buried in her arms. Melody had straightened, he was standing over the body and undoing the top button of his shirt. It looked as if the three had posed for a photograph. Melody was looking down at my father in a speculative way.

He met my eyes as I came in. 'Come on Billy,' he said, and he led me, looking over my shoulder, straight back out again.

In the kitchen, after he had made some phone calls, and given me a cup of sweet tea, he said a few words.

'I predict changes,' he said. 'There are going to be great changes. All I say Billy is that I'm not far away. If you need someone, don't forget me, someone to talk to, someone to stay with, I'll be there for you. If you and your mother don't want to stay in this house, for instance. If you need any kind of help. I'll always be near you.'

I didn't answer, and he didn't say anything more. He took a drink to my mother, who was still in the other room, kneeling beside Eldon.

Twenty

When we left, the sky over the heath was freckled with kites. It was a kite convention and the white sky was dotted with hundreds of colourful kites as if stained by flecks of ink from a fistful of pens.

'Isn't it beautiful?' said my mother.

I watched them, diamonds and boxes and elegant arched gliders, hovering and diving and soaring. A pair of strings flickered in the road in front of us for a moment, and then lifted away in a casual, giant leap into the air. My mother watched as she drove. Her eyes moved from the road to the sky and back again, up and down and from side to side, her head moving too in small quick nods, as if she was affected by a nervous tic.

'Careful!'

I shouted as she veered towards the edge of the road where two boys were standing with their backs to the car. She corrected the movement.

'I saw them,' she said mildly.

I nearly contradicted her, but the last thing I wanted was an argument on the first day we had spoken in a week. That is a small exaggeration. We had said good morning and hello and goodbye, our days had been punctuated by these short acknowledgements. Goodbye when I left for school, and hello when I returned. I cannot say what my mother did with her time. I can say that in a slow but certain progress her thoughts led, one to another, ineluctably, towards a particular point. I can imagine it. I could reconstruct the process if I wanted to. When she arrived at this conclusion it seemed unbearably clear and obvious, and its very harshness, its ruthlessness, made it seem more just, better defined, more *perfect*. Flawless as an egg.

My mother made preliminary sketches of her future, and I went to school. Towards the end of the week I was told off for inattention, and the maths teacher made me stand up in front of the class and solve a quadratic equation. I got it right, and Charlie told me I was a creep. At night I waited for the sound of my father coming home. Numbers and prayers failed to have any effect.

Lucy was wearing a soft brown leather jacket over a pale green summery dress. Her wide lips were pink. No widow's weeds for her. She had been growing her hair, in a gradual and controlled way, and by now it came halfway to her shoulders in a neatly layered cut. Every now and then she moved her head, enjoying the touch of it on her neck. Her mother had once been an apprentice to a hairdresser, and had taught her daughter, so that Lucy was able to arrange a couple of mirrors and cut her hair exactly as she pleased. 'My appearance is in my own hands,' she used to say, when Eldon wondered why she took the trouble. 'I like to feel responsible for it, for everything connected with myself.' Sitting between the two mirrors, looking at him, 'I'm frightened of not being the central figure in my own story.' These remarks make me uneasy, because I have slotted her into a subordinate role in my story, but I am sure that she takes centre stage in her own writing, and I, if I have any part at all, am relegated to a minor role. We were on our way to Melinda's for Sunday lunch, beneath the kite-strewn sky, carrying a chocolate cake. It lay on the back seat on a platter, covered by a dish. It was an unusual treat, because my mother hated baking. I took it to be a significant cake, and I was right, but I mistook its significance.

For the rest of the journey we talked about Eldon's death. I mustered my maturity, Lucy her composure. It was a heart attack, she had been told, and the illness of the previous couple of days could be put down to alcohol, fatigue and stress. There was no mystery. I didn't believe this story even then, and I told my mother so.

'What do you believe then?' she asked.

'I don't know.'

'Nor do I my love. That's the point really, isn't it? There are too many unknowns. It's no good having theories about things, or plans and predictions for the way things are going to work out. Business strategies and life strategies just don't work. Crazy ambitions like your father's, or modest ones like mine, they go awry.'

'What crazy ambitions?'

She was silent, staring ahead as she drove. I was about to speak again when she answered, preceding her words with a sigh.

'Your father led a vivid fantasy life, Billy. Some of it didn't matter much, visions of himself as a powerful publisher, saviour of British culture, all that was harmless. But he liked to think of himself as a high-powered businessman, and that was never really the case. He wasn't as shrewd as he liked to think, nowhere near. And he thought he was the perfect family man, and he was wrong about that too. He was complacent, he thought he had all the right ingredients, in his grand designs, simmering away. That was his joke with you, wasn't it? The alchemist. That's how he saw himself. Don't set your heart on anything, Billy, not dogmatically, you have to be versatile, ready to change direction. Don't ever take it for granted Billy, that you're in control, you have to *assert* that control. I want you to remember what I'm telling you.'

She was driving with care, still looking at the road. I was reminded of Archer's advice, delivered with a nod and a smirk: 'Stay in the driving seat.' There were more questions to be asked about my father, many more, but they could wait. On the whole I was not displeased by her words, rather reassured by her determination. I thought she was considering taking over the running of Eldon's business.

Nothing of the lunch stays with me, except the chocolate cake, which wasn't a very good one. The icing tasted of butter. I would like to say that I remember my mother being particularly affectionate, or at least behaving in some abnormal way, but I can't. There is just the cake, significant because, unashamed by its bathos, it was the best she could manage as a parting gesture, a farewell gift.

After lunch, as arranged, my mother went to visit her parents alone. The note appeared that evening, when she was already late.

It was stained by crumbs and chocolate icing, because it had been laid between the cake and the plate.

Billy look at these words – exciting, extraordinary, exceptional. What do they have in common? That prefix, ex-. Ex, Billy, means *outside*, that's what it means to me. All the exciting extraordinary exceptional things are going on outside my world. I took a wrong turning that's all, I thought I could build things up in a satisfying way but I was wrong. I've gone in search of the X factor, Billy. I nearly asked you to come, I honestly nearly did, but it wouldn't have been fair. You would have said yes. That wouldn't have been fair, to involve you in that way, it wouldn't have been a real *choice* for you, and I'm staking everything on choice at the moment. I want to make something of my life, rearrange it, all the different elements of it, and come up with something new. I don't know if I'm thinking right or if I'm mad, but I don't want a part in someone else's fantasy life any more. Don't forgive me, I'm to blame and forgiveness would only lead to distorting the facts. Melinda is your legal guardian, but granny I know would love to have you. Even Melody, I think, is willing. You choose. Avoid Archer, don't trust him. I love you.

Don't expect my mother to return in either glory or contrition or both, don't look for her body buried in the garden or dredged up from some pond. That's not how it is. She has as much to do with this narrative now as the woman who jumped from behind a bush, called me by someone else's name and gobbed at my back. Somewhere Lucy is in a different story, wading through it at its centre. Only her absence is in this story now.

Twenty-one

At Melinda's, I had a small room and a beautiful bed. It was so big that I felt I could swim in it, across it and from end to end of it. The duvet was big too, so that there was no need to periodically pull it over my shivering bare body, or to have an ankle out in the cold. There was a padded headboard, which somehow was a great comfort. It felt good to lie close to the wall, my head against this soft headboard, with folds of thick duvet on the wide mattress behind me. On the other hand, it also felt good to burrow into the duvet, beneath it, pulling it over my head, creating a warm, dark and breathy space which, I decided, unlike the lamented Lego town, was truly safe.

I am concentrating on the bed because, in the days after receiving my mother's note, I spent a lot of time in it. There was some thinking to do, some adjusting, some rearrangements to be made. I couldn't cope with normal daily life while this process was going on. When I agreed to see anyone, they had to come and sit on the bed to talk to me, or talk at me, depending on my mood.

On the occasion that the GP, the socialworker, Melinda, Kim, Melody and my grandparents all crowded into the small room together and jockeyed for position on and around the big bed, the situation became farcical, like the scene in the Marx brothers' film in which the world crowds into a ship's tiny cabin. Both the GP and the socialworker, by ill luck, were fat. My grandparents, as the most frail of those present, stood at the foot of the bed, nearest the door, and fresh air. Kim was virtually in the bed beside me, and her mother was sitting on it beside her. Louise was standing next to the window, near my head, and Mr Melody, quite portly himself, was sitting on a chair squeezed between the doctor and the socialworker. The socialworker was trying to make notes, while the doctor had been intending to take my temperature and had decided to stay to observe the meeting. He was holding his thermometer in both hands, possibly anxious for its safety.

'Well,' said Louise, 'they did say you shouldn't be on your own too much.'

The mood was one of slightly desperate hilarity, for which I was grateful. It made it that much easier for me to announce my choice. 'I'd like to live with Melinda and Kim and Louise please, if that's all right with them. If it's not, I mean if I'd be any trouble, then I'd like to live with granny. And grandpa.' I remember Roly's face, beneath his more than usually straggly white hair; his lips pursed as if he was suppressing pain, his large eyes fixed on me, not quite readable. Pain because I had not chosen to stay with them? Pain in empathy with my own? Or pain at his daughter's action? I don't know. There were protestations and hugs from Melinda and Kim and even Louise, awkward in the confined space, and that was settled. Then, using the special prerogative that I knew was already wearing out, I asked them all to go away, which they obediently did.

That night I found it impossible to relax. It wasn't so much the effect of the choice I had made, my mind was revolving around a relatively trivial point. I was thinking about the fact that Melinda had always been my legal guardian. It seemed infinitely peculiar that such safeguards should routinely be taken, that a way of life should be so fragile that a reserve one should be arranged, just in case the first one broke down. It made me feel that my complacent, narrow way of looking at the world had been undermined from the start.

I resorted to my old habit of counting, one to 109, and for a while I thought I might find some solace in its familiarity. I did not subtract or multiply, add or divide, I simply counted, slowly. But even as I counted, only just into double figures, I began to feel uncomfortable with the numbers, found them jumbling, found even the primes suspect, containing more variations than they let on. The steady, solid relationships of the numbers were in reality unlimited. Any boundaries I imagined were artificial. The numbers were not to be trusted. There were innumerable ways, I began to realize, for them to surprise me.

I got out of bed and switched on the light. Leaning on the wall of my room was a mirror. As I walked towards it and away from it, my first steps out of bed in four days, I watched my reflection effortlessly climb and descend the crazily skewed floor. Here was a role model, a version of myself unfazed by the most preposterous distortion of his life. Smoothly up the slope, and smoothly down, impassive all the while. Smoothly over the tragedy for the Gunn family, smoothly over the distortions in its wake: abandonment by my parents, the crucial choice of who to live with, and the positive but unfounded knowledge that we had been and perhaps still were being persecuted by Archer.

Now it is neat. Now I have arrived at a place to pause. There is a hiatus. Things settle into new shapes.

WAITING FOR
JOHN WAYNE

Twenty-two

The pause ends as I jump back into the story, with a splash of words and characters.

'No!' cried Kim, as cold water drenched her sun-warmed legs. 'I hate you!'

Phrases lie around untidily, people are in different places, up to different things, moving in different directions. I must gather them up, lay them out, create some order. I should swim less boisterously in these waters.

Kim dived in after me, a graceful swan, hardly a ripple, after my belly-flopping racer's effort. She swam up to where I was treading water. 'Last one to the line's a tampon.' And with this, to me, enigmatic remark, she was off, on her back, arms windmilling expertly, on her way to the line of red buoys which marked out the swimming enclosure.

My desperate, thrashing crawl had no chance of catching her. Time and again I reached out, contemplating grabbing her ankle, and she was a little further ahead of me. 'All right,' I gasped, spitting out a mouthful of water as I arrived where she was hanging on to the line, smiling her complacent pillar-of-the-swimming-team smile, 'all right then, last one to the middle of the lake is a *condom*!' And I dived under the line, took a few underwater strokes in the pale green haze just beneath the surface, and began churning out into the deep water. If I couldn't match her speed I could beat her stamina, and play the old trick of out daring her.

The water beneath me became darker as I progressed, moving further away from the bank. I looked over my shoulder and saw that Kim, after a token effort, was already heading back towards the red buoys. I slowed down to a leisurely breaststroke, but continued heading outwards, wanting to make this an emphatic victory, and enjoying in any case the scenery, the tall pines jostling at the side of the lake, and the sense of freedom. The banks gradually retreating on every side. The sky, implausibly high and wide. It was the middle of the holiday, I was swimming, gently, in the middle of the lake, almost, it seemed, in the middle of the sky.

Only when I stopped and began to tread water, did I begin to become aware of the depth below me, of myself hanging suspended unknown metres above the lake bed. When I began to wonder what might be beneath the surface, my imagination took over: swaying weed and anaemic white fish, sucking mud and crawling water beetles, slimy eels and drifting fungi. Isolated in the still centre of the lake, I found one frightening image after another coming to me. While my head and shoulders burnt in the generous sun, the rest of my body seemed suddenly to be hanging in the water like tempting bait. I shivered. Hidden things. Did something brush my foot? I remembered 'The Journey to the Wreck', and found myself quite unamused by the thought of sea creatures pulling me beneath the water. I imagined long, silver, scaly barracudas with wide and meanly grinning jaws, rows and rows of gleaming needles for teeth, lurking in the depths for decades, maybe centuries. Carnivorous. The word made my teeth chatter. I tried to tread water with my knees level with my chest. I was getting cold.

Why, I asked myself, was that area marked out for safe swimming anyway? What made the rest of the lake unsafe? With an effort of control, I began to head back towards the bobbing line of buoys at a slow pace. I could see Kim at the water's edge, sitting among the pebbles and splashing idly. I began to tread water again. You are twelve, not a baby, I told myself. I know, I answered. Prove it then. How? Dive, dive down to the bottom, or if not the bottom, then as far as you can go. On the bank, Melinda was waving. I waved back. She was not worried, why should I be? Encouraged, and fully aware of the foolishness of my imaginings, I did a forward roll, inverting myself, and slipped head first beneath the surface.

Where coldness and darkness folded themselves around me. My arms pulling me downwards in outward sweeping strokes seemed to be pulling aside thick curtains, one layer and then another, and then another and another. My wide eyes could see nothing, and I could feel nothing, except the water, that seemed to be icy, and the pressure, that seemed to be squeezing my chest. Instantly, I began to expect something to happen, something to bite at my feet, a giant clam to lock itself on to my arm, my face to become enmeshed in the tendrils of a jellyfish. Unsettled, I stopped swimming down, turned around again in an ear popping roll so that I was standing suspended in the water, preventing myself from floating upwards by a timid flapping of my arms. My breath ached to be released. I let out a couple of bubbles and felt them pass my cheeks. The sensation abruptly made me want to laugh. I could let out all the air, empty my lungs, and then take a deep breath . . . a deep breath . . . I could not complete the thought. At that moment something touched my foot and I jerked it back and, panicking, began to swim for the surface. I knew it was only weed, and I knew that that meant that I was almost at the bottom, but even if I had had breath to spare I couldn't have taken the extra couple of strokes down to the clinging sand. Kicking out angrily I swam upwards, arms stretching up and pulling down against the water's resistance, feeling the renewed warmth embrace my body as the dark green faded to a paler green, olive, emerald – now it began to glow – jade, lime, yellow, and finally it was transparent as, chest bursting, scattering spray, arms raised as if in triumph, I broke the surface.

Where I allowed myself to float for a few moments on my back, slowly regaining my breath. Nothing to see but the dazzling sky. I was reminded of the evening of the party years earlier, when the vision of the night so filled my view that it made me dizzy. My fear diminished again, as did all my excitement. I breathed in slowly, and breathed out slowly, floating effortlessly. Now, for no clear reason, I felt like a successful explorer. When I set out for the bank, intending to move at a dignified pace, I found myself racing again, churning up the water again, with an unexpected sense of exhilaration, as if Kim was still racing beside me.

Twenty-three

'So many?' says Melinda.

'They're only very small.' Floyd hefts the box of bottles into the trolley. 'And so cheap. How many are we allowed to take back?'

'I don't know.'

'I thought you were the expert? You were the old hand, you said.'

'I'm not an expert on beer quotas. Wine and cigarettes, I can tell you all about wine and cigarettes.'

Floyd manoeuvres the trolley towards the delicatessen counter. 'I bet.'

She kisses him on the back of the neck as he looks at the different cheeses and cold meats and salads. He is wearing a loose denim shirt and shorts. Her hand strokes his bare thigh, moves a little way inside his shorts.

He turns away from the counter. Cups her face in his palms and growls at her theatrically. The shop girl glances up, half smiles, and glances away again. Gallic insouciance.

Melinda is wearing shorts too, and a loose white cotton blouse. 'When are we going to be alone together?' says Floyd.

Melinda grins. 'We are alone. Look, that potato salad Billy loves has a franc off.'

In the car, in the dusty, sun-drenched, near deserted car-park, he leans over and pulls her towards him, holds her left bare breast as he kisses her. One of her hands moves inside his shirt, the other around his shoulders. Symmetry. Someone watching would not have known immediately which was male, which female.

'I don't like our room,' he says finally, 'it's too small. It seems a shame with all this beautiful countryside around. And I worry that the kids can hear, or are going to come in.'

'You haven't really got used to kids, have you?'

'Not really.'

'It's going to be no use you deciding you want one in a year or two.' Her hands in his hair. 'I've had my lot. I've had my lot and one extra.'

He shakes his head, and her hands with it. 'I'm not going to decide I want one.'

'It's not like going to the shop and buying beer you know.'

'I like your kids. And Billy. I don't want any others. I want you.'

'You can have me.'

'Where?'

'By the lake, on the other side,' Floyd has started the car, 'no one ever goes on the other side.'

It was something more or less like that. As they drive away, preoccupied, they don't notice the red MG which passes them in the opposite direction, stops, turns round, and follows them at a discreet distance.

Twenty-four

Create some order, gather things up, lay them out.

We were in the Dordogne. We had three weeks of idyllic sunshine. What was bad for the farmers was good for the tourists, and we enjoyed the drought enormously, sunbathing daily outside our barn or beside lakes, and walking on scarlet and then peeled and then finally brown legs around castles and caves and medieval cathedrals.

'Now how do you want to feel at the end of this massage?' said Louise. 'Do you want your mind to feel stimulated or your body? Which part of your body? Or parts?'

'We' were Melinda and Floyd, Louise and Kim, and Billy. The new composition. Louise initially had been press-ganged into coming on the holiday, into leaving her boyfriend for three weeks, but once arrived she seemed to enjoy herself. She spent a lot of her time reading in the hammock or sprawled topless in a secluded corner of the garden. I spied on her when I thought I was unnoticed.

'You're in expert hands,' she said. 'I took a course at the institute.'

'I'd like to feel relaxed,' I said, although her hands sent intermittent shivers over my warm skin, as if once again I was treading water in the lake. Kim, ostensibly reading, was actually watching us. Melinda and Floyd were at the Uniprix. 'I'd like to feel completely relaxed.' In a few days time we would be back in London, and I was beginning to feel nervous at the prospect.

'Your skin will melt off your bones,' said Louise, 'I promise you.' Her hands began to move in circles over my shoulders, sliding gently over sun cream. 'You'll be so relaxed that your flesh will simply melt and ooze away until it lies in a puddle all around you.' Her fingers moved underneath me, on to my chest, over my nipples. 'Nothing moves, you are entirely still . . . breathe deeply, deep and slow . . .'

Her hands undermined her words. The disconcerting shiver located itself simultaneously around my chest and buttocks and groin. I had to move slightly and adjust my swimming trunks to get comfortable. 'Be still,' she said. She was enjoying her power. 'Be still,' as her hands moved on to my lower back. 'Be still,' in a reassuring, authoritative tone. 'It's beginning, your flesh is beginning to melt.' Most of it was. Her voice quiet, gently stretching vowels, each one as long as a summer afternoon. 'Every muscle relaxed . . . unwinding . . . every knot untied, in every single muscle.' Hypnotizing, as if weaving an enchantment. 'Nothing exists but the soft pressure of my hands, deep and slow, slow as slow can be, you are melting.'

She was enjoying herself, and so was I, dazed into acquiescence.

'Lulu, can I have one?'

The spell of words broke.

'What?'

'Can I have a massage?'

'No.'

'Why? Why can Billy and not me? You said you would.'

Louise's fingers lost their sureness, and my muscles began to tense. Like someone waking from a happy dream, don't let it stop, I was thinking, don't let it stop yet.

'You two are in love,' said Kim.

And the spell of Louise's touch was also broken, shattered by Kim's words and their resonance of playground mockery.

'That's all,' said Louise shortly, standing up. Something both amused and irritated in her voice. 'I don't want to cause any jealousy between you.' I watched her walk away, down the garden, unbuckling her bikini as she went.

'Well, I didn't mean her to stop,' said Kim, unexpectedly repentant. 'Why don't I massage you, and you massage me?'

'No,' I said, and I rolled over and pulled on a baggy pair of shorts. 'It wouldn't be the same.'

Kim was sitting up, watching me. 'Why wouldn't it?' she said. She wore a bikini like her sister, but it was almost flat against her chest. She was as boyish, in a thin-limbed, smooth-skinned way, as she had been six years earlier.

I pulled on sandals and a T-shirt. I sneered at her with sudden malice. 'Because you look like a *boy*,' I said, without considering the strange process that had made what was once a compliment into an insult. Then, 'I'm going for a walk,' I said, and I ran out of the gate and up the road that led towards the woods, already disliking myself. But it's her fault, I was thinking, she had to interrupt, so it's her fault.

It was August and the Dordogne was full of the English, but Melinda and Floyd had managed to find a quiet part, on the border of the district of Lot. I had been suspicious of this holiday. I was used to snatched, determinedly sybaritic weeks in Mediterranean resorts, late bookings made when my father saw an opportunity to take time off, to spend a few days eating well in good hotels, sunbathing and swimming and, inevitably, reading. My father didn't make sandcastles, he made piles of books. He used to joke that the books, like bricks, might stop the tide if piled correctly. When our week was up, his 'breather' he called it, we returned to real life with equally fast fading memories and tans. 'We', of course, being Eldon and Lucy, and Billy.

I was, at first, unhappy about any variation on this familiar theme. Anything that involved sightseeing or exploring seemed, I thought, unpromising. It took only days, however, to discover the advantage of the longer, more varied holiday. Here was not a brief week spent prone on a beach, here was a small taste of a different way of living. The place was like England, like real life, only crucially different. The warmth and the unfamiliar food and the strange language were just local colour, what made it different was the change in myself that it fostered. A feeling of liberation, a continuous revitalising sense of pressures removed. My parents, school, Archer – none of them belonged here. It was safe. No memories of my mother or my father would be provoked to jump out at me by the barn or the lake, or even by a French supermarket. No one would look twice at me, no one, I thought, would be out to get me. There was room to move. And in three weeks there was time to forget about home. Here was a place I could imagine staying in for a year, or a lifetime, a place where I could create an entirely new real life.

I liked to imagine myself lost in the woods. Like the lake it

141

was an essentially riskless thrill, an artificial fear. On the lake and in the woods strange creatures might be hiding in the darkness, might be waiting to snatch me and take me to their lairs, or I might become lost and suffer from exposure or starvation. These were the fears, the might bes I allowed myself. Archer on the other hand, conspiracy and murder, pornography, and disorientation of a more fundamental kind, none of this was within the bounds of possibility. It was far too remote to consider. I felt that, finally, I had discovered an utterly inviolate region.

I stopped running in order to walk off the track at the familiar spot, where I knew, within a few steps, there would be nothing to see but trees. Breathing heavily, I walked slowly, my hands slipping over trunks on either side. The trees weren't tall, they were barely robust enough for adjectives. They weren't melancholy, they were unfunereal. They were slim and their leaves came from perhaps ten short branches and a lot of twigs. They were young trees with young roots, they had their lives ahead of them, a career of standing. But, they were closely packed, shedding green light, growing spiders' webs, creeping insects and, so I had been warned, vipers. Moving among them, beneath their light foliage, it was easy to imagine myself in a bewildering maze. My affinity with labyrinths was returning to me as, priapic urges dying away, I struck out with more determination than usual away from the path. The trees were Sherwood and Arden and Mirkwood, summer stories and gothic tales. Kicking through long, dry grass, moving through shadows and light, stopping every moment to examine curious patches of lichen or colourful, bulky beetles, I was doing everything but blindfolding myself in my attempt to become lost.

As I moved up the slope away from the track, I listened for any sound of Kim following. I would have liked to be walking with her, to apologize and get things back on a friendly footing. The feelings Louise had roused in me seemed now to be stifling and distorting, unhelpful in an already slightly strained atmosphere. Four months after my mother left there was still an almost imperceptible – was I in fact imagining it? – awkwardness among us all. I wanted Kim to be with me. I was in a mood to cut through awkwardness. Treeclimbing, treasure-hunting games, I thought, would soon dispel it. On the road to the lake we always passed a small stone slab, like an overgrown milestone, on which was a list of names under the heading: '*Fusillés par les allemands.*' This gave an extra layer of interest to the woods, a feeling that French and German ghosts might be stalking strangers. I wanted to be able to scare Kim with this idea, build stories around it, create an atmosphere in which a fifty-year-old war might seem real, complete with its clear-cut good guys and bad guys.

Coming to a suitable tree, taller than the rest, I despaired of company and began to climb, hauling myself up on the lowest of its low branches. It was like a ladder. I got as high as I wanted to go, and I clutched the trunk and looked around. This was not like the tree at home. Not the same at all. Instead of a channel of gardens between houses, I saw, through an overwhelming interference of branches and leaves, only part of the top of a barn, possibly our barn, and in another direction, what may have been the side of a house. Yellowy stone. A spider sat in a web close to my ear. I wished it luck with the flies. Crickets chirped monotonously. Here I was safe, out of reach of snakes. With one arm still around the trunk, I sat down on the branch I was standing on, and began to consider staying where I was, until someone came to find me.

'Valentine! Valentine!'

The shrill French voice almost made me fall off my perch.

Running almost to the foot of my tree came a boy, visible to me as a thatch of blond hair. He looked around. 'Valentine?' This time there wasn't much energy in his shout. While I watched him, I saw Kim approaching. The boy looked at the ground, kicking around in the grass, then picked something up. He had found a long stick and, suddenly, he was sword-fighting, muttering to himself and laughing as he stamped up and down. He stopped equally suddenly and posed opposite a tree trunk, with his back to me. He stood quite still for a moment and looked at it, through narrowed eyes I imagined, and then he parried a vicious stroke and lunged and slashed and parried again then lunged with a gasp of delight and stabbed the trunk conclusively. He leant on his stick and gazed at the vanquished tree.

'*En garde!*'

He whirled round to find me facing him, my own stick torn from the tree which had been harbouring me held out menacingly. My peripheral vision told me that Kim was watching us. He looked at us both, seeing Kim for the first time, and then he turned and ran away.

'Come on!' Here was the kind of game I had wanted, a chase through the woods, cops and robbers, commandos and krauts, Kim following me and the stranger running for it. I sprinted after him, possessed by a ferocious enthusiasm.

We dodged among trees, flailed by twigs and narrowly avoiding obtrusive roots, until suddenly and alarmingly we were out in the open, in the full light of the afternoon, and in the garden apparently of a large and delapidated cottage. I was gaining on the French boy by this time, but I slowed down, glad of the excuse, because it had come to me that I had not an idea in my head what I might do if I caught him. Self-conscious, I stopped and allowed him to escape. He reached the house, the one I had spied from the tree, just as Kim caught up with me. Before disappearing through the front door he looked over his shoulder and, to my surprise, waved and beckoned to us.

'He was just playing,' I said.

'Well, what did you think?' said Kim, at my shoulder, breathless.

'I thought we were going to have a fight.'

'Stupid,' she said, and she surprised me too, laughing, evidently bearing no grudge for my earlier scorn. 'What is there to fight about? Shall we go in? Do you think we should? It's an adventure.'

The house was a curious mixture. The walls were in fine condition, smooth strong looking stone, but the roof looked as if it had been shattered and then thrown back on at random. Pieces of tile sloped untidily over the eaves and lumped together over the door. Tiles had slipped away from the spine of the roof, as if decay was systematically working its way downwards.

Kim was eager, but I dragged my feet on the way to the door. I was abashed by my mistake. Perhaps I myself had violated this inviolable region – sweet stealer, house burglar, ungrateful runaway, liar, jinx whose father died and whose mother left him, fantasist and peeping tom, sneerer at friends, and now bully and lout, a city hooligan in a pastoral scene. I thought of Roly, and for the first time began to believe my grandmother's stories about him.

'Come on,' said Kim, 'come on!'

I was still hanging back. I felt as if my unsavouriness might be contagious, a transforming power. I wouldn't have been surprised if the thick, fading stone had turned out to be sweet, brown gingerbread, sticky to the touch and smelling irresistibly of all things nice. A witch would open the door, and her large, devouring eyes would be welcoming.

So it was Kim who was the more audacious of us, Kim who lifted the faded bronze knocker on the door.

The woman who answered it had long pre-Raphaelite red hair worn loose. She wore a pale blue skirt and a black T-shirt. Her face was pale, her cheeks and her lips, even her eyes were pale. She might have looked witchy but for her distinctly un-occult smile of welcome. Instead, she looked both hospitable and maternal.

'The friends of Phillipe,' she said. 'Enchanted. Have you seen Valentine?'

'Valentine?'

'Our dog. A bad dog. Come in and have a cup of tea. That is what you would like, isn't it?'

I would have liked a colder drink, but I nodded.

'I would like a cup of tea too!' said Phillipe. I realized now that he was only about eight.

'You haven't found Valentine yet,' said his mother, 'find her and then you can have tea.'

'Valentine is my dog,' the boy explained, 'she is indeed a very beautiful dog. She is a very beautiful dog indeed.' He ran out shouting '*Valentine ma belle, ma belle Valentine!*'

Marie was the woman's name. While her son was out we sat down in the kitchen with our tea. There was a fridge and quite a modern cooker, but the table was of old, blistered wood. Marie explained, without prompting, that Phillipe had become lonely living with her on the edge of the woods, and that soon he would go to school in Lyons, where his father lived. She seemed to assume that there was a need to apologize for him. She sat down opposite us and arranged her hair, tying it back with a thin red ribbon, while we drank our tea. Her arms were brown, flecked from wrist to elbow with pale freckles. 'When he goes, I shall have to think things over. But,' she smiled, 'I will have time to think.'

When her son returned a dog was trailing behind him, an ugly, bony animal that scraped at the table and snorted. Phillipe showed off for Kim and me, telling off the dog in slightly skewed idiomatic English, and nagging his mother for a cup of tea.

Kim said something complimentary about the house.

'The tiles are rattling off this roof,' said Marie. 'This is not a modern building, it is ancient.'

'Perhaps you should live in Lyons too,' I said.

'I detest cities,' she said. 'I have a returning dream of all the cities burned down and replaced by trees and tall grass. Not in war you understand, but by their own citizens. Progress would continue without cities.'

Kim laughed. I said 'Where would we live? Where would we shop?'

Marie shrugged. 'People talk about me as "that crazy hermit". Perhaps it will come true.'

It wasn't quite clear from her tone whether she was referring to her dream of the conflagration of the cities, or to the description of herself.

We talked about our holiday, and a little about London. I found myself close to blurting out my life story but Kim's presence inhibited me, so I confined myself to agreeing with Marie about the unpleasantness of cities. Marie had visited London once, and taken Phillipe to see the sights. He was astonished that neither Kim nor I had ever seen the Changing of the Guard. 'Not everyone is interested in war,' she said, compounding my guilt feelings.

Finally, she noticed Kim looking at her watch. 'It is time for you to leave.' She stood up. 'Will you take my address?' she asked. 'And then you can write to me to practise your French.'

We thanked her, and she kissed each of us on both cheeks. When she gave me her address, on a folded slip of pale yellow paper, I felt that I was being given a meaningful and important message. 'Can we visit another time?' I said. 'Next time we are in France?'

She laughed. 'I hope you will,' she said, 'but you will forget me, of course.'

When we were safely back among the trees, walking in and out of bright shafts of light from the low sun, Kim pointed a finger at the side of her head, and turned it back and forth. 'Crazy,' she giggled, 'crazy French lady! Are you in love with her too? I'll tell Louise!' She ran away, hoping that I would chase her.

I had not fallen in love with Marie, but I felt that the piece of paper I was holding was a passport, a secret passage that had the power to magically transport me from the centre of London, the centre of an invisible web created by Archer, to the peaceful, green centre of France where the air was unpolluted and still and there was time to think and room to move. In my mind's eye I disappeared Alice-like down a manhole in a London street, and

surfaced in the middle of the French lake, in my own version of
Wonderland, fresh-faced and grinning abundantly.

We had no difficulty finding our way back, but we hurried, thinking
people might be worried. In fact Louise had fallen asleep with her
book over her face and Melinda and Floyd, laden with shopping,
returned ten minutes after we did. They were irritable, and when
Kim asked Melinda why they were so late, Melinda snapped back,
'Late for what?' as if Kim had been nagging her all afternoon.

After dinner, casting myself as peacemaker, I volunteered for the
unpopular job of going with Floyd to fetch milk for the morning.
My motives were mixed. I appreciated the chance of telling him
my worries about returning to London, and to a new school.

He had mellowed after a good dinner. 'No trouble,' he said.
'After the kind of problems you've overcome recently, this should
be a piece of cake.' He looked at my sceptical expression. 'That's
no help is it? But you've got an advantage Billy,' he said, 'you may
not know it yet, but you have. You can tell what matters from what
doesn't. In a word, perspective. Do you see? You can build, you
can make something worthwhile out of something shitty.'

'I'm scared of Archer,' I said.

'Scared? Why?'

'My father went to him, had his teeth looked at, and it was
just a few days before he died. I think he poisoned him. And
he finds out things, he knows people so he finds out things.
He knows everybody. And dad thought he was Jerome, thought
Jerome looked like him. And . . .'

For the second time that day I was on the verge of blurting out
something I usually kept to myself. This time I nearly mentioned
the photographs I had found in Archer's study, and this time I was
inhibited by the fact that mentioning them involved a confession to
the burglary.

'And?' said Floyd.

'And I don't trust him.' I amended my words. 'Neither did dad
or mum. Neither does Melody.'

Floyd drove in silence for a minute down the unlit road. A pair
of headlights followed us some distance behind.

'He's certainly full of surprises,' he said sourly. 'If it's any
consolation, I've been having a look at Jerome's operation recently,
although as a story it's beginning to look a bit pointless since he's

dropped out of sight. Your Mr Larbey, your friend Charlie's father, did he ever know Archer?'

'No, I don't think so.'

'Mm. Well, I'm still sure he knew Jerome.' We drew up outside the farm. 'Try not to worry about it,' said Floyd. 'I'll tell you if I do find out anything about him. But don't worry, you don't have to worry anymore. Melinda's looking after the legal bit, and she's not going anywhere. Neither am I. Let's get the milk, shall we?'

A little girl on the steps of the house directed us around to the back. There were six cows in a low shed built of dirty white bricks. They had mud caked in large scales on the back of their legs and they were leaning into gaps in a wall, eating hay. The farmer attached four tubes to the udder of the nearest one. The tubes went into a closed pot, like a kettle, and a larger tube left this and joined a pipe running the length of the shed. Strange contraptions. One of the tubes was clear, and I could see milk surging through it. The cow hardly seemed to notice, it shifted its sea monster legs and turned its head a little, revealing a bright orange label in its ear, and watched another cow lick itself like a dog. The milk was poured from the kettle into a churn, a cat mewing and pawing at the metal, and then it was poured into our plastic bottle, through a red funnel.

'My,' said Archer, 'how very elemental.'

I jumped and Floyd nearly dropped the milk. Archer was delighted by the effect of his quiet entrance. He was immaculate in his oatmeal chinos and black polo shirt. 'Well,' he said, 'we are nervy. I thought in the midst of this splendid countryside you would be peaceful and relaxed. Although that wasn't quite how I found *you* this afternoon, I must admit.' He winked at Floyd.

'How did you find us?' I said, mindful of the childish tone of the question.

'I thought you were going home,' said Floyd.

'Bill,' said Archer, as if neither of us had spoken, 'it's good to see you looking so well, positively blooming. That's one of the glories of youth, isn't it? Resilience I mean, flexibility. Give me a flexible youth any time. But didn't he tell you? Didn't Floyd tell you? We stumbled across him and Melinda, almost literally, this afternoon by the lake, enjoying the scenery you know. Astonishing coincidence. Of course I had an inkling you would be in the area, I remember Melinda loving this part of the world of old, but I didn't expect to happen upon you quite like that.'

We had left the shed. 'Anyway,' said Archer, 'yes, the point is we were on our way home when I realized that I had completely forgotten, what with the circumstances of our meeting, and you being a little irked and so on, to give you the invitation. Brain like a tennis racquet, that's me. The point is, I want you to come to my house-warming. I'm glad I'm the first to tell you: I've bought your old house Bill, I always had an affection for it. So you will come won't you? Say hello, Nita.'

Nita was sitting in a red MG. She said hello. Archer climbed in beside her. 'So glad we caught up with you again. See you in London. The party will be in the middle of October I should think – I'll let you know the exact date. Bye-bye.'

And they roared off in a dramatic swirl of dust.

We went into the house to pay. Two women were cooking and the little girl was watching, getting in their way. On the huge, ignored TV in the corner a woman in a leotard with fur trimmings undid a ribbon on a big box and a man in a dinner jacket sprang out, his mouth open wide in a silent shout and his arms raised high.

Twenty-five

The infallible reassurance of supermarkets helped to console me in the first weeks at the new school, that difficult time which Floyd had assured me I would be able to handle with ease.

There were two weekend rituals: Friday night in Sainsbury, and Sunday morning at my father's and grandfather's graves. Friday night in the bad tempered queue at the checkout, Sunday morning alone in front of the headstone. It was a similar feeling, whether I was in the cavernous building, full of people, or in the sprawling field, also full of people, among the rows and rows of shelves of food, or the rows and rows of graves. The two recurring occasions were sanctuaries from the large and small concerns which surrounded them. No pressure in either place, no *thought* of pressure. Life pleasantly diminished. I was all for the shrinkage of life. My attitude was well expressed by a leaflet advertising the life insurance Melinda used:

> CASH if you die, CASH if you don't,
> PLUS a Handy Set of Screwdrivers FREE.

It pleased me to see life made absurd. It still does I think – anyway that's my excuse for the job I presently hold. ('I Talked to Richard Burton's Ghost!') Supermarket and cemetery made life more manageable. If the supermarket was almost a back door, like Marie in France, then the ultimate back door I thought was death, always there, much sampled and, in its way, riskless.

Sitting in my bedroom where the mirror still leant on the wall offering me its casually cock-eyed view of things, I wrote about everything to Marie.

> This school is too big! I will never find my way in it because it has too many floors and passages so I just get lost. The teacher, Mr Sail, who I'm supposed to tell all my problems, told me on the first day that I would get used to it in no time. No time, he said. I think if I'm lucky I might get the hang of it on the day that I leave. But guess who I met today? Well, to explain I will have to go back a bit, quite a long way back in fact.

It happened like this. I was late, running to class through the bewildering corridors after a break spent mooning around in the playground by the fence, watching the cars go by. I played a solitary game with a complex points system which rewarded cars for their size and probable speed and, looking for an unprecedented fifty points, I had made myself late. I wasn't really running, because that was forbidden, but walking as fast as I could, with the awkward gait which that entailed, when a voice I heard through an open door, both the voice itself and a distinctive turn of phrase it employed, brought me up short so that I nearly tripped over my feet.

'Listen to me, you little bleeder, mark my words well . . .'

I never heard the words that some anonymous boy or girl was supposed to mark because the voice changed tack at the sound of my stumbling.

'You out there! Who's staggering about out there? Come in.'

When I obeyed the peremptory invitation and appeared in the doorway, the scary face, bright red, instantly came back to me. The farm that was full of dogs. Mr Fairfax. He recognized me too, or at least began to, I could tell by the way he peered at me, but nothing he said revealed the fact.

'What are you doing? Are you drunk? Why aren't you in class?'

'I'm late sir . . .'

'Don't state the obvious, I know you're late. Can't stand it when people state the obvious. Have the goodness to close my door, then get off to your class. Now!'

Which I did, seething at this unexpected treatment.

I don't know, I don't know why he had to be like that. Two-faced Fairfax they call him here and they're right. I wanted to tell Greig how I had met him before but I didn't, because I'd have had to say how I ran away. I couldn't tell him that. I can tell you though, I like to tell you things. Do you mind? I hope not, it's just good to be able to talk to someone.

Nothing's changed. I liked getting things off my chest then and I do now. Marie wasn't a great answerer of letters. Her replies to my initial flurry of out-pourings tended to be one page efforts, succinct, offering sympathy and interest and news of how Phillipe was getting on at his new school. Kim wouldn't have said these were letters from a crazy lady. They were models of restraint. Rereading them now I find in them a tolerant tone, tolerant of my self-absorption but maintaining a distance from it, like an adult politely examining the sticky sweet a child eagerly offers her. In the first couple of months after returning, I would send two or three letters in between Marie's replies.

Greig soon became central subject matter. I met him on the same day that I entered Mr Fairfax's class. He was smoking by the bicycle sheds. He was sitting on a metallic blue racer, leaning forward, his forearms on the dropped handlebars, and he watched me walking past. I was on my way to the fence, where I was going to watch the cars again. In fact I was also considering slipping off and missing an afternoon's school. Kim was nowhere around. Thursday, swimming team practise in lunch-hour. I felt almost unbearably nostalgic for France.

Greig turned on the bike's lamp. 'Freeze,' he said, 'don't try to escape, you're covered.'

Standing in the invisible beam, I looked at him, he at me. What did he see? I was very nearly thirteen, thin and a bit small for my age, my hair was untidy and too long – the fashion at the time was short – and I was wearing an unstylish pair of cords and a blue shirt that didn't altogether match. He was wearing grey trousers and, flirting with school regulations, a black polo shirt. His black hair was shaved at the sides.

'I like your brogues,' he said. 'I can never find a pair of real brogues.'

I looked at my feet uncertainly, wondering if he was joking.

'Where did you get them?'

They were a pair of shoes my mother bought for me. 'I don't know. I mean it was before I moved. South.' I had a go at being friendly. 'I like your bike.'

He dismounted. 'Not mine. Have you seen the list?'

'What list?'

'There's a list of names on the noticeboard. There's been a reshuffle. You're in my class, with Fairfucks. Come on, he hates it when you're late. One day he's friendly, the next he's roaring at you. Two-faced bastard.'

He trod on his cigarette, which I had been careful to casually not mention, and we headed for class, leaving the bike's lamp illuminating nothing.

So I sat next to Greig and listened to Mr Fairfax introducing us to the Tudors, and fixed on my face was that same scowl he had seen years earlier when he found me wandering in the park. I was beginning to understand his reputation. He was friendly, made jokes, and called people by their first names – 'No Kevin, *six* wives, even Henry had his limits' – and he knew how to make history come alive. He told us the story of a grotesquely bloated, syphilitic Henry being literally hoisted on to his unfortunate young, final wife. I remembered his kindness in the park. But I wasn't convinced, I wasn't fooled by this companionable exterior. I looked at his face, the prominent cheeks, flushed, and the alert eyes, and I thought of him bawling at some 'little bleeder' and withering me with his sarcasm. It's no good, I thought to myself, I know what you're really like.

After the lesson he asked me to stay behind to talk to him. I sat still as the rest of the class disappeared around me. 'See you round,' I said to Greig, and he nodded carelessly.

Fairfax came and sat on the desk in front of me.

'Billy, isn't it,' he said. 'We've met, have we not? As I recall, you were frowning then too.'

I said nothing.

'I'm your tutor, Billy, you've been moved from Mr Sail's juris-diction to mine. I know we started badly the other day, but you mustn't be over-affected by my temper. It's not my best feature, but you will find you can accommodate it. Would you like to tell me a little about yourself?'

'There's nothing to tell.'

'That's not what I have been given to understand. I have been given to understand that you have had quite a difficult time of it, that you have already had a chequered career?'

'Then you already know.'

He paused, and then continued. 'To be self-contained is laudable, Billy. I noticed the trait in you the first time we met, five years ago was it? But to be closed mouthed and closed minded is not sensible.'

'I don't know what you want me to say.'

'As your tutor Billy, I'm interested in any problems you may have. Academic or personal. It can be difficult to fit into a new school, especially when other people already know each other, cliques have already formed.'

'Yes,' I said, pleased with this insight. 'It is difficult.'

'I have to say that Greig is probably not a very good start, I'm afraid. An antisocial element.'

I shrugged, alienated again by this judgement.

'What are you, Billy?' he said. 'Another antisocial element? A high-flier? A seeker of shelter in books?' (No, I should have said, a seeker of shelter in supermarkets and graveyards.) He sighed. 'As your tutor I hope that we can develop some kind of relationship, Billy. I'll see you next week. You'd better go.'

Greig was at the gate, with a couple of his friends.

'What did he want?'

'Nothing. He said he was my tutor, and could he help about anything. What are you doing?'

He looked at his watch. 'Working soon, I work Friday nights in a café. Do you want a job? You can come along and see the man.'

I shook my head. I was looking over his shoulder at Kim approaching. He and his friends followed my eyes.

'Sister?' said one.

'No.'

'Girlfriend?'

This made me pause. 'Sort of,' I said.

He laughed. 'That means no. She's all right though. Wants to grow her hair a bit.'

'No tits,' said Greig.

So I looked at her more closely, in her yellow sweater and knee-length black skirt, thin-limbed, her bag swung over her shoulder. She had seen me and was trying to work out who I was with, was moving a little self-consciously, aware of being watched. In answer to Greig, in defence of my putative girlfriend, I said, 'Not yet.'

A recent piece of my work springs to mind.

School girl Sherri shows her all! Sexy Sherri gets top marks for her fabulous figure. 'It certainly tantalizes my teachers,' says Sherri.

'What about tomorrow?' said Greig. 'Are you around tomorrow?'

Saturday, Archer's warming of my old house. 'Not really,' I said.

'Suit yourself,' he said, 'we've got to go,' and he and his friends left, just as Kim arrived.

We headed in the other direction, towards home. I told Kim who my new friends were, and gave some consideration to holding her hand. It being Friday, the evening promised a trip to the supermarket which seemed, if not less desirable than usual, then at least less completely rewarding.

Twenty-six

The supermarkets, and the frequent letters to Marie, were a short-lived phase, like the Lord's prayer and the numbers were a phase, slightly longer-lived. But the difference was that these later habits continued to be significant when I became less involved in them: because Marie, as far as I knew, wasn't going anywhere, and the supermarket, solid and tangible, wasn't going anywhere either – because of this it was all right to go to Archer's house-warming, and all right to go down some of the more dangerous and convoluted paths I chose in the years afterwards. There was a safety net available, a back door.

Floyd loved cars. We drove to the house in his Jaguar, a big twenty-five-year-old cream-coloured model of smooth curves and stately aspect. 'My investment,' he claimed, a car that would appreciate like property. Something solid. Kim and I sat together on the red leather back seat, Kim anticipating the garden in lunchtime sunshine, Melinda and Floyd in front, talking opaquely of business matters. We drove to *the* house, neither mine nor truly Archer's I felt, and I looked out of the window and kept at bay memories of similar journeys.

The words of Melinda and Floyd, solicitor and journalist cum private investigator, gradually moved towards something I could understand. The subject was money, and in among the mysterious many-syllabled language concerning contractual obligation, obstructive bureaucracy, debts and interest and shortfalls, reminiscent of Eldon's preoccupied monologues in the months before his death, my father's name abruptly appeared, like a word of English in a French sentence, linked by tone at least to anxiety, and disappointment.

'I'm here too,' I said. 'What are you saying about dad?'

'I'm sorry, Billy,' said Melinda, half turning, 'we were getting involved in the technical difficulties.'

'What difficulties?' Technical? This to me suggested stereo equipment and video recorders.

'Acres of red tape,' said Floyd, with a glance in the mirror, 'there's a whole history that needs exploring.' I saw my father mummified in festive red ribbon, blinded and incapacitated by it.

'What history?' I insisted.

'The history of his company,' said Floyd patiently. 'Companies. The bookshops and the property. He wasn't in complete control, I mean he *was* in control but he didn't wield absolute power. There are other interests involved. A partner maybe. There are

THE ALCHEMIST

things involved we don't yet know about. We haven't found all the documents yet, but we will. We have to fit it all together. A big company Billy, or even a medium-sized one . . .'

'. . . is like a maze,' said Melinda, 'but we're trained, Floyd and I, to find our way through it. It's a question at the moment of making funds available. What we want to do is set up a trust for you.'

This was language I thought I could understand. Mazes, concepts of control, trust. 'Yes,' I said, 'I trust you.'

And here was the house. Set back from the road behind a small pebbled semicircle of bushes and grass, rising up imperiously over a bevy of parked cars. Archer had no intention of converting the building into flats, this was to be his home, his base for operations, his palace.

Bolstering this last image, he stood in the doorway with his hands outstretched, a feudal lord greeting his tenants. He wore the same leather jacket he had worn when he baby-sat for me, five years earlier. It looked better than ever now, a battered brown.

'Welcome home, Bill,' he said. 'Come in. You'll find the place changed a little I think. Still, change is evidence of life. Come in, come in, leave your troubles behind.' He ushered us into the hallway. 'Only time for a quick hello I'm afraid, hostly duties you know. Nita's left me slightly in the lurch, feeling ill, very disloyal. Coats off, make yourselves at home, drinks in the kitchen. I'm sure you'll find some people you know. And don't leave early, whatever you do. Treats in store. Did you know I trod the boards a little as a lad? There's still a whiff of the greasepaint about me you know. Charming car incidentally Floyd, did you get it as payment from some thug?' He grinned and, as more guests approached up the drive he said, 'Bill, why don't you lead the way, I'll join you shortly.'

Kim and I stood by the wall, with our cokes, while we watched Melinda and Floyd move together in to the crowded room. In no time they had split up, Melinda greeting old friends, Floyd engaged in conversation by a woman who had offered him some nuts. I was studying the guests. Here, I thought, must be a good sprinkling of Archer's network. There were plenty of people for Melinda to feel at home with, professionals holding simultaneously glasses of wine, buffet morsels and fluent conversation with practised ease.

156

Floyd, of course, would feel at home with these people too, but his social net was wider. Trailed by Kim, I moved around the room, attentive. That was how I came upon Gary, Charlie's older brother, who was looking smart, if as chubby as ever, in a grey suit, and who had his arm around a girl in a short, taffeta-skirted navy-blue dress. I knew he must be twenty, but her age was unguessable to me, anything between sixteen and thirty-six. They were talking, I noticed abruptly, to Jerome's mafia-style frontman. I looked for Floyd anxiously, and met his eye. He nodded, he had seen him too. The frontman's style had evolved since I had last seen him. He was all in black now, black sweater and black trousers, with just a gold chain around his neck, no other ostentation apart from his fillings. In his convex way, he looked like a beetle. The conversation was on the same subject as the one Melinda and Floyd had had in the car.

'The money,' Gary was saying, 'is in money. Don't make me state the obvious, you know that. And when the going gets tough, you just get into gold.'

Words flowed out of the beetle in response to this as if he was reciting a witty stage patter. 'That's money,' he said, 'but it's boring money. Has J.T. taught you nothing? Show business, that's different, that's, if you like, funny money. You know what I want to be, where I see myself? Quiz show host. I could do that, I could do it well. Bruce, Jimmy, Bob, Max, that's my world. "Donny Bird, King of the quiz shows." I'd call mine "Funny Money". Funny money, there's lots of it about. Deals, for instance. Retail, same thing again, if you do it with a little style. Funny money is J.T.'s gift, making money and having fun at the same time. He's the only man who could have fun being a dentist. Funny money is his genius. What do I hear about the City?' He didn't wait for an answer, he just pointed his forefinger at Gary's chest. 'I'll tell you, boys your age, earning vast amounts and not having a spare moment to spend it. Burning out, that's what they say isn't it? Burning out at thirty. I see stripy shirts, I think no, I see red braces, I think no thank you. No, graft is not J.T.'s style, no way, no way in the world, not even for piles of cash.'

Gary bristled defensively at this invocation of Archer. 'It *is* fun in the City. When you get into raids and takeovers and mergers, you don't think that's fun? I've found out about it, and it's J.T. who's told me all about it. Maybe you start with the dull stuff, cold calling, but if you get in with the right people, the venturers, then it all takes off. I'm finding out more every day. People my age dealing in millions. Who do you think is behind me, my dad? Hardly. Bullion and bullying, that's my dad, he's too old to change his spots. It's J.T., he recognizes the growth areas.'

His girlfriend was nodding and was about to contribute her own thoughts when Kim nudged me and nodded towards Charlie, coming from the direction of the kitchen with a can of beer in his hand. We intercepted him beside the buffet.

'Hello Charlie.'

He stopped, belched loudly, and laughed. 'Hello. What are you doing here?'

Oddly, it was only when he asked this that I became sensitive to where I was.

'This used to be my house,' I said, as if answering him. We were in the room where the Great Pretender had performed his show nearly six years earlier. Upstairs was my father's study, where he had shown off his mastery of computer graphics. We were next door to the dining room where we had had the New Year's Eve dinner party. In the kitchen where the tables were loaded with drinks my parents and I had sat chatting about inconsequential things. In the TV room on the other side of this room, my father had died. There was nothing whatsoever to show for any of this. The map of my past had been submerged, having been stripped bare of its largest and most trivial landmarks. Furniture, from three-piece suites to occasional tables, books, TV and video, cabinets full of papers, the computer and its discs, a wordprocessor and its discs, photographic equipment and exercise machines, sports gear, a typewriter, a conventional oven and a microwave oven, cutlery and crockery, glasses, dishwasher, blender, fridge and freezer, washing machine and drier, beds and linen, all of my father's and many of my mother's clothes, prints and paintings and mirrors, vases and ornaments, clocks, stereo equipment, accompanying records and tapes, lights, a variety of games and old toys, carpets and curtains, a car, some DIY items, garden tools and a bench for the lawn: all this was expensively stored while its fate was decided. It was what was left after I had culled one picture, a small TV and a portable typewriter for my room at Melinda's.

'I'll show you round,' said Charlie, 'if you like.'

'Yes,' said Kim, her mouth now full of duck pâté, 'show us the changes.'

'Upstairs,' said Charlie, 'we have to go up, there's not much new down here, and anyway it's all been cleared up for the party. Come on.'

So I followed him, with Kim, up the stairs of my old house.

'Wait till you see the games room,' said Charlie, 'he's knocked together three rooms, your old bedroom has gone, Billy, you won't believe it, it's so much better than you used to have it.'

He led us into the large, unrecognizable room, large enough to have swallowed my bedroom whole, swallowed it and digested it, so that all trace of it had vanished. It was striped crimson and cream, with a thick burgundy carpet. 'You should see the parties we have in here,' said Charlie, 'crazy.' He watched our faces as we looked around, enjoying our admiration with proprietorial pride. He began an alternative list to the one that had just passed through my mind. 'Cable and satellite,' he said, pointing out a prodigiously sized television screen hanging from the wall, 'hundreds of channels you know, you name it they've got it. It's just like being at the cinema. Snooker and pool, you should see J.T., he's an ace. Videos and video games and computer games, he always keeps up to date with the latest of everything. CD player,' with speakers taller than any of us, 'magazines,' he said this with peculiar emphasis, pointing at some leather binders and winking at me hugely. 'Nautilus stuff,' he showed us his biceps, in a pose reminiscent of his father, 'and of course,' he finished, 'let's not forget the bar.' There must have been about a hundred bottles, and almost as many colours. It was like a laboratory, like the chemistry set Kim and I had once experimented with. I expected alembics and tripods and test-tubes rather than the many-shaped glasses that Charlie showed us beneath the bar. 'What can I make you?' he said. 'Look at this one,' reaching down a bottle, 'it's got real gold leaf in it. Doesn't this man know how to spend money? Doesn't he, though? You've got to admit it.'

We sat on stools while he mixed us something colourful in tall glasses that he promised would 'blow our heads off.' It tasted sweet and not unpleasant. 'Do you remember,' I said to Charlie, 'do you remember the Perfect Sweet? Baked beans and soy sauce?'

He shrugged. 'No. Maybe I do. Who cares?'

'It was like this,' I said, 'a cocktail of things, it was going to make our fortunes.'

'Billy,' Charlie leant on the bar across from me, coming on like an older brother, 'Billy, there are better ways to make money you know. Real ways, to make real, serious money. And J.T. knows them all. I mean look at this, isn't it heaven? I mean, isn't it?'

I didn't answer him, I couldn't think of anything to say.

Kim had taken her drink and was peering through the green slats of the blind at the garden below.

'Look Billy, he's left it all the same, he hasn't touched it. Look at the tree, nothing's changed.'

I joined her. 'Except the hut,' I said, 'he's rebuilt the hut.'

'He's not very interested in gardening,' said Charlie, as he joined us. 'Nita does a bit, but not much.'

'Is he having no guests in the garden?' said Kim.

Charlie shrugged. 'He doesn't want people wandering everywhere.'

So not quite all trace of my room had vanished. The window had been enlarged, but the view was the same. The grass and the tree, the hut lost in the bushes. All of it strangely deserted after the crowded room downstairs. The wider view was unchanged too: extensive gardens, bounded by more houses. My nostalgia took a turn and landed me in France, at the top of a tree, suspended a safe distance from real life, glimpsing the roof of the barn and the side of Marie's house and nothing else but grass and leaves and branches.

'Come on,' said Charlie, 'wait till you see what he's done with the bathroom, sunken bath all in black and gold, and downstairs I forgot to tell you, there's a jacuzzi . . .'

'Can we go outside?' said Kim interrupting. I was grateful to her for being unimpressed by Charlie's tour.

He seemed deflated. 'No one's out there. Let's have another drink and play something.'

'Are we allowed?' said Kim.

'Of course we are.' Charlie and I answered simultaneously, both proprietorial now, in our different ways. We looked at each other uncertainly, and then laughed.

A little later, headachy but pretty sure I had discovered a hitherto unsuspected expertize in pool, I was lining up a stripe into the middle pocket when Kim jogged my cue and I jerked it into the baize, causing a long thin strip to tear away.

'Whoops,' I put my hand over my mouth. 'Sorry,' I said to no one in particular.

'Never mind,' said Charlie, 'never mind, we'll just put it back

like this,' he laid the strip back in place, 'and no one will notice.'
He was becoming restless again, as if the house needed our approval
to vindicate his enthusiasm. 'What haven't I showed you yet?'

'The big bedroom.'

'Of course, of course, this way.'

We looked briefly into the bathroom, and Charlie caused a spurt
of water from the bidet to sprinkle us, and then we burst into the
bedroom, formerly my parents', more or less three abreast.

Nita was sitting in a big whicker chair. Her legs were curled
beneath her so that she looked like a sea creature in its shell.
She wore a salmon pink tracksuit in a soft material. Her hair
had changed colour, it was blonde now, or yellow anyway, and
straight.

'Oh! Goodness, am I being invaded?'

We apologized in confusion.

'No, no, don't go away, how lovely to have some company, I've
been lonely up here, and I'm feeling so much better now, won't
you stay and chat?' Without moving her body, she reached out
her hand towards us. 'Billy, you must tell me what you think of
the changes, I do want to know.'

'Very nice.'

'I am glad, I am glad you like it, there's so much rubbish about
isn't there? I haven't forgotten my idea about the skyscrapers.
Horrible great phallic things cluttering up the view. Sink them,
lock stock and barrel, sink them into shafts. Make sure the lifts
work, and the lights, do them up a bit, and there you are. Top
class property. And what's more, you can build a park on top.
I mean have you seen those buildings in the docklands? Have
you, Billy?' I was shaking my head. 'They aren't the answer.
Take it from me, they're tacky. Like beached ocean liners, with
cabins and portholes. Bathrooms all of a piece with little slabs
of soap in them. Dull. That's the skyscrapers,' she continued
without pausing, 'but you're probably wondering what's going
to happen to the estates aren't you? You know the big estates,
with the walkways, where the postmen refuse to deliver? Holiday
camps, theme parks; we'll turn them into tourist attractions. Flood
them to make lakes or swimming pools, underwater cities, adapt
them to make attractions, haunted houses, helter skelters. I haven't
thought it through properly yet, but you can see what I mean, can't
you?'

I nodded, we all nodded, but since none of us said anything, she pressed us.

'You do see what I mean?'

'I think we should go and find everybody,' said Charlie.

I was reminded of the beetle, of his fluent patter, and also perhaps of Charlie, his enthusiastic guide to the house, but I was nagged by some other correspondence, and it took me a moment to place it: Archer of course, with his endless, relentless flow of words, mocking, self-justifying, almost self-defining. In Nita the difference was that the words tumbled out without calculation, as if she was in a hurry to say the next thing simply for the sake of saying it, whatever it was, in order to fill the gap, to replace the silent moment.

'Would you like to come down with us?' Kim seemed concerned.

'With you? What now? No, no, I'm quite cosy up here, thanks. Couldn't be cosier, curled up here with my book,' although there was no book in sight, 'in my lovely chair in my lovely room. Like an oyster, that's what J.T. says, like an oyster. I won't tell you about the pearl.' She laughed. 'You go and find him, tell him I'm full of ideas. He has his off days too, you know,' looking at us shrewdly, 'he's not always on the ball. I'll be down later, I'll see you later. Bye-bye now. Bye.'

There was a respectful hush for Archer as he entered the room, draped in a long, loose fur cloak with wide embroidered sleeves. He had an unruly white beard. He looked like Eisenstein's Ivan the Terrible. It was the room where the Great Pretender had performed his act, but Archer had no stage, he stood in a cleared space and we sat or stood to watch him, with our drinks and food on precariously sagging paper plates.

He had a commanding presence. 'Forgive me,' he said, 'if I jump speeches a little.' And then he began.

He only spoke about twenty lines before he was interrupted, it wasn't clear if he had intended to go on longer. As when my father held forth in his bath, I understood little of what I heard. The occasional word, such as a puzzling reference to 'punks', and once, a couple of lines:

> This is the day wherein, to all my friends,
> I will pronounce the happy word, "Be rich!"

As far as I could tell, it was the same old theme that had been cropping up all day: gold, success, money. His voice had altered, become deeper, almost vibrating with greed. It wasn't his own voice, but it wasn't Jerome's either – I was alert for any hint of that. One thing was clear: he was enjoying himself. His guests, I think, were unimpressed, a little uncomfortable. Unable to see merely their friend J.T. in front of them, exhibitionist as ever, they were also unable, without a stage with a stranger on it, to make the complete dissociation required of them. Probably only I was impressed. Not by his acting, if it could be called that, but by his nerve, by the fact that somehow around sixty people had been arranged into a group, subdued into silence, and persuaded to watch his exercise in self-indulgence. It seemed to me a tremendous feat of control. What came to my mind was a memory of the playground, when I was about five, just starting school. Another boy, who like me was just starting, was striding up and down with his head flung back singing in a tuneless raucous voice just two words over and over: 'Fuuu-cking hell, fuuu-cking hell.' He wasn't looking where he was going but he was striding up and down regardless of anyone around him in the crowded playground, confident, and rightly so, that they would keep out of his way. That was the image that Archer brought to my mind, a performer almost by default, someone so self-possessed and self-absorbed that his self-belief engulfs others within its circle, controls their movements. Self self self; there, I thought, is a definition of Archer.

The interruption was Nita's arrival. She opened the door with an unguarded eagerness, smacking its leading edge into the spine of a woman in a backless red cocktail dress. With a scream, she threw wine in one direction and food in another. Farcically, as people jumped out of the way, there were more collisions and upsets, cries of pain and indignation, rippling outwards from the open door, where Nita stood unmoving, biting one side of her lip in childish dismay. I noticed Floyd dabbing at the beetle's black polo neck with his napkin. Mr Larbey was watching, much amused. I could not see his wife.

Archer, perhaps recognizing the limits of his powers, had simply disappeared. He returned quickly however, immaculate in a blue striped shirt and blue trousers, and his presence reinstated calm. 'Upstaged,' I heard him saying, with a rueful shrug. 'Sorry about this appalling mess.'

Nita had seen me and Kim and, working her way through the disturbed guests, had come straight over to talk to us. 'I haven't told you my best idea yet,' she said, without preliminaries. She took hold of Kim's arm. 'Imagine if women could only have children after the age of forty. Think for a moment about the consequences. No unwanted babies. Children brought up by mature parents who had been waiting for years for the privilege. And think what it might do for relationships. Their whole structure would change, because instead of getting frailer as they went on, they'd get stronger and stronger as the years of childbirth approached. You see? Your mother Billy, she'd still be around if you hadn't even been born yet, and if there had been no miscarriage. And there would be no fear that it was getting too late, that time was running out. Oh, *everything*,' she said, releasing Kim's arm to make a wide, dangerous gesture, 'everything would run so much more smoothly. It would be a neat, sensible way of doing things. No confusion, everything predictable. J.T. would like it too, as a kind of steady background. He needs one you know, more and more. You probably don't understand, but you don't know him like I do. You haven't seen him in action at all unless you've seen him at the City.'

Archer's hand on her shoulder interrupted her. 'There's going to be an awful lot of clearing up to do, isn't there?'

She looked around vaguely. 'People are so messy.'

'I thought you were going to stay upstairs?'

'I was feeling so much better J.T. – Kim and Billy said I should come down.'

He looked at us. 'Did they? Kim and Bill don't understand that you aren't well,' he said. 'I want you to apologize to everyone my love, for your clumsiness, and then go back upstairs. Because you're still very tired. Will you do that for me?'

'Yes J.T.'

She moved away, and we heard her saying immediately, to the first person she saw, 'I'm sorry about the mess.' She then headed straight for the door.

Archer smiled at us, as if he had forgotten her already. 'Everyone will be leaving soon,' he said, 'everyone except a few select guests I intend to ask to stay. Charlie tells me he has informed you about the parties in the games room. Are you tempted?'

Kim and I looked at each other. 'We probably ought to go when my mum does,' said Kim.

'And is that your feeling too, Bill? I would particularly like to persuade you to stay. Charlie will be here of course. And others. Boys and girls. New friends.'

I looked up at him. His face was serious now. I felt that something important was being offered to me. If I am going to investigate, I was thinking, like a real investigative journalist, then I should be there. And part of me, unadmitted, was thinking, If I want a girlfriend . . . I was about to speak, Archer's smile was already beginning to return, when Melinda and Floyd turned up.

'Lovely party,' said Melinda, 'time we made a move I think.'

'Yes,' I said, 'I'd better go.'

Archer sighed, and suddenly looked angry. 'I suppose I should have expected nothing else,' he said. 'You know you haven't yet said sorry for ruining my pool table, Bill. Were you intending to?'

'It was an accident,' I said.

'Well I assumed that it was,' he answered, and with a few strained politenesses we made our escape. Archer turned away a moment before we did, and began talking to Gary, who had materialized next to him. I heard him say, 'Timidity must run in the family.'

Outside, I picked up a pebble from the drive, tossed it from hand to hand, once, twice, and then threw it as hard as I could at a lamp-post which, to my surprise, it hit and then ricocheted off, landing silently in somebody's garden. Melinda and Floyd turned to me, but I didn't look at them, I ran off before they could speak, towards the car.

Twenty-seven

Now perhaps it is time to trespass on private, entirely unknown territory. I would like to know Archer well. That gives the wrong impression; I would like to know Archer, that is more accurate. In the end he had plenty to say for himself, I shall come to that, but there is no telling from his words what is true and what is pose, imposture, or play. That is the most transparent part of his message, that there is no telling what is true. With Archer, only what happens in the absence of a public can begin to be reliable, and that can only be guessed at, or gleaned from secondary sources such as the eminently unreliable Nita, or the Larbeys, or others given partial views behind the scenes.

The most realistic course is to start with a dream, a genuine one from the night after the house-warming, and then elaborate, extrapolate, simply see where it leads.

Archer is sitting in front of a mirror, an actor's mirror ringed by lightbulbs. His head is in his hands. Slowly, very slowly, he lowers his hands and lifts his face. In front of him is an array of make-up. Lip gloss, cheek and nostril pads, face powder, rouge, hair spray and gel, mascara, some kind of oil with which to stain teeth. There is a plastic case of attachments for fingernails which look like shavings from a candle. There are several small boxes containing contact lenses. On a shelf beside him there are wigs and whiskers on white dummies' heads. Archer's face, free of make-up and lit up mercilessly by the naked bulbs, is white too. Chalk. (In my dream, my face is beside Archer's in the mirror, and we are each looking at the other, but that is not relevant to what I am trying to do.) To one side of him there is a screen, four panels in dull gold, depicting swans and garish flamingos, flying over khaki leaves. Behind him, reflected in the mirror, is a rail on which clothes hang. A lot of clothes, and almost as many styles as there are items. Dinner jacket, city slick three-piece, white suit, conjurer's cloak, colourful casual jacket . . . there are too many to enumerate. A similar variety of shoes and boots beneath the clothes, some with heels, some with hidden lifts. At a glance it looks as if a row of people is standing behind Archer, watching his preparation.

Archer has a towel round his neck and a towel round his waist, otherwise he is naked. His face is a blank sheet, without complexion or expression. Slack and unmoving. His body is as white as his face, floury, less than human. Eyes steady, as if he wishes to out-stare his reflection.

He picks up the powder, but before he can dip a finger into it, Nita enters. She is halfway into, or halfway out of, a cotton dress. White with black polka dots. The skirt is in place, but the rest hangs around her waist.

'I've tidied up J.T. I don't want to stay up, I'm going to bed.' A pause, while she stands in the doorway. 'Is that all right?'

He answers with surprising gentleness, 'Yes, go to bed Nita.'

He has not looked at her. While she spoke his finger hovered over the jar. As the door closes, the finger dips into it. He applies make-up in a meticulous way, with a fingertip, with a small brush. The expression that has arrived on his face is one of total concentration, as if he is working on a canvas. This goes on for some time, as layers are applied, colours are shaded in and details are added, until finally something new is created. Experimentally, he smiles. He shakes his head and the smile vanishes. He tries again, slightly less curve in the lips, and he seems to be satisfied. Now a third smile appears, different again, a smile of approval such as any vain person might give to their reflection.

The face in the mirror is the face of a stranger.

His guests are waiting for him in the games room. Charlie, Gary and their father, not their mother, Gary's girlfriend, the beetle, whose name is Donny, other men and women, different ages and classes, who I never knew. Four are playing pool on the damaged pool table, others are playing snooker, an overweight man has taken off his shirt and tie and is showing off in his vest on the exercise equipment. Mr Larbey, watching him with a superior air, frets while he waits for his turn. Charlie and a young girl are looking through the bound collection of pornography. They are both drinking cocktails like the ones we had earlier. I have to assume that at the bar, in place of snacks, there are joints and pills, piled like Smarties in glazed bowls, and there is a large elegant snuff box containing cocaine on the polished bar. Always, with Archer, a certain style. There is a small round of applause when he enters, only it is not Archer, it is a younger man, who is also slightly shorter, and whose curly blond hair falls down over his eyes. He wears baggy trousers and shirt, with a piratical crimson sash separating the two. He is carrying photograph albums. At a nod from him Donny leaves, heading for another room where he is going to set up the video equipment.

Where in those paragraphs does the dream end and the extrapolation begin? I don't know precisely. I know that I am mixing up what was then the future with what was then the present. I don't particularly want to know. Now it is all the past, and I am uncomfortable with this material; it smacks of my daily work. 'Sex monster sold videos of son!' When I am not writing of busty Beatrice, I am usually writing either of monsters or of heroes. It is an odd world I inhabit, from which human beings are for the most part absent. I thought I was escaping from this world, or limiting it at least within safe boundaries, instead I think I am broadening it to include earlier years, my childhood, all of my past.

Twenty-eight

Although I had begun to look at Kim in a new light, our relationship did not change. My friendship with Floyd however, gradually developed. He did not live at Melinda's, at least he was not there every night, he was often, as Melinda used to say with a mocking smile, 'out investigating'. I decided that his position in the house was something like mine, an honorary member. He gave me Raymond Chandler books on birthdays and Christmases, but he remained unforthcoming about his own activities, whether in relation to Archer or to anyone else. He would just repeat, with a fluency that made it clear it was a formula he had perfected, that he dealt in divorce, repossession of vehicles, the commercial probity of individuals and companies, and more divorce. His tools, he said, were not a coat, a hat and a gun, but bugs, wires and a camera.

'And,' he once added, 'a fondness for jigsaws. In the more interesting cases it needs a little lateral thinking, an ability to put people together in the right combinations, effectively to be the villain, so you can see how it works. Significant combinations are the secret. Of course sometimes, there's no motive, and no villain either.'

'What do you mean, "to be the villain"?'

He smiled. 'Poacher turned gamekeeper Billy, that's me. Imagine me wriggling through the undergrowth, with my lens as long as your arm, after the first shots of the new Rover. That's how I used to earn my bread, scoops and exclusives, not for magazines but for rivals. Industrial espionage, perhaps a step above taking pictures of a pregnant Princess Diana, but that's about all that can be said for it. So who better to employ as a Security Consultant? Funny isn't it, how these things happen, from good guy to bad guy, just like that.'

Our friendship developed, but his investigation didn't. There was no progress on either Jerome or Archer, in spite of the intriguing combinations on display at the house-warming. Floyd would shrug. 'I'm trying to get something together,' he'd say, adding pointedly, 'in my spare time.'

Melody came round in January. We had passed his shop occa-sionally in the meantime, and looked in the window, and once we had met him on the street, exchanged greetings and promised to be in touch, but I had barely been aware of his existence since my father's death. I hadn't forgotten my father's words about him, but I hadn't made sense of them either. 'Keep both eyes on him. Melody is a man I thought I could trust.' Nor had I forgotten Archer's startling imitation of him years earlier. It was just that passing time did not leave these memories in isolation, it mixed them with others: myself hugging Melody's legs, his first aid for the boy in the road accident, his distrust of Archer, my guilt at stealing from him, his kindness when I was running away, his presence at my father's death, frantically trying to save him, followed by his generous words to me. What was I to make of this man? Writing from my present perspective I know the answer, even having read this far, granted this partial overview, an answer presents itself but, in the midst of things, nothing at all was clear cut.

Melinda answered the door.

'Ms Sexton,' he said, 'how nice to see you.' She looked at him blankly. 'I do hope it's not inconvenient,' he said, 'but I thought I'd call and, as it were, renew old acquaintance. You see I'm North of the river these days as often as I'm South.'

Melinda apologized. Kim and I were called downstairs, and in no time we were all sitting round a table with Melody, who was effortlessly taking charge, pouring some tea. Nothing about his appearance had changed: the red hair, as thick and wavy as ever, the chubby cheeks enlarging the outline of his face, making it into an almost perfect circle, the lips, not quite as sensual as my mother's, but thick and red, topped by the small, thick moustache. Glasses with red, circular frames. A shorter man than Archer, of a heavier build. The conspicuous clothes, a liquorice allsorts sweater today, over black and blue striped trousers, giving him the air of a showman.

I suppose it was because I was looking at him so closely that, when he met my gaze and smiled, I was for a moment frightened. The effect was that I spilt the mug of tea that he was handing me. I got a paper napkin from the kitchen, and slid it under the tablecloth, to protect the waxed wood. After that my attention was continually drawn to this small lump, like a tumour on the table. Kim, who for some reason was watching me as closely as I was watching Melody, made some comment about my clumsiness, which I could not answer. She seemed in all ways more able than me, when it came to the tiny competencies that make up most of every day. Somehow for instance, after a meal, her napkin was always spotless and uncreased, whereas mine was a suspect shade of grey, screwed up into an ugly shape. It would lie by my plate like a small mouse I had discreetly throttled and crushed.

'I see you two young people get on just as well as you ever did,' said Melody. 'Most gratifying. What do you think, Ms Sexton, is there a romance in the making here?'

Melinda laughed, and Kim blushed. Melody continued undaunted.

'Very late I know, but I've brought you a little birthday present, Kim, and since I forgot yours altogether, I've brought you one too, Billy.'

From a black leather duffel bag, Melody drew out two parcels. 'Don't you think a red coat and a white beard would suit me?' he said, chuckling.

We opened our parcels to find two personal stereos, pink for Kim and blue for me. 'I hope you don't mind the colours,' said Melody, 'but I'm very old-fashioned, I'm afraid,' a rueful pout, 'one of my great weaknesses, I'm afraid.' He paused, but no one contradicted him. 'They're waterproof you know,' he said, 'depths of . . . oh, I don't know, quite considerable depths. Clever little things.'

Kim I knew already had one, but she thanked him graciously.

'You never come to see me in The Circus of Delights,' said

Melody, in mock complaint, 'and it's just around the corner, as Billy well knows. It has changed enormously, Billy. Didn't you enjoy your visit that time? Do you remember it? The video?'

I was nodding, but Melinda looked suddenly alert. 'What video?' she said.

'Oh, a harmless thing,' said Melody, 'a game we had.'

'What game?' Melinda insisted. 'What kind of game?'

'Well,' said Melody, taken aback, 'I think you told a joke. Isn't that right Billy? Did you tell a joke?'

I nodded, slightly taken aback myself. 'I think so.'

'Knock knock,' said Melody abruptly.

'Who's there?' I answered.

'Boo.'

'Boo who?'

'There's no need to cry about it,' said Melody, and then laughed, a hearty sound quickly diminished to small titters when he realized he was the only one reacting.

'I see,' said Melinda, straight-faced. She lifted her cup and took a few sips of tea. All three of us followed suit, and then there was a pause.

Kim looked at her mother, who did not look up.

'How's school, Billy?' said Melody finally, indefatigably cheerful. 'Are you fitting in?'

'Yes,' I said, 'I've made some friends.' I mentioned Greig. I now saw a lot of him and his small circle, although I still didn't socialize with them outside school hours.

'Greig,' said Melody, musing, 'black-haired boy, tends to dress in black too?'

'Yes,' I said, 'how did you know?'

'Rather surly, I thought. He's been in my shop once or twice, with his friends. Oh, I keep my eyes open Billy, I notice things. It's a helpful thing in my business, in retail. I'm like your poor father was Billy, if you don't mind my saying so, I have big ideas you see, I think in terms of nationwide chains, megastores, so forth. Eldon was just the same. Big ideas. That was always the great thing about Eldon, he was never prepared to say "This is what I do. This is what I am." Never static.' Now he paused, as if slightly dismayed at how much he had said. 'And how's Kim? Still the heroine of the swimming team?'

Kim looked at him blankly for a moment, as if not quite sure

171

who the question was addressed to. She was like my mother in her attitude to Melody, she was polite enough, just, but she refused to be drawn into matching his jolly tone.

She nodded. 'I want to be in the tournament at the end of the year.'

Melody left amid more protestations that, without doubt, we would meet again soon. Floyd, arriving shortly after, narrowly missed seeing him. On his arrival, Melinda quickly suggested that Kim and I had homework to do, and ushered us out of the kitchen. We left immediately but, to Kim's surprise, I remained by the door.

'What are you doing?' she whispered. '*You* can't spy on them.'

I was amused by her inflection but I just said, 'It's important.'

From Melinda's reaction to the mention of videos, and from her impatience to get us out of the way, I knew that something worth hearing was going to be discussed. Gingerly, I leaned towards the door, my ear an inch or so away. As I said, a born eavesdropper.

I heard, 'He made a film of Billy.'

'Doing?' Floyd's reply was mild.

'Doing a joke or something, I don't know exactly.'

'Well that sounds harmless. Don't jump on things too eagerly. We're talking about guesswork if you remember, the whole idea is crazy. There's plenty more research to be done. Anyway Billy's sensible, he's a sensible boy.' There was a sound. A laugh. 'I got quite the wrong idea.'

'What?'

'I suppose it was wrong.'

'What?'

'When you got rid of them so quickly, I thought what's she up to?'

'You might not have been wrong. Not altogether. What about your interest in Nita?'

'Purely professional. Research, didn't I tell you? And yours in Archer? I'm not sure you could say the same.'

'Water under the bridge. It was an aberration. History. Most of us have histories we're not entirely proud of.'

More sounds. Embarrassed, I moved away from the door, trying to understand what I had heard. It made no sense to me, suggested only that old feeling of immanent danger, that sense of something pertaining to me being hidden or held just out of reach. It was the usual price extracted for eavesdropping: clues, imperfect knowledge. Only then I noticed that Kim was trying to peer through the keyhole. I dragged her away and, giggling, we ran upstairs. We sat on the top step.

'Do you know what they were up to?' said Kim.

'Yes,' I said.

'You want to ask me out, don't you?' she said.

'Yes,' I said, reflexively.

'Go on then.'

'Will you come out with me?'

'Yes,' she said, and kissed me on the mouth, a brief, wet touch, and then ran into her room and shut the door.

Twenty-nine

So began my second love affair with Kim. Weekday evenings, after homework, if there was nothing on TV, we would go up to her room and kiss a little. I think we did just about everything that is possible mouth to mouth. That phrase is apt, because at first, kissing Kim always conjured up that image of Melody's mouth clamped on my father's. It wasn't helpful, it didn't exactly encourage my lust. French kisses drove that vision away, the wet surprise of the inside of her mouth, the touch of her tongue in mine. We would sit on the beanbag in her room, uncomfortably squashed together, and my hands would move over her body, tracing circuitous routes that led always, no matter how they detoured, back towards her breasts. Which were more noticeable than they had been. She would allow my fingers to come close, she would allow them to brush over the curve of her sweater or her shirt, and then she would move my hand away. I would return to my room unsatisfied.

At weekends we went to the cinema. Screen kisses are noisy, and tend to sound like people eating. Our kisses sounded like paper bags being crumpled. Perhaps because of this, I would kiss Kim's cheek chastely and quietly, she would not even turn her head. In the sanctioning dark, she would allow my hand to rest on one of her breasts, unmoving. My sensitive palm would dream of a nipple tickling its lifeline.

As time passed, I continued to get more frustration than fulfilment from our new relationship. Apart from my recurring problem concerning Melody and my father, I was beset by self-consciousness. The problem was the points system. My friends the numbers, which I used to love counting to reassure myself, had taken on a new significance. Greig and his gang, and I, used to sit in a classroom on Monday lunchtimes and discuss, in detail, the points accrued over the weekend. It was ten for what we called, clinically, Full Penetration, and no one had quite had the nerve to claim this yet, but Greig regularly awarded himself eight which meant very nearly everything but. He was working, he would say, on Magic Nine, the blow job, it was just a matter of time. My own efforts would have scored a humiliating four, so naturally I lied a little. I gave myself six, which meant full, unimpeded contact with the breasts. I was always urged, as I was in my academic reports, to try harder, to make that extra effort required to reach the elusive seven, the hand job. The constructive advice I was given included finding a different girlfriend. My loyalty was scoffed at, and Greig helpfully offered me names of girls he could assure me were more cooperative than Kim. I turned down the offers, just as I turned down occasional invitations to parties. I kept up my pride by making my descriptions of my own modest, and imaginary, achievements more interesting than Greig's reports of his greater successes. From some angles, you could look on my present job (the pen job?) as a vocation.

Why did I turn down invitations? I have never liked parties, never liked drunkenness, never liked things that threaten my control of myself. The way I conducted my life used, for a while, to reflect the way I tried to define it, in small, strictly limited terms. I placed faith in routines. Homework, evenings with Kim, films at the weekends, visits to my father's grave, Sunday lunch with Melinda and Floyd, perhaps an outing in the afternoon, with Louise too if she was around and willing, to a park or a museum or the zoo. My room became very tidy. If the waste-bin was out of place I became aware of it, and if I didn't move it, it hung in my mind like a heavy weight held in one hand, tugging at me, preventing composure. If the doorbell rang unexpectedly my heart would sink. Disruption of my routine could only be feared, because routine was something to rely on, in an unreliable world.

Dear Marie,
I imagine a fort, one of those square wooden cavalry forts in Westerns, do you know the ones? They are surrounded by Indians and running out of supplies, and no one knows if the relief column will get there in time. I am waiting for John Wayne. I start thinking that things are cleared up, or faded away, or safe in Floyd's hands, and they aren't. They never are. Melody might be involved, but I'm not really prepared to think about how. I don't want to tell you anyway, because you'd laugh, you'd think I was mad. Melinda and Floyd are maybe hiding something from me. Archer is doing God knows what. Charlie and his parents, where are they in it all? I used to think I liked labyrinths. I don't. If I was where you are I'd be happier, no one else would know, and we'd walk in the woods and swim in the lake every day.

Nothing is simple, that's the trouble. School still isn't simple. Mr Fairfax is friendly but every now and then he has these furies in class. He's famous for them. And as for Greig, I've no idea if I like him or not, I mean I really don't know. I see a lot of him in school but I always make excuses when he says come to a party, or let's go to a club or anything.

The point of this letter really was to say I hope we haven't lost touch, because I really don't know where I am, but I know where you are, and almost nobody else I know does, and that's why it's good to write to you. It's good to have my own secrets. Hoping you're feeling well and the weather is good,

Billy Gunn

My signature is an illegible looping thing, underlined twice. Some of it fell off the end of the page. I wrote the letter in a rush, because Floyd and I were on our way out, visiting the Larbeys. At least, I was visiting Charlie. Floyd, who was taking me, might, he said, stop and chat with Charlie's parents, or with his brother for that matter, whoever happened to be there, just to talk a little about this and that.

It was Mrs Larbey in fact who met us at the door, and the way she greeted Floyd did not suggest that it was a surprise to see him.

'Mr Floyd,' she said, 'so pleased you could come. Hello you,' to me, 'come in, he's upstairs, up you go.'

Charlie was waiting for me at the top of the stairs. 'Hi,' he said, and, as soon as we were out of earshot, 'what's he doing here?' He was nodding back down towards Floyd.

I shrugged and made a face, elaborately innocent. 'Nothing. How should I know? He just brought me.'

I was unconvincing. 'Why did he?' said Charlie. 'And why's he talking to my mother? What does he want?'

'Charlie,' I said, 'what are you on about? I mean, what's wrong?'

We were in his room now. It was Gary's old room, and it reminded me instantly, irresistibly, of the occasion some seven years ago when Charlie had brought me in here, and we had examined the secrets hidden in the wardrobe. Not much had changed. Charlie, pasty faced, had become more overweight as he had grown. There were different, but similar posters on the wall, a stale smell, a dirty ashtray by the bed. A key concealed beneath it?

'Nothing's wrong,' said Charlie, sitting at the end of his bed. 'What shall we do?'

It was a fairly gruesome afternoon. I had phoned Charlie at Floyd's request, saying that it had been nice to see him at the house-warming, that we should meet up again, suggesting that I come over. Charlie, surprised but perhaps a little flattered by this attention, had agreed. Now, without the context provided by the house-warming, we both felt exposed. It was the same awkwardness which had developed with Kim for a while, when she had moved away, a diminishing of friendship. It felt this time as if something not quite explicit had been clarified.

We talked for a while about the past, but it wasn't very fertile ground. We seemed to have quite different memories of it. I recalled reading out my story in class, Charlie, indifferent, said, 'What story?' I mentioned climbing the tree in my garden, wondering if he remembered our fight, and he said, 'We played some stupid games. When I saw that tree again I thought it had shrunk, I used to think it was so big.' And when, finally, I brought up our illicit entry into Gary's room he became impatient. 'You haven't changed, have you Billy? You're always on about things that don't matter, I don't think you live in the same world as the rest of us, I really don't. You don't care about anything that's really happening, that's why you didn't care about J.T.'s house, because you thought it was still yours, that's why you'll never get anywhere probably, because you don't hardly ever think about real life, you don't care about it, you'd rather think about the past or writing a story or something. When are you going to grow up?'

Am I putting too many words into his mouth? This sounds a little too much like what my father might have said if he had lived to see me now. Certainly when I saw Melinda, quite recently, she mocked me gently in terms not very far removed from these, 'You people live in a different world from the rest of us.' But Charlie must have said something like this, or I wouldn't have been moved to tell him about Greig, and the points system.

As I told him he began to smirk and when, in answer to his question, I told him I had six points, the smirk became a sneer. When I told him that Greig had eight points he just laughed. 'Kids' stuff,' he said finally. 'I've scored a hundred on that system, regularly, every weekend. Like I said Billy, you'll never grow up. J.T. even asked you to a party, I didn't want him to, but he did, and you went home with Mel and Floyd and Kimmy like a good boy. Six points!'

I was both infuriated by his scorn and silenced by it. I felt sure that Greig would have an answer for him, but I could think of nothing to say. It occurred to me in fact that he and Greig might get on well, in the right circumstances. There was something of the spirit of the chemist, or of the alchemist, in this thought. Putting the ingredients together, observing the reaction.

Secure in his superiority, Charlie had moved to a patronizing tone.

'If you don't like parties that's all right,' he said, 'not everything depends on parties. I could show you some things, I could show you the places to go. Have you heard of Video City?'

I said no, and simultaneously remembered Nita's words about Archer at the City.

'Course you haven't,' said Charlie smugly. 'I'll take you there, shall I?'

'Me and Greig?'

'Whoever. I mean it's just a video shop, but you'll meet some interesting people and, you know, see a bit more of the world at least. Trust me, it'll be worth your while, you've never seen anything like this place. Will you come?'

'Yes,' I said, reassured by his words, 'all right.'

So it was agreed, just as it had once been arranged that I would shoplift with him, and, as if Charlie was right and I hadn't grown up, as if no time had passed at all, no seven years moving by with their large and small events, their supposedly growing experiences, I found myself returned to childhood, quelling exactly the same reservations and fears.

Thirty

A death provided some breathing space for me. My unnamed baby brother, Joseph, Eldon, and now Roly; I was in danger of learning to take funerals in my stride. Roly's was possibly the best of these deaths, a heart attack at seventy-seven; a numbing pain, a breath in, a breath out, and then no further movement. Ethel woke, she is convinced, at the precise moment. Then she lay beside him for three hours, not wanting to start into motion in the middle of the night the clumsy mechanisms which would take him away from her. She told me that she had intended to spend the time until dawn in reviewing their life together, but that she only managed to do this for about half an hour. For the rest of the time she thought about other things: the necessary arrangements, the neighbour who was visiting that afternoon, the social awkwardness of grief.

I spent a weekend with her. Over our cup of tea at the kitchen table, we discussed the tapestry. She was catching up with the present, she said, at an alarming rate, she was just finishing the wedding of Lucy and Eldon.

'A lovely occasion dear,' she was looking at me but dreaming of something else, 'we did so like your father, when we got used to him. And Lucy, Lucy knew how to wear a dress, she knew how to carry herself.' She paused. 'I'm being thoughtless,' she said, putting down her cup, 'perhaps you'd rather not talk about it at all.'

I shook my head. 'No, I'd like to hear about it, I'd like to hear

178

all about it.' I was eager for souvenirs of my parents, anything to add to the mental file which I tried to maintain.

She began however, to pursue a different line of thought. 'Yes,' she said, 'it's good, isn't it, to preserve a few memories, to keep them intact. It's good to have a sense of movement in your life, of what's behind and what might be in front. I don't know about you William, perhaps you don't think this way at all, but I rather like to think that my body is no more reliable than our old Mini, which was never serviced quite as much as it should have been. One day it goes along quite well, rattling a bit, the next it stops with a bang and you think it'll never get going ever again.' She said this as if it was a joke, and then paused. 'And you find you're somewhere else, somewhere with different perspectives and small rewards that you would never have noticed before, like the absence of pain.'

She was looking out of the window, squinting slightly at the sun, and still smiling. Wrinkles on wrinkles. I tried to imagine her skin as smooth as Kim's or mine, and couldn't.

'The wedding, grandma?' I said.

She looked round and laughed, and said, 'Your grandma's in a different world, isn't she? The wedding, William. Well, I don't know what I was going to say, except that your parents were so happy, gazing at each other all the time. They were, if you know what I mean, very passionate about each other, anyone could tell that, anyone who wasn't drunk. Roly, and indeed Joseph, bless him, bless both of them, they were a little drunk. Couple of layabouts. There's something about men in suits getting drunk at weddings, isn't there? Something timeless. Give him his due though, he did a very nice speech, Roly did, though not a patch on your father's. Literary allusions, you see, Eldon's speech was full of them, or so Lucy told me anyway, I'm afraid it was all over my head. Your father and your mother sat there in the middle of the table at the top of the room like a king and a queen. They both looked so absolutely *right*, you see, as if they'd reached a place they knew they had been aiming for. Do you see? It was like the culmination of something, perhaps that was a problem, it was a culmination even more than it was a beginning. I cried. I cried and cried.'

In the evening, Ethel showed me where I was sleeping. I carried a mug of hot chocolate, Ethel had a nutty smelling liqueur in a

179

thin glass. It was my mother's room, still containing the old toys and games. Ethel turned on the light while I sat on the bed. She remained in the doorway, and for a moment neither of us said anything. This was different, four years on this was different from my last visit to the room. My mother was no longer bounded by my strict definition of her, she had broken down those walls and forced me to open my eyes to any clues I might be offered to what she was really like. So I looked.

'What happened to the doll?' I asked.

Ethel was licking out the bottom of her glass. Her tongue was squeezed so that it looked like a fat slug on a window pane, or in a test-tube. The sight gave me an odd surge of affection for her, and for a moment I wished that she would sit on the bed beside me, so that I could hug her.

'Doll?' she said. 'What doll?'

'There was a doll here I thought, a rag doll, you said it was my mother's favourite.'

'No.'

'I'm sure.'

Ethel was shaking her head and then, abruptly, frighteningly, as she shook her head I saw her tears shining on her cheeks. I could not move, I sat and watched her, all thought of hugging her dispelled by her distress. I sat and watched stupidly.

Finally Ethel spoke. 'I'm sorry,' she said, 'sniffles, who would have thought it?' And she snorted in a way which might have been a laugh. I took the cue with relief and laughed with her. And she sat on the bed and, finally, I put a clumsy arm around her shoulders.

I said that only my mother's absence would be in the rest of this story, that remains correct. But in her absence she still exercises an influence.

'I wasn't going to tell you,' said Ethel, 'she asked me not to tell you, that she came up here before she went. I don't know why I wasn't to say anything because nothing important happened. She just spent some time up here alone, and when I came up I saw her, all she was doing was touching everything, the bed, and her old books, and she was holding that doll and the photo. She said she was taking them away and now I could burn everything else. Of course I didn't know then that she was disappearing, but even so I said she couldn't have the photo, after all these years I wanted to keep it, so she just gave it to me and said I should get rid of everything else. She was saying goodbye to everything you see. She came here to say goodbye to Roly and me, and also to her old room. Her past.'

We sat together on the bed and looked at the photo, the one Ethel had not wanted Kim to look at and had not wanted Lucy to take away. My mother, a year or so older than me, sat in the branches of a low tree doing, by the look of it, an impression of a chimpanzee, while her parents stood on the ground below her. Ethel was trying to stare the camera down, Roly was looking upwards and sideways, his smile strained, as if he was trying to get a glimpse of his daughter, but was unable to move his feet.

'Funny sort of a picture.' Ethel was toying with her glass, turning it round in her long, blue-veined fingers, tapping it with her yellowy grey nails. 'It was around O-level time. Your mother surprised us all by doing well in her O-levels, ever so well. We thought she would drop out, get involved in, you know, those things that were going on then. Flowers. We never thought she had the motivation. Your mother was always fascinated by other people's lives. Scatterbrained, I thought.'

The picture would have been taken in about 1969. Lucy was wearing a tight stripy T-shirt, flares. Her face was screwed up in a ferocious angry chimp scowl. It was the face of a chimp whose banana had just been stolen, or of a particularly primitive, camera-shy chimp who thought that its soul was being sucked away through the lens.

Leaning back on the pillows with the bedside light on, I continued to look at the photo when Ethel had left. My mother, Lucy Gentleman, a fifteen-year-old girl, my mother up a tree. What kind of a view had she had? Had she fantasized flying away? Or climbing higher and refusing to come down? Her father looking pained, her mother determined to brazen it out. It was hard to imagine the three of them together, it was hard to imagine any kind of connection or communication between the three. Doting father, determined mother, recalcitrant, drop-out daughter. Except she hadn't dropped out, she had surprised them all, she had confounded expectations by conforming, steering clear of the alternatives that had for a while attracted her. She went to university, ten years after this picture was taken she was married, to an older man ('We did so like your father, when we got used to him'), another few months and I had arrived. She had attained respectability, as near as makes no difference. A place on her mother's tapestry. She was in the world of her mother, who pretended nothing was wrong, and her father, who wanted to help, but couldn't quite act. Until, at nearly forty, she had finally fulfilled everyone's expectations, and dropped out. My father's airy complacency, my narrow definition of her, the death of her second child, it must have accumulated over the years. My mother, Lucy Gentleman, a fifteen-year-old girl, my mother up a tree. Her identity was not as fixed as I had thought, as I had wanted to think. It was unreliable, like that of Roly, the reformed layabout. Perhaps he was thinking about that as he looked wistfully up at her, thinking that things came all right for him in the end. With Roly, and Melinda and Floyd, my mother was just part of a pattern. But it's too late to understand, I was thinking, it's too late for insights. Somewhere she is looking for new perspectives, and perhaps for the small rewards (absence from pain?) of a different kind of life.

The next day, I tried to express to Ethel my sorrow, and sympathy over Roly's death.

'Oh Lord,' she said, looking up from the tapestry and taking off her glasses, 'thank you, I mean thank you for your kind thoughts but, I'm philosophical. He hadn't been well, you see, he kept it to himself but he hadn't really been very well. We didn't like to tell you, William, to be honest. But I'm coping, I think I'm coping rather well. I have my friends, you must meet some of them some time. You think *I* am old and frail, you'd be surprised.'

'I don't think you're old and frail.'

It was true. She was in fact just grandma, or Ethel, I had no adjectives to give her at all. I had once been intrigued by her powerful-looking legs but, with the passing of a few years even these had ceased to have any effect on me. I realized with a start that I was guilty of imposing the same narrow definitions on her as I had once imposed on my mother. No wonder her stoical attitude to Roly's death surprised me. Almost any detail about her would surprise me, because it would stretch my image of her. Even physical details were unfamiliar. The slim length of the fingers holding the needle, the carefully-applied coral lipstick, the attractive dress, a discreet shade of blue. I had an urge to slip under the table and have a second look at those legs, but I thought she might not understand.

'What are you staring at, young William?'

Quite a thin face, with foggy grey hair. All those wrinkles. Was my mother's face hidden somewhere in that flesh?

'Nothing.'

'You don't want to worry about me,' she said, misunderstanding, 'I really am philosophical. No use moping. My philosophy is to live in the real world, to get on with things.'

I was reminded of a story Archer liked to tell. I had heard it in his surgery. 'I hope you don't believe in Father Christmas,' he said, leaning over my face. 'I hope you haven't been taken in by any of that trash. Especially, more than anything else, the Tooth Fairy. Do you believe in the Tooth Fairy, Bill?' I shook my head. 'I hope not,' he said. 'I had a little boy once who wobbled out his second teeth so that he could put them under the pillow. You don't get any more after your second teeth, Bill, it was dentures for him, for the rest of his life. His parents' fault. Tooth Demon they should call it, if they have to call it anything. Live in the real world, Bill, that's my advice, I don't believe in making any concessions to kids, they don't want them and they're not good for them. Never mind myths. Live in the real world.'

I nodded at Ethel, agreeing with her philosophy, but she had put her glasses on and she was bending over her tapestry again, working with infinite care on the lacy hem of my mother's wedding dress. I looked at her, and then looked at my watch, wondering when Melinda would arrive to take me away. I was feeling restless. Thinking of Archer had reminded me of Video City, and other real worlds than the ones in which I felt at home.

Thirty-one

The mirror was misted and I seemed to see myself behind gauze, a dim figure whose expression could not quite be read. I imagined myself to be looking at my father. Dripping after my shower, towel half draped around me, Kim knocking on the bathroom door, I fantasized again. An ordinary fantasy: me talking and him listening. 'Preserve a few memories,' Ethel said. I didn't need the advice, I preserved plenty of memories, many of them memories of things that had never happened. I was always changing Eldon, persuading him not to drink, persuading him to moderate his ambitions – in my mind they were an over-stretched military column, like Alexander stretching his conquest a continent too far – I persuaded him to wear glasses which would correct his long-sightedness. Comforting fantasies indulged in at luxuriant length. Sometimes, if I worked at it, or if I made no effort at all, the demarcation between fact and fantasy would blur, and become irrelevant. He loves my mother more openly, more demonstratively, and so she stays, never dreams of leaving.

'What is the point after all,' I am talking and he is listening, 'of grand schemes? Grand schemes don't change people. Things much more intimate, more personal, change people.' In my displaced passion I imagine I would be irresistibly convincing. He is thinking: what a son I have. He is like a joke Jewish parent: my son the professor of logic. 'Have you considered the variety contained in that one word, "people"? It must be the most all-embracing word in the language. Stroll down the streets with your eyes open, different streets, and then think again about your grand schemes conceived in your study and conceived surely – won't you admit this, dad? – with the purpose of conferring honour on yourself. You want something more tangible, less cerebral, to actually change someone. *Smellier.*' I am speaking and he is listening, nodding solemnly.

'Billy,' he says, 'you're right. You're right of course.' I can see him with business cronies, in a boardroom, he's saying, modestly smiling, 'I think I'm a pretty good businessman, but it's taken my son to set me straight on a couple of points, he's put me back on the tracks.' Proud father. To me again, nodding now, because everything, like a skilful conjuror's trick, has suddenly become clear, and wonderfully simple. 'I haven't been open to experience, have I? My eyes, as you aptly put it, haven't been open. I'll change my ways, Billy, now that you've shown me my mistakes.'

Kim's knocking finally disturbed me. I opened the bathroom door to a funny look, a look containing female scorn. I wonder what she thought I was up to. I could have told her that fantasies concerning my father were threatening to displace altogether the less elaborate but more energetic fantasies involving her and Louise.

Charlie led Greig and me out of the tube. He wore a grey jacket, its collar turned up, and he walked with a swagger. 'I always seem to be showing you things, Billy,' he had said on the train. He had barely nodded at Greig. 'This way, this way,' he said now. The station was at the junction of five roads, surrounded by shops. I thought we had arrived, but we went straight past these, heading down a hill lined by large houses. 'Flats,' said Charlie, 'flats all the way down here, quite nice ones, and then down the hill and round the corner, it all changes.'

We followed him, without much to say, and before long we found ourselves in a different street. The same kind of houses that had been made into expensive flats were here apparently empty. Dirty brick, peeling paint, broken windows. 'Squats,' said Charlie, 'and hard-to-rent council houses. In the estate over there,' he waved a hand vaguely, 'they don't have postmen, or milkmen, or anything like that. It's a no-go area. Police go round in fours, four-packs. Come on, it gets better on the precinct.'

I need a change of perspective here, I need to pretend for a while to be a real journalist, perhaps not the one my father envisaged, but one with a better than fourteen-year-old understanding.

This, as I say, was a different street, one where I saw a girl of my age, of Kim's age, talking to a man in a car which had just drawn up, and then getting in with him. 'Whore,' said Charlie, in his offhand way. Years later I did an interview with such a girl, for a big feature, centre pages, on child prostitutes in the city. Colour pictures, lots of detail, probing questions. 'Have you had sex this week?' I asked. 'No, just dates.' Fourteen and she had had three venereal diseases. Divorce and abuse in her background. At least on the street, she said, you get paid for it, they don't pay you at home. 'What do you want to be when you grow up?' 'I don't know.' 'What do you want to be?' 'Nothing.' But later, as if she had been thinking about it in the meantime, she said she wanted to be rich and have a small family; by which she meant her brother, her 'real' father, and her mother. She wasn't at an age to consider husbands or children of her own. 'Maybe we could live on a farm.' 'What disgusts you?' I wanted to know, intrepid reporter. Easy. She had a friend who was adopted, the friend sometimes wondered if she did it with her father, without even knowing. Echo of her own background, 'poignant' underlined in my notebook. And children, this young adult told me, people who did it with children disgusted her. I smelt something on her. 'What perfume do you use?' 'Meadow Violets. Cloudy Blue.' I felt slightly nauseous when I left her, and it was only partly to do with what she had been saying to me. The headline for this piece: 'Young Virgins on Sale to Sex Monsters'.

At fourteen I had no angle, no perspective of any kind. I was an uptight, narrow-minded, short-sighted spectator of things. I had little knowledge of any world outside the one familiar to me. I was scared in this area although, this is still a few years before the turn of the century, it wasn't yet as bad as all that. Video City itself was in fact mildly reassuring. Its name shone out dimly in the sunlight in red neon tubes above the words, in Gothic script:

Import, Export, Sale and Rental
Mail Order Our Speciality
Every Taste Satisfied

but inside it was a bit like Mr Melody's sweet shop, Sweet Surrender. A treasure-house of trays and shelves and glass-fronted cupboards crammed with multi-coloured, brightly-wrapped familiar and mysterious videos. Jay, who ran the shop, considered it an island of respectability in a grotesque area. He was talking to a policeman when I came in.

'Look at this. Have you seen this one? Look at this now, it was a "fifteen" when it came out, that's the certificate right, and I sell it here to anyone who wants it, that's my job, but look at this now, I know my duty, read this.'

He didn't wait for the man to read it, he read it aloud, perhaps conscious of the new audience which had just entered. It was a round red sticker on the front, emblazoned on Sylvester Stallone's swollen chest. ·

'"The management of Video City warns clients that this film contains scenes of violence which may disturb and corrupt." How's that? Hard hitting, isn't it? I'm serious about that, I don't want people to walk down the street killing people. Bad for business." He laughed, and looked over at us, to see if we appreciated the joke. His eyes passed over Greig and me without much hesitation. 'Hello Charlie, all right? Seriously officer, bad for morale generally.

I can make serious money legally. Imagine if I had the sole cassette rights to this, over a big chain of shops? Do you see what I mean? I'm a businessman. I help the community, you know that,' a shrug and a smile, 'I raise the fucking tone around here.'

Jay was wearing a pale blue shirt, cloudless blue, and a red bootlace tie in a buckle shaped like a heart. I was almost certain that he was Archer.

He brushed his blond hair out of his eyes. On his finger there appeared to be a third eye, encased in a ring. 'You have to try to see my position if you can. It's difficult for an honest man, trying to make some money.' He moved his hand away from his hair, and it fell back down over his forehead. He picked up another video, a naked girl on its cover, another red sticker. 'It's society,' he said, 'that's what I blame. I'm not joking. I mean it's a sex-admiring society, you can't argue with me. So it makes it hard to know where the boundaries are, what's permitted and what isn't, what's approved of and what's supposed to be horrifying. I mean do *you* know? I tell you what, I bet you don't go asking your senile old judges for advice, the ones who let rapists off with a chuckle and a wink.'

The policeman was unimpressed. More words were exchanged and then, 'If there's anything to hear,' said Jay, 'I'll hear it. You know that. And if I hear anything, I'll tell you. Cross my heart. OK? I mean is that OK?'

When the policeman left, I was going to approach Jay, but he disappeared immediately into the back of the shop.

Charlie was getting excited. 'Isn't it great?' he was saying to Greig, 'you've never seen a selection like this, and the thing is, there's more out the back, I expect that's why the filth was here, because of the stuff in the back. And Jay's got a chain of them, I didn't know he'd be here because he's got Video Jungle and Video Zoo and Horrorshow, which is only horror films, so you hardly ever actually see him because he's so busy all the time. In fact this is where J.T. gets some of his stuff, so it has to be good, you haven't met J.T. but you might, and,' turning to me now, 'guess who owns half of this shop? You'll never guess . . .'

'Charlie.'

The eulogy stopped abruptly and we all, with a surprise that must have been gratifying to him, looked round, to see Gary standing behind the counter, where Jay had been a few moments before.

He wore an open-necked striped shirt, red braces, the smirk learnt from Archer was imprinted on his face.

'Charlie, what are you *on*? Calm down for God's sake, stop showing off.'

'I'm not, I'm just explaining.'

Gary was looking at me. 'I know you.'

He recognized me, but he seemed to want to imply that I was too insignificant to remember.

'Billy Gunn,' I said.

He laughed. 'Billy the kid, how could I forget? Cat burglar. You tend to pop up fairly regularly, so I hear. Weren't you lurking around at the house-warming? Casing the joint were you?'

'It used to be my house.'

'Used to be. You let it slip through your fingers. Shouldn't do that, shouldn't let a nice piece of property slip away, someone isn't looking after your best interests, Bill. Might pay to change allegiance, Bill.'

'And I'm Greig.' He seemed to think it was time to assert his presence. 'I like your shop. What did the cop want then?'

Gary was clearly pleased to be asked. He shrugged with studied indifference.

'They like to hassle us. Seem to think we're crooks, gates to the underworld. Every now and then they have a look in the back, or in our cinema, makes them feel they're doing their job. They've got some funny ideas, the filth around here, ideas about distribution of drugs and porn, God knows what, if it's not one thing it's another. How's a man supposed to do an honest day's work?'

I said, 'You work in the City.'

'Diversify,' said Gary, 'take my advice Bill, diversify, spread your wings, spread your net wide, wide as you like. Have you any idea how much the big players in this game stand to make? Have you any idea?'

The similarity to Archer's manner and even his actual words was unnerving. I had to remind myself that this was Gary, Gary Larbey, Charlie's brother, who I had known vaguely for most of my life. Archer's ubiquity seemed to extend to possession. I may not have been right about Jay, I was thinking, but Archer is *here*, he *is* present. I thought about my imagined lecture to my father, about sensitive, intimate contact with people, so you can meet their eyes and smell their sweat. Archer was the master of such contact, the communicator, the man who could connect with people, any people, infinitely versatile. Yet somehow, I thought, simultaneously self-contained, islanded, sending out his flamboyant messages from an unruffled, still centre. I was ready to swallow any number of contradictory ideas about Archer, he contained contradictions, permitted them, it was one of his tricks. Extrovert chameleon. I felt myself involved in spite of myself, physically part of his network, the network he had first told me about seven or more years earlier, a wide and growing thing, a spider web, or a long fingered hand extended innocently, ingenuously, as if in greeting.

'So can we have a look in the back then, or what?' Greig wasn't satisfied with patronising hints and winks, he wanted to see the evidence.

'You can look at the studio,' said Gary, 'but if you break anything,' he paused and laughed, relishing his role, 'I'll have to break you.'

Gary was giving me a peculiar feeling. It was something about the way he was enjoying himself, the petty pleasure he was taking in his role. Something about his swagger. The feeling was envy. It seemed so easy to play the villain, as Floyd had suggested, the lines came out so smoothly. I wanted that sense of poise, that sneer hovering about the lips that Charlie was working to perfect. It was an attractive idea, to be a powerful man in a restricted area, on the fringes, as I thought, of normal society. This was a kind of place I had never guessed at. The underworld, Gary had said. It was as mysterious and yet as *close* as the plague victims beneath the heath, as the pipes running underground, as the murky bottom of the lake in France. Gary was a pike in this lake, swimming around happily, baring its teeth now and then. Archer was a big shark, in its prime.

'The studio' was a grand name for a bare, medium-sized room with a large double door, padlocked, which Charlie said opened on to a back street. There were metal briefcases along one side of the wall, some lights next to what looked like a large white umbrella in a corner, and a video camera on a tripod facing the doors, as if waiting to capture on film anyone who should happen to force their way in. Against another wall there was a TV, a video and some other equipment. A big locked cupboard, like a wardrobe. It all looked functional, and undramatic.

I heard Melinda again, interrogating Melody, 'What video? What game?' telling Floyd, 'He made a film of Billy.' I ignored the voice. I would be careful, watch but not get involved. Investigative journalist.

Greig and Charlie were taking the camera off the tripod, Charlie bragging about his knowledge of it.

'You and Bill do something,' he said, 'I'll film you.'

This had the effect of leaving us speechless. We stared at each other self-consciously.

'Do something then,' yelled Charlie, 'say something, have a look in the cases.'

Greig, nettled, opened one of the metal briefcases while I watched. Camera equipment. He picked up a lens and looked at Charlie through it, I picked up a camera and took a picture of him looking at Charlie, who continued to film both of us.

'Let me try filming,' said Greig, '*you* do something, big mouth.' Greig took the camera and settled it on his shoulder. 'Go on,' he said, mocking, 'do something then.'

'Watch me now,' said Charlie, opening another of the cases, trying to keep the initiative, 'watch me now.'

Unlabelled videos, uninteresting black boxes. Charlie took a few out and turned them over, talking to me or to himself, 'Not much here, don't know about these . . .'

'Why don't we put one on?' I said.

'Go on,' Greig was eager, 'go on put one on the TV.'

He swung the camera inexpertly from side to side as I fiddled with the TV and video and Charlie continued to work his way through the cases. The fuzzy screen abruptly revealed a small bare bottom moving up and down. Charlie looked over his shoulder and wrinkled his nose scornfully. 'That's crap, J.T.'s got much better stuff than that, a whole library of it in his shed.'

Greig told him to shut up and open another case.

'This is more like it!' I looked round to see that the case was full of magazines. He was making appreciative noises as he turned the pages. Greig began to move in for a close up.

'My turn to film,' I said.

I took the camera, made it comfortable, put my eye to the viewfinder. I adjusted the focus, placed Charlie and Greig as I wanted them in the frame. Greig was grabbing a magazine from Charlie. The feeling was disarming, the sense of security in having my face obscured by the camera, the sense of control, to be watching them, dissociated from them. I panned around the room a little, ignoring their noise, and when I looked again they were throwing punches at each other. This was not like the childish fight Charlie and I had once had, this was more earnest violence. As I continued to film, Charlie, kicking wildly, came in close to Greig and tried to wrestle him to the ground. Greig, without much trouble, moved inside his arms and got a hold round his neck. Suddenly, he was holding Charlie's head firmly and was punching him repeatedly in the face. All Charlie could do, dripping blood now, was try to ward off some of the blows.

Still, behind my camera, I did not intervene. I was more curious than concerned. Both my curiosity and Greig's ferocity seemed inappropriate, opposite extremes, but we continued to do what we were doing.

The voice came from behind me.

'Are you getting the hang of it, Bill? Are you getting a feel for it?'

Hampered by the camera, I turned round slowly. Archer stood in the doorway, an eyebrow raised. For once his face was almost expressionless, noncommittal, as if he hadn't yet decided on his reaction to what he saw. What did he see? Three young boys in a mess of pornography and video equipment, one filming, two fighting. What could he do, a man like Archer, but smile? Confounding my expectations, he remained impassive. His voice, when he spoke again, having left me a decent time to answer, was solemn.

'It seems you have hidden depths Bill, doesn't it? What a good film-maker you might become, so short of scruples. What would Melinda say? When I knew Melinda, her standards were high. I even suspected her of lowering them in order to allow me to touch her. This man Floyd, this dull, inquisitive man she has taken up with, he is her type. He wouldn't approve of this either. Nor, I need hardly tell you, would your parents, although, God knows, Lucy and Eldon had more to recommend them than Melinda and Floyd. They wouldn't be very proud of you, would they?'

In my experience of Archer I had never seen him so subdued. I didn't know how to react. Fortunately it didn't matter, for once he was not pushing and prodding for a response, he seemed to require no reaction. Eyes on me, he was silent, apparently following some private line of thought until, taking a couple more steps into the room, he visibly altered his mood, looking now at Greig who had released Charlie, but was still looking belligerent.

'Greig,' he said, 'delighted. I must have Charlie invite you to one of my parties, I think you'd find it interesting. There are some people you should meet. Meanwhile, why don't the three of you clear up a little,' he had managed to work up to some faint amusement by now, 'or I have a feeling Gary might lose his temper.'

Until I was about seven or eight, I misheard the word 'terrorist' as 'terriblist'. Terriblist bomb kills thirty. Terriblists storm ferry. Terriblists in hostage crisis. When that was eventually cleared up for me, ('For goodness' sake,' said my father, 'haven't I told you about the importance of words?') I became confused about people claiming responsibility for murders. Why not arrest them then? I assumed claiming responsibility was like owning up, and it made you immune because you had done the decent thing.

I'm not sure that my grasp of world affairs has noticeably improved since then. Today's paper lies beside me now. (Most apt of verbs.) Here is some more of the dross from which I make my money.

Tiny Tina has terrific tits! They wouldn't let Tina be a nurse because she's too small. Small?!! Looks to us like she's bursting out of her uniform!

That is my daily work, read by millions. Alliterative patter for the near illiterate. The product, in a sense, of everything that has happened to me in my life so far. Discomforting, to think that the years of my experience have combined to produce those lines. A long gestation period for something (no offence meant, Tina) so unattractive. More a case of constipation than of pregnancy. It would be interesting if my reminiscence uncovered a reason for my present work, but it would not really be relevant to my purpose. My purpose, as far as I understand it, is to do something my father might be proud of. I never changed him, failed to save him, so what else is there? When I look at the paper beside me, the old question, What would my father say? returns to me. Archer would laugh. He always had a disconcerting ability to expose other people's frailties.

Thirty-two

'I don't want to play at being your father, that's a role I don't cherish.'

'So don't. Don't play at being my father. My father is dead.'

I might not have spoken. Dull, inquisitive Floyd continued to look into his tea. 'But I have to say a few things. I have to ask a few things. What were you doing there, messing around with videos in a place like that, with people like that? Do you think it's a game we're all playing?'

'I don't know what you mean.'

'You do know.'

'I don't know what you're talking about. Who are you anyway? Who are you to be telling me about my friends and where I can and can't go?' His reluctance to show any kind of reaction was a goad, just as it had been when I used to try to please him. 'Melinda's lover,' I said, and curled my lips like Archer, or like Gary imitating Archer. 'Big deal.'

I don't know quite how we had got to this point, I admit things haven't proceeded smoothly up to this confrontation, but that's how it was, it just happened. The whole exchange was a non sequitur. I told Melinda where I had been, she told Floyd, and he started talking to me, all of a sudden, as if he was my father.

He made a small 'tch' sound, but his forgettable face remained expressionless.

'Billy, you and I have got on quite well together . . .'

The 'tch' was encouragement, a chink in the armour of indifference.

'Sure, you mean I've hero-worshipped you and you've patronized me. We've got on like a house on fire.'

Now a pause. A click of the tongue, and a significant pause; not bad. 'I've been trying to help you, Billy, that has always been my intention. If you have felt patronized then I'm sorry. Put it down if you like to unfamiliarity with children.'

It would have been nice to spot some acid in his voice at this point, but there was none, just an exasperating matter-of-fact tone. 'But you haven't *been* helping. Not as far as I know. What have you been doing? Nothing has been happening. It took *me* to find Jay and tell you about the studio and the shop and Gary.'

Floyd's eyes finally met mine. We looked at each other for about four seconds, and then he looked away, just before I was going to.

He said, 'Video City is one of eleven shops that Jay owns or part owns around London. Jay, who, at the very least, knows a lot of the same people as Archer. Significant combinations. I have photographs and a poor quality tape of him in a meeting with some shady people. Donny, Jerome's compère and Archer's house guest, may be some kind of liaison with them. I'm not yet clear who he works for. At first glance it looks like if any of these shops met difficulties it's the partners, people like Gary, who would get into trouble. Jay could probably claim to be clean. The speciality seems to be child pornography; the operation neatly covers recruitment, production and distribution. Drugs are probably involved to some extent too. That's the kind of company you've been keeping, and the kind of world you've been dipping into.'

A piece of shit on a school desk. This is one of those moments that still floats to the surface of my memory now and then to humiliate me. At the time however, my reaction was ungracious. I shrugged, and nodded slowly, as if unimpressed, until a thought occurred to me.

'My father wasn't involved in all that.'

'No.'

'Then why did he die?'

'I don't know, Billy. Why does anyone? It's possible that he found something out, or that he turned down an offer of some sort. Your father's retail proliferation might look very attractive to Archer. Or maybe Archer had always borne a grudge, and he found himself able to do something about it. Or maybe Eldon died naturally. This isn't a detective story, Billy, it's not a TV cop show. Don't expect clues and logic and a developing picture, neatly fitting pieces of a jigsaw. It can be like that, but it won't be with Archer. Archer is enjoying himself, and that changes everything. You can't hope for sensible motives from someone who's doing something for the fun of it. Expect fuzziness and blurred outlines. Motivation is the last thing you should expect to find. Aren't you beginning to get a picture of Archer yet?'

I remembered Donny's words, the little beetle dressed all in black, 'Funny money is J.T.'s gift, making money and having fun at the same time.' And I remembered the boy in the playground striding up and down, creating a channel in the crowd, 'Fuuu-cking hell.' 'Yes,' I said to Floyd, 'I suppose I'm getting a picture of him. It's hard to remember it all, it's hard to understand it.'

'Just be grateful if you get a hint of chronology, the syntax of events. That's a good start, if you can get that much. Don't worry about meaning. Don't look for the source of the river, that's someone else's job, you're after which way it's flowing and where it's going, that's hard enough.'

I nodded again, not really understanding. 'I'm sorry for what I said.'

Floyd had finished his tea, and had no tea leaves to examine. He looked up, pushed out his lower lip a little. 'I haven't really been keeping you informed. You should be aware of developments at least, if only to persuade you to be a little more cautious. All I'm saying is, don't do anything without talking to me first. Will you promise me that much?'

I promised, insincerely. I was impressed by what he had said, by the seriousness he had lent to my suspicions, but I felt no fear. I had seen nothing but a glimpse of a video, the sex of its participants almost indistinguishable, let alone their age. Some photographs years ago. The magazines were sometimes funny, and elsewhere more baffling than shocking. I was unrepentant about what I had done. I felt unthreatened. This underworld so far looked no more dangerous than the lake in France.

I asked, 'What's your next plan?'

Floyd, for the first time, smiled. 'My next plan is to test this absurd theory of ours about Archer. If there's any truth in it at all then we might see something interesting. I've enlisted some support.' His smile was generous, complicitous. 'It's always pleasing to be able to move on to the offensive.'

A creak in the dark made me sit up in bed with an intake of breath. Unthreatened? My perceptions changed at night. I gazed at the dim shapes in the light provided by the slim gap in the curtains. A bulky cat, a hunched man, a sack stuffed with something unmentionable. Nothing there. I told myself perhaps it was Kim at the door, Kim coming to wake me and slip in beside me, to give our slightly stagnant relationship a jolt. I lay back, intending to dwell on this thought, but my mind was travelling independently down a receding chain of associations. I was looking at the sky in my garden with Kim, it was before a dinner party, at a time when my life was uncomplicated. The consoling height of the stars, taller far than any earthbound giant. The spooky shed, smelling of decay, which now housed according to Charlie, Archer's private video collection. I left the shed, made uneasy by that thought, and looked up to find the stars changing, becoming linked by thin lines of light, a net above me, I was one of the stars in it, linked to Charlie and to Greig, to Kim and to Gary, to their parents and my parents and Floyd and Melody and Jerome and Jay, the net just spread and spread from the moon at its centre, and the face in the moon was Archer's.

THE ALCHEMIST

Thirty-three

Deaths, nightmares and ventures into different worlds notwith-standing, school continued. Its character gradually changed for me over my first year there. It ceased to be a source of anxiety and became something like the supermarket or the graveyard: a source of reassurance, a place to relish for its predictable demands, for the continually renewed knowledge that its ups and downs involved no risk.

Two-faced Fairfax to his class: 'There will now be an oral examination.' A shift in his tone as we rumbled discontentedly: 'I don't care if it's the end of term. I wouldn't care if it was the end of the second millenium *today*.' His raised voice was not too worrying, he didn't seem to be in a mood to work himself up into a rage. 'History,' quiet again, 'as should be obvious,' smiling now, 'goes on.'

The subject was the causes of the Civil War, which we had been studying for most of the term. He began to fire questions at people, randomly picked. These tests were notorious, nothing was worse than to be picked and get a question wrong. He would ask another question, and if that couldn't be answered another, all the while getting redder in the face, more disgusted, his affable tone becoming full of rage, as if each silence or incorrect answer was an insult to him, until it became impossible for his victim to think rationally or to remember anything at all.

'Do we have your attention, Billy?'

'Yes sir.'

'And your answer? Would you care to favour us with that?'

To be put on the spot like this would usually be enough to make me nervous at least, but today I looked straight back at Mr Fairfax without concern.

'Could you repeat the question please?'

After a short pause he said, 'You are a tenant farmer in Durham.

You have been plucked from your quiet life to fight for Oliver Cromwell. How do you feel about this?'

With immaculate timing, the bell for the end of the period went at that moment, punctuation to Fairfax's question. There was silence in the room. All eyes on the teacher.

'Stay in for a few minutes please. Everyone else can go.'

The rest of the class disappeared, with surreptitious laughs or commiserations.

'Tell me Billy, what's your philosophy?' I was sitting at the front, Fairfax was leaning on the edge of his desk. He asked me this while the door was still closing on the last person out of the room. He continued before the door had quite shut. 'Never mind philosophy, never mind politics or religion, tell me *this*,' suddenly in his eagerness he was like Jerome interrogating a sinner, 'do you believe in a world outside yourself? Do you think I still exist after you've left the room?'

I was caught unawares by this line of questioning. A world outside myself. What came to mind was not so much Kim, who was swimming in the tournament in the afternoon, or Melinda and Floyd, worrying about my rash actions, what came to mind was Video City, a world outside myself and outside most of my experience, just touching me marginally, like the first symptoms of a disease.

'Yes,' was my impatient answer to Fairfax, 'of course I do.'

'Good,' he was pleased with my impatience. 'I can't stand talking to solipsists, waste of time and breath. All right then Billy,' he stood up and looked down at me, face creasing like crushed paper, 'I'm supposed to be your tutor, whether you like it or not, tell me how your life-plan is mapping out.'

'Life-plan?' I shook my head, surprised again. When was he going to ask why I wasn't concentrating in his lesson? 'I don't know.'

'Very wise, most of it happens by default anyway, to most people. But think about it, if you believed in them, and you had one, do you see what I mean, how would it be mapping out?'

Someone had scratched their name on the desk where I was sitting. My finger followed its grooves, and my eyes followed my finger. 'I don't know,' I said, 'I don't feel that much in control of things, to say how they're mapping out.' I looked up, but I found his pouchy face inscrutable. His tone was friendly enough, but I couldn't tell if he was still nursing his irritation. 'Two-faced' didn't seem quite the word for him. I remembered the Great Pretender's old adage: we have more skins than a shop full of onions. Fairfax made me unsure how to react to him. He made me curious. 'What's *your* philosophy?'

'There was an advertisement on television once,' he said promptly, 'in which a former Police Commissioner announced of some tyre, "I am convinced it is a major contribution to road safety." Now I can no longer hear anyone in public life, any philosopher, fellow teacher or friend begin a sentence with the words "I am convinced . . ." without hearing them gravely continuing, '. . . it is a major contribution to road safety."' He was smiling now, pleased with my interest or pleased with himself. 'As you don't believe in life-plans, so I don't believe in philosophies. Not all-embracing ones anyway. Is that clear? Crystal clear or mud clear?'

'Mud,' I said, and he nodded as if that was satisfactory.

'Try to get in control of things,' he said. 'You need to if you're going to make something of your life, anything more than a name scratched on a school desk that is.'

My mother's phrase: 'Make something of your life.' Associated for me with thoughts of alchemy. 'Make something worthwhile', my father's words. The trouble is, I thought, but didn't say to Fairfax, the ingredients haven't much improved since I was using soy sauce, baked beans and cat's piss.

'You'd better go and have your lunch,' he said. His eyes were almost slits as he looked down at me. 'I suppose you're going to this awful tournament business. Think about what I said though, try not to take any wrong turnings.'

I found Kim in the dining hall having a salad, and talking to a boy I didn't know very well. I sat beside her and, to my satisfaction, she soon turned to me.

'This is Robert,' she said, moving her chair back to allow us to see each other, 'do you know him?'

We looked at each other with a degree of wariness. We shared one or two classes. 'No,' I said, 'not really.'

Being a friend of Greig's tended to exclude me from knowing many other people. School cliques were rigid, and to belong to one meant defining myself, at least in other people's eyes, quite narrowly. Greig and his friends were neither athletic nor academic, they – we – wore clothes that didn't quite conform to regulations, smoked in the café where he worked and talked relentlessly about sex and music and films we should have been too young to have seen. In fact, if I was objective, I understood Charlie's contempt when I had talked about Greig, and partly shared it. Charlie and I knew about more substantial non-conformity, guessed at more interesting infringements of the law. As a result I found myself trying to lead a double life, or a multiple one, as a member of Greig's clique, boyfriend of Kim, some compromise between the two when necessary, and an interloper in Archer's world. Increasingly, I made myself nervous: I had led Greig to Video City, had discovered the pleasure of filming, failed to prevent a fight between two supposed friends of mine, and had been intrigued by the videos and the lurid magazines. 'Don't look for a motive,' Floyd had said. Even my own motives were not entirely clear to me. To be at home in the bedroom I continued to keep obsessively ordered was still an ideal, because there nothing was asked of me, and there were no responsibilities to consider. Tension could be relieved in irregular scraps of diary, and equally irregular and now seldom answered letters to Marie.

All of which is simply to explain why I had to tell Kim that no, I didn't know Robert very well, and to explain also, at least in part, why we looked at each other without friendliness, with a degree of wariness.

'Robert's swimming this afternoon, too.'

I nodded.

'And we're doing the chemistry project together.'

Robert, to give him his due, was beginning to look uncomfortable, but Kim seemed suddenly determined to elicit some reaction from me. I just nodded again, and then turned my attention to some lumpy mashed potato on my plate.

Kim and her friend exchanged some words, and then Robert got up and left, with a short 'Bye'. Kim moved her chair back in. She was wearing a black skirt and a red cotton sweater. The last time we had touched was a couple of days ago, a goodnight kiss.

She said, 'Billy, it's stupid, we've got nothing in common really and I see too much of you anyway. I just want to be your friend, I don't want to go out with you.' She paused, but I was still slow to react. 'Is that all right?'

'Yes,' I said, 'I know what you mean. I think you're right.' Our second romance had lasted six months. The first thing I thought was that I was destined to be stuck for the foreseeable future on four points. The second thing was that I was doing a pretty poor job of staying in control of things. We finished our meals in silence and then I wished her luck in her races.

The splash of a dive, fumes of chlorine, echoing shouts, echoing back and forth as if in some indecipherable aural game; the sounds and smells of a swimming pool always induce in me now a mixture of feelings. Jealousy, fear, different kinds of excitement.

Backstroke was Kim's preferred stroke, and from the gallery where non-competitors and a few parents were sitting, I watched her, apparently effortless, pull ahead of the others in the race, arms sweeping back, brushing her ears. I could just about see her face, she was alternately biting her lip and dragging in breaths. Her breasts were moving underneath her turquoise costume. Her legs straight, her feet hidden under a white bowl of water. Dolphin. I wondered if she knew how graceful she was in the water, if anyone had told her. Robert, perhaps, who was sitting with the other swimmers on a bench beside the pool in his brief black trunks.

After she had won her race and received her applause and her medal she went to sit next to him. They chatted.

There was a click and the whirring of an automatic wind-on beside my ear. 'Hasn't she done well? Melinda will be proud.'

Melody wore a black cotton suit covered with eyes. I tried to conceal my pleasure at seeing him. Floyd had hoped he would be present. It was the first stage of his plan, our move on to the offensive.

'Do you like my suit, Billy? Hand painted you know.' As he shifted to give me a better look, some of the eyes seemed to wink at me. 'Not by me I should say, not one of my talents I'm afraid, although good Lord, I've tried and tried. Is it something you've put your hand to? Painting?' He answered himself before I could open my mouth. 'No, I'm forgetting, what am I thinking of, the written word is your field, isn't it? That's where you shine brightest, like your dear father, although of course he never quite realized his greatest ambition, to write novels like the ones he loved. But so few of us do, don't you think? Realize our greatest ambitions I mean. That's a gift that is given to so few of us.'

He raised his camera again as the boys lined up for their race. His round face and large hands made the camera seem even smaller than it was. But his long fingers had a delicate touch.

'Just look at them,' he said, 'I wish I was still as thin as that.'

Melody might have appreciated a recent feature of mine, headlined: 'How Mums To Be Can Stay Slim. Pregnancy Without Those Extra Pounds!'

'I expect you have some friends among them, Billy,' he said. 'Is Greig a swimmer?'

'My friends aren't really interested.'

Melody gesticulated as the boys dived in. 'But it's so invigorating! What *are* you and your friends interested in, Billy? Cameras? Books? Computers? Gadgets? You must come to The Circus of Delights you know, I do like to see young people there. And it's changed rather a lot since you were last there. I think I can promise, if you'll excuse my pride, you'll be impressed.'

'I'd love to come,' I said, and registered his surprise. 'Will you be there at all this weekend?'

'Yes,' he recovered himself quickly, 'Sunday would be particularly convenient, if you're agreeable.'

'I can't make Sunday, I am sorry, I was thinking of Saturday afternoon. I've got a dental appointment, but I might come after that.' Melody was looking thoughtful. Already I felt I had him on the defensive. 'I'll bring some friends with me of course.'

He nodded. 'Of course. Of course. Well I have some other commitments, at Sweet Surrender you know, but I'll try to be there to meet you. I wouldn't want to miss you.'

He grinned. The grin was his trademark as the smirk was Archer's. My sense of control, which had just begun to materialize, promptly fled. Even when he left, shortly afterwards, I felt that he was still watching me, through the eyes that covered his back.

Thirty-four

Mrs Larbey, for a variety of reasons, felt ill at ease. First of all, she was not only over the water, in

North London, but she felt herself to be in a hostile zone. The
kind of place that one read about, or saw on the news. Hardly the
kind of place to visit. Prudently, she thought, she had chosen to
wear no jewellery and carry no handbag. As a result of this, she
was annoyingly conscious of her hands and she had decided, in
spite of the warmth, to put them in her pockets. She clasped her
jacket protectively around her middle. Even more unsettling than
the area itself was the purpose of her visit. She was to confront
Jay, who when they had last met had seemed so charming, with
her fears about her sons. Well, not Gary. He was old enough to
look after himself, for better or worse, but Charlie's behaviour was
becoming alarming. His attitude to his parents, his absence from
school, his drinking, his unsuitable girlfriends, his erratic moods.
She strongly suspected him of sniffing glue.

The list of Charlie's misdemeanours lengthened as Mrs Larbey
proceeded. She cut it off with an equally unconsoling thought: what
was worst of all was that she didn't know who to turn to. Not her
husband, who ridiculed her anxiety and barely spoke now to either
of his sons. Not Archer, who she knew to be a friend of Jay's, and
whose parties she had heard hints of from Charlie. That left Floyd,
the stranger who had seemed to know all her fears even before she
had expressed them.

She almost wished she had worn her watch. She guessed that
she was going to be early. That meant that she would have time
to somehow kill before her appointment. Nervously, she looked
about her. Deep in her pockets her hands were clasped into pudgy
fists.

Floyd deliberately arrived half an hour early, in order to have a look
at the place before I came. He didn't particularly expect Melody
to turn up, but he always thought it best to be prepared. Some
boy scout, he thought, as he searched in his pocket and found
only one inadequate twenty pence piece for the parking meter.
Above the door of the shop, in florid fairground style script, were
the words Circus of Delights. Foolish name, he thought, inviting
anticlimax. The July weather was muggy, the warmth like a layer
of clothing, promising a storm. His shirt stuck to his spine. Inside,
the refreshing coolness of the air made him smile briefly.

The interior was spacious, and the restrained displays were
apparently organized with aesthetic rather than commercial values

in mind. The shop had a theme which changed every month or so. This month it was the jungle, so creepers and lifelike snakes wound their way around the pillars and furnishings, and silks and cottons with African prints hung from the walls. In one corner there was a glass case, like a fish tank, containing tarantulas. Even after staring for a while, Floyd couldn't make up his mind whether the dozy, furry creatures were real.

He wandered like a curious shopper around the various displays. There were still some whimsical toys which might appeal to children as well as to executives, and one of the computers on show was devoting its high quality graphics to a game involving a car chase, but the character of the place had moved decidedly upmarket. Melody had extended his range, but he offered only a small choice within that range. He sold what was fashionable, whether it was cameras, textiles or designer accessories. He wanted to sell a lifestyle, he probably saw himself, Floyd thought, selling it to the very rich, on Sloane Street or the Brompton Road. Melody Pour La Maison. What made this idea interesting was that it didn't seem altogether consistent with Melody's character.

Having seen everything that was on show, Floyd left and walked around to the back of the building. He entered a café and had a word with someone who was nursing a capuccino and reading a paper, and then he returned to his Jaguar, parked at the front. He was satisfied that if Melody did appear, he or his employee would see him arriving.

Melinda, her feet on her desk, injected a little anxiety into her voice.

'I'm sorry, I know we only talked yesterday, but I just wanted to confirm that, what's his name, the Great Pretender will be able to make it.'

The voice on the other end was managing to contain its impatience. 'He's very reliable, madam. We do our best to provide an efficient service. In fact we only have reliable acts on our books.'

'Yes I know, you were very highly recommended by my friend, but you see it's an hour before he's due to appear and I expected him to come early, to, you know, to prepare and so on. There's no problem is there?'

'No problem at all, madam. And I do assure you that if there is any difficulty you will receive a full refund and a free booking of any other act from our agency at some time in the future.'

'Thank you, that's very reassuring.'

Melinda put the phone down and then, after a moment's thought, picked it up again and dialled another number. 'Pat? How's it going?' She listened for a moment, and laughed. 'Yes it sounds dreadful, thank God Kim and Billy are too old for that sort of thing. Listen, I don't think he's very likely to get there, is that going to be all right? Do you have contingency plans?'

Melinda listened for a moment and then said her goodbyes. She took her feet off her desk and looked up at the clock thoughtfully, as if making calculations. She smiled.

Archer was back on his old form. 'How's Nita?' I asked, just before he had me open my mouth for the entry of his probe.

'Nita is a disappointment, Bill. I warn you, never take a woman at face value, never put your trust in one, they just can't take the pace. She's not interested in dental surgery, she's not even interested in any other surgery, not any more, she's decided it's too intense, too competitive, too this, too that. I tell you this is not the woman I met, not the ambitious woman with a head on her shoulders and an attractive streak of ruthlessness. Words, Bill, it was all words. She's got no grit, and what's even worse, no ideas, no drive. I tell you that woman, she still talks about being a consultant, aiming for a professorship, but it's all talk and no action. You watch, she'll settle at this rate for being a country quack GP. All she's ever been after is a family. She's unstable is what she is, I'm afraid, there's no point in mincing words. No, don't talk to me about Nita, our relationship is on the rocks, I don't mind telling you. You just learn from my mistakes Bill, that's my advice.'

All this was interspersed with comments on my teeth to his nurse, who he invariably addressed as 'darling' or 'my love'. He straightened eventually and looked down at me.

'You could be in for some expensive work here, Bill, I hope Melinda can afford it. I'm surprised at her sending you privately at all in fact, it's not like her.'

I had my answer ready. 'I wanted it to be you. I hate their dentist up there, he drills everybody.'

Archer raised an eyebrow. 'Flattering. I knew a real butcher once. He gave his patient an anaesthetic that was slightly too strong. This woman had a bad habit of chewing at the inside of her mouth, tugging at the skin. Well she couldn't feel a thing you see, the side of her face had gone completely numb. Can you see the punchline coming? She couldn't. Chewed all the way through her cheek.' He laughed. 'Still, you don't want to hear grisly stories do you? That's not why you're here at all.' Now he winked knowingly. 'We'll just clean them up a bit for you.' He re-entered my mouth, and re-entered his monologue. 'Yes, I'm afraid I've run out of patience with Nita. Now me, as you know, I'm an ideas man. Ideas in action, that's me. I'm in a long line of people like that. Role-modelling, you know, is crucial. Were you aware that Newton was going to turn Cambridge into a centre for the study of alchemy? Another ideas man you see, another willing to put things into practice. Like your dear old dad, two of a kind Eldon and me, except that he was no businessman. Not that I hold that against him. What I liked about him was that he was always *reaching*. Over-reaching perhaps, eventually, but that's always the hazard. He should have teamed up, that would have saved his skin. His ideas, my business brain.'

Coincidentally or otherwise, this was the moment when my mouth became free again. 'He *was* a good businessman.'

Archer's amusement was unfeigned. 'Are we talking about the same Eldon Gunn?'

'He used to tell me, he was always telling me how he made a mint with his shares, and then got them all out at just the right time, and how he bought property and then that went up and up as well.'

'Did he boast about it? Well, we all have our foibles. He wasn't a modest man, your father. Quite right mind you, modesty is the last refuge of under-achievers.'

'Are you saying he lied to me about it?'

'Bill, your father's dealings were a combination of sheer luck and my advice. He didn't like his money being in shares, just making more money, he wanted it in something concrete. Fair enough, I told him, what about property development? That's how it happened. He was a dreamer your father, never a businessman.'

I was going to argue, when I remembered Eldon's extended fantasy about infiltrating Mills and Boon. Hesitating, I thought of something else. 'He never discussed business with you, he told me so. It couldn't have been your advice. Melody's maybe.'

Archer had his back to me. After a moment he turned round. 'Run along Bill, time you were on your way. I'm a busy man, I've got patients to see.'

'He told me he never discussed business with you.'

Archer was ushering me out. 'Don't believe everything you hear,' he said. 'I thought you knew that, Bill.'

Had he slipped up? Surely my father wouldn't have said such things to him. 'I like Archer,' he had told me, shortly before he died, 'but I don't really trust him.' He trusted Melody, or he seemed to at least until that final meeting. 'Keep both eyes on Melody.' I stored the idea away as something to tell Floyd, and then looked at my watch. It was four o'clock. At five o'clock Melody was supposed to be meeting me at the Circus of Delights in North London. At the same time, Jay was supposed to be seeing Mrs Larbey four miles away at Video City. At six-thirty the Great Pretender was due to give a performance at a children's party in West London. Meanwhile Archer had appointments to keep him busy until six. I imagined him abandoning a patient with a mouthful of mirrors, probes and polishers with a polite 'Just a moment, I'll be right back', and then dashing out of the surgery and jumping into his Mercedes, ripping off his white coat as he went, like Batman caught on the hop.

The thought made me smile, but I did not feel complacent. Archer had seemed calm, if more than usually intense. Was it possible that he would find a way to weasel through the elaborate test we had set him? If not, if Melody or Jay or the Great Pretender simply failed to show up for any of his meetings, then it was proof of nothing, but it would at least support our theories. But if everyone appeared, unruffled, at their appointed times, then Floyd and I would have to reconsider all our plans and suppositions.

Mrs Larbey smiled with relief. She wasn't as early as she had thought. She had only been looking at the videos for five minutes or so and here was Jay, a little breathless, as if in fact he was late, smiling his winning smile.

'Come into my office, Mrs Larbey. Do you have the time by the way?'

'I'm afraid not.'

Jay looked at his watch. 'Pity. I make it just past five, but I think I'm a bit slow. Anyway,' he looked up and ran a hand over his hair, pushing it off his forehead, 'good to see you, very good to see you. I can't give you long, I'm afraid, I've got to get down to Video Zoo by half five, I've got a manager whose dipping his hand in the till, they're not all as good as your Gary unfortunately. So how can I help you? Incidentally, is it all right if I call you Rose? It seems silly to be formal, I feel like a friend of the family.'

Taken aback, Mrs Larbey was slow to answer. Jay looked businesslike, in his baggy jeans, his bright tie with pink shirt and braces. His brusque air of efficiency was intimidating. She took her hands out of the pockets of her beige jacket and tugged slightly at the neck of her blouse.

'A drink,' said Jay, 'you must have a drink with me, Rose.' He opened a fridge by his desk. 'Beer, wine, Martini?'

'A small glass of white wine, thank you.' Jay poured this and opened a beer for himself while she continued. 'It's about Charlie, I'm rather worried about the company he's keeping and some of the habits he's acquiring.'

The wine was ice cold, and very refreshing. She drank it quickly. They talked, for about fifteen minutes she later estimated, about her younger son. Jay was helpful in a casual sort of way. His tone was objective, as if really the problem had very little to do with him, and Mrs Larbey felt unable simply to accuse him of being a bad influence. By his manner rather than what he said, he made her feel that there was nothing really to worry about. She was unprepared for this man, he had her off balance. Somehow, she thought, the interview doesn't quite have the right tone. But what did she intend? It was Floyd's fault, egging her on, and never telling her what she should say. Somehow it had seemed much clearer when he was explaining it. She stopped listening to what Jay was saying, just watched him, like an audience of one trying to puzzle out the plot of a difficult play: is he being flirtatious? Or mocking me by calling me Rose? Or hiding something?

Jay took a final swig from his bottle, and then stood up. 'Well, I hope I've helped. I want you to feel you can always come to me Rose, if you need advice, or anything at all. I'm well known in this area, for my advice.'

He held out his hand, and Mrs Larbey shook it. 'Thank you,' she said.

He looked at his watch. 'Twenty past five, must dash, do look around some more if you like.' As she opened her mouth to object he said, 'I insist. Ask the chap behind the counter. Got to go.' And he was gone.

At five-fifteen Melody came out of his office and greeted me with an extravagant wave. It looked as if it was an effort to lift his heavy red sleeve. He wore a long green coat, with a black collar, red sleeves and blue cuffs. On his head a large black skull cap, from which protruded a few wisps of his red hair.

'Billy, so glad you could come. What do you think of my little empire? Do you like it? I don't mind telling you I'm proud as a peacock.'

'It's lovely,' I said.

'Good, good, good. I knew you'd be impressed. Sorry I'm late, I've been incarcerated in that office for goodness knows how long, and now I have to rush off to Sweet Surrender in fifteen minutes. It's all go when you're a tycoon you know. But guess who I saw outside, from my window. Mr Floyd! He seems to be just sitting there in his car, shall we go and say hello?'

Not waiting for an answer, Melody marched out of his shop and across the road to the Jaguar, with me in his wake. His coat flowed about him, giving him the air of an impresario.

'My dear Mr Floyd,' he said, 'what ever are you doing out here? I've been looking at you sitting here since, well, it's an hour, isn't it? Would you care to come in, or are you happy in your beautiful old car?'

Floyd got out of his Jaguar. 'Has it been an hour?' He said. 'I was meeting Billy, I lost track of time.'

We all returned to the shop. I was almost running to keep up with Melody's demanding pace.

'Why don't you two have a browse, I must just pick up some things from my office.'

Melody moved away but Floyd accompanied him, and I followed them.

The office was painted in blocks of primary colours. Even his desk was inlaid with coloured panels. He sat behind it and then lifted its top and brought out some cans of diet coke, looking suddenly like an exuberant schoolboy in a classroom. 'Drink anyone? No?' He put the cans back and took out an old brown leather briefcase. I recognized it from the times he had been to see my father, to discuss business.

We all filed out of the office again. 'Well,' said Melody, 'we do seem to be running around today, don't we?' There was an extra quality in his exuberance: nervous energy and a sense of triumph bubbling together. Hadn't he guessed that Floyd would follow him now, on his supposed trip to Sweet Surrender? 'What can I show you now?' he was saying. 'I only have five minutes left. Mr Floyd, I expect you're interested in cameras, are you?'

For five minutes Melody played the salesman, with a relish that suggested it was a natural talent. With the generous discount he was offering – 'Well, a friend of Billy's is a friend of mine' – he very nearly succeeded in selling Floyd an expensive Nikon.

At precisely five-thirty however, like Cinderella hearing the chimes of midnight, he couldn't be persuaded to linger.

'Wait a moment,' said Floyd, 'just another moment, I'd like to see the new Pentax, to compare the two, haven't you a minute to show me that?'

Melody motioned an assistant over. 'I'm so sorry, I do have to go, if only you had come in earlier. Goodbye, goodbye, see you both soon I very much hope.'

As soon as he was out of the front door, swinging his case jauntily, Floyd gave the camera back to the assistant and followed him. We gave him a wave as we crossed the road, watching him get into his Alfa. He gave us a wave back. Floyd, still watching him, got his car keys out.

'I've had enough of discretion,' he said, 'we'll follow him bumper to bumper.'

'Floyd.'

'Mm?'

'I don't think we will.'

The Jaguar was clamped, a notice stuck to the windscreen warned us not to attempt to move it. Melody, doing a U turn in the road, gave us another cheery wave as he passed us.

Thirty-five

The post-mortem on our operation, our failed effort to get on to the offensive, was depressing. Melinda came home after us, by which time Floyd had made some calls, and pieced together the picture. He poured her a drink and refilled his own glass. Robert the swimmer was away that weekend, so Kim was there too.

'Fiasco,' said Floyd, 'we're no better off than we were before. All the appointments were kept, but in such a way that our theory isn't any less plausible than it already was.'

'How is that possible?' said Melinda.

'Dodgy alibis. Archer has a lot of friends. I just spoke to his nurse at the surgery. According to her, Archer saw no more patients after you Billy, although there were five scheduled. He claimed a stomach upset and closed the surgery.'

'Well, surely that's what we want to hear?' said Melinda.

'Not quite. When I told her I needed to know exactly where Archer was between four and seven, this nurse seemed happy to tell me. After closing the surgery she and Archer, wait for it, made love on the dentist's chair. Quite a common occurrence apparently. I mean with these two, not with dentists in general.' He sipped his drink. 'Although you never know I suppose.'

'She's lying,' I said.

And simultaneously, 'What about Nita?' said Kim.

Floyd answered me. 'I think she's lying too,' he said, 'but the point is not what we think, it's what we can prove. Or at least what creates a definite hole in Archer's story. That's what we're after, holes in stories. Archer's or Jay's or Melody's.'

Melinda: 'What about Jay then?'

'Mrs Larbey wasn't wearing a watch. I don't know if her sons advised her not to, or if it was just Jay's good luck, but it means that she is unreliable on timing. The assistant manager of Video City says that Mrs Larbey arrived at five and that Jay showed up a few minutes later and stayed for almost half an hour. Mrs Larbey had the impression that both she and Jay were early for their appointment, and that it may only have lasted about twenty minutes. But Jay seems to have confused her. She couldn't even tell me what he had said.'

'Confused her?'

'Somehow. Possibly something in her wine, although she was pretty agitated in the first place. Billy saw Melody at five-fifteen. We both saw him leave at five-thirty. I didn't see him arrive, although I was watching both doors, so we can't prove he wasn't in his office, as he said, and as his staff agree, from four o'clock.' Floyd finished his drink and settled deeper into his chair. 'Are you following me?' By the look of her face, Kim wasn't, and even I, who had been in on all the plans, was getting confused. I didn't mind confusion, it felt appropriate to what we were doing.

'Finally,' said Floyd, sounding weary now, 'the Great Pretender appeared out of thin air, appropriately enough, in a puff of smoke, at five past six. Unless we think that your friend Pat and eleven children are all in the conspiracy too, we have to accept that. His act incidentally went down very well. And Pat sends her regards.'

There was a short silence. The chink of ice, the sound of Kim swallowing her coke.

'And Jerome?' said Melinda. 'Couldn't we have roped him in?'

'How? Where is he? Who is he? Jerome seems to have gone underground.'

Underground. Perhaps he was down among the pipes criss-crossing beneath my feet, still preaching his message, 'Division is human, unity divine,' in subterranean caverns, to large-eyed cave dwellers. Somewhere beneath us these credulous people were worshipping, people who had surrendered their autonomy. I felt as if I was one of them, somehow implicated in Archer's grand design, and simultaneously I felt a great surge of impatience with Floyd's careful manoeuvring. Hadn't I caught Archer out myself earlier that day? Couldn't I do it again? After all by now, I thought, I am becoming familiar with the underworld.

'Shall I sum up?' Melinda had broken another silence. 'We've got Archer in his surgery from four till seven. We've got Jay at Video City from five till five-thirty, and thereafter at the Video Zoo. We've got Melody at The Circus of Delights from four till five-thirty and thereafter at Sweet Surrender, and we've got the

Great Pretender at Pat's party from five past six till quarter to seven. Witnesses include Mrs Larbey, you two and my friend Pat. Not a hole in sight, for all our suspicions. Who wants another drink?'

'What would be a hole?' I said.

'A hole,' said Floyd, 'would be an inconsistency. Someone failing to be somewhere where they should be. Or someone behaving in an uncharacteristic way. Melody and Archer turning out to have business links beneath their supposed enmity, Archer turning out to be at the bottom of Jay's video operation. You see what I mean? All we have at the moment is a few acquaintances in common between them – you, the Larbey family, this man Donny, some others I've come across. Not proof of anything at all, let alone our more far-fetched theories. You and I, Billy, are going to have to do some serious research. I want you to come on a visit with me.'

Melinda looked displeased at this, as if Floyd had transgressed some agreement between them, but I was not much concerned. I would go on Floyd's visit, but my fluctuating faith in him had diminished again. My mind was on his earlier words: someone behaving in an uncharacteristic way . . . links and significant combinations. There were fragments of ideas in my mind, disparate events and snatches of conversation that I needed to fit together to form a plan. I remembered Floyd's image of a jigsaw puzzle with pieces missing, and false ones thrown in. I like analogies, they make things seem so much more manageable. It was just a question of putting things together in the right manner. Disappointed with Floyd, I was confident that I had the skills. Not just a familiarity with the underworld, but also my well-remembered affinity with labyrinths.

Thirty-six

We drove down a narrow road lined by vans in front of forecourts on one side, and by the high, dirty shutters of the warehouses on the other. 'I'm bored', written in the grime. No one was there; the vans and forecourts were empty, railings encircled nothing but bare gravel and tarmac, and the jointed metal shutters looked like fused, immovable fixtures. Still, I felt uncomfortable in the slow moving Jaguar, conspicuous. Grey, apparently opaque windows stared at us; the sky, the same grey, seemed to conspire. Floyd's words, 'These will all be flats soon, warehouses are heading out of the city,' sounded treacherously surreal.

Occasional splashes of colour trumpeted company names and logos, in red and blue, two shades of green, brown and orange. 'uality at low prices' announced one torn poster. I pondered this as we passed it; it seemed to take ten minutes, and all I could think of was the word 'Duality'. Duality at low prices? I broke the silence and asked Floyd, but he just laughed at me.

He parked the car outside a warehouse that seemed indistinguishable from all the rest. Once I was out of the Jaguar's luxurious interior, I felt that it fitted in better with its surroundings: dirty cream on grimy grey. He took a key from his pocket, a single small Yale, and faced the shutter. Watching him, I felt an unbidden touch of pity, it seemed so absurd to stand in front of such a big door with such a small key. Unhesitating, he fitted the key to a lock and pushed open a realistically sized door within the larger one. He stepped in and turned on a light, and I followed him, blinking as the fluorescent bulbs flickered, revealing the preposterous contents of the warehouse.

'Here we are,' said Floyd, 'home.'

There was a game I used to play, with Kim or Charlie or both, which involved constructing shelters out of complex arrangements of tables, chairs and blankets. We barely used one or two rooms, so it was possible to appropriate them, drag in extra furniture from elsewhere, strip beds and create a different world inside the house. There was a tartan blanket which did odd things to the light, particularly electric light, colouring it, making it glow, and excluding it in patches altogether. We used to crawl in semi-darkness among the furniture, and we devised elaborate games, with passwords and costumes involving old and mismatched clothes filched from my parents' wardrobes. But mostly I remember sitting or lying beneath the blanket, talking or dreaming of being in another place. In a refugee camp, like the ones I had seen on the news, in a cavern underground. I found that I could scare Kim, and even Charlie, if I got into my stride with a vivid fantasy. After Joseph's death, one in particular became a favourite: we were in tunnels beneath a cemetery, between the coffins, among the bodies. Here was a shaft of light from a grave waiting to be filled, look up and see the faces of the mourners looking down. I can still see them now, elongated, bony and white, large eyed, more scary somehow than corpses. I was always an enthusiastic fantasist.

Charlie's visions were less gothic and more violent, Kim's had a touch of the surreal. The shelter was on the back of a huge elephant, she said, lumbering up the motorway to visit my grandparents in Romford. Couldn't we feel it swaying from side to side? Or it was on a towering pillar rising out of the street next door to my house. If we left the shelter we would fall and fall and fall, and land eventually in the tree in my garden. Then why is it dark? I wanted to know. Because we are so high we are in space, she said, among the stars.

But the carpet was always beneath our fingertips, soft green pile, no matter what we said, and when we did leave the shelter it was to have a biscuit and a cup of tea, or to watch television, or to find a game in my room, or to tell my mother that we were bored. 'Well, clear up your mess in there,' she might say, or, if she was bored too, she might come and admire it. Once she crawled through it with us, an honorary player of our game. 'What is it?' she said, 'Isn't that obvious? It's a space shuttle, rocketing away to the furthest edge of the universe. Just don't touch anything, because it's fragile, don't even breathe too hard, or we'll never even get off the ground.'

None of our fantasies seemed much less likely than what I saw now. The same tables and chairs stacked in new shapes, partly covered by dustsheets but, by the look of things, still in use. Empty coffee cups stood around, leaving rings on the polished wood that would have infuriated my parents. All the furniture of the house was here. Sofas and armchairs gathered in paranoid clusters, chests of drawers piled on top of each other like oversized filing cabinets, beds propped upright, looking foolish and exposed, their blankets folded into packing cases. Carpets in musty smelling rolls leant against each other, lanky confidantes. It was like a proof I had always suspected, but never really expected to find: the fragility of my life was on show here. This *was* my former life, removed from me and stored away. I felt a surge of despair rising from my stomach up through my chest, locating itself in my throat in a nauseating ball of pain. It was the starkness of the electric lights that hurt me. It was the random, flung together state of things. The casualness, the casual brutality of it. I thought of the toy town I had built in my room, and then recklessly destroyed one day with Charlie, and I felt again my furious, impotent, too late repentance.

'Come on,' said Floyd, not looking at me, 'it's possessions we're after, not furnishings.'

Desolate, I remembered Archer's description: dull, inquisitive Floyd, and I felt that it was just. I followed him reluctantly.

The next room was not so big, and was even more cluttered. Cases three deep, full of books and bric-à-brac, lined one wall, while the white boxes which were the fridge and cooker and dishwasher and washing machine advanced from the other. The computer and the word processor sat on the freezer, owlish. We made our way along a narrow cleared path through this room to a final one, a small office, in which my father's photographic equipment had been set up. The enlarger stood on the desk next to a sink, beside which there were some plastic trays, a clock, and a black plastic bag. On a shelf there were three large bottles.

Floyd had closed the venetian blind over the only window, and was now hanging some black material over it.

'I thought while we were here I might get you up to date on some of the bits and pieces I've gathered so far, including the latest snaps. Have a look at these while I get things ready.'

While he arranged various containers and bottles, I sat by the door and looked through the photographs he had given me. Donny, with his back to the camera, looked like a fist with a thumb sticking out of it. In each of five hardly varying pictures, he was standing at a bus stop with two men. In another four pictures he was walking in a park with, or at least near, another man. 'The two at the bus stop,' said Floyd, 'used to run a magazine for paedophiles. You know what they are?' I said I did. 'The one in the park has served six years for extortion and assault and almost certainly works for a North London gang.' He took the photographs back and gave me a few more. 'The reason I want you to see these,' he said, 'is to remind you that we're not playing Emil and the detectives. Here's Jay with another man from the same firm. They handle drugs as well as pornography. Jay's shops, with or without any connection to Melody, Jerome and Archer, make excellent distribution centres.'

One of the pictures had caught Jay very well. One hand was in his hair and the other was gesturing. His flowery tie was slightly off-centre and his whole demeanour was defensive. At first glance I thought he looked almost distraught, but when I looked closely at his wide eyes, and his mouth, in the act of speaking, I realized that it was excitement that was animating him. He reminded me of pictures used to advertise rollercoaster rides, faces transfixed by pleasure and fear.

Floyd was changing the lightbulb, replacing it with a red one.

'Right,' he said, 'these are the latest pictures. Close the door, Billy.'

I closed it, and Floyd, in complete darkness, began to unload the film from its cassette. At first I was bored. I had no idea what he was doing. I heard some snips as something was cut, and then some small, unidentifiable noises. I stopped trying to make out what was going on, and I was surprised when, within a couple of minutes, he suddenly opened the door, to let in the light from the next room. 'Now we're ready for developing,' he said, showing me a plastic tank like a miniature dustbin.

Three tall beakers, each containing a measured quantity of liquid, stood in a bath of warm water. Floyd tested the temperature of the first with a thermometer, and then poured its contents into the tank. He pushed the lid on and began to shake it as if it was a cocktail, referring now and then to a clock with a large second hand on the desk. After a short time he poured away the first liquid and added the next, and then quickly poured that away and added the third. He never explained what he was doing, beyond a few muttered words marking stages of the process, and I felt no inclination to ask him. Apart from the fact that I was still annoyed with him, my interest was growing, and an explanation might have ended it. What intrigued me was precisely my ignorance of the significance of his actions, his strict obedience to the clock and the thermometer, his manipulation of the different chemicals.

When he had placed the tank into the sink, and directed a hose into the bottom of it, he stood back with a satisfied nod. 'We have a little while. Shall we have a look at the computer now?'

We went back together into the room full of packing cases and electrical equipment. 'I'm told there's a point somewhere back here,' said Floyd. He slid, irreverently I thought, over the dishwasher and then sprawled across the freezer as he reached down behind it. This was worse than the coffee stains on the table. My mother would never have allowed him to do this. I imagined him in our kitchen lying across the units with his legs in the air while Lucy tried to find the right words to deal with his unusual behaviour.

'Got it!' he said finally, and then he slid back towards me, into the narrow path between the cases and the freezer, and he switched on the computer.

'There's something you might be able to help me with,' he said, 'with a bit of luck.'

'Oh good.'

If he noticed my sarcasm, he didn't show it. From an inside pocket of his jacket he produced a disc. 'Do you know what this is?'

'Of course I do,' I said, 'I use them at school.'

'Of course you do,' he said, and loaded the disc. 'This is your father's, one of many. He seems to have relied quite heavily on his computer, I've found software relating to his work, his financial situation and the state of his backhand. It hasn't really done anything other than help me get to know Eldon rather better than I ever did before he died.' He glanced at me and I nodded, not allowing my face to change. He continued, 'This disc is different.'

As he spoke, some writing appeared on the screen: the name of the computer, the drive being used, and the number of kilobytes of memory remaining on the disc. The cursor winked in front of an arrow, waiting for a command.

'I'll show you the directory,' said Floyd, typing in some letters. Out of the blankness appeared columns of words, filling the screen. Reading them at random I saw 'ACCNT.FILE', 'DEV.FILE' and, to my excitement, 'JT.FILE'.

'Let's look at the J.T. file,' I said.

'OK,' said Floyd. 'Let's try.' His fingers moved over the keyboard again. The directory disappeared from the screen and, after a moment, the winking cursor reappeared beside the arrow, below a single word: 'CODE?'

'It's the same with every file,' said Floyd. 'Your father protected this disc with a codeword, or a code number, so I've never found a way in. I've used combinations of your name and his and Lucy's and your grandparents', I've tried dates of births and anniversaries, I've interrogated Mel for every significant place, time and person she could think of. Nothing. I can't find the key. I was hoping you might have some ideas.'

'Have you tried Archer? I mean the name, "Archer"?'

'Yes.'

'And Jerome?'

'And Melody, and everyone else you can think of, including Charles Dickens and most of his major characters. I thought Krook might be a good bet, but no.'

'Can it be more than one word?'

'Could be.'

'How about "Division is human, unity divine"?'

Floyd smiled slowly. 'The benefits of a fresh mind,' he said, and typed in the words. He typed quickly, using all his fingers. 'You should have asked me before,' I said. The computer hummed and the screen went blank again for a few moments and then another message appeared. 'INCORRECT CODE. WOULD YOU LIKE TO TRY AGAIN?' Beneath this were the letters Y/N, and another arrow, with the indefatigably winking cursor beside it. Floyd tried again, with the single words, 'division', 'unity' and 'divine', and then 'divine unity' and 'human division'. Each time the computer paused for a few tantalizing seconds, and then repeated the same message: 'INCORRECT CODE. WOULD YOU LIKE TO TRY AGAIN?'

When he had exhausted the different permutations of the phrase, Floyd gave up. 'Let's go back to the dark room,' he said.

He took the plastic tank out of the sink and withdrew from it, like a conjuror with an endless line of handkerchiefs, a dangling length of negatives. Using a clip he hung these from a coathanger beneath a shelf.

'Hair-drier,' he said, 'did your mother have a hair-drier?'

In a spirit almost of self-mockery, we went out again to face the piles of packing cases next door. By now it was familiar enough to seem homely.

'It'll be here somewhere,' said Floyd, 'everything electrical seems to be. I remember seeing it when I found the discs, months ago.'

'Maybe she took it with her,' I said, but even as I said it, I knew it was unlikely. It would be banal, it would be unpropitious, to take a hair-drier along when creating a new life for oneself. I suppressed a smile at this thought, and we began to look.

'I knew an old lady,' said Floyd, 'who left her neighbour, in her will, the contents of her fridge. It turned out to be frozen peas, a tub of margerine, and a half-empty tin of cat food.' He picked up a coffee percolater, looked at it, and replaced it. 'The neighbour was very touched.'

This time I laughed out loud, or giggled anyway. 'She wasn't the only one. I'm sorry,' I said, 'that's not funny at all.' But there was an edge of hysteria to my mood now. I found the stereo system, and an accompanying box full of records, tapes and compact discs. I looked through them, feeling like I was in a shop, in Melody's shop. I only had to imagine finding a sticker on a record, '£5.99, Bargain Buy', to start giggling again. Floyd found the video recorder, and a video of *The Maltese Falcon*. 'Shall we take this home?' he said, 'it's years since I saw it.' In one box, along with a kettle and a dismantled wine rack, I found a robot which, when switched on, shuffled forward a couple of steps, machine guns rattling in its chest, before expiring with an unhealthy croak. I had never seen it before, I assumed it was a private toy of my father's. I could imagine it marching across his desk, guns blazing, annihilating his rivals and the enemies he never talked about.

My mood swung unnervingly. I recalled the resolution I had reached the previous Saturday, after Archer had evaded our trap. More than ever I felt that it was time to prove my autonomy, time to take action of my own.

Floyd found the hair-drier, and within five minutes he had dried the negatives. Now for the first time he had a look at them, holding each end of the strip, his arms stretched wide, and moving it in front of his eyes. Now and then he nodded.

He laid out three shallow trays on the desk, and poured different liquids into each. The dark room began to smell of chemicals. I closed the door and there was a moment of near complete blackness before Floyd, darker than the darkness, switched on the faint red light. He adjusted his curtain to cut off a chink of daylight, and then he was ready to begin.

I watched with increasing excitement as my eyes adjusted. Floyd took a piece of print paper from a packet inside the black plastic bag, and placed it beneath the enlarger. He put the negative into position and then, checking his clock, he exposed it to the enlarger's cone of light. I was becoming excited because, for all Floyd's assured movements, I had the sense of an experiment taking place, one subject to time and temperature, involving darkness and light and different chemicals, judiciously applied. I was reminded of old games with sweets and chemistry sets. My father would have approved of Floyd's methodical style. Floyd took the print and slid it into the first tray. We watched silently. After about five seconds, something began to appear out of the whiteness. As the outlines took shape I thought again of Eldon, sitting at his computer years earlier, showing off its graphics to me. Out of the whiteness, the lines and shadows of the picture gradually appeared, becoming sharply defined, and Archer's face became recognizable. Simultaneously, I thought of another codeword for Floyd to try.

He took the print out of the first tray, allowed it to drip dry, and then put it into the second. He rocked it around for a while, and then lowered it into the third. 'Rock the tray for a while,' he said, 'and then take out the picture and give it a wash under the tap. I'll get on with the next one.'

Soon there were six large prints lying beside the sink, clammy to the touch, like cold, damp skin.

'Nita took them,' said Floyd, 'Nita has left Archer now.'

'Why?'

'I think she decided her life didn't suit her. That's what she said. And she gave me these.' He indicated the photographs.

On one arm of an armchair sat a boy, a year or two younger than myself. On the other arm was a girl, of about the same age. In between was Archer, smiling like a proud uncle.

Jay, in unmistakably the same surroundings, sat talking to Donny, whose hands were outstretched, palms upwards, as if he was explaining something.

A more general picture, a party in its early stages. I recognized Charlie and Gary, and the two children from the first picture. Donny had a video camera perched on his shoulder like a small animal. He had a drink in his free hand, and he appeared to be interviewing someone.

The last three pictures, perhaps selected by Floyd to avoid anything too shocking for me, showed the party degenerating into an orgy. Without hesitation, because hesitation would probably have changed my mind, I said, 'I've seen pictures like these before.' And I told Floyd about the burglary of Archer's house years earlier, the things I had seen there, photographs of strange games, and the fact that my father, just before his death, seemed to have been told about

223

it by Melody. It was an unburdening for me. The secret had been carried around for far too long. I should have told my parents the night after it happened, Archer should have allowed me to confess in his surgery shortly afterwards, I should have told Melinda and Floyd. Although I had ceased to worry about retribution, I had never forgotten the episode. Without any logical reason, perhaps just as an echo of my feelings at the time, the thought of it made me nervous and induced almost painful feelings of guilt.

Floyd, taking it for granted that Archer had engineered the burglary, was interested in his motive. 'He's always taken a personal interest in you,' he said, 'and in your family. Charlie was there too of course. I suppose it was a kind of test, and a way of scaring you both, making you think he had a hold on you.'

He was putting things away as he spoke, the trays and the chemicals which had reminded me of childhood games and experiments, and the old joke between my father and myself. 'Floyd,' I said, 'I've thought of another codeword. Try "Alchemist".'

In the next room, the machine hummed again, pausing again, as if reluctant to relinquish its secrets, then on to the screen came half a page of writing above a graph spotted with dates and figures. The document was headed 'J. T. Archer'.

Thirty-seven

The journey home was almost silent. I couldn't relax, inside I wasn't silent, I felt like a badly-tuned radio, receiving at various volumes incompatible voices, each of a different age or humour. The image of the warehouse was still echoing inside me, setting up new echoes and old memories, alongside thoughts about what we had discovered there, and what remained obscure.

The Archer file had been impenetrable to me, and Floyd, skimming over it, predictably had explained nothing. The file was his, not mine, he was in charge. He left me feeling like a child, unable to contribute to problems beyond my understanding. Dimly, I knew there was no logic to this: before I had resented him for doing nothing, now it was for doing too much. But logic was irrelevant. Archer had scared me for years, for all of my childhood, with his schemes and his presence. A movement of his lips. He had involved me in petty crime, inspired me to run away from my parents long before they left me. He had, possibly, killed my father. It was primarily Archer, I was convinced, who had systematically dismantled my life, displaced me, tipped me out of one existence and into another.

Logic was beyond me, all I had was an overpowering wish to build something new out of the rubbish of the old. This was the only logic left, to look forward, to step out of the warehouse. But before there could be a beginning, there had to be an ending. He had evaded the trap set for him by Floyd, but I had another idea, an altogether more audacious one than Floyd's. This idea began to grow above the other voices, in it I found increasing coherence, the invigorating simplicity of decision. If audacity was measured by climbing a tree, as Charlie and I used to, as my mother once did, then this idea, I thought, would take me to the highest branches.

In my bedroom I explained what I had in mind to Kim. There was potentially a part for her in my plan but, more importantly, I wanted her to be with me, because it was only right that she should be, in the old places, treasure-hunting again as we used to years ago, when our friendship was uncomplicated and effortless. I was self-conscious about what I was doing, closing a chapter, giving myself room to move on, and this made me feel justified, in control of events. It was as if I was starting to write my autobiography, starting a few steps, a few months, in advance of myself.

The neat circularity of my plan, I thought, made it flawless. It was 'The Journey to the Wreck' all over again, the unlikely assertion of normality, the even keel. What was needed, Floyd had said, was a connection between Archer and Melody, something to indicate at the very least that there was not necessarily enmity between them. I thought I could provide this.

'It's dangerous,' said Kim. This was a homework evening, not one on which she would be seeing Robert, and I had dragged her away from geography revision. She had a test coming up, and it was hard to make what I was saying sound more urgent than the questions she was worrying about.

'It might be dangerous,' I said, the solemn commando type, planning a vital mission, 'but I need your help. We'll leave a note for Floyd and Melinda, so they can find us if anything goes wrong.' I couldn't maintain the rational style, 'Don't you want to go back there? He's got no right to live there anyway, you know that, it's my house. And all I'm asking is that you sort of look out for me, it's not dangerous for you. We're not even going into the house, just into the shed. In and out in the dark, no one will see anything.' I sounded plausible, as Gary had in persuading me to break into Archer's house. In retrospect, the parallel between the two situations seems uncomfortably close, but at the time I didn't think about this. I was too overwhelmingly sure of what I wanted, too positive to allow any misgivings.

It was the same sense of what was right that made me want to visit my grandmother once more, before we carried out the plan. On the phone she said that was fine, she'd be delighted to see us, but that two of her friends were coming, two of her network, and we mustn't mind if they overlapped. I said we wouldn't mind. I liked the idea of meeting my grandmother's friends, of seeing a different side of her. In my earliest visits there had often been other people there, to whom I had been proudly introduced. As I got older however, and certainly since my move to Melinda's, space had been made so that Ethel and Roly could see me without distraction. With Roly's death, things would swing back to the way they had been, and my grandmother would surround herself with her friends.

'Things would swing back to the way they had been', this feeling existed alongside my wish to start afresh, somehow not contradicting it. I felt competent, large enough, like Archer, to contain contradiction. My eyes were open wider than usual, I was looking more closely at things and people. More than at any other time, I was playing the role of an investigative journalist, someone who could examine things closely and dispassionately, making something out of them, someone making something of his life.

Ethel's two friends were in their nineties, around the same age as the century. One was explaining to the other as we came into the room, 'His father died of something dreadful.' Ethel ignored this and breezily made the introductions before finding another two cups. No one felt ruffled. The age of Ethel's friends seemed to excuse them from any taint of social embarrassment. There was a touch of the hostess about my grandmother, a touch of formality in deference to her guests.

The tapestry was on the table in front of us, layered into a thick pile and unfolded to reveal its earliest scenes. Ethel in 1921, a baby in a white silk christening gown, family heirloom, beginning the long sequence.

'It looks as if everything that follows is the baby's dream,' said Kim.

Ethel's friends were interested in the period detail, commenting on the clothes of the family, parents and two brothers, who stood stiffly beside the baby.

Ethel apologized. 'This was early days of course, with the tapestry I mean, I hadn't got into my stride really. I copied from photographs you see, and didn't bother to change much. That's why they look a bit stilted.'

The features were crude, an expression defined by a couple of large stitches, but they were evocative. Self-conscious dignity. I seemed to see beneath the stitching the photograph, grainy purplish grey, shadowy, the four figures captured for one untypical moment and stuck that way for ever, in the gaze of their descendants. Beneath the photograph I saw the people, posing in the studio on a Saturday afternoon, bullied or flattered by the man behind the tripod. Like Archer, photographing me while babysitting, like the photographers I know now, with their naked models. My great grandfather, I was sure, would stand for no nonsense, 'No we don't want costumes, a plain backdrop thank you, just as we are I think, thank you.' For just a moment I had a sense of vertigo as I looked at this first scene of the tapestry. Baby, parents, grandparents. I saw the sequence moving, not forwards through the tapestry towards the fluky culmination of myself, Billy Gunn, but backwards in its inevitable process, stepping backwards indefinitely through generation after generation, becoming harder and harder to perceive. Torchlight, fading in the darkness but continuing, invisible, to climb the sky.

'It's good to preserve a few memories,' Ethel had said last time I was there, when I had learnt a little about my mother and a little about her. 'It's good to have a sense of movement in your life.'

I hadn't really understood her, absorbed in myself I had thought melodramatically only of my own experience, the effects of malign influence, death and abandonment, the difficulties attendant on change. Jolting, comfortless movement. This was different, movement as process, a new perspective. Something my father had tried to tell me when I was seven, visiting Joseph in his hospice. It was the perspective from the top of a tree, where there is infinitely more to be seen and more to be taken into account. My vertigo evaporated, replaced by a new feeling, one I had come across before, lingering in graveyards. Consolation.

Ethel's friends had begun to remember. Ethel, judging by her apologetic smile at Kim and me, had heard it all before.

'When I was four I was given a doll and I took it home and sat with it beside the stove, because it was warm there and this was Christmas. Winter. I sat the doll down beside me. And I was watching the goings on, it must have been busy, there must have been a lot going on in the kitchen, because I forgot all about my doll for a while. And then I looked at it, I picked it up and looked at it, and its face was melted. It was wax so it had melted and it was ugly.' She smiled at the clarity of the vision. 'I cried. Wept my heart out.'

Her companion had heard it before too, needed only a slight pause to acknowledge it. 'Do you remember the meat parcels?'

'Liver and kidneys, a chop and a sausage. Sixpence.'

'Cakes were four for thruppence. We joined the sweet club at Christmas, a penny a week for twelve weeks. Father gave us a halfpenny on Friday nights, and we were to save a farthing and spend a farthing.'

Their conversation became embedded in the first decades of the century. Kim and I, and even Ethel, just listened, unqualified to take part. Each encouraged the other, collaborated, as if they were not remembering but creating, trying to out-do each other in a storytelling game. It reminds me of me, except that I am more garrulous, less restrained. Like them I feel, often, more at home in the past than the present. I am still sometimes surprised at the job I find myself doing, the way I spend my time. I like to think I couldn't leave. It is reassuring to believe I have no options, it is an alibi. I need an alibi for the things I write. But, if nothing else, then from all these words I should glean the moral of responsibility. The events that I am leading

up to taught me that, taught me that actions cannot be dis-
owned.

Ethel's friends continued. There were small events and large characters, but more than anything else, there were prices. It became a
litany: shoes ninepence, socks fourpence ha'penny, tuppence for a
haircut, five Woodbines for tuppence, a big carpet for a pound,
whisky at half a crown a bottle, ha'penny fares on the tram, a
penny on the bus, tuppence for the elite who sat downstairs.

Kim interrupted with a compliment about their memory. This
was tolerated with a small smile, and seemed to move the game
into a different direction, 'Do you remember the day the First
World War began? It was a Sunday . . .'

When they had finally left, Ethel apologized again. 'They did
rather dominate the conversation, I'm afraid. As you get older,
you see, you care less about things like that, about the social
conventions. It makes you wonder why we ever really bother
about them, don't you think? As you get older you just worry
less and less about what is expected.'

I agreed, thinking of my mother, and of Archer, both of whom
had decided not to care about conventional behaviour, at an age
when their choices might still substantially affect their lives. My
mother had taken seriously the exchanges between my father and
myself, about alchemy. New conditions, new ingredients, a new
outcome. All the things in fact that I have been considering while
writing this.

It was with an effort that I returned to the present. We decided
that we needed a walk, fresh air, the noises, sights and smells of
the nineteen-nineties, to remind us where we were. We stood at
the pelican until it peeped at us, allowing us to cross, and then
moved slowly up the high street, slowly because of Ethel's pace, and
because of the crowds of shoppers, and because of the temptation
of the windows. After our morning of reminiscence, I was hoping
for nostalgic thoughts from my grandmother, perhaps about the
shops Lucy used to visit, buying clothes and records. I knew that
she was at university in the early seventies. Romford, I thought,
might have seemed a little confining. I was always eager to hear
anything new. Not today. Ethel's mind was elsewhere. She talked
with Kim about the clothes in the windows, 'naughty nineties'
fashions, and she talked about the radical changes to the street we
were walking in, before the war, after the war, after development,

after redevelopment. She moved back and forth in the decades with ease, and without lingering in one particular period. She seemed to have no favourites. But her daughter remained unmentioned, a small void in history.

I walked with them along the high street, among busy Saturday morning shoppers, feeling quite apart, contained in a bubble of self-consciousness. I used to feel revitalized on a visit to my grandparents. It used to be as if I had stepped out of the real world for a while, opted out of normal cares surrounding school, friends and family. This was different, because I was so scared about what was coming next, which far transcended normal cares.

One more thing seemed necessary. Back at home I wrote a letter to Marie, the first for months, composed with a fine sense of occasion. The commando again, implying, in his strong silent way, that he may not return from the next mission. I skim over that part of the letter and come to what is more interesting, and sits oddly beside it.

Marie, I am trying to remember who you are, but it is difficult. Nowhere seems further away now than where you live, nowhere is more remote. You say, then why continue to write to me? It is because I like to conjure you up, to think about your dream: flood the city to create the lake, plant hundreds of trees in the West End, for the wood, and build your cottage in the middle of them, with the roof still slowly sliding off. It is pure selfishness I know, but I like to put you and Phillipe inside it, just as you were when Kim and I visited. So yes, you're right, day by day what I conjure up becomes less and less realistic. As a conjuror I am a failure, always have been, producing either nothing at all or something with no bearing on reality. I promise I will try again, try harder. Something is about to happen which, I hope, will allow me to start again, clean sheet, from scratch. Meanwhile my self-absorption, you have already noticed, is still here. But I am hoping for great things, great changes, very soon.

Thirty-eight

Time was getting on, and my effort to appear confident was getting a little strained.

'Treasure-hunting again,' I said to Kim.

She didn't answer, she just gave a snort which seemed to suggest that she at least was too old for such childish games. We had reached the rusty old rail between the gardens, we were in the middle of thick, clinging bushes, it was cold, and getting dark. Kim shivered as she tried to bend back the spiny twigs around her middle. She sighed impatiently. I nearly suggested that she should go home if she wanted to, but I stopped myself, because I thought that she probably would. For a couple of minutes we hesitated, caught between moments like a diver on a high board. It had rained earlier, and the ground was muddy, clinging, like the bushes. Tempting not to move, tempting just to stay where we were, where we could search for treasure indefinitely, secure in the knowledge that there was none to be found.

The rail left a dull red stain on my palm.

'Well come on then.' Kim swung a leg over the rail, and half climbed half rolled into Archer's garden.

I followed, attempted a vault to lift my spirits, but caught my toe and lurched forward into a pile of leaves. I lay still for a minute with leaves plastered to my face, breathing in their wet, mouldering smell. Then Kim began to giggle and, after a moment, I joined her, snared by the pure, unexpected pleasure of it: to be lying here, in my garden, in the soft leaves among the bushes, with Kim beside me laughing at my predicament. The house was far away, some thirty metres, and we were invisible from its high windows. I felt myself not a commando but a prince, reinstated into his kingdom. Or on the verge at least of reinstatement.

The shed had changed. Archer had cleared the bushes from two sides of it and had rebuilt it. It was a house of bricks now, not

231

straw. Its door had two locks, and its small window was of thick reinforced glass. It was compact and uniform, like a picture of a furnace from a text book on the industrial revolution. The window was open.

'It's a trap,' whispered Kim.

'Don't be stupid,' I said. 'How can it be?' Kim said nothing. It was refreshing to realize that I could still quell her doubts with a little judicious scorn. I followed up my advantage, 'Do you think you can fit through that window?'

'I'm just here to keep watch, remember?'

'Kim, I can't fit through it, and if you won't try then we'll have to give up and go home.' Over the years I had discovered more than one way to persuade her to do something against her better judgement. 'I'm depending on you,' I said, 'and I won't ask anything else, I promise.'

She took off her anorak. 'I don't know why I'm doing this,' she said, 'I don't know what I'm doing here.' I stood with my back to the wall and she put a foot into the stirrup of my hands. I lifted her. Disarming intimacy. As her hands moved from my shoulders up to the window sill, her face and breasts and stomach passed my eyes. Scratchy sweater on my cheek. I pushed her up, and she pulled herself through, disappearing slowly, jerkily, like a small, reluctant animal being swallowed.

I watched her disappearing legs with a pang of guilt. She was right after all, there was no good reason for her to be here. In the moment of being alone I felt a renewal of fear, and wondered briefly if Archer had fitted an alarm on his well-protected shed.

The door opened and she stood in front of me, breathless, shining her torch on to the ground at her feet. She was holding a key ring from which dangled two gold keys, a Yale and a Chubb. 'There was a spare set on a hook, why would he leave keys in here?'

'Why not?' I took the keys and put them in my pocket and took the torch and shone it on to the walls. They were black, unresponsive to the light. The shed was lined with videos, there must have been about five hundred there, on shelves on every wall, making space only for a video recorder and a small television. A few had spilled beneath the window, where Kim had climbed in.

'We've found the treasure,' I said. 'Somewhere in here we'll find Melody's video of me telling him a joke, the one we made in the back of his shop when I ran away. That's the significant combination that we're looking for.' I shone the torch at Kim, who had heard it all before. Her lack of reaction didn't dampen my eagerness. 'That's the link that proves Melody and Archer are connected. Do you understand? We've found the treasure.'

'It'll take for ever to find it,' said Kim, 'even if it's here.'

'They're labelled. We just have to read all the labels. Then we can play it on the TV.'

'What if I've hidden it somewhere else?' said Archer, laconically. 'What if I've been hoping you'd come so we could have a last little chat together?'

He leant against the door casually, one leg bent. A sardonic smile inevitably on his thin face in the bright light he had just turned on. 'Yes,' he said, cool as any adult confronted by misbehaving children, 'the fullness of time has finally elapsed.'

With something like a squeak of surprise, I stepped protectively in front of Kim. Archer's smile widened, showing teeth, becoming a grin.

'Do you think I want to hurt you? Don't be obtuse Bill. What do you think I am? What do you take me for? Hm?' He paused and stared down at me, widening his eyes, appearing to genuinely want an answer. His air of authority might have squeezed some words out of me, if I wasn't still semi-paralysed with shock. Archer continued smoothly, in a tone of injured innocence. 'Do you think I'm going to break your windows and crap on your carpet? Beat you up and rape your girlfriend? Or you? Steal your money? Con you? Kill you?' He smiled again, pleased with his fluency. He was making no effort to disguise his pleasure at finding us. 'What am I, a hooligan? A law unto myself? A sociopath? Do grow up Bill, and stop standing in front of Kim like that. Come out and be sociable Kim, stand up for yourself. I've always treated you like a grown-up, Bill, so do have the grace to behave like one.'

'I don't know what you're talking about.' He'd given me plenty of time to think, but it was the best I could come up with.

'We want to go now.' Kim's contribution was at least a bit more direct. Archer remained standing in the doorway. Big, black-rimmed eyes. Dilated pupils. He was the one all my childhood rituals had been designed to protect myself against. He was the creature finally surfacing from the bottom of the lake.

'You simply can't leave until you've had a look at my collection. It's unique.' He gave a proud flourish as he said it. 'I love videos, don't you love them? I do, I love them. One of our greatest advances I think. I like something you can hold in your hand, something substantial. Not flimsy photographs, like your friend Floyd, and not magazines. Don't quote me, you'd ruin my reputation, but I find most dirty magazines just embarrassing to tell the truth, don't you?'

He paused again, politely, for an answer. He was absolutely in control of the situation, enjoying himself immensely. No longer the adult patronizing children, he had become the host with favoured guests. Nothing, apparently, could be more right than that we were here and he was here, and that we had a whole night ahead of us to chat together. He had always loved monologues.

'Now videos,' he continued, 'videos contain real human life. Of course I don't mean actors, I don't mean a couple of idiots getting paid. I mean amateurs. Amateurs are the glory of videos. I know you understand the attraction Bill, the fascination. It gave me a real surprise to find you filming Charlie and Greig, at their games. That's in here somewhere. And I have you clambering around in my house in the dark, all those years ago, playing Oliver to Gary's Sykes. And of course, just as you hoped, I have the tape you're looking for, which contains not just your joke incidentally, but also your confession to theft. That would make an interesting piece of evidence wouldn't it? And now you're trespassing on my property again, just to bring it up to date. You're a real hardened villain, aren't you? Lovey dovey teenage detectives, you're such a sweet pair. You're too good to be true, Bill, you always have been. Still, son of Eldon and Lucy, what should I expect? They were so much more interesting than Melinda or Floyd. Big ideas, energy, an independent frame of mind. I did love your parents. I do ad*mire* Lucy.'

He subsided at last into quietness, a small smile lingering on his face, as if he was now dwelling in some fondly remembered portion of the past. I remembered Floyd's words, 'Don't look for motive. Don't look for motives and alibis and methods. It isn't like that.' He was right, nothing so calculated. Archer enjoyed extremes, he had a taste for manipulation, and no regard for rules. That, I think, was the extent of his motivation, and his method. The playground image in the end is the one I revert to: the wilful child swaggering along his own path, breaking a channel in the crowd.

'What are you going to do?' Kim again. Half-hypnotized by

Archer, I seemed to be speechless. There was too much to say, the questions were too big.

With a swelling of his cheeks and an inward turn of his shoulders, Melody answered. 'My dear Kim, I'm going to leave.' Archer's face, Melody's demeanour and voice. A hybrid chuckle. 'I'm going to vanish in a puff of purple smoke, if you'll forgive the allusion. Your lovely mother's friend, Floyd, and I'm sorry I just can't bring myself to like that man, however I try, has sent me a long and probably actionable letter, full of insinuations, warnings and suggestions, complete with photographs. His *file* on me.' He said the word with fastidious distaste. 'No evidence of course, not a shred, nothing more than circumstantial anyway but, well, enough to irritate. Jerome, you know, has been itching to get back on the road, and there are golden opportunities waiting for him across the sea. That's always been an advantage of Jerome's, he's so eminently exportable.'

He looked at me expectantly, lips pursed as if repressing an indiscreetly self-satisfied grin. He was trying to prod a reaction out of me, approval for his performance. When I still didn't speak, he continued.

'Actually I have a yearning to buy an island. You can pick up a very decent one for around a million. Less if you shop around a little. I deserve a holiday. Doesn't that appeal to you, Billy? Isn't that the sort of fantasy to appeal to a bookworm, a loiterer in cemeteries? For a little while now I've been resisting an urge to drop out, cede all the ground I've made and just drop out, disappear.' A small, conjuror's wave of the hand. 'I may decide to live somewhere quiet, off my considerable savings, and build walls around myself. Relax a little.'

I still didn't have the words. Cautious, stumbling over my thoughts because they sounded so absurd when finally stated to his face, 'And are you . . . and are Melody and Archer . . .'

'Spit it out Bill,' he said genially.

'Have you played more than one role?'

'Oh good God, yes.' In the fluorescent light his face was unnaturally pale. Perhaps I hadn't seen it before without make-up. Somehow his casual admission made his mood, near elation, appear suddenly brittle. I found a new interpretation of his pleasure at seeing us: perhaps he was relieved, perhaps he needed me for something, some last trick. Restricted by the confined space, he stretched his arms out suddenly, and let them drop back to his side. 'It's been such fun. You've no idea how nice it is to tell you. I've had such fun. And haven't I been good? If you were writing reviews, you'd have to admit it, wouldn't you? I do think I carried it all off rather well. Of course, I confess to a certain amount of shorthand with Jerome, and broad brushstrokes with Jay. But Melody now, Melody has been my most complete, if also my most anile, creation. Mind you, that's a bit simplistic. I might as easily say Archer has been my most complete creation. Do you know what I mean?'

'And you were the magician, the Alchemist?'

'Well it would only be appropriate.'

'Were you?'

'I'm a great believer in what is appropriate Bill. Decorum, it used to be called.'

'But no one knew you. My father recognized you as Jerome, but never otherwise.'

'Because I let him. I'm such a tease, aren't I a tease? I let him recognize me. But my dear Bill, it's amazing what people don't notice. At least twice I wore my Archer lifts as Melody, and no one remarked on the fact that I'd gained a couple of inches in height.'

Kim, impatient, interrupted what threatened to be another long monologue, 'But what for? What was the point of it all?'

'Ah Kim, ever the pragmatist. No beating around the bush. Do you know, excuse me for saying so but I knew you and Bill wouldn't last, as a couple. You're just not really compatible, that's my opinion, no offence intended. What was the point? Oh, I don't know Kim, is there ever any point? You wouldn't find Bill asking that question you know. In fact if you have to ask it, you don't really understand, I'm afraid. Why did I do that impression of Melody for you, Bill, at the New Year's party? And why that piece of acting at the house-warming? Rather rash, in the circumstances. Put it down to high spirits. Put it all down to high spirits. Where would I be without them? Where would anybody be? Melancholy. Isn't that your least favourite word of all? That's where I'd be, drowning in melancholy. I'm not quite as egregiously fun-loving as you two may think, with your rather superficial view of life.'

He was barely even looking at us, just rattling on now without need of prompting. 'Still,' he said, 'I don't think I ever really overdid it. I think I managed to avoid the temptations of excess, for the most part. Take France for instance, such a temptation to pop up there as a local yokel, straw in mouth and a thick accent. So easy to slip from comedy to farce. Control is the secret, the ultimate secret of success. I'm the one-eyed man in the kingdom of the blind. I'm subtle. The knave among fools. You may not like it but you have to admire it. The way I high-step it among the plodders, cock of the walk.' He took a couple of short steps, his bent arms swinging jauntily, to illustrate his point. 'That's the thing, to be that step or steps ahead, then you're in control, you're laughing. I hope you noticed that incidentally: Melody, Archer, Jay, the Alchemist, smilers all of them, incorrigible smilers. And didn't they add a bit of spice to your life, Bill, a bit of zest? I've been the tonic in your mortifying gin, the colour to your dull monochrome. I'm the ogre who eats children, didn't you recognize me from the stories? You have to cherish a good villain, you really do, you just have to love him.'

For this performance, Archer was wearing black jeans and a tight sweater, and over it the battered leather jacket he had been wearing when he babysat for me, years earlier. At his feet was a suitcase and a stuffed plastic bag, 'Quality at low prices'. He saw me looking, and went off instantly at another tangent.

'All my worldly goods,' he said, 'more or less. And there's a face or two in here even you haven't seen.' He sighed nostalgically, remembering good times. 'Time to move on,' he said. 'The network seems to be melting away now. My authority isn't quite what it was, sad to say. What with poor Nita such a nervous wreck these days and going over to the opposition, along with dear old Rose Larbey. And Charlie turning into a young alcoholic. He's a little too keen to be his brother that boy. But Gary's in trouble too, of course, thanks to your persistent friend. As for Donny, Donny seems to be less of a liaison these days and more of an agent for . . . well, you know who for, don't you? What seems to have become the other opposition. The villains, as Mr Floyd quaintly calls them. Perhaps I got in a little deeper than was wise. These things seem to acquire a momentum of their own. You just don't know who your friends are these days, that's the problem. It's tiring, it has all become rather tiring, and tiresome. You know it's time for a change when you need a drink or a pill to replace the old enthusiasm.'

'*You're* the villain, you just said so.'

'But I'm not, Bill,' that open-handed gesture of Jerome's, 'that's just the way you've chosen to see me. I'm a businessman, same as your father tried to be. That's what I'm saying to you, your father and I had a lot in common. Not as much as Lucy and I, Lucy and I were two of a kind, but I was always basically just a businessman, like Eldon. What did it say in that tedious letter? Recruitment, production, distribution. That's about right. I'm a small business, only not particularly small. I'm three different legitimate limited companies and I have two or three thriving illegal enterprises. And a dentist's practice of course, when I can fit it in. In fact that's probably the only area of my work in which I hurt people. All my young people are willing you know, Bill. I don't think they're even exploited. I just happen to have idiosyncratic views about pornography. And about the age of consent. And about what constitutes abuse. If you want to know about misery,' he said, with a change in tone, as if Kim or I had just mentioned the word, 'you think about what goes on in those secret places, behind the doors and the windows. That's where the horror is, the real horror. Small scale tyrannies, all the more painful for being small scale. Allow yourself visions, tales of ordinary despair. You've seen it in the news, the baby starved by its parents, the years of misery. I don't deal in that, the kids I recruit know what they're doing.' He became less heated again. 'In fact, tell you the truth, I don't believe in children anyway. Or at least, the age of becoming an adult has got lower. Ten, eleven, twelve maybe, in sheltered cases. It'll be out of double figures soon. They know what they're doing, all the boys and girls.'

'Like Charlie? No wonder you're the expert on misery.'

'And anyway, who are you to accuse?' he said, ignoring me. 'What about you? You've seen my secret places, I've seen yours. Burglar and thief, spy and false friend, conniver, bully, hypocrite. You seem to think I'm a dangerous man, but you didn't scruple to bring Kim along with you, did you? Don't be too glib with your accusations Bill, that's always a big mistake. You know me, and I know you.'

I didn't need Archer to remind me that many of my memories were associated with feelings of guilt: stealing from Melody and Archer, pushing Charlie out of the tree, relishing his fight with Greig. From the trivial to the serious, from the exhilarating violence of the birthday party, to being implicated in my mother's leaving.

And at last my chain of memories led me to a point where I could speak. It wasn't Archer's game anymore, it had nothing to do with fairytales. I had discovered the words I needed to unblock my throat, and, I thought, to irredeemably condemn Archer. He was taking off his jacket, idly looking at the videos nearest to him.

'Did you kill my father?'

Never one to miss a melodramatic effect, Archer didn't answer immediately, he continued to take off his jacket. He lifted it to his face and sniffed the leather, seemed to gain confidence from its strong odour. 'Ridiculous,' he said at last. 'Is that what you think? I was afraid that you might. Eldon died of a heart attack. The pressure on him at the time didn't help of course, things he found out, but I hardly think that counts as murder. What upset him was that he was helping to finance my operations. He didn't like that idea at all. You see, my policy has always been to throw out hooks, lodge them firmly in people, in areas of business and personal life. I got a couple of good sharp hooks deep in your father's flesh at an early stage. As Archer I advised him, even lent him money once or twice, as Melody I was his friend and confidant.'

'You never lent him money. First of all he never borrowed money, he said so, and second he never trusted you. You're lying.'

'Never borrowed money? How do you expect him to make any without borrowing any? I'm afraid not, Bill, it's Eldon who was lying. He lived in a dream world that man, as I've told you before, and he wanted you to live in it with him. I played him, to be frank, like a big stupid fish, just as I pleased. I won't deny that it was useful to me that he died when he did. Floyd pointed that out of course, rather tastelessly, in his letter. Having finally seen the light, Eldon was planning to withdraw investments from Melody's businesses, and to withdraw from other partnerships, involving property. When he died the trust very sensibly left his money where it was, rather than use it to try to prop up his slightly creaky retail empire.'

'What do you mean, "creaky"? He built it all himself.'

'Well more or less, yes.' Archer sighed. 'I can see the responsibility for puncturing illusions has fallen to me. Eldon had no flair for business. He was a good marketing man, none better, and he had a useful streak of ruthlessness, but that was it, that was the total of his business acumen. Terribly limited. He once told me, or Melody . . . anyway one of us, that the more successful he got the more worried about it he became. Then in the next breath he was on about some airy fairy idea of starting a publishing house. Or finding the time to write a book. That was your father Bill. Dreamer. Head in the clouds. A lot like you Bill, in some ways. But I'm rambling a little, aren't I? The answer to your question is no, I didn't kill him, and I must say, I rather resent the idea. In fact this is all becoming a bit boring now. I'm afraid it's always been a tendency of yours Bill, to get a bit tedious, a bit monotonous. That must be why you and Floyd get on so well. Tell me though, if you really want to talk about your parents, what did you do to drive your mother away from home?'

My turn for a short pause. Then I said, 'I'm going to kill you.'

He laughed. 'Yes, yes, well I'm just trying to make a point, let's not get adolescent about it. I'm sure we can still be friends, you and I.'

'And I don't believe you anyway, I think you did kill him.'

'That's your privilege, Bill. Although since you've just said you want to murder me, I'm not quite sure what makes you feel you have the moral high ground here. If it makes you feel better though, I won't say any more about it, but do just remember Melody did his best to save Eldon's life. Melody never lifted a finger against you, was a good friend to you in fact.'

'What are you going to do with us?'

'Kim, dear girl, I'd nearly forgotten you were there. How nice to hear from you again. You're just as persistent as Floyd, aren't you? Much prettier though. Just think of the money you and Bill could have made as junior partners. Anyway, yes, good question, what *am* I going to do with you?' There was a pause. He seemed not to have considered this before. The pause lengthened, and became a silence. Nothing to hear but our breathing. Each of us was slowly reminded that it was late at night, we were at the bottom of the garden, and no one was nearby. Archer finally spoke quietly, lounging again, as if all his febrile energy had drained away. 'I suppose I could lock you in here, couldn't I? The trouble is I want to burn all this, heart-breaking though it is. Wouldn't want to burn you too. Couldn't have that, I suppose. Could I?'

'You said you weren't a murderer.'

'Indeed I did Kim, and I meant it. I'm not unscrupulous. Single-minded is what Bill's father used to call me, but it's a terrible simplification, not surprisingly if Eldon said it. You may think it's true, multiple identities and a single mind, you may like to think of it that way, but it does miss the point. Part of me is Jerome, I really would like people to know what they can do, if they only try. Perhaps that's why I've been chatting away for so long tonight. My evangelistic tendency. And then some seedy corner of me warms to Jay. Quite a large part is Melody of course, because I love people, I really do, I love them. I'm the absolute opposite of a misanthrope. And part of me is Archer. Wolfish, I think, is the adjective that fits. It's criminal not to take advantage of the weak, how else will they learn? I'm a performer who believes in every role, I'm a man of integrity. But look here,' Melody again, suddenly reappearing, 'I can see you two young people are getting restless, so here's my suggestion: Billy, you can get out of the way, nip outside for a minute, and Kim and I will burn all this trash, and then join you. I assure you she's safe in my hands, safe as houses. You know me and children. How does that sound? Does that sound satisfactory?'

He took our silence for consent. 'Come along then, we haven't got all night you know, you've kept me chatting too long already.'

I looked at Kim, shrugged, and walked past Archer and out of the shed. He kept talking. I stood a couple of steps from the door, looking on. 'Good, good. Time, as I said, to move on, things here have gone far enough, time to extricate myself I'd say. The fun's gone out of it, that's the thing, time to start all over again, or perhaps to retire to that island I mentioned. End my days there, that would suit very well, Napoleon on Elba.'

He was holding Kim's arm while sweeping cassettes off the shelves, and pulling shiny ribbons of tape out of them. In the plastic bag, wrapped in rags, there was a can of petrol. As he tried to get at this, Kim bit his hand and wrenched away and ran past him out of the shed. She ran past me too, shouting, 'Come on!' I backed a couple more steps away from the door, still looking in. Archer was squatting on the floor of the shed, nursing his hand. He looked over his shoulder at me, surrounded by a pool of tapes, all in black like a crouching chimpanzee. 'You know where you end up, don't you Billy? Don't you, Billy?' I didn't know who it was talking to me, his voice was unclear, shifting in tone and register, neither Melody's fruity tenor, nor Archer's sardonic bass, neither Jay nor Jerome. He seemed to require an answer. 'No,' I said, 'where do I end up?' He had pulled off his sweater now, he was bare chested, white as a sheet of paper. The smell of petrol overwhelmed the smells of the night as he began to pour it out of the can. 'You end up in a box, Bill, a box which, but for its distinctive design, might just as well contain a vacuum cleaner.' He laughed quietly, whoever it was, pleased by this conceit, and then he bent over and with a burning rag started the fire. 'Like your poor old father,' he said. 'Six foot down and his bones have turned to worm food.'

Flames flared up quickly, making him recoil, painting him in streaks of red and livid purple, bathing him in gold. As I moved back towards the door I saw that he was undressing completely, ready for another costume change I thought, although I wouldn't swear to it. I don't know quite what to make of his last actions. As I closed the door he turned again and caught my eye, without any doubt saw what I was doing. There was a trace of a smirk, as if I had confirmed something for him, and he winked. I turned the key in the lock and then threw it into the bushes, into the darkness.

Thirty-nine

Verdict: death by misadventure. I ran away along with Kim, the door swung spontaneously shut on Archer, he was burnt to death in the fire of his own making. That was the version the inquest heard. Everything came out: Floyd's impressive file, Archer's underworld connections, the various fates of members of his networks, everything but the fact that I closed the door on him, locking him into the furnace, taking on myself the position of judge and jury. Melinda and Floyd thought it was best to elide the part I had played. They thought that the truth was an unnecessary complication. If the police knew that the door had actually been locked, then they too thought it best to keep the knowledge to themselves.

The papers loved it. Headline: 'The Devil in Disguise'. Lurid photographs and stories composed of speculation, exaggeration and lies. Much emphasis on Kim, plucky schoolgirl, pictured in her swimming costume. I read it all with interest, marrying in my mind for the first time my twin ambitions of writing stories and being a journalist.

This is what really happened. When the noise started I ran away, halfway down the garden in a record breaking sprint, toes digging into wet earth, propelling me forward so that each step saved me from falling flat on my face. Not fast enough, though. I stopped, stumbled and then froze, agonizingly poised, and then turned and ran back again, back down the garden and into the bushes where I had thrown the keys. I couldn't find them, I could scarcely even see anyway for tears, and the noise very soon ended. I was left alone. Just the sound and the frightening smells of the fire, breaking through the roof of the shed now, flames reaching up long fingers to the sky. Archer's alchemical experiment, gone grotesquely wrong. While Kim roused the neighbours and the police, I stood in the bushes and watched the shed blaze. Thinking myself likely to be arrested, I considered jumping back over the fence and running away again, a fugitive's life seemed briefly attractive, but I didn't move, instead I held on to cold, clutching twigs for balance and looked up at the sky, as if it might offer some guidance. It offered me nothing. As I began to feel dizzy, I took a step back and touched something on the ground. The torch. I sat down with a bump in the middle of the bushes, as if hiding, and I shined the torch up into the sky, where the beam dwindled and evaporated, like the over-ambitious flames. Down among the fallen leaves, the smell that filled my nostrils was the smell of earth.

Even after all my hesitation, I didn't start this in the right place, because if things were going to unfold in order, I should have started with my father's first meetings with Archer and Melody. That was the crux. He was right, he was like my parents. That was why Eldon liked him and Lucy was afraid of him: they saw themselves in him.

I am not finishing this in the right place either, sitting here where I write mindless headlines and jokes about topless women for a living. My own alchemical experiment, the long process, has also gone wrong, went wrong somewhere about the time of the big lie in the court and all the small lies in the newspapers. I am coining the money, no problem, but something, some vital part of the process, has failed to happen. I dream about a flat, a penthouse, overlooking a London park. Quiet. My ideal compromise of town and country, activity and tranquillity. I still dream about ideals, ideal places and attitudes and modes of living, I still linger in cemeteries, still distance myself, a step back, two steps back, from people and events. So I haven't changed much at all. I am not even convinced any more that change is possible. If it is, then the process demands a grand design, more time and more self-conscious effort than I have given it, and even then it would be unpredictable in the manner of its outcome.

When Ethel's tapestry got up to date, she continued it, into the future, mapping carefully her remaining years or months. I am taking this as my model, not my father's big dreams or my mother's blind jump. I am putting my faith after all into plans, because I still hope, with Mr Melody, that something worthwhile can come from the most unpromising materials. Like my grandmother, who has weathered decades of storms, I am sewing, at this point between past and future, I am sewing what is ahead. For a start, I have plans to write a children's TV series. It will concern a family on a trip to a lighthouse, who are kidnapped by sea-monsters. Plenty of action, plenty of characterization, great settings. I have high hopes.

A NOTE ON THE AUTHOR

Mark Illis was born in Blackheath in 1963, and educated at University College London, and the University of East Anglia. His first published short story was a runner-up for the Whitbread Prize for Young Writers; subsequent stories have been published in the *London Review of Books*, *London Magazine* and *Fiction Magazine*. *A Chinese Summer*, his first novel, was published in 1988. Besides teaching and reviewing, Mark Illis is working on a third novel. He lives in London.

ACKNOWLEDGMENTS

Archer uses some of Ben Jonson's lines, preferring them to his own. I would like to express my debt to the makers of the film *Streetwise* and to those who appeared in it, inhabitants of a more horrific real world than any I could invent.

Mark Illis